ONE
DARK
NIGHT

ONE
DARK
NIGHT

A NOVEL

HANNAH RICHELL

ATRIA PAPERBACK

New York   Amsterdam/Antwerp   London
Toronto   Sydney/Melbourne   New Delhi

ATRIA
PAPERBACK

An Imprint of Simon & Schuster, LLC
1230 Avenue of the Americas
New York, NY 10020

This book is a work of fiction. Any references to historical events, real people, or real places are used fictitiously. Other names, characters, places, and events are products of the author's imagination, and any resemblance to actual events or places or persons, living or dead, is entirely coincidental.

Simon & Schuster strongly believes in freedom of expression and stands against censorship in all its forms. For more information, visit BooksBelong.com.

For information about special discounts for bulk purchases, please contact Simon & Schuster Special Sales at 1-866-506-1949 or business@simonandschuster.com.

The Simon & Schuster Speakers Bureau can bring authors to your live event. For more information or to book an event, contact the Simon & Schuster Speakers Bureau at 1-866-248-3049 or visit our website at www.simonspeakers.com.

Manufactured in the United States of America

1 3 5 7 9 10 8 6 4 2

Library of Congress Cataloging-in-Publication Data has been applied for.

ISBN 978-1-6680-8133-4
ISBN 978-1-6680-8134-1 (ebook)

For Gracie and Jude

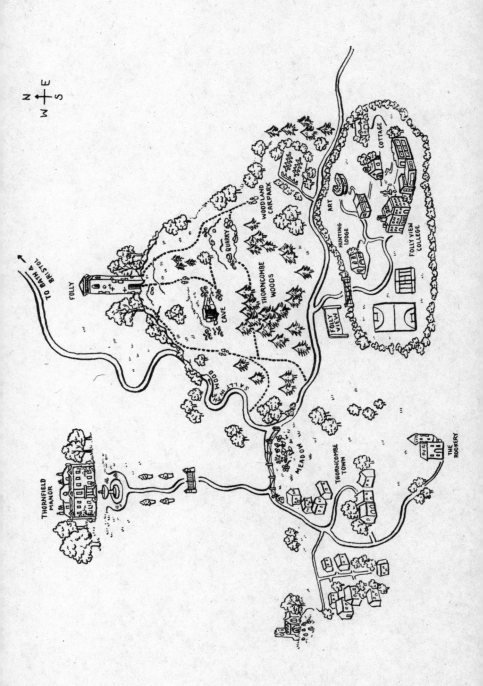

Folly

noun: folly; plural noun: follies

> lack of good sense; foolishness
> a foolish act, idea, or practice
> a costly ornamental building with no practical purpose;
> > especially a tower or a mock Gothic ruin

Definition from Oxford Languages

Prologue

They crowd beside the bonfire, faces cast in flickering orange light, backs turned to the dark unknown.

"It's not true. Sally wasn't real."

"It *is* true," insists the boy. "Sally was here. Her name's scratched on the walls of the old hunting lodge."

They lean into the story, his words holding them captive.

"She was a local girl. Engaged to be married, until her fiancé caught her cheating. He murdered her at the folly on their wedding day, left her body for the crows. They say she haunts the woods now, a girl in a white dress, luring people to their deaths."

"Like I said, just a stupid story."

"There's one way to find out."

They circle the board, hands reaching for the glass jar. The boy waits until the only sounds are the crackle of the fire and the soft breeze whispering through the trees. "Is there anyone out there?"

A giggle is stifled.

"Is there anyone there?"

There's a jolt as the jar shifts on the board, a spasm of movement beneath their fingers. Someone gasps.

"Shhh."

"You moved it."

"I didn't, I swear."

"This is horseshit."

They wait until the jar begins to slide, gliding smoothly to the letter S.

It slides again. This time to A. Then L. L. Y.

"Sally," whispers one of them. "She's here."

There's tension in the circle, an invisible noose holding the teenagers in place.

"What do you want, Sally?"

They watch as the jar shifts. D. A. R. E.

One of the girls jerks backward, breaking the circle. "There's someone out there," she says. "Up by the trees."

"That's not funny."

"I'm not joking. I saw them."

The boy leans into the board again, the firelight caught in his eyes. "Who's there?" he asks, and they're all silent as the jar glides beneath their fingers in a smooth, steady pattern, bouncing from letter to letter, spelling out a single word.

SALLY

SALLY

SALLY

Chapter 1

The two women spill from the back of John Slater's taxi into the triangle of light falling from a streetlamp. The blonde tugs at her skirt and straightens the flashing devil horns perched on her head, then promptly drops her keys in the gutter, cursing loudly. Her friend giggles and staggers toward the house, calling for her to hurry up. She's busting for a pee. John waits until they are safely inside, lights on and the front door closed, before turning the car around.

The last fare of a rowdy night. Job done and into the home stretch. Alone now and yawning, John cranks up the radio and opens his window a few inches, hoping a blast of cold air and Lionel Richie will keep him alert. If he's lucky, he'll get a couple of hours of shut-eye before the wife wakes him.

He leaves the market town behind and takes the snaking road toward Bath, his car cruising down into the valley, past the turning for the fancy private school where he sometimes drops rich kids with their freshly-pressed blazers and their monogrammed luggage, before heading deeper into the woods. A paper-thin moon flickers between the tangled trees. He rolls his shoulders and blinks to focus.

It's not as if he believes the stories about this particular stretch of road, but you can't argue with traffic statistics. Known to locals by its peculiar nickname, Sally in the Wood, the route has seen far too many cars careen off into the dense woodland over the years. He's read about the tragedies. A young female driver killed a few years ago in a head-on smash. A promising young rugby player paralyzed after coming off his motorbike. It's sobering to realize he's just a moment's lapse in concentration away from the steep drop to his left. He's not taking any chances, no thank you. He's looking forward to sliding into a warm bed and curling around his wife. Thanks to her nagging, their suitcases are already packed and waiting in the hall. This time tomorrow they'll be fast asleep, lulled by the sound of the Atlantic Ocean drifting through their balcony door.

His fingers drum a beat on the steering wheel. He checks the dashboard clock, notes it's 02:38 a.m., catches movement in his peripheral vision. Something white flitting between the trees. An animal, he thinks. An owl ghosting through the night. Or a deer, perhaps? He glances sideways, trying to fix the image in his mind, but it's already gone and the dark, serpentine road is rushing at him, demanding his attention.

He grips the steering wheel, taking the bend a little too fast. Clearing the corner, he lets out a cry. A streak of white is caught in the blaze of his full beams, something darting across the tarmac. *What the hell?* He slams on the brakes.

There isn't time for anything other than instinctive self-preservation. The car wheels lock, the steering unresponsive in his hands. He swears as he skids toward the lip of the road, knowing with awful certainty that the car is going over. He's going to plunge into the steep valley, following the path of whatever that thing was. His knuckles blanch. The tires screech. At last, the steering responds to the desperate yank of his hands, the car veering away from the drop and back onto the road.

Christ. His heart thuds in his chest. That was close. Sweat beads pop on his brow. What the hell was that?

He chances a quick glance in his mirror. The black road slides away behind him. All he can see are the dark trees painted lurid red in the glow of his taillights.

Sally in the Wood. He shudders. A deer, he tells himself. No reason to spook himself with silly ideas of ghostly girls rushing out at him. Not at this time of night. All those Halloween devils and zombies he's been ferrying around have messed with his mind.

He drives the rest of the way home at a cautious speed, his hands still clammy as he puts his key in the front door. The sight of the waiting suitcase offers some comfort, and by the time he has poured himself a generous whiskey, gulped it down, undressed, and crawled into bed beside his wife's soft, slumbering body, he's almost consigned the episode to a forgotten corner of his memory.

He won't think of it again. Not for a few days. Not until he sees grim headlines splashed across the British newspapers piled high at the airport as he waits for his flight home.

Chapter 2

They hike in pairs up the steep woodland track, eight Girl Guides with their boots thumping in the dirt and the beams from their flashlights bouncing off the knotted tree trunks. High above their heads, the thin autumn canopy quivers in the damp air. One of the older girls holds her flashlight beneath her chin and turns back to the others, the shadows contorting her face. "I'm Sally," she says, making the others shriek and giggle. "Sally in the Wood. *Wooooh.*"

Their unit leader, a sensible, middle-aged woman dressed in Gore-Tex, snaps at them to stop being silly. The quiet only lasts a moment before the girls pick up the thread again, whispering their ghost stories and the name "Sally" like an incantation through the trees. On reflection, thinks the leader, a "sunrise hike" scheduled the morning after Halloween probably wasn't the best idea for the troop's adventure badge. "If you lower the volume, you might just hear the birds," she says. "Listen."

The girls fall still, but the woods remain cloaked in an ominous silence and when they start walking again, all that can be heard is the steady thud of their boots and their labored breath.

"My brother told me the birds never sing in these woods," whispers one girl. "Not even in summer."

"They're quiet because it's still dark," says another. She tries to sound convincing, but they hear the waver in her voice.

A tree root sends someone sprawling. "Stick together," the leader pleads, falling back to tend to a grazed knee. "We'll open our thermos flasks at the folly."

But the girls aren't listening. They press ahead, eager for the summit and the promised dawn view.

"Look," says a girl at the front of the pack. She points to the dramatic stone tower rising in the distance, a pillar jutting from the treetops, black against the lightening sky. "There it is."

She nudges her partner and they put on a sudden burst of speed, the two girls breaking away from the group, rushing the final incline until they are standing at the base of the folly, craning their necks to peer up at its vertiginous, lichen-spotted walls.

It's even more startling close up, dark and imposing against the dawn sky, a thin, rectangular tower with a peaked roof.

"I feel dizzy just looking it," says the younger of the girls. "Are you really going to climb it?"

Her friend nods and disappears.

Left alone, the girl gazes up again, awestruck, her eyes fixed on the arched opening gaping at the top, yawning like the black, toothless mouth of a giant. It reminds her of a place she's read about in a fairy tale, somewhere to lock up a maiden, imprison her for a hundred years, or force her to spin straw into gold. She reaches out a hand and rests it on the stone. It's cold to the touch, strangely clammy in the early morning air. "I still don't hear the birds," she calls.

There's no reply, so the girl walks around the base and comes upon her friend standing rigid, eyes wide, her mouth hanging open. She's staring at something sprawled on the ground before the tower entrance, something hard to make out in the half-light, though it looks like a sack, or a pile of stained white fabric. "What is it?" she asks.

Her friend's answer is a strangled cry.

Stepping closer, the girl sees it's not a sack, but a long white dress, two hands folded neatly, crude black marks scrawled onto bloodless skin, strands of long blond hair. Her gaze travels higher, looking for a face, finding only blue lips parted as if to take a final breath, before the face morphs into a mass of glossy black feathers, a hooked beak glinting in the dawn light. A puddle of liquid leaks from beneath, like a can of spilled paint.

The girl stares and stares as the confusing pieces of the scene fuse together. When her scream comes, it echoes through the empty chamber of the folly and flies out across the valley like a flock of startled crows.

Chapter 3

Sunday, 8:30 a.m.

Rachel Dean runs fast. She runs with her legs burning, her heart pounding, and her lungs screaming. She runs as if her life depends on it.

It's become something of a habit, getting out early on a weekend, before Ellie stirs and the rest of the school has risen. It's her release. Her way of clearing her head after a bad night, of silencing her brain, of coming back into her body and reducing herself to muscle, sinew, and bone. It's been her way of reclaiming the weekends, giving them new shape, since Ben left and she and Ellie relocated to the staff cottage.

This early on a Sunday, there's a rare stillness across the campus, the residential students tucked in dormitories, their pastoral problems stowed safely with them, for the time being at least. Morning worship will eventually drive them from their warm beds, but for now, the grounds are hers alone. She passes the grand, ivy-clad buildings; the assembly hall; the English department; and the state-of-the-art science block, all locked and quiet, before detouring down a path lined with neat box hedging to where the art department nestles into the cleft of the hills, a

sleek low building with a sedum roof and huge glass windows angled toward the trees. Here she loops back to join the long gravel
drive, crunching toward the wrought-iron gates leading out onto
the lane.

The urge to move is stronger than usual, and not just because
of the bottle of red wine she'd opened last night while cooking
dinner, for one. There'd been no one to share it with, no one to
warn her not to overindulge, and Rachel had found herself topping up her glass, telling herself that the wine would help her
sleep. It had, until she'd woken in the small hours, her dry tongue
heavy in her mouth as she'd moved her hand across the mattress,
reaching for Ben, her fingers grazing the sheet, finding the cold
empty space where her husband once lay.

The shape of her life had returned to her then. Her ex-
husband sleeping across the valley in another woman's bed, and
their daughter, Ellie, spending her second weekend with him, as
agreed in their polite but decidedly tense separation negotiations.
No doubt he'd rolled out the red carpet, playing happy families
with Chrissie in that way it was so much easier to do as a part-
time parent, without any of the daily grind to negotiate. She tries
not to be bitter. It's good for Ellie. A weekend with her father is
probably just what she needs. God knows, she's struggled to get
through to the girl. Ellie's latest stunt had landed her with a three-
day suspension from school. If she isn't careful, she'll lose her
scholarship and any chance of a place at the London art college
she's hoping to attend next year.

Gritting her teeth, Rachel increases her pace. She fixes her
gaze on the tall gates at the end of the drive, but as she nears
the exit and the former Hunting Lodge hunkered low next to
the stone pillars, she pulls up short. The school's entrance is no

longer a picture of immaculate splendor. Splattered across the gravel is a mess of orange pumpkin rind, pulp, and seeds, while a dozen or so eggs now decorate the front of the Lodge, yellow yolks dried in an impressionistic smear over the porch and windows, several more dotted across the school's welcome sign. Rachel stands with her hands on her hips, breathing heavily as she surveys the damage.

It's obviously a mindless Halloween prank, though whoever's decided to decorate their head teacher's residence with such a brazen display must've been feeling brave—or reckless. Rachel glances up and sees the curtains at the Lodge are already drawn, a light on inside. Perhaps the Crowes have already spotted the mess. No doubt it would be Malcolm, Margaret's long-suffering husband, who'd be out later to clear it all up. Such a shame. It only took a few kids to ruin it for everyone.

A dark silhouette passes an upstairs window, then returns, a tall figure, pencil-thin, backlit from within. Malcolm. She lifts her hand to wave, a little embarrassed to have been caught peering up at their home, but he doesn't appear to be looking down at her. His head is lifted, she realizes, his gaze fixed on the wooded hills rising in the distance.

Rachel takes the opportunity to duck away, dodging the mess strewn across the drive as she leaves through the gates and follows the lane to the start of a trail winding up into the woods. The sun is higher now, chasing the darkest shadows from the hills. She finds her rhythm weaving up through the trees, losing herself in the thud of her feet, the crunch of the copper leaves, and the white clouds of her breath, only breaking focus when a figure looms out of the trees, stepping onto the path in front of her.

Rachel gives a startled cry, one hand flying to her chest. "You frightened me," she says, the words exhaled between breaths.

"Sorry, ma'am." The man is broad shouldered, dressed head to toe in a dark uniform, with a shock of blond hair. There's a roll of something blue and white in his hands. Police tape.

She bends over, hands on knees. "Are you closing the trail?"

The officer nods and stretches the tape across the path, winding it around a nearby tree trunk and back again. "'Fraid so. No access to the folly until further notice."

"That's a shame." She glances up the trail, unable to see anything obviously different behind him. Her usual route is a challenging hill climb, taking her a mile or so to the top of the escarpment, past the folly, then dropping down through the other side of the woods to the nearby town of Thorncombe, before circling back along the lane to the school. "What happened?" she asks. "I hope no one's hurt?"

The officer glances around, then leans a little closer. "I shouldn't say, but it looks as though a Halloween party got out of hand last night."

Rachel frowns. "I'm Head of Student Welfare at Folly View College. None of our kids were involved, I hope?" She thinks about the excited buzz that had filled the corridors as Halloween had loomed closer, the mess at the school's entrance that morning.

"I'm sorry, ma'am. I wouldn't be able to say, even if I did know. Which I don't," he adds quickly. "My orders are to stop anyone heading up to the folly."

Rachel feels a prickle of unease. Boarders weren't supposed to leave the school grounds without permission, but she wasn't naive. She knew their residential students found ways to bend the rules, especially at weekends. It would be a nightmare for the faculty if any of their kids were found to have been involved in something illegal off campus. She wipes the sweat from her brow with a sleeve. "Well, I hope you won't be out here too long." She glances about. "It's rather gloomy, isn't it?"

"It's the quiet I don't like," the officer admits, gazing up at the trees. "Not sure you'd get me partying out here after dark."

"No," agrees Rachel. "But then where else do the local kids have to hang out?"

"Shame that skate park didn't get the green light."

"I have a seventeen-year-old who would agree with you on that."

She waves goodbye and retraces her steps back down the trail, catkins and twigs cracking beneath her sneakers, breaking the quiet. It's unnerving to think of something amiss so close to the school, happening right here in the woods. At least Ellie had been safely at Ben's. She finds herself suddenly grateful for their arrangement. At least that's one less thing to worry about.

Thoughts of Ellie and Ben and their weekend together fill her mind until her feet hit the tarmac at the bottom of the woods and she slides her phone from her pocket. She types a brief message. *Hope you're having a great time with Dad. Love you x*

It's too early for a reply. Ellie will be fast asleep.

Leave it, she tells herself. Don't go there. But her fingers seem to have a mind of their own, swiping to another thread. *Hey. Hear there's been some trouble in the woods. Anything the school should know about?* She reads it back, pleased with its perfunctory tone, and presses send. Then, almost immediately, before she can stop herself, she types another line. *Hope you and Ellie had fun last night. x.*

She hits send again, then stares at her screen. Oh god. That kiss. She definitely shouldn't have put a kiss. Ben's probably lying in bed right now next to Chrissie reading the messages out loud, the two of them rolling their eyes, laughing at her needy early morning texts. Almost as if she didn't have a life of her own.

She shoves her phone back into her pocket. For god's sake. She's a grown-ass woman. Time to start acting like one. Turning back toward the school, she can feel the sweat already cooling on her skin. All adrenaline and enthusiasm for the run has left her now; it's just her tired body loping back to an empty cottage and her regret trailing her like a small, lost dog.

Chapter 4

Sunday, 9:30 a.m.

Detective Sergeant Ben Chase's car is being waved through the police cordon when he hears the notifications on his phone, two high "pings" in quick succession. He guides his mud-splattered 4×4 into the space beside Detective Chief Inspector Hassan Khan's pristine sedan and reaches for the cell phone. Two messages. Both from Rachel.

Just the sight of her name makes him grip the handset a little tighter. He scans her messages and bristles. A kiss? Really? As if that's going to soften the fact she's messed up their weekend. No excuse or apologies. He punches out a curt reply. *Can't talk. I'm at work.* He hesitates, then adds: *We have a schedule for a reason. Changing it last minute doesn't work for us.* He catches his error just in time, backspacing to delete "us" and replacing it with a far more tactful "me."

A rap on the window brings his attention back to the woodland parking lot. He waves at DCI Khan, looming through the glass, reaches for his jacket, and steps out into the chill morning air. "Morning, boss."

"Sorry about your day off," says Khan, already gesturing to

the start of the walking trail and the direction they are headed. "Ferguson's off sick and this one's going to need careful handling. Hope I didn't drag you away from anything important?"

"As luck would have it, no." His phone buzzes deep in his pocket as he falls into step beside the shorter man. He ignores it. He hasn't got time for a snippy back-and-forth with Rachel. "What've we got?" he asks, zipping up his jacket.

"A body up at the folly. Young. Female."

"Shit." Ben winces. "Suicide?"

"Doesn't sound like it. I'm told the scene is 'unusual.' Silverton and her team are setting up now. We've started closing the main trails up to the tower, but given the way the woods sprawl, we've got a job on our hands protecting the integrity of the site. There's clear signs of activity up here last night."

Ben tries to conjure the topography in his mind. Their rendezvous point, a small parking lot at the lower eastern edge of the woods, offered the easiest vehicle access to their destination. From there, the shortest of the steep walking trails wound up approximately half a mile or so through the woods to the top of the escarpment where the abandoned stone folly sat high above them. There were incredible views across the Avon Valley, for anyone brave or foolish enough to climb the internal spiral staircase to the platform at the top. Heading west, away from the tower, you could descend a number of longer paths to the winding road known to locals as Sally in the Wood. Once at the road, you could head south to the private school, veer north toward Bath, or take a turnoff heading further west into the nearby town of Thorncombe.

Ben hasn't walked up to the folly in years, but he remembers the forbidding stone tower, sitting like an axis point at the top of the woods, as well as the hills below littered with a series of abandoned quarries and caves, which had provided much of the local building stone, back in the day.

Ben turns his jacket collar up against the chill and follows Khan along the start of the trail. It's been an unseasonably dry autumn and the ground is mercifully hard beneath their boots. The morning air holds earthy notes of timber laced with the faintest trace of woodsmoke and something heavier, something dank and fetid, almost fungal, autumn's organic matter already in decay.

"I used to come here years ago as a teenager," Ben tells Khan. "Back then it was *the* place to come—the only place, really." Memories return of dark, damp nights, spitting bonfires, music playing on a portable CD player, cheap, too-sweet bottles of wine, and kids hollering and cussing, their cries echoing through the trees.

"Doesn't look like much has changed," says Khan, kicking at an empty cider bottle poking from the undergrowth.

"This is what Ellie's been banging on about," says Ben. "She's been saying for months that there's nowhere to go. She's dead keen on the skate park plans, but it seems the new housing development's put the final nail in that coffin."

"I heard," says Khan. "Shame, but money talks round here."

Ben's legs begin to protest at the steep incline and the two men fall silent, preserving their energy to tackle the hill. Khan, the shorter of the two, drops back a little and Ben subtly slows his pace to allow his boss to catch up.

The last time he walked this trail would've been with Rachel and Ellie. A spring day, he remembers. There were muddy puddles, branches coming into bud, and Ellie, probably around eight years old, scampering up the trail, dragging a long stick behind her. Gemma had been staying with them, visiting from London. "Auntie Gem" as Ellie had called her, the two of them playing hide-and-seek among the trees, hunting for animal tracks and imaginary fairy doors, while he and Rachel had ambled along behind, hand in hand.

It's startling to remember how different everything had been. How simple. Before Gemma's death. Before the end of his marriage. Before Ellie's brush with the law at that protest in Bristol last month. Before the slow, slippery slide of life. Too many mistakes. He won't make the same ones with Chrissie. He swallows to think of her, and their conversation with Ellie out in the garden last night, Ellie's unreadable face staring at him in the dark, the merest flicker of emotion in her eyes before she'd regained her composure. She'd been a closed book, hadn't given anything away, not even when he'd taken her to one side and asked if she was *really* OK. Just that infuriating, blank expression and the rigid line of her shoulders turning away.

"Christ, I need to get back on my Peloton," puffs Khan. Ben spins and sees his boss's sweaty brow, narrow shoulders hunched in his woolen coat, his black, usually slicked-back hair falling into his eyes. Khan was a sharp dresser, designer gear, always immaculately turned out, but tramping through the woods on a Sunday morning, he looks almost comically out of place in his smart suit trousers and brogues.

Khan had said the victim was a young female. Thank god Ellie had been home last night, but someone's daughter hadn't been and now there was a job to be done. No time for wallowing in the past or ruminating on his own problems. "You said the scene's 'unusual'?"

"You'll see . . . when we get there."

"Who found her?"

"A couple of Girl Guides. Part of a troop . . . ," still puffing, Khan pauses to take a breath, ". . . out on a sunrise hike."

Ben winces. "How are *they* doing?"

"As you'd expect. I've sent DC Maxwell to liaise with the girls and their families."

Ben nods. Fiona Maxwell was one of the strongest constables on their team, a sparky, energetic recruit originally from Manchester, now relocated to Bath. "I'm sure she was thrilled to be woken so early on a Sunday morning."

"Maxwell's a workhorse. Never complains. Her girlfriend, on the other hand," says Khan, "I could hear in the background giving me a colorful earful."

Ben's grin is short-lived. "Dealing with a bunch of traumatized kids and their parents. That's not going to be easy."

"No. Fortunately, the patrol leader managed to keep most of the girls away from the scene, once she'd realized what they'd stumbled on. Maxwell will be asking for discretion, but it won't be long before word gets out. Small town. People talk."

Ben nods, conserving his energy as they press on up through the woods.

"It's an odd place to bring a group of young girls at daybreak," puffs Khan. "I'm surprised they weren't frightened out of their wits walking out here in the dark."

"That was probably the fun of it. You remember what it was like as a kid? All the ghost stories . . . horror movies."

Khan throws him a disapproving look. "I don't like that stuff. Never have. There's enough darkness in the world without adding to it. Some things should be left well alone."

"I didn't have you pegged as a superstitious type."

Khan shrugs. "I'm not, usually, but you've got to admit there's something off about this place." He glances around and Ben is surprised to see his boss shiver.

"These woods are full of stories. We'd frighten each other with them as kids," admits Ben. "But it was the folly that gave me the creeps. There's an old folktale about a girl murdered by her fiancé up there on her wedding day; left her at the tower in her bloodied wedding dress for the crows to pluck out her eyes." Seeing Khan's grimace, he nods. "Some say she's the 'Sally' that the road on the other side of the escarpment is named after, the ghost in a white dress that drivers report rushing out at them from the woods late at night."

Khan nods. "I've heard the stories."

"That's all it is. A story. Something made up by the locals to scare kids and tourists, and to explain the road accident statistics." Ben feels Khan's keen glance in his direction and knows what he's thinking. "People always want to find a reason why bad things happen." Ben's hands clench into fists. "You and I both know the truth. If you're driving under the influence with a phone in your hand, you're going to come off that road, and chances are, you're going to take someone else with you." Ben's jaw has locked tight. He swallows, trying to shift the hard knot at the back of his throat. He moves a pace or two ahead on the path, so he doesn't have to see Khan's sympathetic look. "It doesn't take a ghost story to explain that."

"Have you climbed the folly?" Khan asks, sensing Ben's desire to shift the conversation.

"Not much of a head for heights. Vertigo."

Khan smirks. "So, our resident action hero does have an Achilles' heel."

Ben rolls his eyes. Ever since he'd hit forty, shaved his head, and joined the local gym, the team had taken every opportunity to rip into him about his cliché midlife crisis. He wasn't stupid. He was self-aware enough to recognize that the changes were, in part, due to his marriage ending; an attempt to fight his softening "Dad bod"; a way to keep up with his younger girlfriend. Even so, he was proud of his new abs and he certainly appreciated the extra stamina on a morning hike like this, even if it meant the relentless mocking from the team.

"Have you seen it?" Ben protests. "The steps spiral all the way up. No handrails. No barriers. There's a platform at the very top, and a huge floor-to-ceiling opening. Amazing views, but nothing to stop you falling."

"Sounds terrifying, even without vertigo. Can't think why it's kept open."

"It's a bloody nuisance. The council installed a steel safety door a few years back, but it didn't last long. Vandals—or kids—broke it down. The tower's been open to the public ever since. One of those abandoned buildings that no one wants to be accountable for. A haunt for errant kids with nothing better to do—and a health and safety nightmare that seems to fall beyond anyone's jurisdiction. The council don't want a bar of it." Ben comes to a sudden stop. "Do you smell that?"

Khan sniffs the air. "Smoke?"

"I caught the scent of it earlier. It's stronger up here."

They detour a few steps from the path to peer over a low drystone wall. Below them they see the carved basin of an abandoned stone quarry, dug into the side of the rocks. The shallow basin stretches like a scar three hundred or so feet across, ringed by trees and toppled, moss-strewn rocks. "Still party central up here then," says Ben, pointing.

Down in the hollow among the fallen leaves and broken tree branches lies the carelessly discarded detritus of a recent party. Empty cans lie among silver vape cartridges, shards of broken bottles glinting in the weak morning light, the blackened remains of a bonfire slumped in the center. An abandoned pumpkin snarls at them with a carved toothy grin from a rocky ledge, while high above their heads, a forgotten T-shirt, hoisted like a flag, droops in the morning chill.

"A Halloween party, from the looks of it. Kids from town? The local private school?"

"Hope not. That's the school Ellie attends."

Khan whistles through his teeth. "Jesus, Chase. You remortgaged your house or something?"

"Nothing to do with me. It's all Ellie. She won a scholarship. Her talent got her there." Ben narrows his eyes, a splash of vivid red catching his attention. He jumps the wall and clambers down the steep slope of the quarry until he is standing in front of a large rock at the edge of the basin. A single word has been sprayed across its surface in red paint. SALLY. He studies the scrawl before reaching out with a finger to touch the letters. "It's dry, but recent."

"Let's circle back later," says Khan. "Once we know what we're dealing with at the folly."

Back on the path, they hike the final stretch up through the woods, until their first glimpse of the folly emerges between the thinning trees. The sky, now visible above them, is scattered with gray clouds, intermittent streaks of sunlight glancing off the tower's high stone walls.

"How tall is it?" asks Khan, regarding the folly, hands on hips. "Thirty-five, forty feet?"

Ben nods. "I'd say so."

"What's the point of it, standing up here in the middle of nowhere?"

"That's one of the few things I do know. It was a vanity project, built by a local quarry owner in the mid-nineteenth century to show off the quality of his stonework. The tower kept his laborers busy during a downturn in the industry."

Khan grins. "Man erects gigantic, phallic monument to show off his business prowess. A tale as old as time."

They emerge onto the escarpment to see the forensics team already assembled, mid-briefing. Trish Silverton, their Senior Forensics Investigator, a small, birdlike woman with short, white-blond hair and flashing green eyes, gives them a wave but doesn't break from her spiel to the gathered officers. Ben nods his greeting and zips into a white crime-scene suit before ducking beneath the tape secured in a large square around the base of the tower.

He approaches the scene with care, skirting the folly and a small heap of black ash—the remains of another recent bonfire—stopping when he sees the body lying in the dirt. He crouches down, taking it all in, forcing his breath to slow and his mind to focus.

It's a disturbing sight and his first impression is that she isn't real. That this isn't a girl, but rather a posed mannequin or a wax figure laid out for display. His gaze sweeps across the details. The white gauze dress, old-looking and detailed with lace, like a Victorian nightdress or undergarment, torn at the neck, exposing the hint of a slender white shoulder. Pale arms folded carefully across her chest. Long, fair hair falling tidily around the shoulders. Feet placed together, the toes of her sneakers pointing neatly skyward.

Ben swallows. He can see significant blood spatter across her chest, and more staining the neckline of the dress, as well as a dark pool of it leaking like oil beneath her skull. With a breath, he allows his gaze to travel to the most disturbing detail. Only half her face is visible, just the bruised jaw and blue lips, before the girl's head seems to morph into a distended black beak, raven feathers ruffling against her fair hair. A mask, Ben sees, with a grotesque hooked beak, half Venetian ball costume, half plague doctor. The sight is unnerving, made all the more unfathomable by the words he can see scrawled over the girl's limbs, daubed in black along her bare arms and calves. PUNISH. DESTROY. REPENT. The words repeat over and over along her skin. Ben shudders. So, this is what Khan meant by "unusual."

Even without seeing the victim's face, it's obvious that she is young. A teenager, probably no older than Ellie. Her hands are unlined, pink glitter polish daubed onto fingernails, a silver pendant—half a heart—hanging limp on a chain around her neck. It's the sort of necklace he knows comes in two halves, a pendant to split with a best friend or a boyfriend. Somewhere, someone has the matching piece.

The ache in his chest swells. This girl has taken care with her appearance, excited about her Saturday night. Preparations for a party or a date. Too young. Far too young to be lying here alone in the woods.

"You ever seen anything like this before?" Khan asks, crouching beside him. "The words on her skin . . . the mask . . . the pose."

Ben shakes his head.

Khan indicates red scratch marks on the girl's arms and a mottled bruise on her jaw. "Looks like she put up quite a fight."

"The mask isn't attached, look." Ben points to the elastic dangling loose on either side. "It's laid over her face."

"What are you thinking? Halloween night. Some dark occult shit?" Khan glances up at the tower above, the opening set high into the stone wall.

A light breeze skims the ground, rustling the dry leaves at their feet. Strands of the girl's hair lift, then resettle on her shoulders. Ben frowns, trying to find a word circling in his mind. "Reverence," he says, the word dropping into his mind like a coin in a slot machine.

"What?"

"The way she's been laid here suggests . . . I don't know . . . a sort of care or artistry. They've taken their time. The words. The mask. They have to mean something. We need to work out what."

Khan calls out to one of the officers nearby. "Have you found anything yet? A bag? A phone? Anything to tell us who she is?"

"Nothing yet, Chief."

Khan frowns. "Name one teenager you know who goes anywhere without their phone?"

Silverton, having wrapped her briefing, strides toward them. "We're ready to set up the tent."

Khan nods. "Be my guest."

Ben stands back to allow the technicians to move in, watching as the metal frame and white canvas walls are erected like a shroud around the girl's body, as they swab and scrape and photograph. He notes their professionalism, their care. Another form of reverence, he thinks. As they prepare to lift the mask from the girl's face, he takes a step closer, his breath tight in his chest.

"Careful," says Silverton, overseeing the technician using a long pair of tweezers to lift the feathered object.

Ben notes the shake in the man's hand as he peels the bird mask away to reveal the face beneath—only it's no longer a face, not really. Half the skull is a mess of bloody pulp and bone.

"Oh Jesus," says Khan, turning away.

Silverton throws them a grim look. "Identification could take longer than we thought." She nods at the high stone walls of the folly looming beyond the tent opening. "It's a long way down."

"She fell? Jumped?" Ben already knows the answer. Nobody jumps forty feet off a tower and lands like this, neatly arranged on the ground. His eyes drift over the words daubed on the girl's skin. PUNISH. The scenarios in his mind make him shudder again.

Khan clears his throat. "I want a full grid search of the area," he says. "From the woodland parking lot up to the folly, and all the way down the other side where the woods meet the road. I want anything out of place marked. And let's get a technician up there." He jerks his head at the tower.

"What about all the splinter routes and trails zigzagging through the woods?" asks Ben. "There must be a dozen at least."

"We've got our work cut out, that's for sure. We'll have to move fast. It's going to be impossible to restrict the area. As soon as word gets out about the body, we'll be overrun with journos and wannabe Miss Marples. We've got a jump on them, but not for long. One sniff and they'll be all over this like flies on the proverbial. I want to know who was in the quarry last night, who was at the party. The school's close by—could she be a student?"

Ben nods, his gaze drifting from the victim's damaged face to focus on other details. The girl's freshly washed hair. Her glitter nail polish. The gleaming silver pendant at her throat. He imagines a bedroom, one with makeup spilling over a dressing table, a jewelry box left open, discarded clothes and peeling posters, a bed, currently empty where a warm body should be. It is not any teenager's bedroom he is imagining, he realizes, but Ellie's, back in their old home, the one he used to share with Rachel.

"We need a victim ID. We need it fast."

Someone somewhere will be missing this girl. Hopefully it won't be too long before it's called in.

Chapter 5

Philippa Easton stands in the bay window of the drawing room sipping espresso from a small earthenware cup. From her position she can see across the formal gardens, all the way to the paddock beyond where the horses gallop and buck, tossing their heads, feathered manes streaming in the breeze. The sight of their joyful cantering brings a hollow ache to her chest, a heavy longing. It's a strange sort of day, the wind up, agitating and bristling, creating a momentum she's not ready for. The pills she took last night linger in her veins. She's waiting for that first kick of caffeine to hit her system and drag her into the day.

She checks her Rolex and sees it's almost eleven. Time slides away so quickly these days. Christopher was up and about early, as usual, but the girls shouldn't lounge about in bed all morning. They should try to make something of the day. With a sigh, she rests her cup in its saucer and makes for the winding staircase.

Upstairs, her daughter's bedroom door is firmly shut. Philippa knocks softly and waits before opening it a crack. "Olivia," she calls, her voice cajoling. "It's time to wake up."

The room is dark and silent, a heavy stillness hanging in the air. The smallest chink of light falls from a gap between the heavy velvet curtains. She steps inside. "Olivia," she says again, "it's nearly eleven."

She skirts the detritus scattered across the floorboards, navigating shadowy piles of books and clothes and a school backpack spilling its contents onto a sheepskin rug. As she draws closer, she lets out a sharp breath. Her daughter's bed is empty.

She blinks in the dim light and takes another step forward. Panic seizes in her chest, but no. She's there, her slim body is pressed up against the wall, tucked into the bedsheets, barely visible but for one telltale foot poking from beneath the covers. "Olivia," she says, relief making her voice loud. "It's time to wake up."

The covers shift. A groan rises from the bed.

"How was the party?" Philippa walks to the window and pulls back the curtains, allowing bright daylight into the room.

Olivia's incoherent grumbling increases in volume.

"I didn't hear you come home. Just before midnight, your father said."

Her daughter's wan face emerges from the covers. She rubs her eyes as Philippa picks up a discarded tulle skirt lying in a puddle at her feet and folds it neatly. "You really should tidy your clothes away," she says. "You have such lovely things." She presses the light fabric to her face, inhaling the scent of something cloying and musky, then wrinkles her nose. "Have you been smoking?"

"No one smokes these days, Mum. We vape." Olivia squints at the window, then rolls away onto her side.

Philippa sniffs the skirt again and pulls a face. "This definitely smells of smoke."

"There was a bonfire." Olivia reaches for her phone on the bedside table. The screen casts her narrow face in blue light.

"I hope you haven't forgotten you girls promised to come into

Bath with me? Sarah should call her mother before we go. Diana says she's not heard from her all week."

When Olivia doesn't answer, Philippa fills the silence. "Shall I wake her, or do you want to?"

For a moment, it looks as though Olivia might slide back beneath the covers, but then she pushes herself up, swinging her bare legs out from beneath the duvet. "I'll go."

"Good. I'll make tea and toast." She throws her daughter a knowing look. "It'll help with your hangovers."

Philippa is pouring boiling water into a pot of tea leaves when Olivia appears in the kitchen, still in her short nightshirt, her long blond hair falling from the messy knot piled on her head. "What is it?" she asks, the half smile on her face faltering at her daughter's expression. "What's wrong?"

"It's Sarah," says Olivia, a tremor in her voice. She wraps one long, bare leg around the other, lifts the necklace hanging at her throat to her lips. "She's not there."

Philippa frowns. "What do you mean, 'not there'?"

"I mean, she's not in her bed."

Philippa stares at her daughter, trying to make sense of the words. "Well, where is she?"

Olivia shakes her head. "I don't know. The bed . . . it doesn't look as if it's been slept in."

"What? Not at all?" Philippa feels a prickle of unease pierce through the soft haze of her mind and travel as a shiver down her neck. "But she came back with you last night. She must be here somewhere."

Olivia's gaze drops to the floor. "Not . . . exactly."

Philippa places the teapot back on the countertop, the prickling sensation moving down her spine. "What do you mean, 'not exactly'? Are you saying Sarah didn't come home with you?"

Olivia eyes her mother, then shakes her head, her face beginning to crumple.

"You need to tell me what happened last night. Do you hear?" She moves across the room and seizes her daughter's arm. "Tell me right now."

Chapter 6

Ellie is burrowed deep in the bed, her limbs tangling in the covers as she flips the pillow, seeking the cooler side to press against her too-hot face. There's a drum beating in her head and her tongue lolls like the stinking inner sole of one of her school sneakers. Traces of the night before ooze from every pore.

Opening one eye, she sees her clothes—denim cutoffs, ripped black tights, and her favorite gray hoodie—lying in a crumpled heap on the floorboards of Jasmine's shared dorm room. A rust-brown stain arcs across the front of the hoodie, a mess she's pretty sure isn't going to wash out. She swallows. She doesn't want to think about that right now. She doesn't want to think about anything to do with last night.

Across the room, Jasmine lies in an identical single bed snoring beneath a duvet covered in small yellow daisies; one slender, brown arm flung above her head, her mouth gaping wide. An old iron radiator clanks and groans in the corner.

Rolling onto her back, Ellie can just make out the posters tacked to the wall beside her, the smiling, sparkly-eyed faces of pop stars grinning back at her. They're not Jasmine's posters.

Jasmine wouldn't be seen dead with Harry Styles or Ed Sheeran over her bed. These belong to Zara, Jasmine's roommate, helpfully away on a weekend home visit. On Jasmine's side it's all Greenpeace, Extinction Rebellion, and Bob Marley. Much better.

Squeezing her eyes shut to block out the white-veneered smiles beaming down at her, Ellie burrows back beneath the covers. She wants sleep, craves the blessed absence of being, but sleep won't come. Not now. Not now she is remembering. There's the drink, the sweet–sour taste of it lingering at the back of her throat. The flames leaping against the dark night. The scratch of branches. The taunts and the jibes, words stinging like hot metal sparks. White fabric twisting and tearing in her hands, warm blood gushing over her fingers.

Sweat prickles on her skin as the awful fragments wheel through her mind.

What has she done?

She could burn her clothes. Drop them into an oil drum, soak them with gasoline, and set fire to them in a flaming roar. Just walk away without a backward glance like you see actors do in the movies. But where do you find an oil drum and a spare jerry can of gasoline? They aren't exactly the sort of thing you find lying around at a school like Folly View.

Outside the window, two girls walk by, their voices bouncing cheerfully off the stone walls. There's a high giggle, followed moments later by the sound of running footsteps. The scent of fried eggs carries on the air. Soon the chapel bell will ring, beckoning the boarders to Sunday worship. Ellie's stomach flips. There's going to be no sleeping this off. She'll be stuck with her hangover and the sour taste of self-loathing all day. And the consequences of what she did last night? They could last a lifetime. A surge of bile floods up her throat.

Ellie should learn to control her impulses.

Ellie needs to practice self-restraint.

Ellie should think before she acts.

Words from past school reports float through her mind. Act first, think later—it's always been her problem. "You get your red hair from your mother, but you get your fiery spirit from me," her dad had told her once, ruffling her hair, Ellie leaning into his hand like a cat. "Passionate. Impetuous. It's a good trait . . . sometimes," he'd added, with a grin.

He hadn't been quite so enthusiastic when her passionate spirit had seen her cut school to join the oil protest sit-in on the superhighway into Bristol, or when she'd been caught scrawling graffiti on a fast-food chain's posters in town. She'd been given a three-day exclusion from school, an official warning from Mrs. Crowe, and a stern talking-to by her parents, both of them all sad, soft eyes and cloying disappointment.

But all of that was nothing compared to last night. Last night, she'd gone too far.

You're fucked, Ellie Chase.

Ellie's heart thumps painfully in her chest, her throat closing. She'd lost complete control. Frightened herself. What she'd done was unforgivable—and this time it could cost her everything.

Surrendering to full consciousness, she reaches for her phone. There's a message from her mum, a text full of obvious false cheer about the weekend with her dad. A pang of guilt rises but she shoves it away. She wouldn't have had to lie if her parents hadn't messed everything up. She could handle the fact they didn't want to be married anymore. What she couldn't handle was having every aspect of her life micromanaged, being shuttled between them like a six-year-old. It was bad enough that she had her mother hovering over her at school all week. She didn't want them squabbling over her at weekends too. She was seventeen. It wasn't right that they dictated how she spent her free time.

Ellie ignores the message from her mum and switches instead to Snapchat, scrolling through stories of Halloween selfies; impressive carved pumpkins with leering, toothy smiles; a three-second video of Jasmine with her tongue rammed down a boy's throat, arms snaked around his neck; Danny and Saul posing in front of a bonfire, grinning as they flash the hang-loose gesture, a bottle of vodka passing between hands. Another shaky video follows, the screen mostly black, the thump of electronic music playing from a speaker, before the camera swerves to a crackle of flames. A sour taste fills Ellie's mouth. She wants to drop her phone, but she can't tear her eyes from the screen. "Sally," she hears, the name like a taunt. "Saaaally!" There's a flash of trees and white fabric, a glimpse of blond hair and a close-up of a wide, straight-toothed smile. A scuffling noise ensues and the camera veers chaotically before it cuts.

She could carry on, torment herself with her doomscrolling, and see what else has made it onto the feed, but the fragments she's replayed are enough to tell her she doesn't want to see any more. At least this time tomorrow the stories will have disappeared, automatically deleted by Snapchat's servers. She jumps instead to her private texts.

Hey, where'd you go? You ok? 😶

Last night was MESSED UP.

Damn girl. You were on a mission. 😈 😈

She swipes the app closed. There's dirt on her hands and something reddish-brown lodged beneath her nails. The sight of it brings another violent wave of nausea. She pushes the covers away and staggers to the window, wrestling with the catch on the old sash before wrenching it up, cold air rushing over her skin. She breathes deeply. Behind the identical residential block on the opposite side of the quad, she sees the wooded hills rising in the distance. Somewhere, right at the top, stands the folly. Ellie closes her eyes and takes another deep breath. Fuck.

Bedsprings creak on the other side of the room. "Hey," Jasmine groans. "What time is it?"

Ellie swallows bile. "Gone eleven."

"Shit. I'll be late for worship. What are you doing at the window? It's freezing." She throws a dramatic hand to her forehead. "My head's banging."

"Mine too."

"What even happened to you last night? Do you remember getting back here?"

"Not really."

"You were lucky I heard you. If Matron had caught you outside . . . she'd probably been at the gin again." Jasmine wrestles herself up onto an elbow with another labored groan. Her headscarf has slipped, releasing a rogue braid. "So, where'd you go last night?"

Ellie closes her eyes, but it's as if the bone-white trees and the stone tower are painted on the inside of her eyelids. "I just walked it off. Went round and round in circles, I think. What time did I turn up here?"

Jasmine shrugs. "No idea. I was wasted."

"I owe you one."

"Yeah." Jasmine grins. "You do."

Ellie turns back to Jasmine. "I do remember one thing."

"What's that?"

"You and Saul."

Jasmine's brown eyes go wide. She makes a gagging sound, then hides her face behind her pillow. "Saul. Gross."

"That's not what you said last night."

"Beer goggles."

"Did you two . . ." Ellie throws her a meaningful look.

Jasmine nods, a sheepish smile creeping over her face.

Ellie thinks for a moment. "Do you reckon Danny's OK?"

Jasmine raises an eyebrow and Ellie blushes but doesn't look away, tries to style it out.

"He'll be fine," says Jas. "It was time he woke up to that girl. Do you think *she's* all right? I mean . . . Connor. Really? Even Olivia looked pissed about that. No wonder she left early."

Ellie doesn't want to think about that. She doesn't want to think about any of it. "No one can let on I was there," she says. "I'll get in so much shit."

Jasmine nods. "Don't worry. We got you. Everyone knows to keep quiet."

"I hope so." Ellie angles her face back to the cool air drifting through the open window. The sun is climbing over the wooded slopes, the hills looming over the campus, a hard shoulder butting up against the school. She can't help shivering. "I've got a really bad feeling."

"That's your hangover."

"Is it OK if I lie low here a bit longer? Clear my head. I can't face Mum yet."

"Where does she *think* you are?"

"Still with Dad."

"Well, that's something. You're lucky." Jasmine sighs. "Divorced parents are so much easier to play. Not like in this prison."

"Hmm," says Ellie, but as she reaches for her clothes and wrestles one leg into her ripped tights, she knows she isn't lucky. In fact, staring at her grimy hands and her ruined clothes, she feels certain that any luck she might've had has just run out.

Chapter 7

Sunday, 1:00 p.m.

Rachel is sitting at the kitchen table wrestling with a PowerPoint presentation on her laptop when she hears the soft click of the front door. "Ellie?" she calls. "Is that you?"

"Yeah."

Just one word, but from its flat delivery she knows that Ellie has returned tired and cranky, in one of her especially tricky moods.

Rachel has spent the morning working on a student presentation about the dangers of recreational drugs. Given a recent overdose incident at the local high school across town, it had seemed pertinent to move the topic as a priority into the term's personal health program. She'd argued to Margaret Crowe that it would be naive to assume the prestige of Folly View College was in any way a shield for their students. If it was happening at the local secondary school, then it was almost certainly happening at Folly View too.

She slides her laptop across the table to join a plate of discarded sandwich crusts. "You're earlier than I expected," she calls. "Dad got called into work?" Her question is met by silence, so she tries again. "I didn't hear a car. Did Chrissie drop you back?"

Ellie acknowledges the question with an indecipherable murmur that is neither "yes" or "no."

Rachel has only met Chrissie once, during an awkward doorstep exchange she'd insisted on, knowing that Ellie would be spending time with the woman at her home. She'd seemed perfectly nice, if a little nervous to be standing face-to-face with Ben's ex. Younger than her by a good few years. Blond curls and a pretty face, with immaculate eyebrows and bright red lipstick, the sight of which had made Rachel feel frumpy and disheveled. An office administrator from Bath, Ben had told her. She's desperate to know what Ellie makes of her and can't help a small, uncharitable flutter of pleasure that she's chosen to return home early—to her—rather than hang out with Chrissie in her neat new build on the other side of town.

Still, it hardly fills her with joy to think of Chrissie dropping Ellie home, hovering outside in her car, scoping out the cottage. The place was lovely in the warmer months, the tiny front garden blossoming with roses and a scrambling clematis that shrouded the peeling paint and flaking window frames. But come late autumn, the cottage grew decidedly gloomy, the woods crowding oppressively close, as if they would reach out and one day entirely swallow the stone building from view. Inside, it was drafty and lacking insulation, with old iron radiators that never quite seemed to warm up and a temperamental hearth where the fire would smoke and spit, whenever she could be bothered to light one. Still, of the staff members who lived on campus, she knew she was one of the luckier ones. Some resident teachers lived in apartments attached to the boarders' dormitories. At least out here on the fringes they were afforded a little more privacy. If Chrissie wants to judge their living arrangements, she can't exactly stop her.

Hearing Ellie's footsteps creaking toward the stairs, Rachel calls out again. "Wait, I want to talk to you."

There's a pointed sigh before her daughter's ashen face peers round the door, violet shadows and yesterday's eye makeup still smeared beneath her green eyes, her short red hair springing up in its usual wild nest. "What?"

Breathe, Rachel warns herself. She doesn't want to start with an argument, not when Ellie's just walked in the door. This is an adjustment for them all. She fixes a smile to her face. "So? How was it?"

"Fine."

"Come in here. I missed you."

She sees Ellie's eye roll as she emerges from behind the door. "Your hoodie's on inside out. You must be tired. Late night?"

Ellie doesn't reply.

"So . . ." she says, hating the false note of cheer in her voice, "what did you guys get up to?"

"Nothing much."

Rachel purses her lips. "I know you're annoyed about missing the party, but it was important you spend time with your dad."

"I know. Is that all?"

Rachel's about to wave her away when a distinct scent carries across the room. She sniffs pointedly. "You smell of smoke."

"Chill out, Mum. It's charcoal. Dad bought a pizza oven. He was cooking in the garden last night."

"Oh. Nice. And it was OK? You're OK?" Rachel eyes Ellie. Something isn't right. She can feel it. Ellie is avoiding her gaze, shifting uncomfortably by the door, a look in her eyes. Guilt. Fear. She can't tell. "Ellie, if there's something you want to talk—"

"Is this about the baby?"

Rachel frowns, thinking she's misheard. "Baby?"

"Because if it is, I'm totally fine with it. You don't have to do one of your 'therapy' numbers on me."

It's like a punch to the guts. "You don't mean . . . ?"

"Dad's a free agent. He can do what he likes. Have as many babies as he likes, with whoever."

Rachel's momentary relief to realize this isn't *Ellie's* baby they're talking about evaporates. *Ben's baby.* The truth is another fist slamming into her. Ben and Chrissie are having a baby? They've only been together five minutes.

"Honestly," continues Ellie in her flat delivery, her hands burrowed in her sleeves, twisting the fabric, "I know you won't believe me, but I don't care. I'll be leaving as soon as I've got my A-level results." She narrows her eyes. "You did know about Chrissie being pregnant?"

"Sure," she lies. "Course."

"So, was there something else?"

"Um . . . I . . ." Rachel's mind crackles with static. Logical thought seems to have escaped her. A baby? Ben's having a baby with Chrissie. She scrambles for something to cover her shock. "Have you eaten?"

"I'm not hungry."

"What about homework?"

"On it."

Still distracted by her daughter's unintentional land mine, she lets Ellie duck away, her footsteps thudding up the stairs. At the sound of the bedroom door shutting firmly overhead, Rachel slumps in her seat and stares at the Folly View screensaver logo bouncing haphazardly across her laptop screen, the small stone tower performing a chaotic dance that seems to mirror the pattern of her thoughts.

Chrissie is pregnant? Ben told Ellie yesterday at a cozy pizza night and he didn't think it appropriate to at least warn Rachel? To give her a polite heads-up? Didn't think that their complicated, emotional daughter might need a little support from her mum to process this huge life change? Eighteen years of marriage and Ben thought so little of Rachel's feelings that he didn't think she might like to hear it from him, directly?

My God. She shakes her head in bewilderment. That man was something else. How galling to spend the best part of your life with someone and to only now realize that you barely knew them at all.

She reaches for her phone and sees her last message to Ben still hanging unanswered. The single *?* she'd sent that morning in response to his nonsensical reply about schedules. The solitary punctuation mark seems even more apposite now. As tempting as it is to fire off a stinging dispatch, she'll wait for him to grace her with a reply before she opens this whole new can of worms.

Unsure what else to do, she fills the kettle, then stands for a while looking out the window at the scruffy garden with its tilting wooden fence, at the dead seed heads of summer's long-gone flowers waving in the autumn light, at the dark wooded hills rising toward the sky. Standing there thinking about Ben and Chrissie and the pregnancy they hadn't had the decency to tell her about, she lets her anger rise with the piercing scream of the kettle.

Chapter 8

There's a woman waiting at the entrance to the manor house. Ben sees her as he navigates his car around the stone fountain and parks next to a racing green Jaguar on the gravel drive, its hood gleaming in the soft November sunshine. She stands by the huge wooden door, her bobbed ice-blond hair tucked behind her ears, a camel-colored cardigan drawn tightly around her slight frame.

He's come straight from the woods, as soon as the station had radioed through about the reported missing girl, calling Chrissie en route in an attempt to placate her. It hadn't worked. They'd had a terse conversation, Ben's mind distracted and already racing ahead into the investigation. "Are you even listening?" Chrissie had asked him, the hurt evident in her voice.

"Sorry, yes."

"You left so early this morning. Is everything OK?"

"Not really. It's going to be a long day."

"What's happened?"

"I can't say—not yet. Sorry." He'd gripped the steering wheel. "Are you OK?"

"I guess."

He could tell from her voice that she wasn't. "Is this about last night?"

Chrissie had released a long sigh. "It's just I had it all planned out. I thought Ellie might be a little happy for us, that it might bring us closer. Instead . . . well, the night didn't go exactly how I'd hoped."

"She'll come around. It's a lot of change for Ellie." *For all of us*, he'd nearly added, stopping himself just in time.

"You should've told Rachel 'no.'" A petulant note had entered Chrissie's voice. "You let her walk all over you."

Ben had felt torn. The previous night hadn't gone how he'd imagined either and yes, he'd been annoyed with Rachel too. He hadn't wanted Ellie to leave any more than Chrissie had, but he'd seen how thrown his daughter was at their baby announcement, as much as she'd tried to hide it. He'd felt guilty about adding to Ellie's emotional distress. He hadn't liked to say as much to Chrissie, but secretly he'd wondered if it was Ellie who had phoned Rachel and asked her to make up an excuse, so that she could leave. He supposed he could've challenged her, but the sight of his daughter's pale, tight face had made him think the kindest thing to do was to drop her back home to Rachel. To give her time.

"I think we need to be patient with her. Listen, I can't talk now," he'd said, watching as the ornate electric gates to Thornfield Manor slid open, a long gravel drive unfolding before him, "but I'll speak to Rachel. I promise."

Leaving the car, he heads toward the woman on the top step, his gaze sliding surreptitiously across the front of the imposing Georgian house rising behind her. Three stories high, built in honeyed Bath stone, with thick branches of wisteria clinging to the facade. Everything in his eyeline screams money and status. It's not often he gets called to a place like this.

"DS Ben Chase from Avon & Somerset Police," he says, holding out a hand in greeting as he reaches the top step.

Her handshake is limp, a frown creasing her narrow face, worry visible in her blue eyes. "Philippa Easton. Come in, please." She turns and leads him into the vast entrance hall. "My husband and daughter are waiting in the library. This way."

She walks with a stiff gait, he notices, a drag to her left foot, as if one of her neat leather loafers is slightly heavier than the other. He glimpses polished flagstones, a wall of painted family portraits, and a glass console table holding the biggest vase of lilies he's ever seen. The flowers fill the space with a cloying scent. "This is us," she says, ushering him into a dark, book-lined room.

A tall man with a thatch of salt-and-pepper hair stands by the window, his back to the door. Nearby, curled onto a low-slung leather sofa, is a blond girl, aged about sixteen or seventeen, Ben guesses. She looks up as he enters, wide-eyed and pale.

"Goddammit," the man says, and Ben realizes he's talking into his cell phone. "I thought the fence would keep them out. What sort of mess are we talking about?"

"Dad," the girl says, pulling at his sleeve. "Dad, the police are here."

The man holds up a finger to silence her, still listening intently to the voice down the line. "See that you do. No more delays, do you hear?" He jabs at the phone to end the call, then turns, his expression shifting in an instant from deep frustration to polite greeting at the sight of Ben. "Hello," he says, offering a firm handshake. "Christopher Easton. Thank you for coming." Ben sees the glimmer of recognition. "Have we . . . ?"

Ben nods. "DS Ben Chase. We met at the town hall consultation last month." Ben thinks it politic to get any potential elephants in the room positively identified. "My daughter spoke up on behalf of the skateboarding community. The redhead," he adds.

"Ah yes. The firecracker. I thought she spoke quite well, all things considered."

Ben nods, bristling ever so slightly at the man's condescending tone. He'd been proud of Ellie that night. She'd argued a strong case for the benefits of a dedicated skate park in Thorncombe. Not that it was going to do much good, by the look of things.

"Forgive me," says Christopher smoothly, "I'm usually good with names but there were a lot of faces there that night. Quite the evening," he adds, with a hint of self-congratulation. He's solidly built, broad shouldered and muscular, with the remnants of an expensive summer tan and a gold signet ring on his little finger. In his neatly pressed shirt and mother-of-pearl cuff links, Ben recognizes a man who takes pride in his appearance. "It was good to canvass local opinion and get everyone singing from the same hymn sheet," he adds.

Ben nods again, though his recollection of the meeting is a little different. The fiery session, hosted by Easton's development company, had been an attempt to placate the local community over a proposed new housing development earmarked for a strip of countryside on the far edge of town. Personally, Ben had been on Ellie's side. Thorncombe had already met its new housing targets and appeared to be struggling for infrastructure and services; there were complaints about pressures on the town's schools, transport, and health services. Though for a man like Christopher Easton, he imagines it's quite easy to resign yourself to tearing up great swaths of countryside when you're king of your own castle, surrounded by acres of private land. Not even the local conservation group seemed to hold much sway when it came to the town planning process. It appeared Christopher Easton was a man with friends in high places and enough cash to grease all the necessary palms.

"You've already met Philippa, my wife." He nods at the blond woman hovering at his side, then turns to the teenager. "And this is my daughter, Olivia."

The girl is huddled on the sofa, swamped in a huge burgundy sweatshirt pulled low over her knees, bare feet sticking out from beneath. "Hello, Olivia," he says, throwing her a sympathetic look. "I'm DS Chase."

She greets him with a quiet, "Hello." Ben sees the same olive skin as her father, the blond hair and fine features of her mother; handsome rather than pretty.

"Can I get you anything, DS Chase?" asks Philippa, a strangely vacant look in her eyes. "Tea, coffee?" She slips into the formal conventions of a social occasion.

"No, thank you. Let's get straight to it, shall we?"

Philippa lowers herself onto the arm of the sofa. Next to the bulk of her husband, she appears even more delicate and insubstantial, like a piece of paper ready to flutter to the floor. He flips open a notebook. "You've reported a teenage girl missing?"

"Yes," says Christopher, taking control. "We discovered this morning that our niece, Sarah, hadn't returned home from a party last night. We're rather worried." He shoots a look in his daughter's direction. "Home by midnight, we told the girls. We only realized Sarah hadn't come home *at all* when Olivia went to wake her this morning and found her bed empty."

Ben frowns. "Sarah is visiting you?"

"No, Sarah lives with us. My sister, Diana, is a partner at an international law firm in Dubai. Sarah used to live out there too, but after her father passed away—cancer, very sad—Diana thought an English boarding school might be a good option. It was the girls," he gestures to his daughter, "who suggested she come here."

Olivia brushes loose strands of hair from her face.

"They're very close," adds Philippa. "More like sisters than cousins."

"We agreed that Sarah could live with us while she finishes her education. She transferred to Olivia's school for the start of Year Twelve. They're day pupils. My sister, Diana, travels back and forth to visit, as much as she can."

Ben mentally grapples with the family tree. "I see. So where is Sarah's mother right now? Dubai?"

Christopher nods.

Olivia's fingers are worrying the cuff on her burgundy sweatshirt. Ben spots the tower logo embroidered on the chest. He addresses Olivia with his next question. "You and Sarah both attend Folly View College?"

She nods.

"What year?"

"Thirteen."

"It's a big year for you." He keeps his voice light, but inside, a hammer has begun to beat against his heart. It's the same school—the same year—as Ellie, and the same school where Rachel works as Head of Student Welfare. If the girl in the woods *is* Sarah, Ben knows it's going to impact everyone terribly, the noose of their investigation sliding a little tighter around their small community. "You might know my daughter, Ellie?"

"I know her." Olivia tilts her head, her gaze silently assessing. "You look alike."

"I don't think Ellie would be too pleased to hear you say that,"

Ben admits with a small smile. "So, you and Sarah attended a Halloween party last night?"

"They *said* they were going to a friend's house," Philippa chips in, clearly miffed. "Only it seems they weren't quite telling the truth. Olivia, you explain."

Olivia avoids his gaze, tugging a loose thread on her sleeve between her fingernails.

"Where were you last night, Olivia?" Ben's voice is gentle. "You're not in any trouble, but I do need to collect as much information as possible so that we can find Sarah."

"Tell DS Chase," urges Christopher.

Olivia's voice, when it comes, is soft and tremulous. "We went to a party in the woods. At the old quarry."

Ben nods. "How many people were there?"

"I don't know." She shrugs. "Fifteen. Twenty. Maybe a few more."

"All kids from your school?"

"Mostly."

"And you spent the whole evening there? With Sarah?"

Olivia nods. "Until our curfew."

"When did you last see Sarah?"

Olivia thinks. "I stayed until around 11:30 p.m. I was worried we'd get into trouble if we left any later." She glances at her mother. "I *told* Sarah we had to leave, but she wouldn't come. I didn't know what else to do. I couldn't exactly force her."

"Olivia walked home on her own!" Christopher interjects, with a disapproving look.

"But Sarah stayed behind?" asks Ben, looking to Olivia for confirmation.

The girl nods. "She *told* me to go. Said she wanted to stay. So I came home alone."

Ben glances at her parents. Philippa shrugs. "I was asleep in bed." She defers to her husband. "You were still up, weren't you, Christopher?"

"Yes. I heard Livvy come in as I was drifting off. I assumed it was both girls and fell asleep."

"Did you have any contact with Sarah after that point, Olivia?"

She nods. "Sarah still wasn't home as I was getting into bed. We follow each other on that Find My iPhone app, so I checked to see where she was."

"What time was that?"

"About quarter to one."

"Could you see where she was?"

Oliva nods. "Still in the woods. I couldn't believe it. I sent her a message. See."

Olivia opens her cell phone and angles the screen to show him a message on Snap, timed 00:49. *What the hell Sarah! You must have a death wish.*

"You can see she's read it," says Olivia. She points to the "opened" status. "I waited up a bit longer, hoping she'd come home, or at least reply, but I guess I fell asleep." Olivia hangs her head.

Philippa rubs her daughter's back. "You tried your best."

"This isn't your fault," adds Christopher. "Sarah is being rather selfish, worrying us all like this."

"Does Sarah have a boyfriend?"

Olivia clears her throat. "She was seeing a boy at school—well, sort of. On and off."

Christopher folds his arms across his chest, eyes narrowing. "Well, that's news to us." He leans forward. "Who, Olivia? Why didn't you mention it?"

"It seemed more 'off' than 'on' last night. His name's Danny Carlisle," she adds, glancing up at Ben. "He's a boy in our year."

Christopher sighs. "Right, now that Olivia's finally thought to mention this Danny kid, we'll try him next. We certainly don't want to put you out, Sergeant, or involve you in silly teenage shenanigans. Sarah's inconvenienced us quite enough already."

"You're not putting us out, Mr. Easton. A teenage girl hasn't returned home. You did the right thing calling us. How did Sarah seem to you last night, Olivia? Anything out of the ordinary?"

Olivia frowns. "To be honest, she was being kind of annoying." She glances across at her parents. "She'd had a bit to drink and was showing off."

"Showing off how?"

"Dancing. Flirting." Olivia's cheeks flush pink.

"She was in high spirits? Happy?"

Olivia nods.

"Do you remember what she was wearing?"

"Of course. It was fancy dress. Sarah went as Sally."

Ben frowns. "Sally?"

"Yeah. Sally in the Wood. You know," she glances up at him, "the ghost story about a local girl killed at the folly. Sarah thought it would be funny."

A cold sensation runs through Ben. Sally. The folly. It was only a few hours ago that he'd been relaying the bare bones of the same story to DCI Khan. If that is Sarah lying dead at the top of the woods, what was this? A sick coincidence? Or something more sinister? He tries to focus. "What did Sarah's 'Sally' costume look like?"

"She wore a white dress—a lacy thing. One of mine," she adds, and Ben glimpses a hint of irritation in her face, imagines teenage girls tussling over clothes. "We smudged black around her eyes to make her look like a ghost. She left her hair loose, and on the way to the party, she messed it up with leaves and twigs and stuff. She looked really creepy."

Ben clears his throat. "Did she paint anything else onto her skin? Any other marks? Words, perhaps?"

He's tried to ask the question casually, but Olivia looks startled at the suggestion. "Words? No."

"What about a mask?"

She shakes her head again. "Sarah's costume was spooky enough without one."

"And Sarah definitely had a phone with her last night?"

Olivia nods. "She won't go anywhere without it."

"Can you describe it for me?"

"It's an iPhone. In a rose gold case, personalized with her initials."

"That's helpful, thank you. I'll need the number."

Christopher nods. "No problem. We've rung it several times, of course, but it's going straight to voicemail."

"I looked on Find My iPhone again this morning," adds Olivia, "but her battery must be dead. It just shows her 'last seen' location in the woods."

"I know you were partying in the quarry last night, but what about the folly?" he asks lightly. "Did any of you walk up through the woods to the tower?"

"Not while I was there. We stayed near the bonfire and the music." As Olivia shifts on the sofa, his gaze catches on her bare feet and her toenails, painted a familiar hue: sugary pink with flecks of gold glitter catching the light. The heavy feeling in the pit of his stomach intensifies. He turns back to Christopher. "Has your sister, Diana, been notified of Sarah's disappearance?"

Christopher and Philippa exchange a look. "We thought it best to wait until we'd spoken to you. We didn't want to worry her unnecessarily. We thought Sarah might have . . . overindulged. She could be sleeping off a hangover somewhere. Maybe she's forgotten to call, or is stuck somewhere with a dead phone battery."

"It's the most obvious explanation, don't you think?" Philippa is seeking reassurance. "I do hope we haven't wasted your time."

"Not at all. I'll need a recent photo of Sarah, if you have one?"

Christopher frowns. "Do you think that's really nec—"

"Yes," says Ben quickly. "It would be helpful."

Philippa places a hand on her daughter's shoulder. "Olivia, you girls are forever taking photos. Perhaps you have one of those 'selfies' you could share with DS Chase?"

Olivia's phone, as if on cue, chimes on the seat beside her. She picks it up and starts to scroll, leaving Ben to address her parents. "For my paperwork, can I confirm where you both were last night?"

"Yes, of course," says Christopher. "As I already said, we were here at the house all evening."

Ben waits.

"I was tired last night," says Philippa. "I watched some TV, then took myself to bed. I took a sleeping pill around 10:00 p.m."

Ben gets the distinct impression from Christopher's and Olivia's carefully neutral expressions that Philippa Easton is well acquainted with her sleeping pill bottle.

She turns to her husband. "You were working in the study, weren't you?"

Christopher nods. "Tying up loose ends. It's crunch time for the development. We should've had the approvals wrapped up by now. Poor Livvy," he says, patting his daughter on the shoulder, "I've been rather distracted in recent days, haven't I? We had to postpone our autumn half-term holiday," he explains to Ben, "but I've told her, as soon as this silly resistance settles down," he frowns, "I'll be back in Dad mode."

Ben nods. "So you were working at home last night. What time did you go to bed?"

"Around 11:45 p.m. and, as I said, I heard Olivia arrive home around midnight. I assumed it was both girls." He shakes his head. "I wish I'd checked now. Did you find a photo, Livvy?"

Olivia is staring at her phone; what little color she had in her cheeks has drained to white.

"Olivia?" says Philippa. "Did you hear your father?"

Olivia ignores her mother and turns to Ben. "It's from someone at the school," she says, a tremor in her voice. "She says there are police in the woods."

Ben clears his throat. He's been biding his time, hoping to break this news in a more sensitive way. "That's right. I'm afraid we received a call earlier this morning about an incident in Thorncombe Woods."

"What kind of incident?" Christopher asks, rising in his seat.

Ben eyes the man. "I'm sorry to tell you that the body of a young woman was discovered up at the folly in the early hours of this morning."

Philippa's hand flies to her mouth. Christopher bolts up from the sofa. "Good grief. You're not suggesting . . . ?" His gaze darts to his wife, then back to Ben.

Philippa's face is aghast. She glances at her daughter. "Olivia, I think you should leave us."

Olivia shakes her head. "I'm not going anywhere."

"Is it Sarah?" Christopher is fixed on Ben.

Ben chooses his words carefully. "We haven't been able to carry out formal identification yet, but I should ask you to prepare yourselves for the fact that it could be."

"Christ." Christopher turns to look at his wife, startled. "What happened? Was there an accident?"

Flashes of the scene return to Ben. The carefully folded arms. The blood spatter across the girl's chest. The grotesque mask laid over her smashed face. "We won't know for certain until the forensics report is filed, but it doesn't look that way. No."

Olivia lets out a small whimper. Philippa reaches for her daughter's hand, gripping it tightly in her own.

"I'd advise you to phone your sister," he prompts Christopher. "Right away."

Philippa leans against her husband and allows him to wrap one arm around her narrow shoulders, his other snaking about their daughter, so that the three of them sit huddled together. Watching them, Ben feels a heavy sensation settle in his chest. It's never easy breaking news like this. He understands better than most the trauma he has just unleashed on this otherwise picture-perfect-looking family. "Olivia," he says, "it would be helpful if you could draw up a list of everyone you remember attending the party in the woods last night."

Olivia frowns. "I don't want to get anyone in trouble. Not everyone was allowed off campus."

"She'll do it," says Christopher.

"One last thing." Ben opens his phone and swipes back to a photo he'd taken at the crime scene. "Could I ask if any of you recognize this?" He angles his screen to show the close-up detail of the broken heart pendant hanging from a silver chain. Olivia lets out a sob.

"Livvy," says Philippa, her voice cracking with emotion. "Show him."

With trembling hands, Olivia reaches for a chain hidden beneath the neck of her sweatshirt, raising it so that Ben can see the dangling pendant: half a silver heart, a reverse match for the one in the photo. "Did you give the other half to Sarah?" he asks gently.

Olivia's eyes fill with tears. "No. Sarah gave it to *me*. A birthday gift." She turns and buries her face into her mother's shoulder.

"If you could forward me a photo of Sarah—text or email is fine . . ." He lays his card on the coffee table between them. "I may need to request a DNA sample too . . . hairbrush, toothbrush, that sort of thing." He trails off at the sight of their anguish. "I'm sorry. I'll be in touch as soon as I have any news or further questions. But please, call Diana."

Ben leaves them huddled in the library and retraces his steps back to the car. The recent clock change sees twilight already stealing down from the woods, wrapping Thornfield Manor in a bleak light as he slides into the driver's seat and slams the door shut. He sits for a moment, staring out at the darkening world.

It's the worst part of the job. Always. And this case feels closer than most. He's not afraid to admit that he is shaken. Shaken that this has occurred in their sleepy, rural area. Shaken by the age of the girl in the woods—so young—potentially the same age and school year as Ellie. He feels for Olivia Easton. That silver broken heart emblem is lodged in his mind as he navigates back down the gravel drive. Something like this isn't just going to affect a family. It's going to rock their close-knit town. The fallout will cloak the whole community in suspicion and fear.

Remembering his earlier promise to Chrissie, he considers calling Rachel. He imagines driving onto the school campus and knocking on their cottage door, sitting at her kitchen table, talking through the awful details of the day. He has a strong urge to draw Ellie close—to warn his feisty, street-tough girl about the myriad of dangers out there. She still carries the naivety of youth, a belief that she can beat anyone and anything that comes her way. He knows she thinks him overprotective and fearful, but you don't do a job like his for twenty years and remain oblivious to the fact that there are dangerous people out there, that it only takes a minute for lives to unravel. But turning up unannounced is not a good idea. It's not as if he can divulge the details of this case to anyone—not yet. And it's not as if he'd be welcome in Rachel's home, even if he could.

Bone-tired and with Chrissie already upset with him, he can't handle having it out with Rachel today too. Not after this. He needs to keep a clear head for the case, because whatever happened up at the folly last night is the stuff of every parent's worst nightmare. Until they work out what has happened and who is responsible, he can't honestly say, hand on heart, that anyone is safe.

Chapter 9

It's still early when Ellie grabs her school backpack, a favorite beanie, and her skateboard from the hall and slips quietly from the cottage. Pulling the woolen hat low on her head, she makes for the campus perimeter and glances around before slipping through a narrow gap in the tall laurel hedge. It's a quick stumble down the roadway's grassy shoulder onto Thorncombe Lane and then she's on her board, skating toward town.

It's a relief to get away. She'd startled awake in the early hours to the shrill sound of the phone, followed by her mum's concerned murmurs. A phone call that early was never good news. Ellie had waited, rigid in her bed, expecting at any moment for her door to fly open and her mum's horrified face to appear. Instead, the call had ended and was replaced by the sound of the shower. Seizing the moment, she'd dressed quickly and made her escape. There was only so much time. She had to go now if she was going to stand a chance of staying one step ahead.

The lane is deathly quiet, the cold air a welcome slap to her cheeks as she weaves up the lane, rubber wheels gliding along the dimpled asphalt. She'd been exhausted falling into bed the night before, having spent the rest of the day nursing her hangover and her guilt like a heavy sickness, standing for far too long in the shower, scrubbing and scrubbing, removing every last trace of blood from beneath her fingernails. She'd thought she'd be out for the count as soon as her head hit the pillow, the idea of oblivion a welcome one. But sleep hadn't come. As soon as she'd closed her eyes, she'd been back in the woods with the dark towering trees and the flickering bonfire. It was as though the acrid scent of smoke had permeated everything—her skin, her bedcovers . . . a queasy feeling churning violently inside her. When she did sleep, it was restless and short-lived. She'd startle awake with the memory of warm blood sticky on her hands and a girl's name playing on her lips.

You're fucked, Ellie Chase.

The guilt rises from the pit of her stomach. Breathe, she tells herself, forcing her lungs to inhale and release in time with the motion of her foot pushing the skateboard. Breathe.

The autumn trees slide past in her peripheral vision, drifts of leaves turning to a dull sludge at the roadside. A flash of color in the hedgerow ahead catches her eye. Drawing closer, she sees a crisscross of blue-and-white police tape blocking access to the woodland path. Her heart sinks. The police? Already?

Beyond the tape, all she can see are the tightly clustered trees and the path disappearing into the woods. No sign of any police officers. No sign of anyone to stop her. With a final check up and down the lane, she stashes her board behind a tangle of ivy, hoists her backpack higher onto her shoulders, then ducks beneath the tape, starting up the trail on foot.

Two-thirds of the way up to the escarpment, she peels off the main track to take a secondary trail bisecting across the slopes to the quarry. The trees here are in full autumn dress, a palette of Turneresque colors, burnt umber, ocher, and sulphur yellow. She circles the upper rim of the basin, eyeing the dark scar below where their bonfire had burned, the red scrawl of paint sprayed onto rock, but she doesn't stop. Instead, she weaves along the top edge until she is scrambling a less well-trampled path leading beneath the stone escarpment, the solid wall of it towering over her like a predator hunched over its prey.

At the path's end she comes face-to-face with the metal safety grate set into the rock face, tinged with age, the faded sign beside it almost completely obscured by tangled vines and brambles, making it virtually impossible to spot unless you knew what to look for. NO ENTRY. DANGEROUS MINE. BAT ROOST.

Spears of morning light pierce the canopy. It's eerily quiet, not even the faintest trill of birdsong, just the soft sound of the wind moving through the trees, as if the wood is whispering its secrets. Ellie twists the screw holding the grate in place—already loose, as she knew it would be—then tugs at the cover. It lifts easily, up and over in one smooth, well-oiled motion. She turns on her phone flashlight and clambers into the hollow space, pulling the grate shut behind her with a clang.

The air inside is dank and fetid, with hints of wet earth, mushrooms, and burnt wood, as if the smoke from the bonfire they'd lit on Saturday night had somehow drifted here and got caught. She doesn't have much time, but she doesn't need it—she's not going far. She never does. Her stash is hidden near the entrance, tucked in a dark corner. To go deeper into the cave might risk getting lost in the twisting maze of quarry tunnels beneath the escarpment or disturbing the bats roosting down below. No thank you. Up here nearer daylight is just fine.

She grabs her supplies and stuffs them into the empty front pocket of her school bag, then gropes for the plastic bag hidden at the bottom of her backpack to throw it into the depths of the cavern, when she feels a current of cool air slide against her neck. She stiffens, goose bumps rising on her arms. She is afraid to turn around, afraid not to. There's a presence lingering in the shadows. Someone, or something, watching her. She's certain of it.

"Hello?" Her voice echoes, high and uncertain. She swings the flashlight beam. "Is someone there?"

The light illuminates an object deeper inside the cave. A gray bundle slumped on the ground next to a pile of ash. There's something else too, shining a little further back, too far away to make out. She thinks about the bat colony deep underground, leathery little bodies suspended in sleep, black eyes blinking open at the sound of her call, wings unfurling, claws twitching. She is in their space. To disturb them is a crime. She needs to leave.

She turns back to the grate, her flashlight beam bouncing off the surrounding walls, then stops and frowns, noticing something new. Something alarming. A series of dark scrawls covers the rock face, black letters daubed in chaotic repetition, leaping out in nonsensical order. Words and pictures. Things she's certain weren't here the last time she came.

"Hello?" she calls again, more tentative now. Someone has been here. Someone might *still* be here.

The silence is broken by the sound of tumbling rocks. She swings the flashlight behind her again, but the beam isn't strong enough to penetrate the dark and she's frightened now, so she legs it toward the metal grill, wrenching it open and clambering back through, falling into daylight.

It's Saturday night and everything that happened, it's messing with her head. But those sounds. The feeling of being watched. Just the bats, surely? She inhales deeply, trying to calm herself. Still, those words and pictures. Creepy as fuck. And worst of all, she still hasn't got rid of the plastic bag and its contents burning a hole in her backpack. She needs a plan B.

Her unease remains all the way down the trail but checking her watch, Ellie is relieved to see she still has a little time, so instead of turning back to school, she skates further along the lane until she is gliding beside a high chain-link fence, beyond which she can see the overgrown meadow bursting with dry thistle heads and brambles. She reaches out and trails a finger along the metal barricade. It's only been up a week or so and its presence is still jarring. Further along she comes to a huge new advertising board. Her quiet rage begins to swell as she reads its headline. COMING SOON: FOLLY HEIGHTS. EXCLUSIVE NEW HOMES FROM EASTON ESTATES, YOUR TRUSTED LOCAL DEVELOPERS.

The image on the board shows a CGI sprawl of identikit LEGO houses fanning out in a series of neat cul-de-sacs, each one built in custard-yellow brick, each with an immaculate postage stamp yard of fenced grass. There are CGI children kicking a ball on a tiny CGI green as a smiling woman pushes a pram along a pavement. Figuring she's got nothing left to lose, Ellie pulls her beanie a little lower, unzips her backpack, and pulls out one of her cans. With a quick glance up and down the lane, she sets to work.

Five minutes later, back on her skateboard, Ellie spots her plan B. An old grit bin lying half buried beneath the bushes at the side of the road. She swings the lid open and is relieved to find it almost empty, just a couple of potato chip packets and a crushed Coke can resting on top of the dwindling salt supply. It doesn't look as if it's been filled in a while. She pulls the plastic bag from her backpack and stuffs it down into the bin. The lid swings shut with a thump.

A stream of sleek Mercedes and gleaming Teslas are pulling

out of the iron gates as she reaches school, the vehicles, having disgorged their day pupils, roaring back down the country lane, scattering leaves in their wake. As she approaches, another vehicle slides up behind Ellie and slows at her shoulder. She steps onto the shoulder to allow it to pass, her gaze tracking to the words painted onto the side of the white van. AVON VALLEY NEWS.

She wonders if the van will turn through the school gates, but instead it crawls past, then pulls up short and makes an awkward U-turn in the narrow lane. In the front passenger seat is a familiar-looking woman. Chic brown bob. High cheekbones. Red lipstick. Ellie's eyes widen. She recognizes her as a journalist from a local evening news program. What the—? First the police tape barricading the woods. Now a news crew?

She is ten minutes late for registration. Her tutor, Mr. Morgan, or Edward as she's allowed to call him, using teachers' first names a privilege reserved for the sixth form, glances up as she enters the classroom. She braces, but there's none of Edward's usual joshing, no pointed, "Good *afternoon*, nice of you to join us." Instead he's solemn, and the rest of the class sits in strange hushed silence.

He taps his watch and then gestures to the beanie still on her head, which she tugs off, ruffling her hair as she heads for her seat.

Jasmine acknowledges her with raised eyebrows. She spots Danny sitting just behind, his eyes tracking her across the room, the bruise on his cheekbone seeming worse today. She gives him a nod, but he frowns and turns away. "All right?" she whispers to Holly, her usual desk companion. "What did I miss?"

"Nothing much." The girl leans in to whisper, twirling her thick ponytail between her fingers. "Edward was late too. He's in a funny mood. All the teachers were called to a staff meeting first thing." Holly glances around before continuing. "My friend's sister is in the local Girl Guides group and she said something happened in the woods this weekend. Something bad." She narrows her eyes. "Has your mum said anything?"

Ellie's stomach clenches. Hold it together, she wills. She shakes her head and sees Holly's visible disappointment.

Edward has begun to read out the class notices, messages about upcoming games, drama auditions, and a history trip to the French battlefields all delivered in an unusually flat monotone. Most mornings he'd perch on the edge of his desk, an informal air about him as he'd pull a couple of ties from his desk drawer with a flourish, then allow the students to choose which one he should wear. His argument was that a shirt and tie wasn't a look you could successfully pull off while riding a motorbike into work, which Ellie thought was probably right. Most Monday mornings he'd be cheerfully engaged, asking about weekends and sports results, exeats and visits home. He'd tell them about an art gallery or music gig he'd been to, crack a joke or two, and ease them into the week with warmth and humor. Edward was generally all right—all right by teacher standards anyway.

But Holly is right—this morning is different. Edward is different. More formal and somber, his tie already knotted firmly in place, failing even to offer one of his sardonic eye rolls as he reads out a familiar warning from Mrs. Crowe about creative interpretations of school uniform regulations and her plans for a series of random spot checks on school ties and skirt lengths. Seeming to lose track, he frowns, then runs his hands through his dark hair before rifling through the remaining papers on his desk until a knock at the door interrupts.

A red-faced Year Nine student scuttles in and Edward reads the offered note before turning to the class. "Year Twelve and Thirteen are to attend a special assembly immediately after this tutor group. At the bell, please make your way to the school hall. Attendance is compulsory."

A bad feeling rushes at Ellie, like a speeding car coming at her at full speed, the impact inevitable. Her mind drifts back to the fluttering police tape and the news van circling the campus. Holly's excited whispers. *Something happened in the woods this weekend. Something bad.*

Don't look at them, she thinks, but she can't help herself. She throws a sideways glance at Jasmine and meets her friend's alarmed gaze and, over Jasmine's shoulder, Danny's hard stare still boring into her. This is it, she thinks. This is how my whole life comes crashing down.

Chapter 10

Monday, 9:00 a.m.

Ben meets Diana Lawson outside the police morgue. From a distance, stepping from the back of the silver Mercedes, the woman looks polished and elegant, ash-blond hair falling to the cowl-neck of a gray cashmere sweater, tailored black trousers and patent-leather high heels, a handbag and camel coat draped over one arm. It's only as she draws closer that Ben can see the traces of a sleepless night from a long-haul flight and the deep worry etched across her face. He introduces himself as they shake hands.

"Is my brother here?" Diana asks, glancing over his shoulder. "We spoke in the car. He said he'd come."

"Not yet. Would you like to wait?"

Diana shakes her head. "No. I need to know."

Ben is relieved. They all need to know. "I'm taking you to a viewing room," he tells her, leading her through the muted gray corridors of the building, the air heavy with a sterile chemical smell, as if the linoleum floors have only just been mopped. As they walk, he tries to prepare her for what she will see. "She'll be lying on a gurney, dressed in a blue gown, the sort of thing you might wear in hospital. She'll be covered with a sheet. The forensic technician has advised me that they will keep her face covered. Given the extent of the head injuries, they felt it would be less distressing for you." Ben knows it's important to prepare a person as much as possible for a viewing like this, though in this case he's not entirely sure he can.

Diana flinches but keeps pace beside him. "So how will I know it's Sarah . . . if I can't see her face?"

"There's a chance you won't. We'll run DNA samples, but we'd like you to confirm if you recognize any obvious marks or features. If it's too distressing, you just let us know. You can leave at any time."

Diana nods, though her face appears to have blanched even paler. "None of this feels real. Since I took Christopher's phone call . . . I keep thinking it must be a bad dream, that I'm going to wake up any minute."

He nods. It's a refrain he's heard many times over the course of his career, but he relates on a personal level too. Nothing can prepare you for that moment when life diverts without warning onto a sickening new course, one where you are expected to just carry on without a precious loved one. He holds his own painful memory of being walked through this facility, prepared by a police officer, readied to come face-to-face with his own unfolding nightmare. "I'm sorry. I know this isn't easy."

They come to a halt outside a door. Through a small, high-set window he can see the technician dressed in scrubs waiting on the other side. "If you're ready, I'll take you in. Anytime you want to leave, you just say. OK?"

She nods, her mouth set into a grim line.

The tech steps forward to greet them. Diana issues a curt nod, but her gaze is already fixed on the gurney.

The technician lifts the far end of the sheet and pulls it back to reveal most of the victim's body, though as promised, he keeps the head covered, just a few strands of blond hair visible, falling around the shoulders. "Take your time," he murmurs, standing back to allow Diana to move closer.

She takes a hesitant step forward before skirting the gurney, giving it a wide berth at first, as if afraid to go too close. Ben sees her eye the body, slim and frail in the blue hospital gown, pale legs and arms now washed and free from the dirt and the awful, scrawled words that had marked her skin. Here in this room, she no longer looks macabre and frightening. She looks young and delicate. Frail. Helpless.

Ben can see the distress in Diana's face as she moves closer, the slump of her shoulders. She staggers slightly and Ben steps forward to catch her elbow, afraid she might collapse. "It's her," she says, her voice little more than a whisper. "It's Sarah." The handbag on her shoulder slips to the floor, but Diana doesn't seem to notice.

"Are you sure?"

She nods. "That birthmark." Diana lifts a trembling hand to point at the girl's right ankle. "She always hated it. She wanted to get it lasered, but David told her it made her unique. I thought it was nice. Like an oak leaf." Diana's voice cracks. She closes her eyes and tries to draw a steadying breath.

Ben can see she is holding on by a thread. It doesn't get much worse than days like this. It's always more shocking when the victim is young. What a waste of a life. A terrible sadness lingers, swirling with the cool air and that distinct, sterile smell that never fails to tug at his guts.

Diana opens her eyes. "Can I touch her?"

At the technician's nod, Diana moves a little closer and lifts the girl's hand to lay it gently in her own. She traces the skin on the back of Sarah's hand, her nails with their pink polish shining under the bright strip lighting as the first of her tears starts to fall. "I'm sorry," she says. "I'm so sorry. I thought this would be a happy place for you." A moan leaves her throat. Pure pain, Ben thinks, the sound tugging at him. Tears stream down Diana's cheeks as she bends to kiss the girl's hand. The red scratches on her arms are vivid against the bloodless white of her skin.

Ben has to swallow hard, looking up at the ceiling to hide his emotion, feeling a deep ache in the hollow of his stomach. Waiting . . . waiting . . . just the sound of a mother's grief until Diana wipes her face and turns back to him. "You mentioned a necklace? Was there anything else?"

He moves to a table where a silver tray holds the necklace and a ring Sarah had been wearing. "These were found on her."

Diana studies the jewelry. "The ring was a gift, for her six-teenth birthday . . ." Her voice catches in her throat. "I'm not sure about the necklace."

"It's a friendship necklace. Olivia's confirmed she has the other half. Sarah gave it to her."

"Poor Olivia." Diana crumbles again, pressing her fist to her mouth. She turns to Ben, her eyes filled with pain and confusion. "What happened? Who did this to my daughter?"

"That's what we're going to find out." He holds her gaze. "I promise."

Diana stays with Sarah's body until the sound of voices out in the corridor penetrates the silence of the viewing room. Ben looks through the glass panel and sees Christopher Easton with his wife, waiting outside, a wool coat slung over the man's arm, his other wrapped around Philippa's shoulders. Philippa looks as though she's aged several years in the hours since he last saw her, her face drawn and sallow, not a scrap of makeup. "Your family's here," he tells Diana.

Diana Lawson gives a small nod. "Thank you."

He holds the door for her and watches as Diana walks out to greet her brother and sister-in-law, the question evident in their faces. Diana bows her head and allows herself to be enveloped in Philippa's stiff embrace. "I'm so sorry," Philippa says. "I've been praying it's not her."

As Diana collapses into her arms, Christopher steps forward to help support her. "It's confirmed?" he asks Ben.

"I'm afraid so."

Diana is weeping into Philippa's shoulder. "I should never have let her come. She should've stayed in Dubai."

"But she was adamant, Diana," says Christopher. "She was desperate to be here. You remember how the girls begged?"

Ben clears his throat. "How is Olivia?"

"I'm not sure she's slept at all since we found out Sarah was missing. She wouldn't leave her bedroom this morning."

"What do I do now?" Diana gazes at Ben with a blank, tear-streaked face. "What am I supposed to do?"

"You come home with us," says Christopher, placing a hand on her shoulder. "We let the police do their work. We let them catch whoever did this to Sarah."

Ben nods. "My colleagues have been at the school since first thing this morning, poised to brief the staff. Given that the last time we know Sarah was seen alive was on Saturday night at the party, we'll be asking any students who were in the woods to come forward."

"And that boy," says Christopher, his eyes narrowed. "The one Olivia mentioned. Danny Carlisle. You're talking to him?"

"He's first on our list."

Christopher nods. "The Carlisles certainly seem to have an interesting reputation. I've been asking around some of my contacts."

Ben experiences a flicker of alarm. The last thing they need is a man like Christopher Easton, with all his influence, starting a witch hunt for a teenage boy without any evidence of his involvement. "It's important we all keep an open mind at this stage. Danny may well have vital information to share with us, but you need to let us conduct our interviews and gather evidence, if we're going to catch and, most importantly, prosecute whoever did this to Sarah. I know you want answers. Believe me, Mr. Easton, we do too. We're on your side."

Outside the morgue, Ben watches the trio walk toward a green Jaguar, parked in the disabled bay near the entrance. Christopher Easton charges ahead, but Philippa's stiff gait keeps pace with Diana's bowed form. Christopher presses his key fob, headlights flashing, and the two women slide into the back seat, hidden behind tinted windows, but Christopher walks a short distance away, cell phone in hand. Ben watches with a growing unease as he speaks animatedly into the phone. Even at his distance, Ben can feel the anger bristling off the man. He watches until Christopher tucks the cell phone back into his pocket and slips behind the wheel of his car, driving away with a squeal of tires. Ben sighs. Christopher Easton on the warpath adds a whole new level of stress to their investigation.

Chapter 11

Monday, 10:00 a.m.

Rachel stands at the back of the assembly hall and scans the faces of the students filing in. On a normal school day, an unexpected interruption to the standard timetable would generate a buzz among the pupils. There would be giggling and jostling, the low hum of anticipation at the break in routine. Today, however, the sixth-formers are ominously quiet, the only sounds the shuffle of their shoes on the polished parquet floor and the creak of plastic as they settle on the chairs lined up in front of the stage.

Perhaps it's the sight of their formidable head teacher, Margaret Crowe, dressed head to toe in her usual black, a tailored jacket buttoned high over a modest knee-length dress, solid calves clad in opaque tights, polished black high heels shining under the strip lights as she commands the lectern placed front and center on the stage. Her arms are folded across her ample chest, long gray hair coiled and pinned to her scalp, sharp eyes scanning the students, a picture of stern gravitas. More likely, it's the presence of Ben's colleagues, DCI Hassan Khan and DC Fiona Maxwell, standing up there beside her, who have caught the students' attention.

DCI Khan could be any middle-aged businessman, formal in a

sharp gray suit, dark hair slicked back off his face, hands clasped behind him as he rocks on the heels of his brogues; but DC Maxwell is obviously police, trim and athletic-looking, neat as a pin in her starched uniform, the only untamed part of her the cloud of curly brown hair fanning out around her freckled face.

Rachel knows Khan relatively well, having met Ben's boss at a variety of police fundraisers and family socials when she was still Ben's wife. Hassan had always been kind to her, keen to compare notes on the challenges of raising daughters, jovial after a beer or two, and always the first to hit the dance floor, enthusiastically boogying with wild abandon.

Fiona Maxwell, on the other hand, was a more recent recruit. Ben had introduced her at the very last event Rachel had attended, before their split. Maxwell had struck Rachel then as quiet and serious, still figuring out her place in the team, a woman on a mission to prove herself, though Ben had already privately shared with Rachel that he thought Maxwell showed remarkable promise. Rachel remembers how she'd skulked on the periphery of the community hall with her girlfriend, drinking cider and making small talk with Rachel, until a karaoke machine had been wheeled out and Maxwell's girlfriend had shoved her up onto the stage. To everyone's surprise, the reserve had fallen away as Maxwell had belted out a knockout Adele cover. "I always say it," Khan had said, nudging Rachel and Ben, tapping his polished shoes in time to the backing track. "Doesn't matter if it's kids, colleagues, or criminals. It's the quiet ones you have to watch."

Police presence aside, there is no mistaking the gravitas of the atmosphere in the school hall. Rachel's been in a state of disbelief— her lungs tight in her chest, her adrenaline spiked—ever since she woke to Margaret Crowe's early morning phone call. "A body in the woods," Margaret had told her. Rachel, remembering the fluttering police tape barricading the woodland path and Ben's curt text messages followed by his silence, had suddenly realized what he must've been dealing with. "I'm calling an early all-staff meeting to inform the faculty, but as our Head of Student Welfare, I thought you should have a heads-up," Margaret had continued. "This will be a sensitive pastoral situation for the school."

Finding that Ellie had already left the cottage, her backpack and skateboard missing from the cluttered hall, Rachel had gone straight to the teachers' lounge.

It was unusual for the entire faculty to gather as one in the space and the room had felt crowded and airless, dust motes spiraling in the weak morning light as they'd jostled for the comfiest sofas and chairs, waiting for Margaret Crowe.

"What do you think this is about?" someone had whispered. "Drugs?"

"Porn in the computer room again?"

"Maybe Malcolm's finally lost the plot about 'foreign objects' being flushed down the school toilets."

Malcolm, Margaret Crowe's husband, was often the butt of jokes among the staff but Rachel, the only one to know the full story, had stayed quiet and eventually the sniggers had been silenced by Margaret's arrival, her husband's stooped frame shuffling a little behind, ever watchful at her shoulder. Their head teacher hadn't wasted any time.

"Thank you for assembling at such short notice. I'm afraid I have some distressing information to share with you all." Her expression had been even more dour and steely-eyed than usual and the atmosphere in the teachers' lounge had shifted immediately.

"Late yesterday, I was notified by the police that the body of a young woman had been discovered in the woods above our school." She'd waited for the shocked murmurs and gasps to die down. "Her identity has yet to be officially confirmed, but there is reason to believe the deceased was one of our students."

It had been like a pressurized door opening, all the air rushing from the room. One or two had cried out at the news. Mrs. Bateman, the school's administrator, had started to cry. There had been a flurry of anxious questions from the teachers, but very few that Margaret had been able to answer.

"Who is it?"

"I'm afraid I'm not at liberty to say until there has been a formal identification, which I believe is taking place this morning."

"Can you tell us *how* they died?"

"I don't have details at this stage."

She'd told them that the police would address them in due course. In the meantime, the school's crisis management plan would come into play and Margaret would be reviewing their security measures as a matter of urgency. It was her intention to hold a special morning assembly to break the news to their sixth-form students in a controlled environment, before the rumors took hold. Likewise, she would be notifying all parents and guardians of the situation in an email that morning. The police didn't want to waste any time—they'd be conducting on-site interviews with a number of students and staff members that morning.

"But what about the parents? Shouldn't they be present for police interviews with a minor?" one of the secretaries had asked.

"Yes," Margaret had confirmed. "However, all parents, as part of our admissions process, have signed forms authorizing nominated members of staff to act *in loco parentis* in an emergency. I've taken advice and it falls within police jurisdiction to talk to the students today, as long as there is a member of staff present." Margaret's gaze had fallen on Rachel. "I've asked Rachel Dean, in her capacity as Head of Student Welfare, to attend.

"This is going to be a difficult and unprecedented time for our school," she'd continued. "It will test us all personally and professionally. Our students and their families are going to need reassurance and support. Every one of us is going to have a part to play in handling this crisis. It *will* be challenging, especially if, as the police seem to believe, the victim is one of our own." She looks around at them all. "If anyone is struggling, please come and see me. My door is always open."

Any hint of the faculty's earlier banter was long gone as they'd filed from the teachers' lounge and made their way to their respective classrooms to greet the bleary morning faces of their unsuspecting tutor groups. Rachel had just had time to shelve her planned meetings, read through the school's crisis management plan, and review her notes on grief counseling when she'd received the summons to the hall.

Standing there now, grateful for the solid wall at her back, her gaze slides from Margaret and the police officers on the stage to the sea of burgundy blazers seated before them. She is wondering who is missing, trying to spot the gap in the crowd, but she is also searching for Ellie, looking for the red flag of her daughter's wayward hair. She can't help wondering, as a mum, how Ellie will handle such upsetting news.

Edward Morgan, Head of Art, enters the hall and hesitates, his tall physique framed by the open double doors. He adjusts the cuffs on his jacket before glancing around the room, a frown creasing his face. Spotting Rachel he nods his head in greeting and she beckons him over with a wave.

"This isn't going to be easy," he murmurs, taking the spot next to her against the back wall. "I don't envy Margaret."

"It's awful," she agrees. "So sad."

She's glad it's Edward beside her. Not only was he Ellie's form tutor and quite clearly her favorite teacher, he'd been something of an ally to Rachel too since her earliest days at the school, seeking her out on her first day to welcome her, coming to her rescue as she'd wrestled with the coffee machine in the teachers' lounge. "Here, allow me," he'd said, demonstrating with the capsule, standing back as the machine had whirred and steamed, releasing a double shot of espresso into her waiting mug.

"Thanks. In my last school, you'd be lucky to get a working kettle and a mug of instant. I think you've just saved me an expensive repair bill and a serious falling-out with my new colleagues."

"Yes, for goodness' sake, don't deprive the old guard of their caffeine," he'd joked. "You'll make enemies for life. Us 'youngsters' have got to stick together."

It was true, she'd realized; among the portly, gray-haired, tweed-suited faculty gracing the hallowed hallways of Folly View, Edward Morgan stood out like a youthful sore thumb. He couldn't have been more than thirty-five or so, with his dark tousled hair, slim-cut shirt, and an easy smile that crinkled the corners of his brown eyes.

"Between the two of us, we must lower the mean age of the staff room by a decade . . . at least," he'd added, giving her a cheeky look up and down, his wry smile bringing a warm flush to her cheeks.

"I feel like a fish out of water. So many new systems and faces to learn. So many rules to navigate." She'd hugged her coffee cup and looked around at the elegant room with its antique furniture, creaking wooden floorboards, and ornate leaded pane windows. It was a world away from the stained carpet tiles and ripped pleather seats of her last teachers' lounge. "Are they staring?" she'd asked, aware of half a dozen or so pairs of eyes regarding them at the coffee machine. She'd tugged at the brightly colored fabric of her floral dress, the one she'd chosen earlier that morning, certain in front of her bedroom mirror that it had projected just the right amount of confidence and conservative cheer, worrying now that it was a terrible choice in a sea of beige and brown.

"You should've seen their faces when I turned up on my first day in full motorbike leathers. Jaws hit the floor." He'd leaned in a little closer. "They're a good bunch. A little stuffy at times, but kind, once they get to know you. They'll love you in no time. And those rules," he'd given her a small eye roll, "for all Margaret's talk of exacting standards, you'll find subtle ways to bend them. They're kids, not robots, after all. Everyone deserves a chance to be themselves, don't you think?"

She'd smiled.

"Good to have you on board, Rachel," he'd said, clinking his cup against hers.

Since that first day, their paths had crossed frequently. She'd hear the growl of his motorbike announcing his arrival on campus, Edward hunched low over the machine in his matte black helmet and leathers. He always struck her as rather dark and unknowable, but as soon as the helmet came off and he ruffled his hair and slipped a work tie around his neck, he transformed, chameleon-like, into a more familiar shape, the benign art teacher, more often than not surrounded by a group of colleagues or adoring students hanging on his every word in the corridors or the school canteen at break times. Being one of the younger, more attractive male teachers offered a certain cachet to both pupils and staff, though Edward seemed to navigate the attention with care and diplomacy. She respected him for that.

"I keep hoping that the police have got it wrong," she admits, meeting his gaze. "That it's all been a terrible mistake."

He nods up at the two figures beside Margaret on the stage. "I think we should be prepared for the worst. This is going to be a lot for the students to process, however it plays out."

Malcolm Crowe is next through the doors, hands clasped behind his back, his tall, wiry figure stooped in a manner suggesting a lifetime of ducking through doorframes. He ambles toward them, the light glancing off the lenses of the round wire spectacles perched at the end of his nose. With his thinning white hair, hooded eyes, and an unfortunate skin condition that always seemed to worsen in the colder months, he conjures an equal mix of sympathy and revulsion in Rachel, though she tries to be kind, and not just because he's her boss's husband. He's always struck her as something of a lost soul, wandering the campus in his beige anorak, a sort of self-appointed caretaker tinkering with odd jobs or watching the kids' sports games from a bench on the sidelines, all while Margaret valiantly steered the Folly View ship. It was obvious that early retirement hadn't suited him.

"You OK there, Malcolm?" Edward asks, budging up to make room for him against the wall. "Looks like you've done yourself an injury." He nods at the man's shuffling gait, the slight drag of his left leg. "Can I get you a chair?"

Malcolm winces. "I turned my ankle on those blasted stairs in the Lodge. It's nothing. I'll be fine in a day or two." He removes a handkerchief from his top pocket and dabs at his face. "This is a bad business. Forty years of teaching," he says, "and I've never seen a situation like this."

"It's very sad," agrees Rachel. She can hear the rasp of the handkerchief as it moves over his scaly chin.

"Back in my day, children wouldn't have been wandering in the woods at night," Malcolm tuts.

Rachel feels a gentle pressure on her arm, the softest nudge from Edward. Sliding her gaze to meet his, he offers the briefest hint of an eye roll. Malcolm is most definitely of the "old guard."

The flow of pupils eventually slows to a trickle until the doors are pulled shut behind the last straggler. "Same," says Edward, noticing her gaze sweeping the hall for Ellie. "I can't help wondering who's missing."

"Did you see Ellie this morning? She left very early. Did she come to the art studio?"

"Not that I saw. She was late for registration." Seeing Rachel's frown, he leans in. "Everything OK?"

"I think she's putting herself under a lot of pressure with her final year project. She acts tough, but she's soft on the interior."

"I can see that in her work." He squeezes her arm. "It's natural to be worried. Something like this, it makes you wonder what the kids are going through, doesn't it? If they're coping OK? It's a lot of pressure." He lowers his voice. "An accident's one thing. Tragic. But if it's suicide . . ."

Rachel swallows. As Head of Student Welfare, she should know the at-risk kids.

"I hope you're not thinking that this is in some way your fault?" Edward asks, reading her expression. When Rachel doesn't answer, he nudges her gently. "Hey," he says, "I'll keep an eye on Ellie."

She nods her thanks. Across the hall, she spots the broad shoulders of Danny Carlisle, with his close friend, Saul Ayofo, seated beside him. As Danny bends to mutter something to Saul, Rachel notices a bruise on the boy's face, a swelling below his right eye, turning a nasty shade of violet. Saul listens to Danny, then turns, his black Afro brushing against Jasmine Ware's cheek as he bends to whisper in her ear. A tall Year Twelve boy in the row behind Jasmine blocks Rachel's view, but craning her neck, she is relieved to see the back of Ellie's head appear, her distinct red hair bright like a flag. It's no wonder she hadn't spotted her before. Ellie is slumped so low in her chair it's as if at any moment she might slide off into a puddle on the parquet floor.

Jasmine pulls away from Saul and tilts her head down to murmur into Ellie's ear. It's like the children's party game, Rachel realizes, passing a whispered message along the row. She sees Ellie nod and Rachel waits, expecting to see her daughter continue the chain. But she doesn't. She doesn't even look up. Danny's message has stopped at Ellie.

It seems Margaret might be ready to step up to the microphone, when a door at the back of the room swings open and Rachel sees Ben striding into the hall. The jolt of recognition she experiences at the sight of him is visceral, a tugging sensation in her stomach. Ben. The man she lived with for over twenty years. So familiar, and yet these days so other, with his recently shaved head, slim-fit utility jacket, and a pregnant girlfriend living on the other side of town. She swallows, the anger surprising her with an unpleasant surge.

Ben signals from the back of the hall and all of the students' heads swivel as DCI Khan drops down off the stage and goes to join him. Glancing back at Ellie, Rachel sees their daughter's head dip even lower. Poor girl. It's the full family affair today.

Ben and his boss share a brief exchange, the expression on their faces steely and unreadable, before Khan returns to the stage. Margaret covers the microphone with her hand as Khan updates her. Ben looks around the hall. She imagines he's scanning for Ellie, but spotting Rachel at the back, he comes across to join her, greeting her and her colleagues with a polite nod before folding his arms and turning his attention to the stage.

Rachel is desperate to ask Ben what he knows, but before she can, Margaret is tapping the microphone, clearing her throat.

"Good morning, everyone. Thank you for gathering so quickly and quietly. I'm afraid I must share some very sad news with you all." The head teacher takes a breath, visibly steeling herself. "It's been confirmed that Sarah Lawson, one of our Year Thirteen pupils, has died over the weekend." She waits as a ripple of shock travels through the hall, a collective intake of breath.

Sarah Lawson. Rachel closes her eyes. She can picture the girl well. Silver-blond. Blue eyes. Cherry-red lips. China doll pretty. She'd arrived at the start of Year Twelve, transitioning from an international school overseas to join her cousin, Olivia Easton, in the same school year. Rachel had often seen the two girls together, drifting through the school corridors arm in arm, the family resemblance obvious in their fair hair and fine features. They'd seemed to shine, Sarah especially, drawing the gaze as beautiful girls will. What on earth had happened? Sarah had been studying English, Drama, and Psychology and had seemed to adapt to life at Folly View well, given the circumstances of her school move. Had she missed something?

Opening her eyes, Rachel sees the students swiveling in their seats, their shared looks of shock and surprise, but Ellie, she notices, remains still, her head bowed and her gaze fixed on the floor. "Was Sarah in your tutor group?" she asks, turning to Edward Morgan on her left.

Edward's face is pale, his eyes dark with concern. "No, not Sarah. I teach Olivia, her cousin. I met Sarah briefly last year through the Drama club. From what I remember, she seemed like a bright, talented young girl. Everything going for her. Did you know her well?"

Rachel shrugs. "A little. Not well." A hard lump is forming at the back of her throat.

Margaret, having allowed space for the inevitable reaction,

steps back to the microphone and valiantly presses on. "Sarah was a popular member of our sixth form and, I'm sure, a cherished friend to many of you. She made a great impact at the school, particularly among her peers in the Drama department. Our thoughts and prayers, of course, are with Sarah's family, especially Olivia, Sarah's cousin and a fellow pupil at this school."

Rachel searches for Mrs. Wiley, Head of Drama, in the lineup of staff at the side of the hall and spots the gray-haired woman dabbing at her eyes with a tissue.

Margaret pauses again, scanning the room. "No doubt you've all noticed the police presence in our school today. I'm joined up here by Detective Chief Inspector Khan from the local Avon & Somerset police force and his colleague, Detective Constable Maxwell. DCI Khan and his colleagues are with us this morning to make enquiries into Sarah's last known movements."

Rachel frowns. *Last known movements?* She glances across at Ben, but his gaze remains fixed on the stage.

"They will have questions for some of Sarah's friends and teachers and I know we'll all want to offer our assistance in any way we can. I'll let DCI Khan explain more about that in a moment.

"In the meantime, this is an opportunity for me to remind you all of the importance of following school rules. Until the police have concluded their investigation, whether you're a day pupil or a boarder, it is imperative that we know your whereabouts and can ensure your safety. As your teachers, we have a duty of care to your parents. Students found sneaking out of school or leaving campus without the appropriate permissions will face serious consequences. Exeats will be restricted for the foreseeable time. I hope I make myself clear?"

The hall fills with a soft murmuring of disapproval, which fades as Margaret Crowe's intense gaze sweeps over the students.

"It's natural for an event like this to bring up strong emotions and to raise difficult questions, but I expect us, as a school, to conduct ourselves in the coming days with the propriety and respect I know you are all capable of. Counseling will be made available to anyone struggling. I'd urge you to speak to your tutors, house matrons, or of course our dedicated Head of Welfare, Ms. Dean, should you require support. Lastly, I will be sharing details of the funeral arrangements as and when they become available, according to the family's wishes. For now, I would ask you all to continue your school day as best you can, without gossip or speculation."

Rachel bows her head, the lump growing in her throat.

"Are you OK?" Ben leans closer, eyeing her with concern.

She nods.

"What was Sarah like?"

"Smart. Confident. Self-assured. She carried herself in a way that suggested she had the whole world ahead of her." Rachel sighs.

"Any issues you were aware of? Anything here or at home? Safeguarding concerns? Bullying?"

"No. Nothing. At least, not that I knew of." She thinks back. "I met with Sarah when she first joined us. It's standard procedure. I like to keep a close eye on the kids integrating from other schools. I'd flagged Sarah in the admissions process as someone who might need closer attention, after losing her father and moving from overseas. It was a lot of change for a teenager." Rachel frowns. She wonders if she'd missed something vital in her early meetings with the girl, something that might've indicated Sarah was unstable or at risk in some way. "She told me she'd found school in Dubai hard, after her father's death. She seemed happy to be here. Happy for 'a change of scene,' she said. She was close to her cousin, Olivia. You'd see them around the school together."

Rachel swallows, the emotion caught in her throat. "What happened? Was it an accident? Did she . . . hurt herself?"

Ben doesn't have time to reply. DCI Khan is stepping up to the lectern, tapping the mic, and the murmurs in the hall fall silent again as he introduces himself to the pupils. He holds their attention with his gravitas. "We have a number of questions surrounding Sarah Lawson's death and my colleague here, Constable Maxwell, will be speaking later with some of you who may have spent time with Sarah in recent days. We're particularly interested to hear from anyone who attended a gathering in the woods above the school on Saturday night."

There is shifting in the seats. The mention of the woods seems to have generated a stir.

"I'd urge anyone who was there to come forward. In the meantime, we've closed the woodland and ask you all to avoid the area and to continue to follow the school's signing in and out procedures." Khan gazes out at the room. "We ask you to adhere to this for your own safety."

Rachel exchanges a worried frown with Edward before turning back to the stage.

"When something like this happens in a community such as ours," continues Khan, "it's natural to feel shocked or frightened. I want to reassure you that my officers and I are here to support you all. Your safety is our priority."

"Their safety?" she murmurs, throwing a questioning glance at Ben. She can see he's tired, dark circles beneath his green eyes and that crease between his brows that's always more visible after a sleepless night. You can't be with a man for twenty years and not know his tells. He doesn't answer her question. Instead, he leans in again and asks one of his own. "Were Ellie and Sarah close? Were they friends?"

She knows what he's asking. This isn't a work question. This is personal. *How hard is this going to hit Ellie?*

"Ellie's in the same art class as Sarah's cousin, Olivia. But that's it. From what I could tell, they moved in different circles." She glances up at Ben. "You know Ellie. She hasn't had it the easiest since starting here."

Ben nods. It isn't the first conversation they've had about their daughter and her friendship circle, or lack of. Ellie was shy. She had always struggled to make friends. Rachel had held high hopes for Ellie when she'd moved to Folly View on her scholarship, but unlike Sarah Lawson, the fresh start for Ellie hadn't translated into a flourishing circle of friends. Ellie could be socially awkward. She preferred to cultivate a close few. Nor had she had the advantage of a cousin like Olivia to smooth her way. To Rachel's private dismay, the transition to Folly View hadn't proved that much easier than at her former school. Ellie was Ellie. Both she and Ben knew that.

"What happened?" she asks him, unable to hold her worry at bay, unable to ignore that nagging voice at the back of her mind that maybe this could have been prevented. "Was it an accident? Suicide?"

Ben hesitates before giving the slightest shake of his head, but Rachel's relief is short-lived. There is something in his expression that sends a dart of fear up her spine. Her eyes widen. "Someone hurt her?"

Ben seems to consider his words carefully. "You heard Khan. We need to interview all the students who attended the party in the quarry on Saturday night."

Rachel is stunned. Is he implying that a student could have been involved in Sarah's death?

"I'm heading to the Eastons' home to take Olivia's statement, but we should talk later. About Ellie. About the weekend."

Rachel feels a flash of irritation at his sudden shift in tone. "Yes, though if it's about Chrissie and the baby, I already know." She senses Edward, still standing nearby, take a step or two away in tactful retreat. Ben at least has the good grace to look embarrassed. "Ellie told me," she adds, "though it would've been nice to hear it from you. It's an awful responsibility to lay on her shoulders—to expect her to do your dirty work."

"It's hardly 'dirty work.' It's a baby." He tilts his chin, but a tell-tale red flush is rising on his cheeks. "To be honest, I didn't think you'd care all that much."

She stares at him, dumbfounded. "Regardless of my feelings, it's huge for Ellie. I should've known, in case she needed support. We need to communicate better."

"I couldn't agree more. I could've handled it differently if you hadn't altered the plans. We need to stick to our arrangements. For Ellie's sake."

"Altered the plans?" She doesn't know what he's talking about, but if he's trying to take the moral high ground, he really doesn't have a leg to stand on. A student is dead. They should be working together, not against each other, prioritizing the kids. Prioritizing Ellie. "Look, this isn't the time or the place."

"Agreed," snaps Ben.

She steadies her voice. "Come round tonight? We'll talk then. Properly. You can check in with Ellie—I'm sure she'll be glad to see you after today."

He nods, his gaze flicking across the rows of students until it lands on their daughter, who is now filing in a snaking line out of the hall. As Ellie nears the door, she casts a glance in their direction. Ben raises his hand and Rachel sees Ellie's eyes dart between them in alarm, before she drops her head and shuffles out.

Rachel hopes she hasn't witnessed their entire tetchy exchange. "Just tell me one thing," she asks, lowering her voice. "Are the kids safe? Khan made it sound like there could be someone dangerous out there."

Ben doesn't quite meet her eye. "You know I can't say anything."

"But what do we tell the kids?" She glances round and sees Edward has already been encircled by a group of students, four teenage girls gazing up at him wide-eyed and worried as he tries to offer reassurances—reassurances that none of them have.

Ben rubs his chin, his brow creased. "You tell them to be careful," he says. "You tell them to look out for each other. To stay close to school or home, just until we know what we're dealing with." There's fire in his eyes as he adds, "You tell them that we're going to find whoever did this to Sarah, and we're going to put them away."

She watches her ex-husband stalk away to join his colleagues at the front of the hall, shaking Margaret Crowe's hand, offering what she imagines are words of comfort. Not that there is much to be found. He's made it clear. Someone hurt Sarah and until they are caught, they can't assume anyone is safe.

Chapter 12

"If you'd asked me this a week ago, I'd have told you there wasn't a single person in the world who would want to hurt Sarah."

Olivia Easton sits across from Ben at the long oak table in the kitchen of Thornfield Manor, a room he figures must be at least twice the size of the entire ground floor of Rachel's cottage. The girl is curled on a velvet banquette, dressed in leggings and a hoodie, her arms hugging one raised knee. It's obvious the stress and grief of the past twenty-four hours have altered her. Her hair is unwashed, scraped into a scruffy ponytail, and her eyes are tired, red-rimmed, and bloodshot, her nail polish chipped, her skin pale. He feels a pang of pity for her—she's taking Sarah's death hard.

"I keep going over it." Olivia's finger traces a spiraling whorl in the wooden table. "It's like a nightmare you can't wake from. How can she be dead?"

"I'm sorry," says Ben, "I know this is difficult." He moves his case file to the side, pulling his notepad closer, pen poised. "Let's go back to the beginning, shall we?"

They haven't been talking long. Olivia had been the one to open the door on his arrival, and they'd had to wait a few minutes for the girl's mother to join them, Philippa Easton eventually drifting into the kitchen wearing a vacant expression. "Sorry to keep you. I'm not feeling the best today."

"Is Dad coming?" Olivia had asked, eyes wide, imploring.

"No, darling, sorry." Philippa Easton had turned to Ben. "Something's come up. Local protestors causing problems. It's never-ending," she'd explained in a soft, strained voice.

"But he promised." Olivia had looked visibly crestfallen as her mother lowered herself gingerly into a chair at the far end of the table, wincing at the effort.

Ben knew physical pain when he saw it. "Are you OK?"

Philippa had waved away his concern. "I'll be fine, as soon as the medication kicks in." It was clear she hadn't wanted him to press further. "Shall we start?"

So here they sit, the three of them in the Eastons' sleek interpretation of a high-end farmhouse kitchen that could've been pulled straight from the pages of *Architectural Digest*, Ben all too aware of his colleagues waiting at the private school on the other side of the vale for the names he needs to supply them with.

"Take me back a bit, Olivia. Who organized the party at the woodland quarry?"

Olivia considers this for a moment. "I think it was Saul who first mentioned it. It wasn't like you had to be invited or anything. Word just got around. Sarah and I thought it sounded fun. Trick-or-treating is so childish."

Ben nodded. He hated Halloween. It was always a busy night for the force, one when the dark irreverence of the occasion inevitably spilled over into antisocial behavior. If he could fast-forward through the whole damn event each year, he would.

Olivia lifts her gaze and tilts her head at him. "You were married to Ms. Dean."

Ben nods.

"Does Ellie know about Sarah?"

"The sixth form were briefed earlier this morning at a special school assembly. Everyone's shocked and sad."

Olivia's head dips again. She reaches out and brushes at a crumb on the tabletop. Ben needs to steer the conversation. The clock is ticking. "You mentioned there were about fifteen to twenty people in the woods on Saturday night?" He waits.

"Yes, about that. Sarah and I arrived around 9:00 p.m. There was a bonfire. Someone had brought a music speaker. We hung out. Messed around. Played some stupid games."

"I'm guessing there was alcohol?"

Olivia nods.

"Were you and Sarah drinking?"

"We shared a bottle of wine." She throws him a hasty glance. "My parents let us drink, sometimes. Within reason," she adds, turning to her mother, though Philippa doesn't seem to have heard. She is gazing out at the kitchen garden beyond the French doors, seemingly lost to the movement of the swaying ornamental grasses planted in the borders.

"Neither of us were paralytic," Olivia continues. "At least, *I* was being careful. I don't know what Sarah did after I left."

"I understand. What about drugs. Did you see anyone taking anything?"

She gives him a sheepish look. "I saw a couple of joints going around."

"Anything else?"

"I'm not sure."

"Did Sarah take anything?"

Olivia shrugs.

He senses she's holding back. Ben makes a mental note to

return to the drugs issue. A school like Folly View wouldn't be immune to drug problems. He knew rich, bored kids with a disposable income were often the worst offenders. The toxicology reports would tell them definitively soon enough.

"The party was fancy dress, wasn't it? What was it you girls went as?" He makes a show of flicking back through his notes, as if he's forgotten.

"I was a zombie ballerina. I wore an old leotard and long net skirt from the dance classes Mum used to make me go to. Sarah went as Sally."

"Oh yes," he says lightly. "The girl from the local ghost story. Sally in the Wood?"

Olivia nods. "It was a good idea. I wished I'd thought of it." She flicks at another crumb with a chipped nail.

"Any other costumes you remember?" he asks.

Olivia thinks for a moment. "Saul's was the best. He went as the serial killer from that new show everyone's watching. He looked great. Terrifying, actually."

"Anyone else stand out?"

"Max Allen was a Dementor. He's always been Harry Potter mad. His girlfriend, Viola, went as an avenging angel. She looked creepy. To be honest, besides me and Sarah, they were the only ones who'd made much effort. Everyone else was pretty low-key. Vampire fangs, devils' horns, and masks. That sort of thing."

He scribbles Max's and Viola's names onto his list. "Everyone else being . . . ?"

She sighs. Ben can see she's no fool. "Mrs. Crowe is so strict and not everyone had permission to leave campus." She gives him a searching look. "I don't want to be a snitch."

"I understand, Olivia, but this is important. You'd be helping the investigation and you'd be helping Sarah."

She relents with a nod of her head, reeling off some more names. "Jasmine. Saul. Danny." Olivia leans forward. "You've got Ellie's name down already?"

"Ellie?" He frowns. "My Ellie?" Ben feels a compression in his chest. "Ellie was in the woods on Saturday night?"

When Olivia nods again, Ben tries to mask his surprise by slowly adding Ellie's name to the bottom of the list. He leans back and stares at it, trying to make it make sense. Clearing his throat, he turns his attention back to Olivia. "Let's talk about Danny. He's Sarah's boyfriend?"

"Not boyfriend, exactly. Danny and Sarah are . . ." she catches herself, "*were* . . . talking."

Ben recalls a past conversation with Ellie, when she'd attempted to school him in the baffling terminology surrounding modern-day romance between teenagers. He remembers her exasperation at his obvious stupidity as she'd explained the sliding scale. "If you 'get with' or 'link' with someone then you're kissing them. 'Talking' is seeing each other, more casual than dating. It's the sussing-each-other-out stage, before you decide if you want to be exclusive. 'Exclusive' is when you stop talking to other people and only date each other. You have to ask someone to be your boyfriend or girlfriend. You shouldn't assume. You make it 'official' when you post a photo together on social media."

It had all seemed terribly complicated. Not like when he and Rachel got together. Back then, you just made out with each other and, assuming you actually liked each other, you started dating. Bingo. Girlfriend and Boyfriend. Now it seemed kids with their social media accounts and apps faced a continual roulette of new faces and potential partners, varying degrees of relationship status and connection.

"Danny liked Sarah. Maybe more than she liked him. They blew hot and cold."

"Were they hot or cold on Saturday night?"

Olivia chews her lip. "They were fine until Connor showed up."

"Connor?"

"Danny's older brother. Connor Carlisle."

Ben straightens a little in his chair. Connor Carlisle was known to the local force. At twenty-one, he'd already racked up an impressive history of petty, drug-related crimes. Last Ben had heard, Connor was branching out. Diversifying into a nasty little sideline of YouTube videos, modeling himself on controversial influencers like Andrew Tate, trying to monetize his misogyny.

"Connor Carlisle is Danny's brother?"

Olivia nods. "Danny doesn't talk about him much. They're not close. Polar opposites, really."

"But Connor was in the woods on Saturday night?"

She nods. "He turned up with a friend. A big guy. Goatee and a leather jacket. Neither of them had bothered with costumes."

Ben feels a surge of adrenaline, that feeling when something game-changing emerges in a case. "And the atmosphere shifted between Sarah and Danny when Connor arrived?"

"Yeah. Danny and Sarah argued. There was a fight between the brothers." She frowns. "You should ask Danny about it. I didn't stick around much after that. I told Sarah I was leaving, but she refused to come. I didn't want to walk home alone, but I was worried about missing our curfew and getting into trouble, so I left. I was angry with her." She sits back against the bench, deflated, eyes watering. "I never should've left her."

Seeing her rising emotion, Ben changes tack. "Your dad said you were very close. Like sisters. Tell me about Sarah. What was she like?"

Olivia sighs. A small, sad smile plays on her lips, the first to appear on her face since he's arrived. "We looked a little similar, I guess, but our personalities were different. Sarah said I was more of an introvert. Sarah, on the other hand, I guess you could say she was a bit of a magnet. A live-wire. Being around her sometimes felt like a firework going off. Loud and chaotic. Explosions of color and noise. But she was kind too, supportive. I had a big crush at the beginning of the summer, someone I thought had feelings for me." Olivia's face falls at the memory and Ben is reminded of those awful, intense pangs of first love.

"Someone at school?" he asks sympathetically.

She casts a quick glance at her mother, but Philippa still doesn't seem to be listening, her gaze fixed on the garden outside. She nods. "Sarah listened to me drone on about him for hours. She used to tell me to be more confident. She offered to help me. Said she'd give me a 'glow up.' She said I just needed to believe in myself."

"We all need someone like that in our lives. A cheerleader. Especially when our hearts are broken. She sounds like a good cousin. A good friend."

Olivia bites her lower lip, tears pricking her eyes again.

"How did Sarah get on with her teachers?"

"Fine, I think."

"Anyone else she was particularly close to? Or anyone she struggled with?"

"No. She seemed happy. She loved Mrs. Wiley, her Drama teacher. Sarah was hoping to go professional. She was good enough. She brought the house down as Cosette at the end of the summer term last year." She turns to her mother, at the end of the table. "Mum. You came to the closing night. She was amazing, wasn't she?"

Philippa shifts in her seat. "What was that, darling?"

"Sarah, she was good in *Les Mis*, wasn't she?" presses Olivia, a note of exasperation in her voice. "Really stole the show."

Philippa manages a wan smile. "She did."

"That's where she was most comfortable, I think. On the stage. Acting a part. She was good at that." Olivia bows her head as the tears begin to fall.

Ben nods. "I'm sorry, I know this is hard."

"I keep expecting her to walk in at any moment and tell us it's all been a horrible trick."

Conscious of his colleagues waiting at the school to start their interviews, and of not pushing an emotionally vulnerable girl too hard, he decides to wind things up. "You know Rachel . . . Ms. Dean, your school counselor," he adds, seeing her confusion, "she'd be a good person to talk to, if all of this starts to feel overwhelming." He eyes the dark hollows of her eyes, the bitten fingernails, then thinks of Philippa Easton sitting at the end of the table, spaced out on god knows what, her father on his work calls. "Go see her, if you need to talk to someone. Grief affects us all in different ways . . ." He trails off. He doesn't know what to tell her, knows there's something he wants to offer, but feels the fragile landscape between them, the knife-edge of loss she's walking, and fears he'll only make it worse. "Don't struggle through alone. Trust me, it's not the way."

Fearing he might have overstepped, he begins to gather up his papers. "Before I go, do you think it would be all right if I took a quick look at Sarah's room? It might help me to get a better picture of her."

Olivia glances at her mother for approval, but Philippa is away with the fairies again. "It's messy," the girl warns him.

Ben smiles gently. "As the father of a teenage daughter myself, I am well-schooled in the definition of 'messy.'"

Olivia leads the way, Philippa trailing behind them as they take a grand wooden staircase up to the second floor of the house and follow a wide, carpeted corridor until they are standing outside a door. "This is Sarah's room," announces Olivia.

Mother and daughter hover silently in the doorway, watching as he enters. Other than the grand proportions, the high ceiling with its ornate cornicing, the chandelier and the antique four-poster bed, the room looks like any other teenage girl's. Fluffy cushions. Fairy lights. A tasseled duvet cover dotted with tiny gold stars. There are clothes draped on a chair and scattered at the base of the bed. Jewelry spills from an open box. Makeup palettes, perfumes, and bottles of lotion are stacked haphazardly on a dressing table. A toy penguin sits nestled among pillows. He studies a collage of photos tacked to the wall, mostly of Sarah and Olivia, arms draped around shoulders as they grin at the camera, the two girls strikingly similar, though Ben can see that where Olivia is attractive, Sarah is another level pretty, with her high cheekbones and full lips. Amid the selfies, there is a photo of Sarah in heavy makeup and a tatty peasant's dress, part of a lineup of costumed students and a few staff members clearly celebrating the end of a stage production. There's another of a younger Sarah, beaming in a sun-bleached desert, sandwiched between two adults, one her mother, Diana, the other a handsome man he presumes is her deceased father. Looking around at the belongings accumulated in a girl's young life, Ben feels a hollow ache in his chest.

Behind him, he can hear Olivia weeping quietly, her face now pressed into her mother's shoulder. His eyes sweep the clutter on

the desk: books, pens, crumpled pieces of paper covered in doo-
dles, an empty mug. The sight of her scribbles sparks a thought.
"Do you know if Sarah kept a diary?"

"I—I'm not sure," says Olivia, wiping her eyes.

"You never saw her writing anything, a journal or notebook
perhaps?"

Olivia shakes her head.

"Would it be OK if I looked?"

At Philippa's nod, Ben pulls on latex gloves and slides open
the drawer beside the four-poster. He feels beneath the pillow,
runs his hand under the mattress, then looks beneath the bed.
He checks drawers and crevices, all the obvious places a teenager
might hide her secrets, but there's no diary.

Aware of the ticking clock, he decides to finish up. "You've
been a big help today, Olivia. Thank you."

"Will you catch whoever did this?" she asks in a tremulous
voice.

He can see the fear and worry in her eyes. Ben nods. "I promise, I'll do everything in my power to find out what happened
to her."

He can still picture the girl's distress as he heads back to the
car, imagines the emotion mirrored in the hundreds of students'
faces back at Folly View as he dials DC Maxwell's number.

She picks up almost immediately. "Who've we got?"

"Start with Danny Carlisle," he tells her. "According to Olivia, he
and Sarah were romantically involved. They had a big falling-out
at the party, something to do with Danny's older brother."

Maxwell hesitates. "Hang on. Danny Carlisle's brother? You're
talking about Connor Carlisle?"

"The one and only."

"Shit."

"It seems he made a special appearance with one of his meat-heads."

Maxwell lets out a low whistle. "I wouldn't have imagined a party of schoolkids would be Connor's vibe."

"Find out what you can from Danny. I'll track down Connor. Pay him a little visit."

"Who else?"

He reads the list of student names out one by one and Maxwell repeats them back as she scribbles them down.

"Anyone else?"

Ben stares at his notes, his eyes fixed on the final name, the one he can't bring himself to say out loud. He clears his throat. "That's all I've got—for now."

"Fine. I'll keep you posted." There's a pause.

Ben waits, sensing her hesitation.

"One or two of the DCs are grumbling. Have you heard?"

"No. What about?"

"They think Khan's playing favorites. They're complaining about being landed with support work, while I get the interviews."

"Let me guess. You're talking about Crawford?"

"I'm not naming names."

"Well, whoever it is, that's their problem. Every bit of police work in this case is important. We support each other."

"I know that, but they're saying it's favoritism. All this stuff in the press recently about institutionalized sexism and misogyny in the police force. You know, push the female DC front and center to make the team look good? They're implying my role is nothing more than a canny PR move from Khan."

"That's bollocks. Khan gave you the job because you're the best. He trusts you."

Maxwell waits a beat. "Well, I'm not sure the others see it that way. Crawford's had it in for me since I transferred from Manchester. Soon as he found out I was with Steph and immune to his 'masculine charms' . . ." She trails off.

"You don't want to be worrying about what a jobsworth like Crawford thinks. If anything, he should find your work ethic motivating. It's not your problem, Maxwell. Focus on the case."

"Thanks, Chase. I will."

The call ends and Ben sits for a moment, his gaze drifting to the scene outside the windshield. Beyond the long gravel drive, the wooded hills rise up dark and vertiginous, clawing at the gray sky. Somewhere high up on the escarpment stands the folly where Sarah was found. He thinks about the name scribbled at the bottom of his notepad, the one he omitted to give Maxwell, and lets out a groan. Goddammit, Ellie.

Saturday night had been a car crash of an evening. She'd been at his place until around eight, when she'd joined him and Chrissie outside by the pizza oven and announced that she needed to go home.

"But it's our weekend together," he'd protested.

Ellie had flipped her phone screen toward him, showing him, quite clearly, the message from "MUM MOBILE." *I need you back here. Tell Dad. Sorry, but it's urgent.*

"Ellie, is this about the baby news?" he'd asked. "I know it's a surprise, but I'd hoped a little brother or sister would be a nice thing for you?"

Ellie had shrugged. "I'm happy for you both, but I think I should go. Mum's on her own."

The jibe hadn't been lost on him, and while he wasn't exactly thrilled about it, she was too old to keep at Chrissie's against her will. It would be miserable for all of them. Small steps, he'd told himself. It would start to feel more normal for them all in time.

"Fine," he'd sighed. "I'll run you back." He had dropped her, at Ellie's insistence, outside the cottage so that they "could avoid any
awkward run-ins," watching as she'd walked up the garden path,
put her key in the door, then turned and waved goodbye.

Had it all been a ruse? Had Rachel been in on it too? Lying
for Ellie, summoning her home so that Ellie could skip out on
their night and attend the party? Was Rachel playing against
him for popularity points?

He eyes the notebook on the passenger seat beside him, fighting the sudden urge to flip it open and rip the page from the pad,
to crumple it into a ball and shove it deep in his pocket, burying
the evidence. It's what he wants to do. What any father would do,
isn't it?

He thumps the steering wheel in frustration.

They'll have to thrash it out at the cottage later. Right now,
he needs to focus, and while he might not like withholding information from his colleagues, he can't see the point in diluting
police efforts with unnecessary—and potentially incorrect—
information. Not until he's had a chance to find out what the hell
went on with Ellie this weekend. Not until he's corroborated the
facts of her whereabouts, like any good detective would. At least,
it's what he tells himself as he puts his key in the ignition and
steers away up the drive.

Chapter 13

Monday, 2:00 p.m.

A sit-down with a police officer after the sudden death of a friend would be enough to make any kid feel nervous, but there's something in Danny's stooped posture and darting eyes that makes Rachel uneasy. Standing in the open doorway to her office, he looks, for all the world, as if he might turn and bolt.

"Hello, Danny," Fiona Maxwell says, pointing to the empty chair beside the fireplace. "I'm Detective Constable Maxwell. I'm going to be asking you a few questions today."

Danny doesn't move. His gaze bounces from DC Maxwell to Rachel.

"I hope it's OK that I sit in?" Rachel asks, mustering what she hopes is a reassuring smile. "We've tried your mum but she's not answering her phone. So, you've got me, if that's OK?"

"She'll be at the warehouse," he says, his voice flat. "They're not allowed their phones on shift."

Rachel nods. "I'll be acting *in loco parentis*," she explains. "It means as your substitute guardian, if you're happy to proceed?"

He nods and lopes into the room, taking the seat Maxwell has indicated, folding his long legs beneath him and shaking the tousled hair from his eyes. Up close now, Rachel can see the bruise on his cheek, the swelling beneath his eye turning a startling shade of violet.

"Am I the first?" he asks.

Rachel nods.

"Some of the kids are saying she was murdered. Is that what happened?"

"I can't confirm anything at this stage, Danny," says Maxwell firmly. "I'm here to ask you some questions."

Rachel's known Danny for the three years she's been employed at Folly View. During that time, she's watched him shift from a gangly boy to a broad-shouldered young man, tall and muscular, with a strong jaw, piercing blue eyes, and clear skin. Compared to some of his more hormonally challenged peers, he's won the genetic lottery, at least on the days when he doesn't look like he's gone several rounds with Mike Tyson.

"That looks sore," DC Maxwell says, nodding at Danny's face. "When did that happen?"

"Saturday." Danny drops his gaze, his dark hair falling over his eyes. "There are all these rumors flying. Someone said Sarah had an accident, but others are saying there's a serial killer out there." He lifts his head, his eyes darting between them both. "Is there?"

DC Maxwell doesn't budge. "I'd like to start by confirming a few personal details. I understand you've been a student at Folly View for . . . five years?"

Danny, realizing Maxwell isn't going to answer his questions, shakes his hair from his eyes and nods. "Since Year Nine. I used to attend the local comp in town, until I was awarded a sports scholarship here."

"Congratulations. What's your sport?"

"Athletics. Track, mainly. I play a bit of football too."

"Position?"

"Midfielder."

"Any good?"

He shrugs. "I'm all right."

Rachel's tempted to interject that he's a star athlete at county level and a lynchpin player on their league-winning football team, but she knows it's not her place to speak. Instead, she catches his eye and gives him an encouraging nod. She's always had a soft spot for Danny Carlisle, perhaps because, like Ellie with her art placement, he was one of the school's few scholarship students. She knew, firsthand through Ellie's experience, that it wasn't always easy for these local kids to assimilate. She liked to keep a close eye.

Danny, to his credit, had seemed to manage the transition relatively seamlessly. It wasn't exactly fair, but Rachel knew that's how it went. Whether it was private or state school, there were always going to be popularity hierarchies, and in a school like Folly View, being a sport hero carried a weight far greater than that of a shy outsider like Ellie. Danny, with his athletic flair, humble attitude, and natural good looks, seemed to have that rare ability to garner popularity across the different student cliques. Nor did he have any problem attracting the attentions of the girls, if her hunch about him and Sarah was right.

"You're a day pupil?"

He nods.

Maxwell turns to Rachel for clarification. "What's the general split between boarders and day students here?"

"We're about sixty percent boarders, spread across four houses."

Maxwell turns back to Danny. "So, where's home?"

"Thorncombe. 18 Woodleigh Rise."

"Who do you live with?"

"It's just me and Mum. My brother moved out six months ago. I don't see my dad."

DC Maxwell scribbles the details down, then taps her pen onto her notepad. "Let's talk about Saturday night, Danny. Specifically, the party in the woods." Maxwell's tone has shifted. The small talk is over. "Run me through your movements on Saturday?"

"Sure. I had football training on Saturday morning, here at school. Then I went home to finish my coursework."

"Go on."

Danny clears his throat. "I'd arranged to meet Saul near the school gates around eight o'clock. We walked up to the quarry together. I was there for a few hours with some other kids and then . . . I left . . ." he stops to think, ". . . I guess around midnight. I was home a little after."

"Did you interact with Sarah Lawson while you were at the quarry?"

Danny tosses his head and glances in Rachel's direction. There's a reddish smudge of a love bite just below his left earlobe. She wonders if Maxwell has seen it too. He clears his throat. "Yeah. Sarah and Olivia arrived around nine, I think. Olivia left a little before me. Sarah was still there when I left." He swallows and looks down at his hands. "I don't understand how something like this . . . I mean . . . is she really dead?"

Maxwell's voice softens a little. "I'm afraid so, Danny."

He slides lower in his chair, his eyes visibly watering, his body rigid, as if the effort of containing his emotion requires every muscle in his body. If he was romantically involved with Sarah, then it's going to hit him harder than most. Every instinct, as both a parent and a school counselor, makes Rachel want to comfort him, to offer some kind of counsel, but Fiona Maxwell had been clear: "You're just sitting in, Rachel, in a guardianship capacity. Just be a quiet, reassuring presence." It pains her to stay silent, but she knows she mustn't interfere.

Maxwell leans forward. "Do you need a minute?"

He shakes his head. "No, I want to help."

"OK. I gather you and Sarah were quite *friendly*?" Maxwell puts a suggestive emphasis on the last word, lets it linger in the room.

He meets her gaze. "We'd been talking. Off and on."

"And were you 'on' or 'off' at the party on Saturday night?"

"I thought . . . I mean . . . I don't know." He rubs at a mark on his sleeve, his emotion visibly rising again. "I heard she was found up at the folly. Did she fall?"

"I know this is upsetting, Danny, but I need you to focus on my questions."

"Sorry."

"I'm guessing you and Sarah spent a bit of time together at the party on Saturday night?" Maxwell's eyes flick to the love bite on his neck.

He nods. "A bit. Yeah." He meets Maxwell's gaze. "We had a . . . row."

"What about?"

Danny frowns. "I blame Connor showing up."

"Connor is your older brother?"

"Yeah."

"Why was Connor in the woods on Saturday night?"

Danny throws up his hands. "Beats me."

"Does he have a link with the school? Ex-pupil, perhaps?"

Danny lets out a dry laugh. "No chance. Connor dropped out of Thorncombe High a few years back. He didn't get on well at school and there's no way Mum could afford the fees for a place like this. The only reason I'm here is because of my scholarship.

Connor's forever ribbing me. He calls this a place for 'posh, brainless twats.' Sorry," he adds, glancing at Rachel, flushing pink. "That's just what Connor says."

"So why did your brother turn up on Saturday night?"

She waits. Danny rubs his chin and glances longingly at the door. "Do I have to answer *every* question?"

Maxwell leans back in her chair, her face neutral, but Rachel can sense the shift in atmosphere. "No, Danny, you don't *have* to answer every question. You can refuse and we can resume this down at the police station, with your mum in tow, where we can go over things in more detail, if that's what you'd prefer?" The picture she paints hangs like a threat between them. "Or you could answer now and help us move our investigation along, for Sarah."

Danny seems to weigh up his options. "Fine. It's on Connor, not me."

"What's on Connor?"

"Look, I was as surprised as anyone to see him there. I thought he'd have better things to do. But he must've heard about the party and . . . I don't know . . . perhaps he saw it as an *opportunity*."

"An opportunity?"

Danny sighs. "You know my brother, right?" The question seems rhetorical and Maxwell doesn't answer. "Mum won't hear a bad word said against him, but the truth is he's kind of an asshole."

"Go on."

"He turned up on Saturday night with one of his mates. Big Kev. Built like a brick shithouse." He catches himself, glances at Rachel again. "Sorry. But he's huge. I think they'd got it into their heads that my 'posh' friends would have money, because, you know . . . private school." He shrugs. "He probably thought he'd come along and sell to my friends."

"Sell?"

Danny winces. It's obvious he's not enjoying ratting on his brother. "Yeah, just weed . . ."

"And?"

He throws up his hands. "I don't know. Pills."

"So, Connor shows up at the party in the woods with Big Kev. What time was this?"

"Maybe ten. I think it was around the time the games started."

"The games?" DC Maxwell's voice is neutral, but Rachel notices the shift in her posture, the rise of her eyebrows. "Tell me about that."

"It was dumb. Halloween night. Everyone was dressed up in costumes. Sarah had come as the ghost of a local girl . . . Sally . . . and—" He falters, clears his throat. "I guess that started the ghost stories. Saul was trying to scare us all with the 'Sally' story. He told us she was a local girl who'd been murdered in the woods." He swallows. "Up at the folly."

"Go on."

"Someone came up with the dumb idea that we try to contact her." He lifts his gaze. "I know. I don't believe any of that stuff, but Saul was on a mission. He made a dodgy Ouija board out of an old cardboard box and a jam jar he'd found. It was just a stupid idea to scare the girls. We played with the board for a bit. Someone kept moving the jar to say that Sally was there and that she wanted us to do dares." He swallows again. "But then we stopped when Jasmine said she'd seen someone. She said someone was watching us from the trees above the quarry."

Rachel feels a prickling sensation shoot up the back of her neck. Maxwell's pen, she notices, has gone still over her notebook. "Someone was watching you?"

Danny shrugs. "Like I said, Jasmine said she saw someone in

the trees. She was properly freaked out, so Saul and I went to check. We thought we'd chase them away."

"Did you find anyone?"

"No. We looked, but there was no one there. Just Jas's imagination running away with her. Saul started teasing the girls, calling them chicken, and then Sarah said we should do the dares. To prove who was actually chicken." Danny sighs. "It was just a game, you know? Like truth or dare. But we made it 'Sally Says.'"

"You mean like 'Simon Says'?"

"Yeah, exactly."

"What kind of dares?"

Danny winces. "Stupid stuff. It started out tame. Viola had to swap clothes with Max. Saul long-jumped the bonfire. Someone ate a worm. There was some kissing . . . and er . . . other stuff." He's blushing furiously. "It was just a bit of fun, until Connor got involved. Connor made things weird."

"Your brother got involved in the dares?"

"In a sense."

Maxwell waits. "What do you mean?"

Danny squirms in his seat. Locked in the laser beam of DC Maxwell's questions, he looks like he'd crawl under Rachel's desk, if he could. "Sarah dared me to take one of Connor's pills."

Maxwell keeps a neutral tone. "And did you?"

He shakes his head. "No way. I wasn't going to risk my place on the team—my scholarship here at the school—by taking shit like that." He catches himself. "*Stuff* like that. She knows how much this means to me. How focused I am on going to uni. I was annoyed she'd even suggest it."

"How did Sarah respond when you refused?"

Danny's eyes flash with anger. "She was drunk, so I don't think she meant it, but she called me a pussy." He bows his head. "I re-fused her dare. Took two shots instead. I thought that would be the end of it."

"Did anyone give Sarah a dare?"

Danny nods. "Connor went next. He gave Sarah one."

"What was it?"

Danny swallows. "He dared her to kiss the boy at the party she fancied the most." Rachel can feel the anger bristling off Danny.

"Who did she kiss, Danny?" DC Maxwell's eyes slide down to the raspberry love bite on his neck.

He drops his head, his voice low. "Connor. She made a big show of it."

Maxwell lets his answer sit for a moment. "That must've been difficult, seeing the girl you like—the girl you've been *talking* to—kissing your brother."

"Yeah," says Danny. "Connor thought it was hilarious, obvi-ously. He couldn't drop it. Kept saying 'posh chicks' always go for the bad boys. Said it was well known that the Folly View girls put it about. That's when I punched him. We had a bit of a scuffle." He points at his face. "As you can see."

"And if we were to talk to Connor, he'd tell us the same?"

Danny's head snaps up. "He might not admit to being punched by his younger brother. Or the drugs. But yeah, I reckon he'd tell you the gist of it. Sarah and I argued. I'd already had my suspi-cions she wasn't being honest with me and then I . . . I saw some-thing on her phone that made me think she was taking the piss."

"What sort of something?"

"I wasn't looking for it, but it was there on her home screen. A message that said something like *miss you . . . I want to be with you*. I read it out to her, but she snatched the phone away and refused to tell me who had sent it. I was sick of being treated like a fool, so I left. I wasn't having fun anymore. I was pissed at Sarah and I wanted to go home."

"An anonymous message?" Maxwell sounds circumspect.

"Yeah."

"No idea who sent it?"

"Nope. She wouldn't say. The name wasn't really a name. Just a bunch of random letters. You could check her phone?"

"Well we would if we could, but there's a problem, you see. We have no idea where it is."

Danny frowns. Maxwell, Rachel notices, holds his gaze and Danny is the first to look away. The detective leans back in her chair and considers her notepad for a moment. "Danny, did any of these dares take your group up to the folly on Saturday night?"

"To the tower?" He shakes his head. "Not as far as I know. Someone might've mentioned going, but I don't think anyone fancied it. We stayed in the quarry."

Rachel can see it in his face, any hint of bravado gone. She can only imagine how frightening the woods might feel at night, how heightened the atmosphere would be with them all in Halloween costumes, playing Ouija boards and egging each other on with foolish ghost stories, dares, and talk of watchers hiding in the trees.

"This joke your brother taunted you with. The one about Folly View girls 'putting it about.' Why would he say that? Did Sarah and Connor have history?"

Danny looks alarmed. "No. Course not. He was just being a dick."

Maxwell waits. "Rumors don't usually just blow up out of nowhere. There's often a kernel of truth to them. Are you sure?"

Danny shakes his head, insistent. "If she *was* seeing someone else, I doubt it was Connor. She kissed him to wind me up—to get back at me for refusing her dare."

"What about this?" asks Maxwell, opening up an iPad and sliding it across the table. "Do you know who did this?"

Rachel leans in and sees the word "SALLY" sprayed in scarlet paint onto a jagged rock.

Danny tilts his chin. "I don't know anything about that."

Maxwell eyes him steadily, before pulling the iPad back. "OK. What time did you leave the party?"

"I told you. I got home just after midnight."

"You went straight home?"

"Yeah. I walked back with Saul. We took one of the trails down to Thorncombe Lane. He went back to his school dorm and I walked home."

"And you left Sarah in the woods . . . with Connor?"

He nods. "Olivia had already gone. She'd left in a huff when Sarah wouldn't listen about their curfew. I admit I was mad at Sarah too, but I didn't want her wandering around on her own. I offered to walk her home, but Sarah told me to forget it. She seemed angry, which seemed a bit rich to be honest." He frowns and hangs his head. "I wanted to help her, but Saul told me to 'man up.' He told me not to follow her around like a puppy dog. Said I should leave her with Connor if she was so keen on him. Let her come running back. So yeah, I went home." When he lifts his head, his face is distraught. "I never should've left her there."

"And that was the last time you saw or heard from Sarah?"

He nods. "I snapped her when I got home. I know she saw it, those little ticks showed up next to my message. But she didn't reply. I assumed she was still pissed at me." He shrugs.

"What did your message say?"

"I just asked if things were OK between us. If she was OK."

"That was the last exchange?"

Danny nods. "Look, I'll show you." He slips his phone out of his school blazer and unlocks the screen, navigating to his snap. He angles the phone so that Maxwell can see. "I sent this at 00:53."

"Anyone see or hear you get home?"

Danny thinks. "Yeah. Mum was still up when I got in. She asked me to let the dog out. So yeah, Mum."

"Is there anything else you'd like to tell me about that night, Danny? Anything you think it important we know?"

Danny returns his phone to his pocket. He glances across at Rachel, then looks away again. Tell them, Rachel thinks. Don't hold anything back. It won't do you any favors in the long run.

As if reading her mind, Maxwell adds, "It would be better if you shared everything now. If you knowingly hold anything back, it could be considered an obstruction of justice at a later date."

Danny stares down into his lap, his hands clasped tightly. He shakes his head. "I just wish I'd insisted I walk her home. I wish I hadn't left her." He looks up at Maxwell, his eyes glistening. "But it's a bit late for that now, isn't it?"

Maxwell waits a beat. "Do you think Connor might've had any reason to hurt her?"

Danny's eyes widen. "You think Connor had something to do with this?" He shakes his head. "No way. Connor can be a dick, but he wouldn't hurt her."

Maxwell lets the silence that follows fill the room.

"I know my brother. There's no way." Even Rachel can hear that he sounds less certain. "That's all I've got to say."

"Very well." Maxwell's face is set with grim determination. "Thank you, Danny."

After he's left the room, Rachel leans back in her chair with a sigh. "Poor kid. You can see how hard he's taking this."

"Mmm . . ." says Maxwell, "or he could just be a really good liar."

Rachel turns to her in surprise. "You don't think . . . ?"

Maxwell shrugs. "It's part of the job—keeping an open mind."

"I know Danny. He's a good kid. All my instincts tell me he wasn't involved."

Fiona Maxwell lays her pen across her notebook. "I know you're attached to these kids, Rachel. Your empathy is what makes you good at your job. But in my work, it's important to let the evidence do the talking."

Rachel swallows, feeling chastised. "I just can't believe any of them would . . ."

Maxwell opens her file and shuffles through a series of photos, selecting one and sliding it across the table. "I shouldn't show you this . . . it's the least graphic one in here . . . but it might help you understand what we're up against. Why we can't let emotion sway our judgment."

Rachel isn't sure she wants to look, but the photo is right there on the table in front of her. An image of what is clearly a body. Strands of fair hair. Hands clasped together. Blue-white limbs lying in a bed of autumn leaves. Words streaked across white skin in filthy black. PUNISH. DESTROY. REPENT. She turns to look at Maxwell, eyes wide, a rush of nausea rising in her throat, "This is . . . Sarah?"

Maxwell nods. "Now you see why I'm not prepared to give anyone the benefit of the doubt, not until we've got all the evidence in front of us. Someone killed Sarah and left her like this and right now, we have no idea who they are or what they're capable of. All I know is that they're still out there, walking around, while Sarah lies on a slab in a morgue."

Rachel shoves the photo away. "Sorry," she says, pushing back her chair, "I think I need some air."

"Fine. Let's take five."

Rachel bolts from her office, out into the long, oak-paneled corridor. She pauses for a moment to take several deep breaths, relieved to have escaped the intense, airless room and the horrific image lying on her desk.

"Are you OK, Ms. Dean?" It's Jasmine Ware waiting in a chair by the door, staring up at her with concern.

"Yes," she says. "I'm OK. Are you next, Jasmine?"

The girl nods, though seeing Rachel's expression, she sinks a little lower into the seat.

Rachel tries to rally. "Don't worry." She conjures a weak smile. "Just go in there and tell the truth. That's all you have to do."

Jasmine nods, but Rachel notices how the girl averts her gaze, not quite meeting her eye. Just like Danny, she thinks, remembering his evasive looks. Something happened in those woods, something the kids aren't sharing. The realization chills Rachel to the bone.

Chapter 14

Monday, 4:00 p.m.

Connor Carlisle is pumping bullets into a gang of balaclava-clad assassins when Ben first comes across him. He's sprawled on a faux leather couch, Xbox controller in hand, long legs clad in black joggers stretched out before him, his expensive Nike Airs propped on a glass coffee table littered with cups and empty pizza boxes. "Be right with you," Connor says, though he doesn't look up, his attention fixed on the huge flat-screen TV.

Ben doesn't say a word. He lowers himself onto a nearby leather chair, the foam cushion wheezing beneath him as he sits and looks around. The curtains are drawn, casting the room in the flickering glow of the TV and the air is heavy with the cloying tang of aftershave and sweet vape fumes.

It's been a surprise to Ben that he's gained such easy access to Connor. Given his frequent brushes with the law, Ben had assumed he might find it next to impossible to get an impromptu conversation with the lad. As he'd pulled up outside the riverside flats on the edge of Bristol, he'd considered his options, deciding in the end to play it straight and see where it led. He'd parked in a visitor's space, next to a massive black four-wheel drive, and buzzed up to the "Penthouse" on the door intercom.

After a long moment, a male voice had grunted an indecipherable greeting.

"I'm here to see Connor," Ben had said, glancing up at the redbrick facade. He'd assumed he was being watched on the door cam. Expecting more questions, his fingers had rested on his identification badge, but to his surprise, there hadn't been any further discussion. The front door had clicked open and Ben had slipped inside, taking the elevator to the top floor where a huge man wearing too-tight skinny jeans and a suspiciously glazed expression had waved him into the darkened flat. "He's at the back."

The flat was all monochrome, glass and steel, a bland modern pad in dire need of an injection of color and a good clean. As he passed through, Ben glimpsed a tower of washing-up, unmade beds with duvets heaped and pillows scattered, discarded takeout containers spread across a kitchen table, weights and dumbbells dumped in the hall. Following the sound of grunts and gunfire, he'd entered the back room where he'd found Connor on the Xbox.

Waiting for him to finish his game, Ben looks around and notes the expensive-looking speaker system, a ring light and laptop as well as several cardboard boxes stacked high against one wall. The place is a cross between a student apartment and a pimped-up bachelor pad.

"Who the fuck are you?" Seemingly satisfied with his body count, Connor has lowered the controller and is staring at Ben.

"DS Chase. I'm with the Avon & Somerset Police." He flashes his badge and takes some satisfaction at the lad's obvious double take.

"Jesus Christ," says Connor, glancing in alarm at the doorway. "Big Kev just let you wander in here?"

Ben shrugs. "Well, Big Kev didn't exactly ask for my calling card, if that's what you mean. Pretty lax door security you've got going on."

Connor's gaze darts nervously over the coffee table and then sweeps the room, hesitating momentarily on the stack of boxes towering behind the sofa, before returning to Ben. He shifts in his seat, tries to wrestle himself a little more upright on the sunken sofa cushions, his chin lifting. "I haven't got time for this. I'm busy. I've got a business meeting."

"So I see." Ben throws a pointed glance at the controller in his lap.

"If this is about the videos, I can tell you right now it's freedom of speech. Pure and simple."

"This isn't about your YouTube channel. I'm here to ask some questions about Sarah Lawson."

Ben watches Connor, sees his defiance slide to confusion, cogs slowly turning before recognition dawns in his eyes. "Oh shit." His face splits into a wide grin. "The posh bird?"

The sight of his smile brings a rush of fury. Ben would like to kick Connor's feet off the coffee table and wipe that smug smile off his face. Instead, he leans forward and narrows his eyes. "You know Sarah?"

"She's not made a complaint, has she? For fuck's sake." He reaches for one of the energy drink bottles on the coffee table and untwists the cap. "The rich ones are always the worst. They dish it out, but they can't take it. I told Danny not to get messed up with her. What's she said then?" He takes a swig of the lurid-colored liquid. "Cos I can tell you now, it was all her. No one made her do anything. If anyone should be complaining, it's me. She wasted *my* time."

Ben's hands clench into fists. He waits for Connor to replace the cap on the bottle before he speaks. "She's not said anything. Sarah Lawson is dead."

The drink bottle hovers in midair. Ben studies Connor closely, watching to see how his words have landed.

"She's dead?" Connor's eyes widen.

Ben nods.

"How?"

He doesn't answer, just holds his gaze.

"Shit." Connor shakes his head. Even in the dim light of the room, Ben can see that his face has drained of color. "Does Danny know?"

"He knows."

"Fuck." Connor twists the bottle round in his hands. "What did she do? Top herself?"

"We're treating Sarah's death as suspicious."

Connor leans back in his seat. "Suspicious?"

"Were you involved with Sarah Lawson?"

"Me?" He shakes his head. "Shit no."

"But you were with her on Saturday night? In the woods?"

"With her?" He shakes his head. "I went to see Danny and his mates. I didn't stay long. Should've known it would be a lame-ass party. A few rich kids from that jumped-up school he goes to playing stupid party games in the dark."

"But Sarah was there?"

Connor nods. "She was there."

"We've heard you and Sarah were quite . . . friendly that night."

Connor rolls his eyes. "She was all over me, if that's what you mean." He holds up his hands. "I know. Danny was pissed about it, but I can't help it if women find me irresistible. It's the energy I give off." He looks Ben up and down. "You should watch my You-Tube channel. I teach guys all about this stuff. How to pull chicks. How to get them to do anything you want. It's all about the BDE." He grabs his crotch. "You should check it out."

Ben really doesn't want to think about Connor's self-professed Big Dick Energy. "I'm good, thanks. We've got a witness saying that you took drugs to the woods on Saturday night with the intention of dealing."

Connor folds his arms across his muscled chest. "I didn't sell anything to anyone on Saturday night."

"Did you supply drugs to Sarah Lawson?"

"No." His reply sounds like a yes.

"So, if our toxicology reports come back and show illegal substances in her system, that wouldn't be on you?"

Connor tilts his chin, but Ben can see the flicker of doubt in his eyes. "Is that what you think happened? She took something dodgy? Because I'm telling you, that's not on me. She had a little smoke. That's it."

"What were you smoking?"

"Just some skunk."

"Skunk like the stuff you were dealing last month outside Thorncombe High? Skunk laced with spice that saw three near-comatose kids rushed to hospital."

"You lot tried to pin that one on me," Connor tilts his chin, "but you couldn't prove anything."

"Sarah didn't take anything else?"

"Not that I saw." Connor does a good job of staring him down. "She was fine when I left her. Better than Danny, anyway. Gave him a right shiner. Little prick, coming at me like that."

"We've heard you had an altercation with Danny. What prompted that?"

He shrugs. "His girl was out of control. Thirsty. All over me, like she had a point to prove. Danny didn't like it. Can't blame him, really. Need to keep a chick like that on a tight leash or you're in a world of trouble. Danny came at me and I defended myself. Plain and simple."

Ben swallows down his distaste, tries to keep his voice neutral. "Then what?"

"A few people left, Danny included, until it was just me, Big Kev, and that Sarah girl. She was in a funny mood, agitated. I guess because of Danny, but you know what? I was buzzing. Sounded like she'd been taking him for a mug. I was glad he'd seen the light. Happy to help illustrate the point," he adds with a leer. "I suggested we head up to the folly for a smoke. We hung out up there for a bit, lit a fire, chatted shit until Big Kev got bored and suggested we resurrect the night back in Bristol. We offered to take Sarah with us, good-looking girl like that. I don't mind buying her a few drinks in a club, but she said no. Said she was going to walk home. It was the opposite direction to us, so we left her to it."

Ben bristles. "You left a seventeen-year-old girl alone in the woods in the middle of the night? Not very gentlemanly."

"She wanted us to go. Told us to *fuck off*, if you must know. So Big Kev and I walked back to the car and drove into Bristol. Hit up Lakota."

"What time did you get to the club?"

"I'd say around 1:00 a.m. I got home at 5:00 a.m." Connor looks pleased with himself.

"We can check the CCTV at the venue to confirm you were there."

"Be my guest."

"Can anyone else vouch for your whereabouts that night?"

"Yeah. Kev, until he peeled off. And a chick from the club. Kayla. She was up for it," he adds, his smug grin spreading across his face. "Desperate to come home with me."

"Do you have Kayla's surname? Her contact details?"

"Don't know her last name, but she left her number. Insisted on it. Not that I was planning on calling . . . but I don't mind if *you* do." He leans forward and rummages among pizza boxes to pull out a scrap of paper. "Here. Have it. I won't be needing it."

Ben makes a note of the number, then pulls his own card from his pocket. He throws it onto the coffee table between them. "My number. In case you think of anything else important."

Connor rolls his eyes, already reaching for the Xbox controller in his lap.

Back at the car, Ben pulls out his cell phone and dials the number from the torn napkin. A woman answers on the third ring. "Hello?" She's softly spoken. Tentative. Hopeful.

Kayla goes quiet when Ben tells her who he is, though he senses her interest lift at the mention of Connor. "I was with him. We got kicked out of the club at 4:00 a.m. and went back to his, via a kebab shop."

"And you were with him for the rest of the night?"

"Yeah, I left his place the next day, around twelve. He said he had work to do."

"You've been very helpful. Thank you."

He's about to hang up when she jumps in. "If you're talking to Connor again, tell him he still owes me for the Uber. And tell him he can call me . . . anytime."

Ben sighs. "You sound like a nice girl, Kayla. I know you're not asking for advice, but I'd say the same thing if you were my daughter. You'd do well to stay clear of men like Connor Carlisle."

Kayla is quiet, her silence sullen and heavy, and Ben knows as he finishes the call that she isn't going to listen.

Leaving the concrete suburban sprawl of the city behind him, he heads back along the M4 toward the distant vale of Thorncombe. As he drives, he thinks about Connor, his misogyny, his bluster, his unpleasant narcissistic ego. He knows exactly the type of videos he's been making—the men he's been idolizing. Men who think women are less, there to serve, to manipulate, to degrade. This is the world Ellie is growing up in, the one she must learn to navigate safely. He'd be lying if he said the thought didn't terrify him.

Inevitably, Ben's thoughts segue to Sarah. He remembers the way her body lay on the ground, as if placed there, tenderly, her long blond hair lifting in the breeze. He thinks about the words daubed on her skin. He thinks of that word that had come to him in the clearing. "Reverence." Someone had taken care with her.

Police training and years of experience have taught Ben never to underestimate what a person is capable of, but every mile he drives away from Bristol, he feels it more strongly, more instinctively: Connor isn't Sarah's killer. A young man like Connor Carlisle is basic, brash, full of bravado. As much as he might disrespect and denigrate women, he doesn't have the imagination or the artistry for such a disturbing crime scene. Sarah's killer had more going on in their mind. More intent behind their actions. More they wanted to say.

Chapter 15

Monday, 6:00 p.m.

After concluding the last interview for the day, a drained Rachel and DC Maxwell leave the administration building together. Darkness already cloaks the school grounds as Rachel walks with the officer to her vehicle. "Thank you," says Maxwell, meeting her eye over the hood of the police car. "I know it's not been easy, but I'm glad you were there for the kids."

"I just hope you catch whoever did it."

"We will." Maxwell eyes her with concern. "Are you going to be all right?"

Rachel shrugs. "I think I need to go home and hug my daughter. Will *you* be OK? I know the stress you deal with. I've seen it up close. You police officers act tough," she adds, seeing Maxwell's frown, "but it's a lot."

"Me? Oh sure. That's the joy of dating a hot chef. Steph will shower me with food and affection the moment I walk through the door. She's the perfect antidote to all of this." She hesitates. "I owe you an apology, Rachel. I shouldn't have shown you that photo earlier. I'm sorry—I messed up."

Rachel swallows. She wishes she hadn't seen it either. "I understand why you did."

Maxwell's car is pulling away down the drive when Rachel hears her name being called. She turns to see Margaret Crowe hovering by the building entrance, wrapped in a black shawl. She beckons to Rachel. "Do you have a minute? I wanted to ask how the interviews went."

Rachel frowns. She's almost certain she's not allowed to share the details of what was spoken about, bound by confidentiality to both the police and the kids. "The students were troopers," she says, keeping her reply vague. "A credit to the school," she adds, hoping the praise will appease her boss.

"Were the police satisfied?"

"I . . . I don't know. It was an information-gathering exercise. I'm not sure they'll be satisfied until they've brought someone to justice."

"Of course," agrees Margaret. "I meant, were they satisfied that the school wasn't involved? Nothing arose that might have . . . posed an issue for anyone? No one on the faculty, for example?" She lets the question hang.

The way the light is falling from the building behind her makes it impossible to read Margaret's expression. What is she asking her? Rachel clears her throat. "I think the police have various lines of enquiry to pursue. I'm not across their exact thinking."

Margaret gives a small wave. "I'm sure you understand my concern. I have a duty as head teacher to protect the school. Reputation is everything for an institution such as ours."

A girl has died. It doesn't feel like quite the right time to be focusing on the school's reputation.

"Children can get so muddled," Margaret continues. "Whispers and rumors can be twisted and gather momentum. Students say things sometimes for attention, just to be part of something . . . well . . . exciting. You can't always believe everything they say, can you? I'm sure you understand."

Rachel's not sure that she does.

As if sensing her confusion, Margaret adds, "All I'm saying is that if there was something troubling . . . something that you thought might affect the school, then I'd expect you to bring it to me. Do you understand? Above and beyond. Everyone playing their part. That's what we stand for here."

Rachel nods slowly.

"Good." Seemingly satisfied, Margaret turns back to the building. "I hope you have a restful evening, Rachel. Good night."

Relieved to escape Margaret's interrogation, Rachel darts down the steps and scurries across the campus, seeking out the pools of light falling from lampposts, keen to avoid the shadows and the less well-lit pathways. Her senses are on high alert, conscious of every bush masquerading as a hiding place, startling at every twig crack and the distant hoot of an owl high up in the hills.

It's not like her to feel so rattled, especially in a place that has always felt so safe and secure, but then she supposes the day's not been like any other she's experienced in her career. The corridors had echoed all day with the students' whispers. Perhaps it was natural for Margaret to be concerned about what they might be saying. Perhaps the strange conversation was nothing more than a badly phrased request, coming from a place of pastoral concern, rather than anything more sinister or calculated. They were all hypervigilant, jumping at shadows, wary of the danger looming over the school.

Rachel shivers and pulls her coat a little tighter, relieved when the cottage finally appears through the gloom, the light in Ellie's bedroom window guiding her home.

Letting herself in through the front door, she just has time to kick off her shoes, sling her coat over the banister, and start chaotic preparations for a scrambled-together meal when Ben arrives, announcing himself with three sharp raps on the front door. She slings the tea towel she's been using to waft smoke from the kitchen over her shoulder and pushes strands of damp hair from her face. "Come in," she says, flustered. "Sorry about the smell. I'm burning dinner."

She steps back to let him into the narrow hallway and ushers him past Ellie's skateboard, a stash of shoes, and a muddy hockey stick. "You go first." She kicks an errant sneaker out of the way before following him back into the kitchen.

She knows from the high set of his shoulders and the tension in his jaw that he's readied for battle. It wasn't so long ago that she felt she knew him inside out. When they'd said "I do" in a small ceremony in front of their friends and family, when they'd vowed "for better or worse," she'd thought they meant it. But all those years together had brought about a certain, undeniable malaise, both of them guilty of taking the other for granted. Toward the end, it had been as if she couldn't see him clearly anymore.

This new distance between them, both geographical and emotional, is startling to her. It's as if the lenses of a pair of glasses have been wiped clean, or a camera twisted back into sharp focus. Whenever she sees him now, she feels wrong-footed. He is *her* Ben, and yet he is not. This new version of him standing at the back of the school assembly or walking through her front door feels unknown to her. Other.

It's not just the subtle changes in his appearance—the shaved head, which looks annoyingly good, emphasizing his green eyes and his strong jaw; or the trimmer physique, also annoyingly attractive. It's something in his eyes whenever they come face-to-face. A shuttered expression, a defense mechanism, perhaps, that forms a barrier between them, an unknowable terrain she can no longer step foot into. She wonders if he looks at her and feels the same. Wonders if he sees any changes in her. Wonders if he even considers her at all. Unlikely, she thinks, her sorrow shifting to something sharper, something hot and barbed as she remembers the baby news from the weekend and how badly he's handled it.

"You've made it nice," he says, breaking eye contact, his gaze sweeping around the cluttered, low-beamed room. "Cozy."

Rachel, wrong-footed by the compliment, looks about in surprise, trying to see the space through his eyes. Margaret Crowe had offered Rachel the old worker's cottage as part of her benefits package, in lieu of a raise after her first year of employment at the school. Ellie hadn't been keen to live on the school grounds, but financially it had made sense for Rachel. Rent-free accommodation was more generous than any raise she could've asked for and far better for them emotionally than staying in the home she'd once shared with Ben, full of its memories and ghosts. Only Ellie hadn't seen it that way.

"It's not much bigger than that first place you and I shared," Rachel says to Ben, gesturing half-heartedly at the space.

"But you were always so good at making a place feel like a home." His praise hangs awkwardly between them, loaded with an emotion she doesn't want to feel. Is this a peace offering? Or perhaps, she thinks, catching herself, it's just guilt. A tactic to try to smooth things over after the way he's handled his announcement.

Looking around at the room that comprises their kitchen, dining, and living area, she supposes it has changed since that first week of moving chaos. She and Ellie have put their own creative stamp on it. Some of Rachel's favorite pieces of Ellie's art—abstract canvases of bold, layered color, experimental pieces created out of splashes of oils and spray paint—line the walls. The rickety shelves over the fireplace are filled with tatty paperbacks and recipe books. A colorful woven rug she'd lugged home from a charity shop lies across the worn wooden floorboards, while the shabby fabric sofa she'd requisitioned from their old home is now angled toward the stone fireplace. When it's just the two of them it doesn't feel too cramped, but with Ben's tall frame now filling the space, his head almost brushing the ceiling beams, the room feels tiny. "'Cozy' is probably the right word for it," she says. She waves a bottle of wine at him. "Would you like a glass?"

He looks as if he's going to say no, but then relents. "I shouldn't, but it's been a hell of a day. Thanks."

Rachel pours him a glass and slides it across the counter. "The student interviews were intense. Fiona's like a dog with a bone."

"She's a good detective. Thorough."

Rachel nods. "I like her, personally, but she's not taking any prisoners with the kids."

"She's got a job to do." He frowns. "Is Ellie here?"

"Yeah. Shall I call her down?"

"Not yet. We need to talk first."

She can tell by the tone of his voice that he isn't happy. Any last traces of adrenaline she's carried through the day leach out of her. She's drained, exhausted, ill-prepared for the conversation ahead. "What's up?"

Ben leans against the kitchen counter and folds his arms. "Changing our arrangements at the last minute, Rach. Whatever the reason, it's disruptive and unfair to me . . . and Chrissie."

Hostile words bubble up her throat, threatening to spill, but she catches herself. Let him speak, she tells herself. Just listen.

"I think we need to be very careful about allowing Ellie to play us off against each other. I thought we'd agreed, as annoyed as she was to miss out on a party, that she was to spend Saturday night with me."

Rachel frowns. She opens her mouth to speak, but he is still going.

"I know our news this weekend was somewhat . . . challenging for Ellie. And I'm sure you have your own feelings about Chrissie and I . . . and the baby," he adds, dropping his gaze. "But what sort of a precedent are we setting, if Ellie thinks she can use you as an escape route whenever life gets a little uncomfortable? What lesson are we giving her if we capitulate and let her do whatever she wants whenever she wants, over existing family commitments? It's not fair to play favorites with her."

"Wait." She can't hold back any longer, her anger rising at his irritatingly calm, measured tone, patronizing in the extreme. "I honestly don't know what you're talking about. I didn't give Ellie 'an escape route.' She was with *you* on Saturday night."

Ben narrows his eyes. "She stayed for dinner, but then you sent that message calling her back, so we all had to jump to your tune."

"Wait. What message?"

"I saw it. Your text *demanding* that she come back here. Urgently." He tuts. "If I'm honest, it felt disrespectful, as if you were trying to get one up on me."

Get one up on him? What the hell. Rachel holds up a hand. "Hang on. Are you telling me that Ellie didn't stay with you and Chrissie on Saturday night?"

"I dropped her back here after dinner, just like you asked."

Rachel's eyes narrow. "I didn't *ask*. I was here on Saturday night and Ellie didn't come home." She stares at him. "You dropped her back? You actually saw her walk into the cottage?"

Ben's expression shifts, but she still has no idea what he's talking about. "I'm telling you now," Rachel says firmly, "I didn't send any message. And Ellie sure as hell didn't come back here on Saturday night."

Ben shakes his head. "Then she's played us both."

"Sounds like it. But more importantly, if she wasn't with you, and she wasn't here with me . . . where the hell was she?" Rachel is afraid she already knows the answer.

"The woods," says Ben, his face grim.

Rachel reels. "The party in the quarry? Then she should've come forward today," she adds, her panic growing at the full implication of Ellie's lies. "Maxwell should've interviewed her." And then she remembers: the chain of whispers in the assembly, stopping with Ellie. Danny's awkward glances in her direction during his interview. Jasmine's shifty look in the corridor. They knew. They'd all been covering for her. "I don't understand. Why didn't anyone mention her?"

Ben shifts on his chair. "Olivia Easton did."

"She did?"

He nods. "I wanted to be sure. I left her name off the interview list until I could confirm it."

Rachel stares at Ben. "You what? You're telling me that you already knew she'd been up there? You thought I was in on it too, lying to you, so that she could go? Jesus, Ben. Give me some credit."

He reaches for his wineglass, a faint flush rising on his cheeks. "I'm sorry. I thought perhaps you were angry. Or . . . I guess I hoped there was a chance Olivia was muddled. She's distraught— the poor girl's had a lot to deal with these past few days." He shakes his head. "I needed to speak to you and Ellie first. Get the full picture. But it's not good whichever way you look at it, is it? Ellie's lied to us. Put herself in potential danger."

Rachel simmers silently, still trying to process Ben's thinking. Did he really think her such a shitty parent, that she'd let Ellie duck out of her responsibilities to go to a party, then lie about it to the police?

Ben thumps the kitchen counter. "For god's sake. She could've been hurt, and we would've had no idea where she was. What the hell was she thinking?"

"I need to hear this from her." Rachel strides to the bottom of the stairs and yells Ellie's name. It takes a moment, but eventually their daughter slinks down the staircase, a single white earbud still jammed in one ear. She takes in the scene with a nonchalant gaze. "This looks cozy," she says, nodding at the open bottle of wine. "What's up?"

It's obvious what's up. She might be playing it cool, but Rachel can see she knows what's coming, that she's braced for their interrogation.

"Take that thing out of your ear," snaps Ben. He waits for her to pocket the earbud before he continues. "You lied to us."

Anger ripples through his voice and Rachel sees the shutter drawing down over their daughter's face. Not a great start going straight in on the attack, she thinks. Certainly not a tactic she would've used. Classic Ben. Interrogating her like a police detective, rather than a father.

"About what?" Ellie doesn't blink. She folds her arms across her chest, the mirror image of her father.

Rachel attempts to intervene. "Why don't you start by telling us where you were on Saturday night?"

Ben nods. "Because you sure as hell weren't at my place, and you weren't here with your mother."

"Ben," Rachel warns. "Let Ellie speak."

Ellie shrugs, still playing it cool, though a telltale flush has begun to scramble up her neck. She juts her chin. "I went to the Halloween party."

"You went to the quarry in the woods," adds Ben.

"So what?"

"So what? Seriously?" Ben looks at Rachel in disbelief.

She throws him a pleading look. *Stay calm.*

"You lied to us. Neither of us had any idea where you were all night. Don't you see how irresponsible that was? How dangerous?"

Ellie studies her hands, picking dried flakes of paint off her fingers. "I'm OK, though, aren't I?"

Ben and Rachel exchange another glance. "Ellie, Sarah Lawson didn't come home that night," says Rachel pointedly. "A friend of yours is dead."

"She wasn't exactly my friend. But yeah, I know."

Rachel is shocked at her tone. "Ellie, this is serious. Someone killed Sarah. Someone who's still out there. Someone with god knows what motive. What if it had been you who'd been attacked?" She can see from Ellie's expression that her words have hit home. She wishes she hadn't had to use such blunt delivery to make her mark. "Until we know what happened, we have to assume no one is safe. More kids could get hurt."

Ellie looks chastened.

"You were asked to come forward. Why didn't you?" Ben fixes her with his intense stare.

"What is this? The full police interrogation now?" Seeing her father's face, Ellie pulls it back. "Maybe because I knew if you both found out I'd gone to the party, you'd go off like *this*. I didn't want to get in trouble." She shrugs. "It's not as if I had anything useful to tell the police."

"That may be true, but we still need to rule you out of the investigation, Ellie. The fact that you were there that night puts me in a difficult spot with the team. But most importantly," he adds, "your mum and I can't have you wandering about at night, with us not knowing where you are. You're seventeen. You live under our roofs. You abide by our rules."

Ellie turns back to her dad, anger flaring in her eyes. "Your roofs? You live under Chrissie's roof. Mum lives under Mrs. Crowe's thumb."

"That's not fair—"

"You and Chrissie expected me to sit there on Saturday night, listening to you both banging on about your new baby, acting like I should be *thrilled* about it." Ellie's voice rises as she interjects over Ben. "What did you expect?"

Rachel shoots Ben an exasperated look. Had he really been so tone-deaf to Ellie's feelings?

"You faked a message from your mum, asking you to come home."

Ellie shrugs. "It was Jasmine's idea. I renamed her 'Mum' in my contacts list, then she messaged me to say she needed me home. To be honest, I didn't think it would work but when I showed you the message you just rolled your eyes and told me to gather my stuff. It was like you couldn't wait to be rid of me."

"Ellie, we didn't want you to leave."

"Didn't you?" She glares at him, her green eyes flashing.

Rachel intervenes. She has a more pressing question for their daughter. "You didn't come home until lunchtime the next day," says Rachel quietly. "Where were you?"

"I slept in Jas's dorm room. Her roommate was away. I was fine. Totally safe." She throws up her hands. "I had no idea something bad had happened to Sarah. Can't we just forget this?"

"Forget it?" says Ben, incredulous. "You can't go wandering around, sleeping wherever you like, your mother and I not knowing where you are. Especially not *now*. Not with a murder investigation underway. You've broken our trust."

"But I'm fine. You guys are so dramatic. You always see everything through a twisted lens. It's your jobs. You always expect the worst to happen. It's stifling. I deserve a life."

"Ellie, the worst *has* happened—a girl was killed. Sarah lost her life on Saturday night."

Something in Rachel's plea seems to chime with Ellie. She bows her head, scraping at the flagstones with a socked foot. Rachel watches her through narrowed eyes. She knows Ellie. All this defensive bluster. Something isn't right. "You could've been hurt. I don't want to scare you, but it might still be dangerous. None of us know what happened. Until we do, we need you to be safe . . . and responsible."

Ben sighs. "Tomorrow morning you're going into school and you're going to tell DC Maxwell that you were at the party in the quarry. She'll have some questions for you. Answer them truthfully and that will be that. I'll talk to Khan. I'll tell him you lied to us about where you were. I'll explain you were worried about getting into trouble." Ben hesitates. "That is why you didn't come forward today, isn't it?"

Ellie stares intently at the floor. Rachel feels that sensation in her chest again, a sense of wrongness.

"It's just us here, so I'm going to ask you outright, Ellie, is there anything else you want to tell us? Anything important about Saturday night you want to share, before this is out of our hands?" Ben swallows. "We love you. We're both here for you, no matter what. But we can't help you if you aren't honest with us."

Rachel listens to Ben's words and wonders if he shares her worry.

Ellie's gaze remains fixed on the floor. "I went to the party.

I slept over with Jas. That's it." She lifts her gaze. "Honest." She waits a beat. "You don't think I had something to do with Sarah, do you?" She stares up at him.

"Of course not."

"We just want honesty, Ellie," Rachel chips in.

Ellie doesn't answer.

Rachel has a question nagging at her. The words dance on the tip of her tongue, impossible to hold in. "The dares . . . the stuff some of your friends were doing . . ." Rachel hesitates. "Were you involved?"

Ellie shakes her head.

Rachel lets out a relieved sigh. "Good."

"I don't understand why the police are so fixated on us. It could've been anyone."

"The police need to eliminate you all from the investigation."

"Did they check the woods?"

"Yes." Ben narrows his eyes. "What makes you say that? Did you see something?"

Ellie eyes him, then looks away. "No. I just think if someone hurt Sarah, it's not going to be one of us. More likely to be a random weirdo, right? The woods are huge, the quarry, the caves . . . they're good hiding places."

Ben studies her for a long moment. "If there's something you want to tell us, now is the time."

She shakes her head, her bottom lip caught between her teeth.

It's a look that reminds Rachel of a much younger Ellie, the little girl they would swing in their arms and tuck into bed at night.

"OK." He turns to Rachel and she can read his look: not entirely convinced, but out of ideas. She shrugs. What more can they do?

"Can I go back to my homework?"

Ben nods. "I'll see you soon, OK?" He holds out his arms and Ellie relents, crossing the kitchen and allowing him to hold her, briefly, in a stiff hug. "Bye," she says, the word muffled in his jacket sleeve. As she turns and leaves, Rachel sees Ben's hurt at her curt dismissal.

"It doesn't get easier, does it?" he asks, after she has gone. "This parenting thing."

"No. It doesn't."

"It wasn't that long ago I'd come home from work and she'd throw herself into my arms. Do you remember how she'd cling to my trouser legs, her little feet balanced on mine, as I danced her round the kitchen to Little Mix?"

"She wouldn't be caught dead listening to them now."

He gives a wistful sigh. "She's growing up so fast."

The look on Ben's face pierces her, until she remembers. "You're all right. You've got another round to look forward to. Another chance to get it right." There's a barb in her voice. She can't help it. The thought of him and Chrissie launching into parenthood together after just a few months of dating cuts deep.

"We didn't plan . . ." He falters. She waits, but he seems to have changed his mind and whatever he was going to say remains locked away. He changes tack. "Ellie seems so angry. Is it my fault?"

Rachel shrugs. She's not sure what he expects her to say. "I guess we both hold some responsibility. If it helps, I think she's as angry with me as she is with you."

"Has she said anything about the baby?"

Rachel stares at him. *Really?* "I'm too close to see all of this clearly, but I doubt it's helped." Then seeing his crestfallen face, she adds, "She's a teenager, Ben. She's supposed to pull away. If we love them enough, do a good enough job, then they reward us with distance . . . by leaving. It's healthy, but yeah," she shrugs, "it's painful, and frightening, especially with everything going on right now," she adds. "Try not to blame yourself. You need to focus on the case. And on Chrissie," she adds quietly.

He takes a sip of wine. "I don't imagine I'll be on the case for too much longer."

"Why not?"

"Hopefully Ellie will answer a few questions and we'll all move on." He twists the stem of his wineglass. "But there's a chance my position could be considered a conflict of interest."

She shakes her head. "It's crazy. Things like this don't happen round here."

"Things like this can happen anywhere. You know that, Rach."

"Do you have a suspect?"

"We're following some leads."

"Could it really be one of the students?"

"We're keeping an open mind."

She throws him a look. "You're giving me all the PR lines. Maxwell showed me a photo. I know," she adds, seeing Ben's dismay, "I think she realized her mistake as soon as she'd done it. But I saw her, Ben. I saw what they'd done to Sarah. It looked crazed. Sadistic. Tell me, should I be worried for Ellie? Should we impose a curfew? At least until you've caught the person responsible?"

"I'd love to, but you've seen what Ellie was like tonight. If we go too hard, I think we run the risk of alienating her completely. Hopefully she's smart enough to recognize she's had a lucky escape. To be careful and stay close to school and home, for now." Ben frowns. "We'll catch whoever did it," he says. "We have to."

He finishes his wine and Rachel asks if he's eaten, if he wants to join her and Ellie, but he tells her he should go. Out on the doorstep, moths ghosting out of the dark toward the cottage lights, he turns back to her. "I'm sorry," he says. "I know our news must be upsetting for you."

Rachel gives a small nod, acknowledging his apology.

"I'd go back if I could, you know . . . do things differently. This isn't exactly—"

"Don't, Ben." She doesn't think she can bear what he might be about to say. "Everything changed after Gemma. It's done now."

"You and me, Rach, we're the same. We do our jobs because we want to serve. We want to help people. Do you have any idea what it feels like when you can't help someone you love? To see them suffering, knowing you can do nothing to help, nothing to save them?"

She knows he's talking about the aftermath of Gemma's accident, when his sister lay unresponsive in a hospital bed, dying slowly. She knows how hard it was for him, but she'd been there, right by his side. She'd been hurting too, and he was gone. Locked away. Unreachable. He'd shut her out and his rejection, intentional or otherwise, had been painful. Rachel holds his stare. "I have some idea, yes."

"If you mean me, it's not the same, Rach."

"I wanted to help. You wouldn't let me in."

There's a twitch in his jaw, a flicker of emotion in his green eyes. She can see he wants to fight her, wants to argue his case, the destructive pattern of their relationship threatening to unfurl again, a noose encircling them on the doorstep. "There's no point going over this. Not now." She sighs. "We are where we are."

He nods and steps away. "If you get worried about Ellie, call me. We should present a united front."

"Bye, Ben."

There is an ache in Rachel's chest as she pulls the door shut and listens to the sound of his footsteps fading into the night. She leans her head against the cool wood of the door, the past seeming to rush at her, even as he walks away into his future.

The cracks had started with Gemma's accident, the fissures in their relationship only widening after her death, his sister having succumbed to her injuries four weeks after she'd been airlifted to the hospital. The whole thing had been so sudden, so shocking, the knock at the door telling them that Gemma had been in a road traffic collision. It hadn't felt real. She'd only been with them earlier that day, laughing over Sunday lunch, playing Mario Kart with Ellie, and singing along to the radio in the kitchen while they washed the pots and pans. She'd hugged them all on the doorstep and punched Ben on the arm and told him, "Smell you later, Benny Boy," before driving away in her little yellow Fiat. She'd made it three miles down the road when her car had collided with a vehicle coming too wide on the wrong side of a sharp chicane, a nineteen-year-old kid, stoned at the wheel, texting on his phone. Sally in the Wood had claimed its latest victim, and all their lives had changed forever.

It had hit each of them differently. Rachel had been heartsick and emotional, Ellie alternating between distraught and confused, falling in and out of her grief like the child she was, jumping through puddles. But Ben had been unreachable, consumed with rage, utterly fixated on the court case and seeing the driver punished. Locked in his pain, every attempt she'd made to reach him was rebuffed, until it felt to Rachel as if that damn car had smashed through the safety barriers of their marriage. What remained had seemed to be nothing more than a daily polite dance around each other followed by a cold shoulder at bedtime, both of them more comfortable staring at their phone screens than facing their crumbling relationship.

Rachel grimaces as the memories race back at her. She doesn't want this in her head. Not now. Sarah's death is upsetting enough. She won't let Ben upset her too. She won't rehash the pain. Peeling herself from the door, she turns and calls up the stairs. "Ellie," she yells. "Dinner."

They eat in near silence, pushing their food around, the heavy atmosphere of the cottage punctuated by the scrape of cutlery against plates. Rachel eyes Ellie. "Do you want to talk about the baby?" she asks, unable to stand the quiet any longer.

Ellie shakes her head.

"How do you feel about it?"

Ellie lays her knife and fork down with a sigh. "How do *you* feel about it, Mum?"

Rachel frowns.

"Stop trying to 'therapy' me. I'm your daughter, not your job," she mutters.

Rachel eyes Ellie but decides to let it drop and when it comes time for bed, Ellie disappears with a curt "Good night."

Sitting alone, staring at the empty hearth, she wonders how she might reconnect with Ellie. She is so like Ben. When she pulls up her emotional drawbridge, she is unreachable, which in turn only makes Rachel feel more redundant and alone.

Her phone beeps and perhaps, because she's been thinking of him, she expects to see Ben's name on the screen. She's surprised to see a Facebook notification instead: a friend request from Edward Morgan. She hesitates, her finger hovering over "accept" as she remembers the concern in his eyes at the back of the assembly hall, the reassuring press of his hand on her arm. Social media isn't really her thing. She tries to grapple with it, tries to stay abreast of the various apps her students are glued to, but it's like Whac-a-Mole, a new one replacing the old before she's figured each variant out. Facebook is the only one she's even vaguely maintained—old school—definitely more her style than all these reels and disappearing snaps, but she's not often on it.

She studies Edward's name on her screen, those two words beside it: *Friend request*. There's really no reason why she shouldn't accept. He was more than a colleague; certainly the closest she's got to a friend at the school. She presses accept and almost immediately, her phone pings with another notification.

Hi.

Just one word, next to the circular profile picture of Edward's face, a photo she recognizes from the school website, clean-shaven in a shirt and tie, his dark hair pushed back off his forehead, a half smile making him look thoughtful and approachable. She stares at his expressive brown eyes and his full lips, something warm rising inside her. Then another message, in quick succession.

Are you OK?

Such a simple question. She is surprised by her sudden rush of emotion.

I've had easier days. You?

Same, and I didn't have half the day that you did. Those interviews can't have been easy.

She hesitates, a finger poised over her keyboard, the echo of her earlier conversation with Margaret returning. She supposes everyone's curious, seeking answers. There's really no harm in sharing her own perspective.

It was tough. I feel for the kids. There's a lot of pain and fear right now.

Typing dots, then another message.

And a lot of wild theories circulating! I tried to squash the chatter in class today, but the kids are going to talk.

Rachel knows it's true. Danny had said as much in his interview, and so had Margaret, earlier that evening.

Let's hope the police have some answers soon.

Yes. You take care. Try to get some sleep.

Thanks. You too.

She switches her phone to silent, and after she's showered and changed into pajamas, she goes to Ellie's door and opens it a crack. It's dark inside, the steady rhythm of Ellie's breathing a sure sign she is already asleep.

Rachel creeps forward, careful to avoid the creakiest floorboards and the artwork fanned out on the floor near the bed. She can just make out vivid paint scrawls and cut-out shards of cardboard littering the carpet. A gap in the curtains allows a sliver of moonlight to fall onto Ellie's pillow, illuminating her pale face. Rachel stands for a moment, studying her conundrum of a daughter, noting the familiar curves and contours she has gazed upon for seventeen years, the slope of her nose, the short, tufty hair and scattered freckles. Somehow, in sleep, all the hardness and resistance has fallen away. Beneath her cool teenage exterior, the traces of the little girl she once was linger and pull at her heart. The child who'd refused plasters and Savlon when she fell and grazed a knee, who'd resisted every bedtime, who'd stood in every toddler seat in the supermarket shopping carts and insisted on going up every slide at the playground, rather than taking the stairs. The girl who'd generally insisted on doing everything the hard way.

It really wasn't so long ago that she'd sit on the bed with Ellie curled into the crook of her arm and read her favorite books to her. Stories of adventure, mystery, and monsters, Ellie screaming with delight as wild things roared their terrible roars and gnashed their terrible teeth. It pains her to remember how quick she'd been to reassure Ellie that there was no such thing as monsters. Nothing under the bed or hiding in the forests. But now, with Sarah dead and the shocking photograph of her poor body imprinted on her mind, Rachel isn't so sure. Standing there in the darkness of Ellie's room, with the wind outside whispering through the dark trees, Rachel feels a rush of fear. There *are* monsters out there—monsters doing awful, inexplicable things—and she has no idea how to protect the ones she loves.

What was it Ben had said to Ellie earlier in the kitchen? *If there's something you want to tell us, now is the time.* Ellie hadn't answered and Rachel can't help wondering—was it simply a mother's paranoia rising in her gut, sending prickles of fear through her? Or was it her training, her professional instincts, making her suspicious? Because in that moment, she'd known it as clear as day: Ellie was hiding something, and the knowledge makes Rachel feel inordinately afraid.

Chapter 16

Monday, 11:30 p.m.

Ellie listens for her mother's footsteps leaving the room, waits for the sound of the bedroom door shutting behind her, the soft creak of her moving away down the corridor, before she rolls onto her side and opens her eyes. It's not always easy to fool her mum, but she's good at faking sleep. It's all about the breath. The slow rise and fall of the chest. Keeping a soft face.

She slides a hand beneath her pillow and retrieves her phone, unlocking the screen to her last exchange with Jasmine. *Up?* she types, and waits.

Jasmine's Snap status remains stubbornly offline, and rather than face the silence of her room, she distracts herself with TikTok videos of skateboarders tearing up parks, street artists tagging benches and stenciling their work onto walls, a mundane tutorial about how to perfect a grungy eyeliner.

None of it takes away the sickening fear building in the pit of her stomach. Her parents have told her to tell the truth tomorrow, but what if the truth is what she's most terrified to share? The thing no one will understand?

She's done her best to cover her tracks. Now she must hold her nerve. Stay one step ahead. No one will ever know what she did, because the only other person who did is now dead.

Sleep, she tells herself, laying down her phone. She needs a clear head for tomorrow. A calm demeanor. She readjusts her pillow and is sliding down beneath her duvet when her room lights up with the flash of her phone. A new notification.

She's expecting Jasmine, but it's not her. It takes a split second for Ellie to register the sender's name.

sally@inthewood

What the fuck.

A shot of adrenaline jolts through her body. She reads with a growing sense of dread.

If you go down to the woods tonight . . .

There's no photo to identify the sender. Just a screenshot of the ghost emoji, which somehow feels all the more sinister.

Almost immediately, another message appears on the screen.

Someone's been a naughty girl.

She can see the three typing dots still pulsing on the screen.

Think you're safe, tucked up in bed?

I'd stay there if I were you.

You never know what might be waiting for you outside.

Ellie throws down her phone.

She shivers as she glances about her room. It's as if a stranger lurks in the darkest corners, an evil presence looming at the foot of her bed. As if she's back in that cave, the puff of air against her neck, someone lingering in the shadows, watching, waiting.

She could change her privacy settings. She could block the sender. But if she does that, she won't have a clue what they know . . . what they're planning. Better to keep the line open, surely, than let them plot and scheme in the dark?

Fear and a dark, sickening guilt surges through her. Pulling the pillow over her head, trying to burrow away from the threat that seems to creep toward her, Ellie presses her face into the mattress, the suffocating cotton of the sheet filling her nose and mouth, choking the air from her lungs until there's nothing but the sound of her heartbeat roaring in her ears. *I'm sorry*, she screams, the word a silent roar lost in the mattress. *Sorry, sorry, sorry.*

Chapter 17

Khan calls the meeting for 8:00 a.m. sharp, assembling the full task force at the station. The officers gather, coffee mugs and files in hand, drawing up chairs as Khan calls for quiet. "We've got the media snapping at our heels," he warns. "One of the parents from the Girl Guides troop has gone to the local press. I'd hoped for a period of grace, but the first report ran this morning about 'a serious incident' up at the folly, so I'm expecting the full circus to gather shortly. I'll make an official statement later. Throw them some breadcrumbs. Perhaps the coverage will bring up something useful. We can but hope."

"Something useful?" mutters DC Maxwell in a low aside to Ben. "More like a massive headache."

Ben nods. They all know that the moment this hits the mainstream media, they'll be inundated with calls from the public offering tip-offs, hypotheses, and wild theories, most of them nothing more than a time-wasting distraction.

"In the meantime," Khan continues, "I know I don't have to remind you that the last thing we need in an active investigation are leaks. None of us want a pack of internet sleuths or true-crime podcasters stomping all over our crime scene. *Everything* we discuss between these four walls remains strictly confidential. Am I clear?"

Diminutive Khan, short in stature but huge in character, is a formidable sight when he's fired up, fierce and crackling with energy. Ben knew some of the junior constables had learned the hard way not to judge him solely on the amiable persona he adopted around the station during quieter spells. In the midst of a major investigation, Khan transformed into a terrier. Tenacious, demanding, quick to bite. Certainly not a man to cross. Everyone nods their agreement.

Ben had been hoping to catch his boss before the briefing, but arriving early that morning, he'd found Khan locked away with the department's Senior Press Officer and the opportunity to talk to him about Ellie's presence at the party hadn't yet arisen. There was no way he intended to raise it in a team meeting. He'd have to wait a little longer.

"Let's start with you, Silverton," says Khan, turning his focus to their Head of Forensics. "Kick us off with an update."

Silverton tucks her white-blond hair behind her ears and opens her laptop, beaming several images onto a large screen behind Khan. "Most of the victim's injuries are what we'd expect to see from a high fall: cervical fracture, pelvic fracture, broken ribs, and the massive head injuries. Death would've been instantaneous. In layman's terms, she broke her neck."

"Can we rule out suicide?"

"The pattern of injuries from an intentional jump at this height are, broadly speaking, different. In that scenario, you'd expect extensive trauma to the pelvis, abdomen, and lower extremities. The head injuries and tissue damage we see here are more consistent with a fall. And, of course, that's not taking into account the state the body was found in, indicating postmortem interference. I'll come to that in a moment."

Khan nods. "Carry on."

She clicks to an image of the folly. "The identified site of impact is consistent with a descent from the arched opening up here. The technicians found clear signs of a struggle on the top platform. There are traces of Sarah's blood, a small amount of spatter, and fingernail scratch marks here on the bricks at the opening, which are a match for the scrapings of stone and moss found beneath Sarah's fingernails. We also identified scratches and bruising on Sarah's body," she points to the girl's arms and hands, "wounds consistent with a physical attack."

She purses her lips. "Our most likely hypothesis is that there was a struggle at the top of the tower between Sarah and an assailant. Sarah flailed near the opening, grabbed at the stone walls for purchase, but she was overpowered and pushed to her death. My guess, she was fighting for her life up there.

"Where it gets interesting," Silverton continues, "is down here on the ground." The carousel of images on the screen spins to reveal Sarah lying in her death pose beneath the folly.

"Sarah's body was moved shortly after death, before rigor set in. She was rolled from her front onto her back and arranged into this corpse pose. The bird mask was laid over her face and the words you can see on her skin were written on her arms and legs in soot. The ash appears to be a match for the fire residue located up at the folly, though it'll take a few days to confirm definitively. We found blood spatter *beneath* the black substance to indicate the words were added postmortem."

There are murmurs among the assembled officers. The details are grim and unsettling.

"Olivia mentioned that Sarah had messed her hair up with

leaves and twigs, as part of her costume," Ben chips in. "It doesn't look messy in these photos."

"No, it doesn't," agrees Silverton. "We don't know how long her killer spent with Sarah's body, but certainly this all took place before initial signs of rigor set in, so within the first hour or so after her death."

"Tidy her up? Brush her hair? What kind of sicko does that?" Maxwell throws a troubled look at Ben. He raises his eyebrows back at her, as baffled as she is.

"Any signs of sexual assault?" asks Khan, the question everyone has been dreading.

"None."

One small mercy, thinks Ben.

"There is some good news," Silverton adds, her voice brightening. "Whoever wrote the words on her skin wasn't particularly careful. Most of the prints were smudged, but we did find a partial that we're running through the system now. A match might be tricky, but we could get lucky. We also recovered a footprint in the dirt beside the body. A man's sports shoe. Size 10."

"Just one?"

"The heavy leaf litter has hampered our search for further evidence."

"Any way of knowing if the footprint belongs to our killer?"

Silverton shakes her head. "This site, as I understand it, is popular with local dog walkers, hikers, runners. It'd be hard to pin this case on someone with a single shoe tread, but it could help narrow a field of suspects."

"Toxicology?"

"Should be back later today. Time of death was between 2:00 and 4:00 a.m. on Sunday morning. I'll feed through more details as we have them."

She stops and looks around, waiting for any further questions. When there are none, she nods.

It's important to keep an open mind in an investigation, but Ben senses the frustration around the table. Their field of suspects remains wide open. There's a killer roaming free—someone violent and seemingly unhinged—and it could be absolutely anyone. Someone unknown, or someone close to the kids at school. Someone, for all they know, with an inclination to kill again.

"You've got the reports from yesterday's interviews. Throw out your thoughts," says Khan, opening the floor.

"Danny Carlisle, Sarah's on-off boyfriend, remains a person of interest," offers Maxwell. "He had a reason to be jealous—there's the kiss Sarah shared with Danny's brother, Connor, and the subsequent message Danny claims she received on her phone. Hardly the model girlfriend. Danny's mum has confirmed he returned home a little after midnight, but the lad was upset. Perhaps he snuck out and circled back later, to confront Sarah alone?"

"Any of the other kids mention a rival suitor in Sarah's life?" Khan asks. "Could Danny be making it up? Trying to throw us off? It's not as if we have her phone to corroborate his story."

Maxwell frowns. "It's possible. I had the feeling he was holding something back."

"And the other students?"

"Everyone tells the same story. Sarah, drunk and in high spirits. The argument between Sarah and Danny. Danny and Connor exchanging blows. The party coming to an end and everyone leaving, bar Sarah, Connor, and his friend, Kevin."

"Between the Carlisle brothers it's cut and dried, surely?" pipes up Dave Crawford, a heavyset DC who sat at the far end of the table. "It's gotta be one of them."

Khan turns to Ben. "Where did we get to with Connor Carlisle?"

"If Silverton's right about the time of death being between 2:00 and 4:00 a.m.—"

"I am," interjects Silverton.

Ben nods his apology. "Then Connor Carlisle was twenty miles away in Bristol. CCTV at Lakota nightclub checks out and his alibi—a girl he picked up at the venue—covers the rest of the evening."

Khan frowns. "We're ruling him out?"

"At this stage, all we can pin on Connor Carlisle is possible dealing and being a class-A bell end."

"Let's move on to the faculty. Maxwell, you spoke with Sarah's tutors?"

"I sat down with all three them: Mrs. Wiley, her Drama teacher; Mr. Effeny, English; and Mrs. Hall, Psychology." DC Maxwell refers to her notes. "They all painted the same picture: a bright, popular girl with a promising future ahead of her. Mrs. Wiley described Sarah as a star student, painting sets and running lines with her peers. She had nothing but teary praise for her summer performance in *Les Misérables*."

Khan turns to DC Crawford. "Did you run those background checks on the staff?"

Crawford shakes his head. "Not yet. I was pretty tied up chasing my tail in the woods yesterday, Chief. I'll get to it." Ben notes the merest hint of an eye roll from the man as Khan is turning away.

"See that you do," says Khan, then hearing the man's sigh, he glances back, eyes narrowed. "Is there a problem?"

Maxwell throws a pointed look at Ben, which he acknowledges with a raised eyebrow.

"No, Chief," replies Crawford.

"Anything else from the school?" Khan turns back to Maxwell. "What are you thinking?" he asks, spotting her hesitation.

"There was something in the interviews yesterday. I couldn't quite put my finger on it. Just a hunch, I guess."

"Go on."

"It felt as if a couple of the kids I spoke to were holding back. Hiding something. Danny included."

"Any ideas what?"

Ben stares down at his hands, an image of Ellie standing in Rachel's kitchen ricocheting back to him.

Maxwell shakes her head. "The games and dares. Perhaps Sarah's death was a dare gone wrong? Maybe one or some of the kids pushed it too far. They all feel responsible and are keeping quiet? A conspiracy of silence . . ."

"But the state the body was found in?" protests Ben. "It's hard to believe kids would do anything so brutal to one of their peers."

"You ever read *Lord of the Flies*?"

"Everything we've learned about Sarah so far tells us that she was a confident, popular girl. A ringleader, not a victim. Hardly the type to be coerced into a dangerous dare or set upon by her peers."

"Go on," says Khan, sensing Ben has more to say.

"But the words on her body," he adds, "they feel personal. As if her death—the presentation of the body—had clear meaning. A punishment? Revenge for something?"

"I agree," says Khan. "The staging of the body is crucial to understanding this crime and what was going on inside our killer's head."

Ben's gaze drifts back to the macabre photo of the words smeared on Sarah's death-white skin. "Christopher Easton's caused a few waves in the community with his new development. Could his high-profile position have made Sarah an unwitting target?"

"Have you seen the advertising hoarding at the far end of town?" pipes up one of the assembled officers.

"Not today, I haven't. Why?"

"Someone's taken to it with spray paint. Scrawled the words BLOODY GREED over the illustration of the housing estate. It's clever, the words look like blood dripping down the board. I can't imagine Easton is too happy about it."

"Bloody *lech*, is what I've heard," mutters another of the female constables seated at the table.

Khan's head snaps up. "What was that?"

The officer shrugs. "Off the record, a friend of mine works at Easton Developments. It's common knowledge the boss likes to recruit a certain type of office administrator. Young. Brunette. Ambitious . . . if you get my meaning."

Ben glances at Khan.

Khan nods. "Talk to Christopher Easton. Ask him about any particularly vehement resistance to the development. Anyone causing trouble for the Easton Group. Business conflicts. Personal vendettas. It can't hurt. Anything else?" Khan's gaze moves around the table.

"Perhaps . . ." offers Maxwell, seeming hesitant.

"Go on."

"It's probably stupid."

"All ideas are on the table right now."

"It's just something that occurred to me. The name Sarah. I fell down an internet wormhole last night, thinking about the area, about Sarah's costume and the story of Sally in the Wood. Sally, it turns out, is an old-fashioned nickname for Sarah. Did you know that?"

Most of them round the table shake their head.

"Where are you going with this?"

"As I said, it's probably stupid, but is it possible whoever did this to Sarah was inspired by the local area? By stories of the folly and a girl being killed there?"

"You mean a copycat killer?"

Maxwell shrugs.

Khan turns to Ben. "You mentioned the ghost story when we hiked to the crime scene. A girl murdered on her wedding day, punishment for her infidelity, left at the folly for the crows?"

"That's how the story goes," confirms Ben.

Silence falls around the table as they all turn to the photo of Sarah's body lying at the foot of the tower, her white dress, and the bird mask laid over her face.

Khan glances round at the assembled officers. "DC Crawford," he snaps. "Are you still with us?"

Dave Crawford lifts his face from his phone, a guilty flush rising on his cheeks. "Yes, Chief?"

"You coordinated the search of the woods?"

Crawford struggles into a more upright position on his chair. "Yep. The trails were clear. Mine entrances sealed. We bagged a lot of rubbish from the quarry and sent it down to Forensics. Those kids sure know how to party," he adds with a wink.

No one laughs.

"Any sign of the girl's phone?"

"None, Chief."

"Fine. While you're on the database today running those background checks, search for old reports of anything suspicious logged in the area. Anything with a ritualistic or occult leaning."

Crawford gives a curt nod and mutters something inaudible under his breath.

Ben can't help bristling. Maxwell had said he was disgruntled. She wasn't wrong. It's clear he's doing everything asked of him to the bare minimum, allowing his colleagues to carry him. They don't have room on the team for someone like him.

Khan leans back in his chair. "We need to find that missing phone. The last ping was from the woods at around 3:00 a.m., so we know it was there with her. There's been no trace of it since. If she's anything like my teenage daughter, her whole life is on that device." He fixes the group with his steady stare. "To understand how a person died, it helps to understand how they lived."

Ben's heard this line from Khan before. They probably could've all recited it with him, but as Ben glances around the room, he sees his fellow officers nodding. They all know the boss is right. It helps to get beneath the surface of the victim, to understand their secrets, their desires, their inner lives. It's often where the truth is found.

Khan gathers his papers with an air of disappointment, tapping them into shape on the table. "Right now, we still have more questions than answers. Let's get back to work."

With the meeting drawing to a close, Ben leaps up, intercepting Khan at the door. "Have you got a minute, Chief?"

"Sure, walk with me." He beckons for Ben to follow him back through the reception area, where they are greeted by the sound of a woman mid-rant to the duty officer.

". . . looked like he hadn't washed in days, the filthy bugger. And the smell of him! Everyone's struggling with the cost of living, but he just grabbed the cereal right off the shelf and ran. Not the cheap home-brand stuff either. Big box of cornflakes. Brazen as you like. I'm telling you, Officer, never in all my days have—"

The officer breaks with visible relief from taking the woman's statement as he flags Ben down. "Chase, I've got something you might be interested in."

Khan and Ben come to a halt by the swinging doors. "What's

up?" Ben hopes he's not about to be pulled into the woman's shoplifting complaint. He knows Mrs. Kerridge from the Co-Op. Once she gets going, you're in trouble. You can stand at the register for fifteen minutes just trying to pay for a loaf of bread.

"There's a council worker out there." The duty officer jerks his head at the hard plastic seats in reception. "Says he found something on his morning rounds. Something odd. He saw the local news story last night and brought it in." He nods at one of their empty interview rooms. "It's in there." He looks pleased with himself. "I didn't touch it."

"Good work." Ben turns to Khan. Khan shrugs.

The interview room is empty but for a crumpled plastic shopping bag slumped on the table. Ben pulls sterile latex gloves from a box on the windowsill and opens it, lifting out a bundle of cloth, spreading the items across the tabletop. A gray hoodie. A pair of ripped denim shorts. A tangle of black tights. Nothing so out of the ordinary, except for the arc of what is clearly dried blood spattered across the front of the hoodie.

Khan leans closer. "Where did he say they'd been found?"

Ben steps back from the table. He can't answer. Bile is rushing up his throat.

The duty officer standing in the open doorway answers. "Chap said he found the bag stuffed in a salt bin out on Thorncombe Lane. He was topping up the winter grit this morning and spotted it. Luckily, he was curious enough to open it. He said you'd be amazed what people shove in those things."

Khan nudges Ben. "Get this to Forensics. It could be coincidence. On the other hand, it might just be our first solid lead."

Ben doesn't answer. He can't. All coherent thought has left him. It disappeared the moment he spread the garments across the table and realized they were the exact same clothes Ellie had been wearing on Saturday night when he'd dropped her outside her mother's house. Just before she'd slipped away to the woods where a girl would later be found dead.

"Chief," says Ben, his voice strained. "There's something I need to tell you."

Chapter 18

Ellie is kicking her chair with the heel of a sneaker, thudding it against the metal leg in an annoying, repetitive rhythm. Rachel, sitting at the Formica table beside her, reaches out and lays a hand on her daughter's thigh. Although Rachel knows she's full of bravado, trying hard to appear nonchalant, she can see the fear in her daughter's eyes and the dark shadows beneath.

The night before, she'd woken to the sound of shouting, Ellie calling out in her sleep. Sarah's name, echoing in the dark. Going to her room, she'd found Ellie sitting up in bed, dazed and white-faced in sweat-drenched pajamas. The scene had reminded Rachel of the night terrors Ellie had suffered on occasion as a little girl. "What were you dreaming about?"

Ellie had shaken her head. "Just a bad dream. I thought I was in the woods."

Rachel had smoothed the hair from Ellie's clammy forehead. "I know it's frightening, but they'll catch whoever did this," she'd said, praying it was the truth. "Just tell the police everything and it will be OK."

Ellie had looked as if she were going to cry, but when Rachel had tried to draw her close, she'd pushed her away. "I just want to sleep."

Now they're here, DC Maxwell across from them, a notebook and pen laid in front of her, a recording device whirring to one side. It's a nightmarish repeat of yesterday, only this time they are confined to an interview room at the police station, and it's her daughter sitting beside her, not one of her students.

She'd been flustered to receive the phone call from the duty officer, summoning her to the station. Rachel had presumed Ben would inform his colleagues about Ellie's presence at the party and that Maxwell would find a moment to chat with Ellie at the school later that day, just as she'd conducted the other student interviews. Rachel had never dreamed she'd be notified that Ellie had been picked up from school and carted away in a police car, with the urgent demand that she attend the station too. "Why the formality?" she'd asked.

"Sorry," the duty officer had apologized, "just following orders."

Perhaps it was Ben? Perhaps he'd asked his colleagues to go a little harder on Ellie, to teach her a lesson? It seemed rather over the top, cruel even, and a waste of resources in the midst of their investigation, but of the two of them, Ben had always been the tougher parent. He'd always been the one to enforce clean plates, a tidy bedroom, screen-time restrictions, and early bedtimes. Given Ellie's deception this weekend, perhaps he was right to come down harder on her. Perhaps Ellie did need a wake-up call. Maybe Rachel had been too soft, too gullible. Perhaps this was one of the reasons that they were in this mess right now.

Still, sitting next to Ellie in the overheated gray interview room with its functional chrome wall clock ticking overhead and Fiona Maxwell leaning forward on her elbows, her owlish gaze fixed on her daughter, every one of Rachel's maternal instincts screams in alarm. She wants to wrap Ellie in her arms and whisk her away from the interrogation she knows she is about to face.

"Why didn't you come forward on Monday morning with the rest of the students?" Maxwell asks, her tone light. She waits, and when Ellie doesn't answer, she tries again. "Why didn't you alert us to the fact that you'd been in the woods with Sarah?"

Ellie casts a glance at her mother. Rachel nods. *Go on*, she urges. *Tell her.*

"Because I didn't want to get in trouble. I wasn't supposed to be at the party. I'd lied to my parents about where I was."

Maxwell frowns. "Given what happened to Sarah, did you not feel a responsibility to share your whereabouts?"

"I didn't know anything. I guess I didn't think I could help."

"But your presence at the party couldn't stay a secret forever. It was bound to come out eventually?"

Ellie shrugs. "I assumed you'd have more important people to talk to. If you caught someone quickly, no one would need to know I was there. That's what I hoped anyway." She hangs her head. "I'm sorry."

"More important people?"

"Yeah."

Maxwell leans in. "What do you mean?"

"People who were closer to Sarah." Ellie shrugs again. "I didn't know her that well."

"But Sarah was in your year at school, wasn't she? I've been told there are only two hundred or so sixth-form students?" Maxwell glances at Rachel and she nods, corroborating the figure. "That's small for a secondary school. A warm, collegiate atmosphere is how your head teacher, Mrs. Crowe, described the school to me. A place where 'everyone knows everyone.'"

Ellie shifts on her chair. "That didn't make us friends."

Rachel casts a sideways glance at Ellie. She wishes she would temper her tone a little. No doubt it's nerve-racking answering questions in this formal environment, but fear is making Ellie sound defensive, hostile even. Rachel presses her lips together, fighting the urge to intervene.

"Walk me through *your* Saturday night, Ellie. What time did you head to the woods?"

"I was at Dad's until around 7:30 p.m. I faked a text message from Mum asking me to go home, and Dad dropped me back at the cottage around eight-ish. I pretended to go inside, waited for Dad to drive away, then went to meet Jas at the Drama department. I know." She throws a guilty look in Rachel's direction. "I shouldn't have lied."

"That's Jasmine Ware?"

Ellie nods.

"You'd arranged to meet her?"

"Yes. We didn't have Halloween costumes, so Jas suggested we borrow something from the Drama department at school. We found masks at the back of a costume cupboard—weird Venetian things. Pretty creepy-looking. We took those."

"Can you describe the mask you wore?"

Ellie shrugs. "Sure. It was black with feathers. It had this long, curved beak. Jasmine's was similar, but hers was white and gold."

Maxwell eyes Ellie steadily. "Then what?"

"We headed into the woods. Got there around 9:30 p.m., I think."

"What was happening at the party when you arrived?"

"Nothing much, to be honest. Just a few people hanging around a bonfire drinking, listening to music. I didn't think we'd stay long but then Jas got chatting to Saul. She likes him. She won't admit it, but she does. There was a box of wine. I was bored. I drank a bit too much."

Sensing another guilty glance from Ellie in her direction, Rachel is careful to maintain a neutral face.

"And Sarah Lawson was there?"

"Yeah. They started up with the Ouija board, so I stayed for a bit longer. To watch."

"To watch?" Maxwell sounds puzzled. "You didn't participate?"

To Rachel's relief, Ellie shakes her head. "No, that was Sarah's flex. I wasn't going to play her games."

"Her *flex*?"

She nods. "Sarah's one of those girls . . . used to the spotlight, you know? Pretty, popular. Likes to have the attention on them. She and Olivia would swan around the school like they were the center of the universe, and the rest of us mere satellites, floating by."

Rachel frowns. Ellie sounds angry, bitter even. She knew the girls moved in different social circles, two circles of a Venn diagram occasionally intersecting, but she hadn't realized there was animosity. Had she missed something?

"Sarah traded on being the new girl, at first. But then she set her sights on Danny. Started toying with him."

"Toying with him? Can you explain what you mean by that?"

Rachel runs her fingers around the neck of her sweater. It's too warm in the interview room. She's never understood how Ben could stand these dingy, soulless surroundings. She longs to fling open a window.

"Danny's a good guy. Genuine. Everyone likes Danny, and Danny . . . well, Danny liked Sarah."

Maxwell doesn't miss a beat. "That bothered you? Danny and Sarah?"

Ellie flushes pink. "He's my friend. I don't like seeing my friends being taken for mugs. Sarah blew hot and cold with him. Used him, when it suited. Pushed him away when it didn't. She acted like she was too good for him. I thought Danny deserved better, to be honest," she adds, her voice lowering. "But he didn't see it."

A picture is building in Rachel's head. Ellie had always seemed close to Danny. She'd assumed their friendship had been built on their mutual position within the school as scholarship kids, but perhaps it had been about something else. At least, on Ellie's side. Had Ellie been jealous of Sarah's romantic involvement with him?

"Some of the other students reported that Sarah and Danny argued at the party. Did you witness any tension between them?"

Ellie nods.

"What happened?"

"It was Sarah's fault. She dared Danny to do something she knew he never would, then played up to Connor in retaliation, flirting with him . . . kissing him." Ellie wrinkles her nose. "She knew what that would do to Danny. It was obvious he'd see red. I think she wanted them to fight over her. Another flex. Danny didn't take it well, but you wouldn't, would you? The girl you like snogging your dickhead brother right in front of you."

"Was Danny violent toward Sarah?"

Ellie's head snaps up. She throws a fierce look at Maxwell. "No way! He'd never. Danny went for Connor. And Sarah could've stopped them fighting, but she just stood there, watching, this weird smile on her face. It was a power trip for her. A chance to show off how much Danny liked her."

"Did you get involved in the fight, Ellie?"

Ellie looks down at her lap. "Not really."

Rachel studies Ellie, a feeling building in the pit of her stomach. Maxwell waits.

"It wasn't my fault. Sarah shoved her phone at me so she could do her dare. 'Hold this,' she goes, like I was her servant. I was still holding it when the fight broke out between the two boys. That's when the message buzzed on her home screen. The evidence right there in my hand."

"What did you see?" Maxwell is leaning forward.

Ellie twists the fabric of her school sweater in her fingers. "A message. From some random account. It said something like, 'Missing you tonight. I wish we didn't have to be a secret.' There were a couple of heart emojis too." Ellie shakes her head. "It was obvious she was carrying on with someone behind Danny's back."

"Who was the message from?"

"I dunno. It looked dodgy. A few letters followed by 123. I mean, that's suspicious in itself, right? Definitely a secret account."

Maxwell doesn't answer. Instead she counters with another question. "What did you do?"

"I did what any good friend would do. I showed Danny. As I said, I'd had a bit to drink, and I was pissed off. He deserved to know what sort of girl Sarah was."

"How did Danny react?"

"He wasn't happy, obviously, but I think the fight with Connor had upset him the most."

"Do you remember what happened next?"

Ellie nods. "Danny confronted Sarah and when she wouldn't say who it was from, he left with Saul. I wanted to go after him, but they were fast and I was . . . drunk. Dizzy. I couldn't keep up. I lost them in the woods. Lost my way."

A feeling rises up inside Rachel, fear at the thought of her daughter wandering alone through the woods at night. "Ellie," she says, unable to hold her silence. "What were you thinking?"

Maxwell shoots her a look, a gesture to refrain. "You were alone in the woods. You'd lost Danny. Lost sight of everyone. What happened next?"

Ellie glances down at her lap. "I didn't feel well. All that wine . . . and I'd had a few puffs on something being passed around. I . . . I was sick. I puked and then I lay down for a bit. Just to let it pass."

Rachel shakes her head, still horrified at the thought of her daughter alone and incapacitated with a violent killer roaming the woods. Where were her friends? Why wasn't anyone looking out for her?

"And then?"

Ellie shrugs. "I must've passed out, because next thing I remember is hauling myself up and realizing I didn't know where I was. I had to try to orient myself. I knew if I walked uphill, I'd eventually find the folly. From there, I'd be able to pick up one of the main trails leading down to the road."

"So, you walked up to the folly?" Maxwell's voice has taken on a slightly different pitch. For the first time, Rachel notices the camera set high into the corner of the room, a red light blinking at them. She realizes they are being recorded, with police officers behind the scenes, perhaps watching every move. She's never thought to ask Ben about the cameras, never thought she'd have need to understand the workings of an interview room, but now she wonders if it's Ben out there, if he's watching their daughter squirm and flounder in the interview chair and wishes he could put a stop to this. Wishes he would burst in and whisk Ellie away from these relentless questions.

Ellie is nodding. "I found the folly, found the trail I needed that would lead back to the road, and I walked back to the school campus. I knew I couldn't go home so I woke Jasmine. I stayed in her dorm room and returned to Mum's the next day." She shrugs. "End of story."

Rachel eyes her daughter. A sensation of disquiet rises, an echo from the night before when she'd stood over Ellie's bed and watched her sleeping daughter. The memory of Ellie's nightmare, the sight of her pale and shaken in her bed. *I thought I was in the woods.* Something is off. Ellie is lying. She knows her daughter. She's holding something back.

"You mentioned the bird mask. What else were you wearing on Saturday night?"

Ellie frowns. "Just ordinary clothes."

"Can you describe them for me?"

Ellie gives the slightest eye roll, which Rachel prays Fiona Maxwell hasn't seen. She nudges her daughter's foot gently under the table and throws her a warning look.

"A gray hoodie. Cutoffs. Black tights. Converse."

"She never wears a coat," adds Rachel. "No matter how many times I tell her she'll be cold, she always refuses." She glances at Fiona, trying to lighten the mood, but Maxwell just nods and turns back to Ellie, reaching for an iPad. "I'm going to show you some photos. I'd like you to tell me if you recognize the items in the pictures."

Ellie's head snaps up, instantly wary. Maxwell scrolls until a photograph appears enlarged on the screen. She slides the device across the table. Rachel leans in to get a better look and sees a gray hoodie with a smear of rust brown across its front. A pair of denim shorts, filthy with dirt. Black ripped tights.

"Do you recognize these, Ellie?" Maxwell asks.

Ellie glances at Rachel.

"Are these the clothes you described to me a few moments ago, the ones you were wearing on Saturday night?"

Ellie shrugs. "I don't know."

Maxwell skips to the very last image, a close-up of the inside label of the hoodie, something scrawled there in indelible black Sharpie. *E. Chase.* Rachel recognizes her own handwriting. She remembers the morning quite clearly, Ellie off on a school excursion to an art exhibition in London, Rachel worried that she'd lose her favorite sweatshirt.

"E. Chase. Your name?"

Ellie nods.

"Are these your clothes, Ellie?"

"Yes." Ellie hangs her head.

"Can you explain what the clothes you say you were wearing on Saturday night were doing inside a plastic bag hidden in a salt bin on Thorncombe Lane?"

Ellie stares blankly at Maxwell but her cheeks are glowing red.

"Did you put them there, Ellie?"

Ellie seems to consider her options, before nodding slowly. Rachel is struggling to keep up. "You threw your clothes away?"

"Why not put them in the wash? Or throw them into a bin at home?" Maxwell's stare is unflinching. "Why go to such lengths to dispose of them?"

Rachel gazes at the photos on the iPad. She can't seem to shift her gaze from the horrifying arc of red-brown smeared across the front of Ellie's hoodie that looks for all the world like dried blood.

Ellie clears her throat. "Look at them. They were ruined. I knew Mum would be furious if she saw the state of them."

"They certainly look rather . . . stained. I'm guessing they didn't look like this when you set out for the party on Saturday night? They weren't part of your costume?"

Ellie lowers her head. "No."

"So, can you tell me what happened?" Maxwell points to the smear spread across the front of the hoodie. "What were you doing in the woods on Saturday night to end up with clothes looking like this?"

"It was dirty. It's just mud and, yeah, you know . . ." Ellie trails off.

Maxwell leans back in her chair and regards Ellie for a long moment. "I have to tell you, Ellie, that right now, these clothes are being tested as a matter of urgency by our forensics team. We have technicians looking for any evidence that might link them to Sarah Lawson's death."

Ellie's head snaps up, her gaze sliding to the door, as if desperately willing an escape route to open before her.

"If there is *anything* incriminating on them, anything that you don't tell me about now that you might want us to know about later . . . well, you and I both know it won't be good for you."

Rachel is staring at Maxwell. It's as if a veil has fallen and she sees her clearly; no longer the sweet-faced DC, probing and pushing Ellie to confide her frightening experience in the woods. Behind her soft, northern burr, those warm hazel eyes, and her pretty, freckled face lies a calculating, razor-sharp detective. Maxwell has led her daughter methodically through her statement to this singular point, fully aware the whole time of the evidence waiting on her iPad. Ben had said she was good at her job. But this is too much. What she's implying is illogical. Impossible. Isn't it?

"You need to tell me what happened." Maxwell eyes Ellie steadily. "The truth."

Ellie is rigid beside her, her face angled to her lap, her fingers twisting the sleeve of her top round and round. "Fine," she says at last, lifting her head. "It's blood. All right?"

Rachel swallows.

"Whose blood, Ellie?"

Rachel watches as her daughter appears to weigh her options. In this moment she wants nothing more than to scoop up Ellie and drag her from the room, to protect her from whatever she is about to say.

"It's Sarah's blood," Ellie says at last, the words quiet but sure.

Rachel stares at Ellie in disbelief, even as something chimes in her mind, a tiny whisper that says, *You knew. You knew she was lying.*

Chapter 19

Tuesday, 2:00 p.m.

Ellie rubs her eyes and lets out a long sigh. There is mascara smudged on her fingers when she pulls them away. It's strange, but it's a relief to finally say the words out loud. Like the sudden release of something unpleasant being purged from her stomach.

"Should Ben be here?" she hears her mum ask the detective. "Do I need to call a lawyer?"

Ellie shakes her head, irritated at her mother's bewilderment. It feels as though they've been talking for hours already; she just wants to get this done now. "Don't fuss, Mum. I don't need a lawyer. I can explain. It's Sarah's blood, but," she adds hastily, "it's not how it looks, I swear."

She can see it in her mum's face. The disbelief. The horror. *Sarah's blood?*

But if the police officer in front of her is surprised, she gives no hint. She is dead-eyed, showing no visible emotion. "Tell me how Sarah's blood ended up on your hoodie," she asks. You wouldn't want to play poker with her.

"It happened up at the folly."

"After you'd walked there, to 'reorient' yourself?"

"Yes." Ellie nods. She's not sure why the detective is looking at her like that, like she doesn't quite believe her. "I scrambled up to the escarpment. It was pitch black but as I got closer to the folly, I saw a light through the trees, and I heard voices. I figured it was the others from the party, but I hung back, just in case."

"Did you see who it was?"

"Yes, it was Sarah. She was with Danny's brother, Connor, and that guy, Kev."

"What were they doing?"

"Arguing. They'd lit a fire so I could see the three of them, but I stayed back among the trees. I didn't like the vibe. Connor was clearly angry. He said Sarah owed him money for the joint he'd given her and she was getting in his face, jabbing at his chest. She said it was his fault Danny had left. She looked upset and it was getting heated, but then I saw Kev pull Connor away and tell him not to bother. One of the lads mentioned Bristol, but Sarah shouted that they could 'fuck off' and so they left. Connor called back to Sarah that she could find her own way home. Kind of a taunt, you know?"

Ellie hears her mother's tut, but Maxwell is back to inscrutable Robocop. "Then what happened?" she asks.

"I waited. I thought Sarah might leave too, but she sat down on the stone step at the bottom of the folly, near the fire. I could see her outline. Her white dress. The orange tip of her roll-up."

"Did you talk to her?"

Ellie glances across at her mother and sees her wide eyes, her hand at her throat. "I thought I should check if she was OK. She was alone and I guess . . ." she hesitates, "I guess I thought we could go back together. Finding my way up to the folly hadn't ex-actly been a walk in the park. Your mind plays tricks. The Ouija board game and those stupid dares. I was frightened. I know it's stupid, but I kept thinking about the ghost story. About Sally. There were rustlings in the woods, animals or bats probably, but my imagination was starting to play tricks. I figured even Sarah would be better company than going back through the woods alone." Ellie is aware of her mum shaking her head in dismay. She can't look at her.

"So, you approached Sarah?"

"Yes."

"Was Sarah pleased to see you?"

Ellie thinks for a moment. "I think I frightened her. I didn't mean to. I made her jump. When she saw it was me, she just gave a little shrug and patted the stone step next to her. She offered to share her joint, but I didn't want it. I still felt sick. I wanted to go back. I told her I was leaving, and she could walk with me, if she wanted. But Sarah, being Sarah, wasn't going to make it easy. She said she'd come when she'd finished her spliff, so I waited. I figured we'd walk down to the road together, then go our separate ways."

"Is that what happened?"

Ellie eyes Maxwell. They both know that's not what happened. They wouldn't be having this conversation now if they'd both made it down to the road together safely. "No. That's not what happened."

Ellie knows she should've told her parents everything last night, should've come clean and worked out with them how best to handle this, but last night she'd had no idea that that stupid bag of clothes would show up here. Last night, she'd still thought what happened up at the folly could remain her secret, a terrible act confined to the woods, her only witnesses the silent stone folly, the towering trees, and a girl—now dead. An awful sensation grips her stomach, dread tugging at her insides.

"Go on," urges Maxwell.

"Girls like Sarah always get everything they want. Life just seems to offer it all up on a plate. I shouldn't have raised the Danny thing again, but he deserved better, and I was annoyed to be sitting there, waiting for *her* to decide when we could leave."

"What did you do, Ellie?"

"I told her that she was a manipulative bitch." She doesn't dare look at her mum now, not as she relays this part of the night.

"How did Sarah respond?" asks Maxwell.

Ellie shrugs. "She didn't. Not right away. She just ignored me. I guess that got me even more riled up. I said it again, that she was a bitch and that Danny was going to wake up to her and move on and that I'd be there cheering him on the day he did." She tries to control it, but there's a heat rising in her cheeks. She doesn't want to say all this in front of her mum, but looking at Maxwell's blank face, she knows she's got no choice. Ever since Saturday night, this thing has been rolling away from her, faster and faster. A runaway train. She wants to jam on the brakes, but the truth keeps coming in a rush.

"Sarah's mood changed then. I saw it in her face. I knew I'd touched a nerve. She turned to me with this mean smile and looked me up and down. 'You think he's going to fall into *your* arms?' She was smirking, saying how a boy like Danny would never go for a girl like me. That I was dreaming if I thought that. She started teasing me about the skate park. About how us 'emos' would have to find another place to hang out now her uncle's big development was going ahead. She was bragging about how much money he was going to make. She knew exactly how to get at me. She knew how against the housing development I am."

"Go on."

"I'll admit it—I bit. My temper . . ." She glances at her mother.

"Mum knows. I'm hotheaded. I was so mad. I told her that her family were cutting down ancient trees and killing the local wildlife, causing irreversible damage for their own personal greed. I told her I'd find a way to stop it. I told her that I wouldn't back off until I'd found a way to derail the development.

"Sarah just laughed. 'You think one lame-ass Greta Thunberg wannabe can stop my uncle?'" Ellie swallows. "She said he was doing the community a favor by building affordable homes, social housing, places for 'scroungers' like me and Mum." She closes her eyes, feeling a hot flush of shame. "Sarah told me that I had no place lecturing her when my parents were parasites leeching off the school—off the parents who actually paid school fees. She said scholarships like mine were paid for by families like hers, so maybe I should shut up and be grateful for the education *she* was providing."

Ellie squeezes her hands into tight fists, blinking back tears at the memory. She glances across at her mum for support, but she's not looking at her. She sits with her head bowed.

"That sounds very hurtful," says Maxwell.

Ellie nods. She can't stop now. "Sarah said my scholarship . . . our cottage on campus . . . it was all charity, charity paid for by *her* family. She said when the development was built, Mum and I could move into social housing and stop 'begging' from the school."

Ellie feels her mum's head lift, but she can't look at her now.

"I knew things weren't easy," her mum murmurs, "but I didn't realize to what extent. You should've told me."

"Told you what?" Ellie asks. "Did you really think it would be so easy for a kid like me at a school like Folly View? You only wanted to see the good. The 'opportunities.' What suited *you* best."

"Ellie, that's not true. I thought it was the best place for you and your interests. The facilities . . . the art department. And I did want to hear. If you'd told me, I would've tried to help you integrate with—"

Maxwell interrupts, clearly keen to keep the interview on track. "Sarah's comments sound very upsetting, Ellie. How did you react?"

Ellie stares at the officer. Her voice is still neutral, but she thinks she sees a glimmer of sympathy in the police officer's eyes. "I couldn't help it. I took a swing at her." She hangs her head. "I punched her."

She ignores her mother's gasp and carries on. "Sarah screamed. She was holding her nose, but the blood just kept spurting everywhere and Sarah was freaking out. It was awful. She was shouting that I'd broken her nose." Ellie exhales. "I've never hit anyone before. I was frightened. I tried to help her. I tried to stop the blood. It went all over my sweatshirt, see." She points to the image on the iPad screen. "I said sorry.

"I was still trying to help, when Sarah caught me off guard. She swung at me and we fell and," Ellie shakes her head, "I don't know, we went down in the leaves and dirt until I could get out from under her. We just stood there, panting and staring at each other, and she said, 'You're fucked, Ellie Chase. You're in so much trouble. This is assault. My mum's a lawyer. She'll ruin you. Your mum will lose her job. You'll lose your scholarship . . . your home.' I knew how Sarah would spin it. I was already in trouble for bunking off to go to a Just Stop Oil protest. I'd lose my place at Folly View, right in the middle of my final year. I'd lose my chance at art school."

"What did you do?"

Ellie frowns at Maxwell's question. "I didn't do anything. I told Sarah that she should come with me. I told her that I was sorry, and I was scared, and I didn't want to be in the woods anymore. I told her I was going back, and that we should walk together."

Maxwell taps her notepad with the cap of her pen. "Sarah's just threatened to ruin you and your final year of school, to smash your dreams of art college, to potentially ruin your mum's career and take away your home, and you just . . . offer to walk home with her?" There is more than a hint of doubt in the police officer's voice.

"I wanted to get out of there. I thought we could talk, sort things out on the way back, but she didn't want a bar of it. She just laughed. She told me I was 'an even bigger pussy than Danny.' I didn't want to stick around after that, so I ran down to the road, as fast as I could. I couldn't go home—Mum and Dad didn't know where I was—so I woke Jasmine in her dorm room. I knew I couldn't justify what I'd done. I knew Sarah had won."

"What time was the fight, Ellie?"

She shrugs. "I don't know."

"Best guess?"

"About 1:00 a.m. Perhaps."

"What time did you get to Jasmine's dorm room?"

"I don't know."

Maxwell hesitates for a moment, flicking back through her notes. "What you're saying is that you left Sarah alive and well, bar a busted-up nose, at the folly around 1:00 a.m.?"

"Yes."

"Alone?"

"Yes. She wouldn't come with me."

"And when you left Sarah, how did she seem? Was she breathing? Was she conscious?"

"Conscious? Of course. She was screaming as I ran away. Yelling that she'd make sure I paid for what I'd done. That I wouldn't get away with it."

"Your fight took place at the base of the folly, in the clearing?"

"Yes."

"Not at the top?"

"No."

"You didn't go up the folly?"

"No way. I'm not climbing that thing."

Maxwell waits a beat, before changing tack. "And when you arrived at Jasmine Ware's dorm room, did you explain to her what had happened?"

Ellie shakes her head. "She was half asleep. She wasn't happy. She fell back into bed and was snoring within minutes."

Maxwell studies Ellie for a long moment. "Did you tell anyone else about the fight?"

"No. I was too frightened . . . too embarrassed."

"So, there weren't any witnesses to your fight with Sarah? No one who might be able to corroborate your statement?"

Ellie hangs her head. "No."

"And you disposed of the clothes because . . ." She trails off, waiting.

"Because I figured Mum would have a whole lot of questions for me if they ended up in the wash looking like they did. Questions I didn't want to answer."

Maxwell frowns. She seems to think for a moment, before tilting her head at Ellie. "The mask, the feathered one you took from the costume department at school, were you wearing it up at the folly?"

"It was itchy and the elastic was stretched. It was around my neck for most of the night."

"But did you have it on you when you arrived at the folly?"

Ellie frowns. "I don't know."

"Did you still have the mask with you when you arrived back at Jasmine's dorm room?"

Ellie scratches her head. "No . . . I guess I didn't. Perhaps it came off me when Sarah and I fought? Or when I was sick in the woods. That would make the most sense, right?"

Maxwell taps her pen on her notebook. "I'm curious, Ellie. Why do you think nobody—Danny, Jasmine, Saul, not one of them—thought to mention that you were at the party in the woods on Saturday night?"

Ellie frowns. "They knew I'd lied to my parents about where I was. I assumed . . ." She trails off, fighting the tears again. "I assumed they'd tell you. To be honest, I don't know why they didn't."

Maxwell's face softens. "Maybe they were trying to protect you?" she suggests. "Maybe your *friends* like you more than you know, Ellie?"

Startled, Ellie glances up. She's been wondering since Saturday night why they hadn't told the police. Had they been protecting her? Or, she'd wondered, come Monday morning when the police had announced what had happened to Sarah, had they suspected she was involved? Was one of them behind the sally@inthewood messages she'd received? "Maybe," she whispers.

Maxwell tilts her head. "Ellie, would you consent to us taking your fingerprints today?" Seeing her mother's look of alarm, she adds, "We have a partial print from the scene. It could help us eliminate you, Ellie."

"But she's already told you she was up at the folly . . ." Rachel trails off, then clears her throat. "That she fought with Sarah. Can she say no?"

"She can. We'd only be able to take them without her consent if she were under arrest."

Ellie feels a cold stab of fear go right through her. *Arrest?*

"Which she's not," says her mum firmly.

"No," says Maxwell slowly.

Ellie doesn't like the tone of the police officer's voice. An unspoken "yet" seems to hang in the air.

"I'll do it," says Ellie.

"And we can go home after that?" her mum asks.

"We'd also like to search the cottage."

"What? What on earth for?"

"Ellie, do you recall seeing Sarah's iPhone when you were with her at the folly?"

Ellie is staring wide-eyed at Maxwell. "I don't know."

"But you saw it at the quarry. You said earlier," Maxwell leafs back through her notes, "'I was still holding it when the fight broke out between the two boys.'" She eyes Ellie. "You have no idea where her phone is now?"

"No."

Maxwell turns to her mum. "Do we have your permission to conduct a search?"

"Ellie's just told you—she doesn't know where it is."

"We could get a warrant," Maxwell presses.

Her mum turns to look at her. Ellie shrugs. It seems they'll do it, whether they like it or not.

"Fine," says her mum. "You can go in."

"Thank you."

"But then you'll let her go, right?"

There's a pause. Maxwell leans back in her chair and purses her lips. "Mrs. Chase—"

"Dean," insists Rachel quickly. "I'm Ms. Dean now."

"Of course." She holds up her hands. "Sorry. Ms. Dean, that will be up to my superiors. Given Ellie's account of the night in question, alongside the fact she's admitted to a violent altercation with the victim, as well as evidence that places her at the scene of the crime, we may need to keep Ellie in for further questioning."

Her mother's face is aghast. "But she's told you everything."

"Right now, Ellie's account makes her the last person to see Sarah alive." The fact hangs in the air between them.

"I know it looks bad, but I swear, it wasn't me."

"Of course it wasn't," insists her mum vehemently. "That's not what you're saying, is it?" she asks, turning to Maxwell.

"We're expecting the forensics results. Then we'll have more questions for Ellie. I'm sure you understand."

Ellie turns to her mum in a panic. "Mum? Do I have to stay?"

Maxwell answers. "We'll need to detain you a little longer, Ellie. Yes."

What Ellie sees in her mum's eyes is anything but reassuring.

"Sit tight, Ellie. I'll call your dad. We'll get this sorted, I promise."

Ellie glances back at DC Maxwell. The police officer, she notices, avoids her eye, busying herself with her papers.

"It wasn't me," Ellie says, her voice rising. "You're wasting your time. Someone else did this to Sarah—some sicko—and they're still out there. They could be hunting for another girl right now. They could do it again."

Maxwell doesn't react. Instead she shuffles her files, her voice light as she asks, "One last thing. You wouldn't happen to know anything about the recent defacement of an Easton Developments sign out on Thorncombe Lane?"

Ellie juts her chin, glad that Maxwell's face is still averted and she no longer has to look into her shrewd hazel eyes. "No," she says firmly. "I wouldn't know anything about that."

"Huh," says Maxwell. "Well, OK then. For the benefit of the tape, it's 4:58 p.m. and I'm stopping the recording."

Chapter 20

Tuesday, 4:30 p.m.

Ben knows what DCI Khan is going to say before he's even answered the call. Rachel had phoned him in a panic as she'd left the police station, hastily filling him in on the interview, as well as the more alarming fact that they had decided to detain Ellie while they searched the cottage.

"You gave them permission?"

"It didn't seem as if I had a choice. Besides, it's not like we've got anything to hide."

"But they haven't charged her?" pressed Ben.

"Not yet. They want the forensic results before they continue." He'd heard the distress in her voice. "All these lies, Ben. After bunking off school for that blasted protest . . . the graffiti on that bus shelter. I feel like she's slipping away from us. As if I hardly know her."

"She's our girl. We have to believe her."

"I couldn't bear to leave her at the station."

Ben had seen it in his mind's eye: Rachel driving away with an empty passenger seat beside her, the worry etched on her face. "She'll be OK," he'd said, unwilling to admit that he too was gripped with fear.

Ten minutes later, Khan's name is flashing on his phone. Ben pulls into a turnout, the car engine idling as he braces for the conversation.

"I'm taking you off the investigation, Chase. Just while we figure this out." A gust of wind shakes the trees overhead. Ben watches as a single brown leaf lands on his windshield and slides into the wiper well, before lifting again with the next flurry and disappearing on the breeze.

"But Ellie's explained, Chief. I know it looks bad, I know I sound like a protective father, but the way Rachel tells it, it was a teenage scrap. Sarah was alive when Ellie left her at the folly. Ellie says she wasn't involved in the girl's death. There's no reason not to believe her."

Khan waits a beat. "I'm sorry. I've discussed it with my superiors and we're all in agreement that it would be prudent for you to step back, in the short term. We've been pushing the boundaries of what was acceptable—your ex-wife an employee at Folly View, your daughter a pupil there, the victim in the same school year. I'm afraid this latest . . . development confirms that it's untenable for you to continue on the case."

"She's my daughter, Chief. She didn't do it."

"This is a delicate situation. Emotions are running high. As SIO, you know I have a responsibility to ensure everything is done by the book. One misstep and we could jeopardize the entire case. I can't risk accusations of mishandling."

"You're detaining an innocent girl while a killer roams free. You're sending officers to search Rachel's home when they could be chasing leads. And now you want one of your best detectives sitting at home twiddling his thumbs? How does that make sense?" Ben tries to curb his frustration, tries to return to a more measured tone. "Let me help. Let me prove Ellie didn't do it."

There's an edge to Khan's reply. "I'm sorry, Chase, but that's exactly why I need you to step down. Your judgment is clouded."

"It's in no way—"

"Chase, this is how it's got to be. For now."

Ben knows he can't push any harder. Khan is a decent man. A fair one. But once his mind is made up, it's near impossible to change it. "Is she in a cell?"

"Just for now. I've got to do things by the book. If there's an option to release Ellie tonight, I'll do it."

"Who's the custody officer?"

"Morrow. She's keeping a close eye, Chase, I promise."

That's something, thinks Ben. Fay Morrow is a bustling, maternal type, one of the kinder officers at the station.

The call ends and Ben sits for a moment, fighting the urge to slam his fist into the steering wheel. He knows the custody cells well. Bleak, functional spaces. Hard surfaces. Noisy. Places designed to make you sit and contemplate your life choices, choices that have brought you to a room like that. He can't bear to imagine Ellie sitting there, frightened and alone. But Khan had been clear—he was to step back. He was to ignore every paternal instinct and let his colleagues do their jobs.

Unsure what else he can do, Ben reverses in the turnout and drives back into town, pulling into the gas station to refill before heading home. Out on the forecourt watching the astronomical numbers slide ever higher on the gauge, he replays Ellie's baffling new version of events. A fight at the folly? Had he and Rachel been so distracted by their crumbling relationship that they'd failed to notice their daughter's struggles? Failed to understand how hard the transition to Folly View might've been? Was all this acting out, all the lying and destructive behavior, a cry for help? A plea to be noticed? And if so, what did it say about their parenting?

It takes a moment for him to notice the familiar-looking car sliding up to the opposite pump. A sleek green Jaguar with personalized plates. EASTON1. Ben's heart sinks. The engine falls silent. The driver's door opens.

"Thought that was you," says Christopher Easton, his face appearing over the roof of the car.

He doesn't look happy. In fact, he looks bloody furious. Ben squares his shoulders, stands a little taller. "Can I help you, Mr. Easton?"

"I heard your daughter got hauled into the station today."

Ben frowns. There is no way in the world Christopher Easton could know that. Not unless someone had leaked the information. Easton struck him as the type of man to have a finger in every pie; he just hadn't realized that also included the local station. Bristling, he tries to adopt a conciliatory tone. "Yes, a routine interview, as per all the students who were in the woods on Saturday night."

Easton narrows his eyes. "Not *all* the students were dragged into the police station, though. Not from what I hear."

"I'm not sure who your source is, Mr. Easton, but they're feeding you misleading information. This is an active enquiry. It would be best if you let us do our police work. We'll brief you as soon as anything pertinent comes to light."

Christopher Easton doesn't seem to like Ben's answer. His eyes flash, his fist clenching around his keys. Ben recognizes the signs of a man with a quick temper. "Your use of the word 'we' seems a little outdated. I heard you're off the case."

Goddammit. Ben waits a beat, counts to three in his head, and tells himself there's no point taking the bait. Two alpha males facing off over an emotive matter such as this could only ever end badly. "Everyone's on your side, Mr. Easton. We all want to find out who did this to Sarah and bring them to justice."

Easton eyes him with obvious suspicion. "I certainly hope so, because you're not the one going home each night to your devastated sister, your daughter racked with grief, unable to sleep or eat, and your wife a literal shell of herself. You're not the one," he adds, his voice rising in pitch, "trying to calm jittery investors on a high-stakes project slated for a town with an ugly PR situation on its hands. Have you seen the mess someone's made of our advertising hoarding? I don't see you lot chasing those hooligans down. These eco warriors banging their bongos, damaging private property, causing me major headaches, and keeping me tied up in long meetings and phone calls. They're intent on destroying my business. Why aren't you doing something about them?"

Ben can't quite believe what he's hearing. *An ugly PR situation*? Is Christopher more worried about his family or his finances?

"If there are any parties of interest you think we should be looking at, anyone you think might have a particular vendetta against the project, anyone who might have made Sarah a target, we'd like to hear about them."

"If I knew who they were, I'd tell you. Isn't that your job? To find out?" Easton is throwing daggers at him. "You lot are losing control. Someone needs to be caught. Someone needs to be punished. The sooner they are, the sooner my sister will find some peace and the sooner business can get back to normal."

Ben shakes his head. *Back to normal?* Is he serious? "We all want the same thing, Mr. Easton. Our focus is on bringing Sarah's perpetrator to justice," he adds, with emphasis. "We can't assume anyone is safe until we do."

Christopher Easton points a finger. "I'm watching you. I'm watching you all." He ducks back into his car and leaves the forecourt with an unnecessary revving of his engine and a screech of rubber.

"Asshole," mutters Ben, watching the Jaguar's red taillights fade into the falling darkness.

Ten minutes later he is pulling up outside the house he shares with Chrissie. He turns off the engine and waits, trying to calm himself, unwilling to take the stress of the day inside. Something from his ugly confrontation with Easton has stuck with him. He circles back over their encounter, the man's apoplectic face, his spitting words, his fist clenched around his keys. *Someone needs to be punished.* That word again. "Punish." It brings the memory of the words daubed on Sarah's body to mind. A coincidence?

Three days ago, to any outsider, the Easton family would have looked to all intents and purposes to have had it all, but Ben knows that even the most idyllic facade can hide a multitude of sins. He's seen enough over the years on the job to know that there's no such thing as a perfect family. Easton is a man quick to anger, his rage bubbling visibly beneath the skin. His wife was clearly troubled, doped up on painkillers and sleeping pills. Which left poor Olivia, traumatized and alone, a princess adrift in a palace. He found something in the atmosphere of their family home undeniably unsettling. Could Easton's aggressive bluster be cover for something more sinister? It'd be worth keeping a close eye on the man. At least he would, Ben realizes with a pang of frustration, if he were still attached to the case.

He studies the redbrick facade, the lit-up windows, and terra-cotta pots of chrysanthemums scattered around Chrissie's doorstep. It's a shock to realize that the feeling building in the pit of his stomach feels something akin to resentment. He doesn't want to go inside. In that moment, where he'd rather be is sitting with Rachel, trying to work through the nightmare they're caught in, trying to understand how they can support Ellie.

Chrissie had thrown him just the other week as they'd lain stretched out together on the sofa, her feet in his lap, the two of them watching a frothy dating show she liked where couples met for the first time at an altar. "This is nice, isn't it?" she'd said. "It feels like you're home."

He'd squeezed her toes and smiled his agreement, but it was only later as he'd stood brushing his teeth, staring at his reflection in the bathroom mirror, that he'd truly considered what she'd said.

"Home." As soon as she'd said the word, a place had risen in his mind, and it hadn't been Chrissie's neat new build. It had been the Victorian town house that he and Rach had moved into after Ellie had been born, when she was still small enough for him to carry around in the baby sling, moving from room to room at the property viewing with the pushy estate agent trailing behind.

In those earliest days, after they'd collected the keys and spent their first night surrounded by boxes, giddy with excitement and plans, they'd worked for hours side by side, steaming and stripping the lurid Seventies wallpaper, rewiring, repainting, retiling. Outside they'd dug flower beds and a vegetable patch at the bottom of the long, narrow yard. It was the place where he'd strung a rope swing onto the bough of an old apple tree and pushed a squealing Ellie: *"Higher, Daddy, higher!"* It was the house he'd returned to every evening, sitting at the kitchen table to help Ellie with her spellings and times tables, or stirring Bolognese on the hob—his staple Dad dish—while Rachel had studied late into the night for her counseling qualifications. It was the place where they'd hosted friends and family, where his sister, Gemma, had come to stay—

her "home away from home," she'd called it, appearing whenever she needed to rest and recover from her relentless stints at the hospital, walking through the door every couple of months with a duffel bag and a huge smile plastered on her face. It was the place where he'd last seen Gemma alive.

Don't, Ben tells himself. Don't go there. He leans his head back against the seat rest and shuts his eyes, squeezing away the unwelcome sting of tears. He misses the ease of those days, when everything in his life had felt ordered and in the right place. It baffles him, sometimes, to wake in the morning and realize where he is. He's messed up so many things . . . and now this, with Ellie? Was it his fault for leaving? Was that the trigger for this whole nightmare with their daughter?

He grabs his cell phone and scrolls through his contacts until Gemma's name appears on his screen. Staring at the dial button, he lets the grief expand, dull and heavy like a sandbag in his chest. There's no point calling. The sound of Gemma's cheerful voicemail greeting disappeared years ago, the number reassigned to someone else's phone. What he wouldn't give to hear his sister's voice, to talk to her again, to ask her advice about Ellie.

She'd been there from the very first moment Ellie had entered the world. Rachel had wanted her at the home birth, but so had Ben, relieved when Rachel had suggested it. "A fully qualified midwife and the funniest, kindest person I know . . . bar you of course," she'd added hastily, noting his feigned indignance. "Of course I want Gem there!" It had been humbling and not a little awe-inspiring to watch his sister work with Rachel, coaching her through her labor pains, never leaving her side, a steady, reassuring presence and the safest pair of hands he could've possibly imagined to guide their daughter into the world. He remembers the scene with awe. These women were warriors, he'd thought. There was no way he was worthy, but seeing his love and his fear, Gemma had placed a swaddled Ellie in his arms and told him, "Breathe, Benny Boy. You've got this. You're going to be amazing."

Gemma had always been the one who set him straight. She'd always had an ear for his problems, always held him to account, sifting through his feelings, injecting humor into dark moments, calling him out on his bullshit. She would've had something to say about the current shape of his life—about his separation from Rachel, about Ellie's withdrawal. If she were still alive, he wonders what she'd advise, what she'd take him to task over. He wonders how different life would look.

Ten years. That's all the scum who'd run his sister off the road had been given. Death by dangerous driving. The young man had pleaded guilty, claimed addiction and mental health issues, with his solicitors producing a raft of medical documents. The sentence had been small consolation to Ben. He knew how these things went. The jails were too full. He'd be out in half the time. What sort of a punishment was that for destroying Gemma's life, for robbing them of a beloved sister and aunt?

Most likely, the asshole would be out on parole already. It's one of the things that Ben thinks about as he falls asleep at night. It's certainly tempting to look him up, pay him a little visit, but the fear of what Ben might do to him, should they ever come face-to-face, keeps him away. That way madness—or prison—lies.

Instead, whenever the accident or that scumbag rises in his mind, he tries to remember the times before. He thinks of Gemma at her happiest, sitting at their kitchen table with her hands wrapped around a coffee mug and her hazel eyes shining as she told them hair-raising birth stories from her maternity ward.

He imagines them both as teenagers, Gemma humming along to the radio as they bombed around in his first claptrap car. The little girl he'd walked to and from primary school, her small hand clutched in his, ever the protective big brother. Whenever he feels the rage and sadness building, he tries to focus on her voice, still there in his head, patient and calm: *Let it go, Benny Boy. Don't let it eat you up.*

Rachel had told him to get help. To find an outlet for his anger. To work through his grief. She told him it was like living with a zombie. She'd asked him to stop drinking, told him their marriage might not survive if he didn't. Seems it hadn't made a difference. He'd cut back, found a therapist, and just a few years later they'd split anyway.

She'd needed some time—had essentially asked him to move out—and he hadn't handled it well. "If I go, I'm not coming back," he'd said, a knot of fear building in his chest.

Rachel had studied him, weary and sad. "Just some time, Ben. That's all I'm asking. I need you to face what's happened. To let me in. I can't live with a ghost."

"I'm not the ghost! You are. You're the one who's turned cold, asking me to leave."

"Because I'm trying to help you."

"I mean it, Rach. If you make me leave, that's it. I'm gone."

"Well, that's on you, I guess."

Here he was now, a new relationship and a baby on the way. Life moving at a dizzying pace. He had a responsibility to do the right thing. He and Chrissie would make their own home now—together—with the baby. But sometimes it was still hard to accept how the guillotine could fall, cleaving away all that had gone before. Sometimes, he couldn't help but miss his old life. The brutal truth of it, the one he hadn't been able to admit to Chrissie the other night, was that he wasn't entirely sure he knew where home was anymore.

Opening his eyes, he regards himself in the rearview mirror. God, so tired. He sees the bags under his eyes and the first hint of gray at his temples. Pull it together, he tells himself, stepping from the car, slamming the door behind him. None of his self-pity or navel-gazing is going to help Ellie. That's where his focus needs to be.

Chrissie emerges from the kitchen as he walks through the front door, a surprised smile on her face. "You're early."

She's dressed casually, a long oatmeal sweater, black leggings, gray fluffy slippers. She opens her arms for a hug and he obliges, holding her close, breathing in the perfume of her shampoo, feeling the warmth of her in his arms. He can make this life work.

"Come home to surprise me?"

Ben nods. "Long story."

"Come and talk to me while I make the soup."

Chrissie bustles around the kitchen, chopping vegetables, stirring them into a saucepan, slicing a loaf of bread, placing cheese on a board. Ben gathers cutlery and bowls before sitting on a stool, watching her move around the room. The light from the low hanging pendant over the kitchen island catches in her blond hair. She turns and smiles. "What?"

He nods at the slight curve beneath her top, an almost imperceptible swell pressing against the fabric of her cardigan.

Chrissie smiles and pulls the fabric taut, arching her back to emphasize the tiny bump. "Twelve weeks yesterday. Just starting to show now. The size of a plum, apparently." Chrissie frowns, seeing his face. "What's wrong?"

"They've taken me off the Sarah Lawson case."

"What? Why?"

"Ellie lied to us. After she left our place on Saturday, she snuck out to the party in the woods. Top brass says there's a conflict of interest, so I've been stood down. For now."

"No." Chrissie's face is a picture of shock. "That's awful."

Ben thinks about the stained clothes spilling from the plastic bag. Ellie's evasive answers to his and Rachel's questions the night before. He doesn't want to get into the details with Chrissie. He can't bear to speak his worst fears out loud. "I guess they can't risk the optics," he says vaguely.

Chrissie is still frowning, the wooden spoon hovering over the pan. "It's frightening to know there's someone out there who could do something so violent to a young girl. I've been thinking about it all day."

Ben nods. "We're chasing a few leads, but the case still feels wide open."

"And to think Ellie was in the woods that night! That was sneaky of her to lie, especially when she should've been here with us," Chrissie adds.

"We've talked to her."

"You have?" Chrissie turns to him. "You *and* Rachel?"

Ben nods. "Yeah. Last night."

He realizes his mistake too late. He hadn't told Chrissie about his stop-off at Rachel's the previous night. It had seemed easier not to involve her, but now, of course, it looks as though he's kept it secret. Excluded her.

"I thought you said you were working late," she says archly.

"I was. Then I popped round to see Ellie. It was important," Ben stresses. "I needed to be there for her."

She lifts one eyebrow. "For Rachel?"

"For Ellie," he snaps.

Chrissie purses her lips. He's not an idiot. He understands why it would bother her. It was only twelve months ago that he and Rachel were still living together as a married couple, albeit an es-tranged one.

The soup starts to boil over in the pan and Chrissie turns back to the cooktop, stirring carefully. Ben's cell phone rings, cutting through the deep silence. He sees Chrissie glance at it, then look away. It's not a number he recognizes and when he answers, he is surprised to hear Connor Carlisle's voice at the end of the line. "Connor. How can I help?" He slips out of the kitchen, shutting the door behind him.

"Look, man, you caught me off guard yesterday. I was on the de-fense."

Connor is talking like a phony American gangster and Ben can't help an internal eye roll. In the background, he can hear traffic noises and the low thump of bass and knows he's probably calling from the pimped-up SUV. "I'm listening," he says.

"You said to call if I remembered anything."

"Go on," says Ben, a glimmer of interest building.

"While we were in the woods, one of the girls started freaking out. She said someone was watching us."

Ben's excitement slumps. "Yeah, Danny told us about that al-ready. He said he and a friend went off to investigate, but there was no one there. They said the girl had imagined it."

"Yeah, but they was wrong."

Ben frowns. "Who was?"

"Danny and his mate. They didn't find anyone, but there *was* someone watching us. I saw him too."

"Him?"

"Yeah. Up in the trees above the quarry."

Ben frowns. What's Connor playing at? Is he for real, or simply trying to muddy the investigation, to divert suspicion away from his younger brother? "You saw a man in the woods on Saturday night?"

"Yep."

"Could you describe him?"

"I dunno. It was dark."

"Try."

"So . . . I guess he was older. White face. Sunken eyes. Kind of creepy-looking, but that could've just been the dark. Maybe if I saw him again . . ."

"If I asked you to come in and give a proper description, could—"

"Ah man. Police stations aren't really my vibe . . . You know, it was pretty dark . . . maybe I didn't get the best look at him after all . . ."

Ben can feel Connor backtracking, the lead sliding away. It's not much to go on. If he were to call Khan and ask him to consider this, he'd sound like a desperate man clutching at straws, anything to distract them from their focus on Ellie. "Why didn't you say anything at the party?" he asks, frustrated. "Why didn't you back up Jasmine?"

Connor sighs. "Look, if everyone gets scared, they scarper, right? I figured we were a big group. Some random perv in the woods wasn't going to spook me."

"And if they all leave, you don't have anyone to push your 'product' onto?"

Connor falls into a stony silence, just the heavy bass of the car stereo thudding in the background. "I didn't say that."

"So why tell me now, Connor?"

Connor sighs. "Look, the girl may have been a spoiled brat, but she didn't deserve what she got."

"So, this isn't about covering your arse. Or protecting your little brother?"

"No man. My alibi's tight. And there's no way Danny was involved in this. He's a pain in my ass, but he's not a bad kid."

The conversation breaks with the sound of a blaring horn and Connor yelling, "Wanker!" at full volume. "Look," he says, returning to Ben, "you can believe me or not. It's no skin off my nose. I didn't have to call you."

The line goes dead. It's hardly new information, but it does corroborate Jasmine Ware's statement. Besides, Connor had a point. While Ben wasn't particularly keen to take the lad at face value, Connor had no real advantage to getting back in touch with him. Ben knew from past experience that Connor would do pretty much anything to avoid a brush with the law. Maybe there was a glimmer of hope for Connor Carlisle after all.

He returns to the kitchen table and sits with a still-sulky Chrissie, the air crackling between them as they eat the soup she has cooked, the tension remaining between them until Chrissie announces she's tired and going up for an early night.

"I'll join you," he says, still hoping to soften the mood, but Chrissie won't meet his eye and as soon as she hits the mattress, she flicks off her bedside light and rolls away.

Ben lies next to her in the dark, staring up at the ceiling, wide awake. "Chrissie, I'm sorry. I should've told you I'd seen Rachel."

Chrissie mumbles something inaudible in reply.

"What was that?"

"Go to sleep," she says. "I don't want to argue. Stress isn't good for the baby."

Ben turns away, chastened. It's not fair of him to feel annoyed. None of this is Chrissie's fault. She's been nothing but sweet and decent since the first night he'd met her, when Rachel had asked him to leave and he'd stormed out to find the nearest pub.

Furious at the injustice of it all, he'd downed two pints of IPA and a whiskey chaser in quick succession. Only when he'd raised his head from the bottom of his glass had he noticed Chrissie, right there, perched on a stool at the end of the bar, looking dangerously hot in a black leather miniskirt and knitted cardigan, her blond curls spilling down her shoulders. She'd raised her gin and tonic at him and offered a wry smile. "Looks like you might be having a worse night than me."

She'd been stood up by a Tinder date, it transpired. He had been drunk and morose. Terrible company really, when he thinks about it. God knows why she'd invited him back, but when he'd woken in Chrissie's bed the following morning, hungover and sick with shame, he knew that what he'd done had put the final nail in the coffin of any possible reconciliation with Rachel.

From that night on, it had been easier to look forward than back. He'd kept his blinkers tightly fastened. Chrissie was pretty and fun and he was bruised and hurt and—yes, childish. Chrissie was right there, ready to stroke his ego and make him feel like a man again. She didn't ask searching questions about his emotions or force him to confront painful losses from his past. When he was with her, he didn't have to think about Rachel—or Gemma—and soon, the woman who had started out as a convenient distraction seemed to have become a permanent fixture. It wasn't easy to manage Ellie's emotions or face her hurt at the collapse of their family, but he told himself it was better to be happy with Chrissie than make them all suffer. Chrissie represented an easy life and he was here for it—all in for that easy, blinkered life— right up until she'd told him she was pregnant.

"There is one good thing about you being stood down," Chrissie says quietly, her voice lifting off the pillow beside him, jolting him from his thoughts.

He rolls back to her. "What's that?"

"You can come with me tomorrow."

Ben frowns in the darkness.

"The antenatal appointment. You haven't forgotten?"

There's no way he can admit that in the tumult of the last couple of days, it has clean escaped him. He nuzzles into her warm shoulder. "Course not. I'll be there. Promise."

The solid wall of her back remains, but she relinquishes a hand, her fingers reaching over her shoulder for his. He squeezes tightly and kisses her palm. "I'm sorry, love. I'll do better. I promise."

Chapter 21

Rachel receives a late phone call from the duty officer asking her to collect Ellie at 10:00 p.m. She's told there's been a delay on the forensics report, but that she will most likely be required to attend the station again the next morning. "Don't go skipping the country," says the officer, only half joking.

It's a relief to see Ellie, just a short time later, being ushered through the swinging doors into the station's waiting area. "Come on," says Rachel, wrapping an arm around her shoulders, "let's get you out of here."

They drive home in near silence. Rachel doesn't want to press Ellie about her experience. They are both too tired and Ellie's face remains fixed on the passenger window, only stirring when her phone pings in her lap. She angles the screen away, but Rachel can see the color rising in her cheeks as she reads the message. "Your friends checking up on you?"

"Something like that," she mutters.

Turning through the school gates, Rachel lets out a gasp and hits the brakes. A figure looms ahead on the drive, tall and thin, his face bleached white in the car headlights. He steps up onto the

shoulder, allowing them past with a wave of his hand. Malcolm
Crowe, out on one of his evening walks. "Weirdo," Ellie mutters
under her breath.

"Ellie!"

"What? He *is* weird, creeping around the campus at night."

"He's exercising. Taking in the night air." Rachel tries to sound
reassuring, but when she glances in the mirror, she sees Malcolm
hasn't moved. He stands sentry-like at the gates, a ghostly smudge
in her rearview mirror as he watches them go. "You don't have
any other reason to think he's weird, do you?"

Ellie shrugs.

"Ellie?"

"It's nothing."

A prickle of apprehension rises in Rachel's mind. It does seem
a little odd for Malcolm to be prowling around in the dark after
such awful events, especially on a twisted ankle. Even if he has
taken it upon himself to act as some sort of self-appointed school
security guard, it's hardly the sort of behavior that's going to put
a campus full of jumpy students and teachers at ease. Since Monday's assembly, the bonfire of fear and mistrust has only seemed
to grow across campus. No one, it seems, is free from suspicion,
not even lumbering Malcolm. "Well then. How about a little
kindness? He's an old man, doing his best for the school." She says
it, she realizes, to convince herself as much as Ellie.

They're almost at the cottage when Ellie speaks next. "Do you
think people are inherently good or bad?" she asks, her face still
fixed to the window.

Rachel frowns. She is thinking less about what her answer
might be, and more about what might have prompted such a
philosophical question from her daughter. Were they still talking
about Malcolm? "I'm not sure, Ellie. What do you think?"

Ellie shrugs.

Rachel kicks herself. It isn't the time for a professional counseling approach. Ellie is asking for something from her. Openness. Honesty. She tries again. "I don't think I do believe that, no. I believe we're shaped by our experiences. Our families, our friendships, the things that happen to us . . . those are the things that mold us. Human beings are complicated. Nothing's ever black and white."

"So, you believe in nurture over nature?"

Rachel's still unsure where Ellie is heading with her questions. "I think it's probably a combination of the two. But I don't like to think that anyone is born evil. I can't imagine that. Can you?"

Ellie doesn't answer and for a moment they are both silent, listening to the gravel crunching beneath the tires. "I think some people have a streak of bad running through them. Like an apple with a rotten core. You can't always tell it's there, but it is, waiting to be revealed."

"Ellie, you don't think you've got a rotten core, do you?"

Ellie glances up at her, and Rachel sees something in her daughter's eyes, something hot and bright, which makes her feel a little afraid.

"Because I don't see that in you," Rachel adds. "Not at all. I see a loving, compassionate girl. A girl who feels things deeply. There are some difficult, sad things happening right now. This terrible business with Sarah. And I know you've had a hard time accepting your dad's and my separation. There's Chrissie's baby too. It's a lot right now, but I promise you, it will settle down."

Ellie releases a fierce sigh. "God, Mum. For a trained therapist, you really can be clueless sometimes."

"So tell me, then. What am I missing?"

Ellie shakes her head. "This thing with Sarah. It's terrible. I really wish she hadn't died. That she was OK. But everyone's talking about her now like she's some sort of saint. She'll be forever remembered as this golden girl. I guess that's not the person I knew, that's all."

Rachel falls silent, thinking. "I'm sorry I didn't understand how hard it's been for you, transitioning to this school. I'm sorry I missed that you were having a tough time."

She is sorry. Rachel's always thought the benefits of working at the school, of being in such close proximity to Ellie, would outweigh any negatives, but perhaps Ellie was at a disadvantage having her mother on the school faculty. All the other students had access to her as a counselor. But for Ellie, she'd always just be "Mum." Who else did Ellie have to talk to?

"I know you might not want to open up to me—or your dad. But if you'd like to speak to someone, in confidence, I could arrange it. Someone neutral. Someone private. It doesn't have to be a therapist. Your tutor, Edward Morgan, you like him, don't you? Perhaps we could ask if he might—"

"Drop it, Mum. I don't need anyone." Ellie draws her shutter down.

Rachel, chastised, parks outside the cottage and they sit for a moment, both of them staring out at the small stone building and the wooded hillside rising up steeply behind, cast in moonlight. Somewhere out in the darkness a fox screams, its cry high and unsettling.

Rachel steals a glance at Ellie, noting the familiar slope of her nose, the mirror image of Ben's; those scattered freckles, the new, dark shadows beneath her eyes, the proud tilt of her chin. She wishes she could see inside her, understand her anger and pain.

Ellie turns to meet her gaze. "What?" Instead of waiting, she sighs and slips from the car, slamming the door behind her.

"Nothing," Rachel replies to the empty seat.

She can't shake it. The fear is still there. Every bone in her body screams that something is up with Ellie, that she might still be in trouble. But what can she do? She can't hover over her every minute. She can't pepper her with more questions—it will only push her further away.

Inside the cottage, she finds Ellie standing in the kitchen surveying their ransacked belongings. The police had moved through the premises like a well-oiled machine, but it had already taken Rachel several hours to start putting things back into order. "They didn't find anything," Rachel says, reaching out to squeeze Ellie's shoulder.

Ellie shrugs her off. "I could've told you that."

She slinks away upstairs and Rachel lets her go, returning more of their scattered items to drawers, replacing books on shelves, and adjusting the cushions on the sofa. After a while she gives up, looking for somewhere to settle, something else to occupy her. She is far too wired to sleep.

If she could, she would work. God knows recent events have meant she's slipped behind. There is the statement she needs to draft for the governors' report, notes from a student assessment to write up, reassurances to parents' worried emails. All tasks that have slid in priority over a horrible few days. But the papers she needs for those jobs are still sitting on her office desk, right next to her laptop, exactly where she'd left everything in her hurry to get to Ellie's interview.

She goes to the window and glances out at the night sky. Thin cloud shifts like drifting smoke over a crescent moon. It's hardly an appealing prospect to head out into the dark again, but if she goes now, she could scoop up her belongings and be back again in twenty minutes, with everything she'll need to work from home

tomorrow—or worse, should she be summoned back to the police station with Ellie.

Calling up to Ellie that she's popping out and won't be long,
she pulls on her coat and slips out the front door.

The temperature outside seems to have plummeted as she
sets off across campus and there's nothing for company but the
sound of her boots on the winding gravel path and the ghostly
call of an owl somewhere out in the trees. She shivers. Quick as
she can. In and out. Then home.

In the recent past, the splendor of the school grounds has always given Rachel a thrill, a sort of chest-swelling pride at being a
small part of something so historic, so prestigious. But what had
once appeared as a safe haven, nestled into the shoulder of the
valley, now seems sinister and oppressive. The looming trees, no
longer standing like benevolent, silent guardians, now feel somehow threatening, as if they've closed ranks, hiding a multitude of
dark secrets. There's a pressing claustrophobia. And something
else too—something she recognizes from the too-fast thud of her
heart. Fear. It's as if the school is shrouded not just in darkness,
but in a strange new terror. It's become a place of dread. A place
where something terrible has happened. Where something terrible might still happen.

The hairs raise at the nape of her neck. Just the cold, she tells
herself, but she quickens her pace, grateful when she's finally
standing outside the administration building, putting her key to
the door and sliding into the unlit entrance hall.

Given the lateness of the hour, the whole building is silent and
empty, just as she's expected. Just as she's hoped. No awkward
questions about Ellie's visit to the police station. No nosy colleagues to navigate. She scurries down the dark wood-paneled
corridor, her path tripping a series of security lights, stern eyes

boring down at her from the dour portraits of former head teachers lining the walls. When she reaches her office, Rachel stops.

It's a surprise to see a narrow band of light shining at the gap
beneath the door. She frowns. Had she, in her hurry to get to Ellie,
left her office lamps on?

Standing there trying to remember, she is plunged into sudden
darkness. She stifles a gasp. The security lights in the corridor
have timed out, but behind the office door she can hear a soft
shuffling noise. Like soft footsteps moving across floorboards, or
papers shifting on a desk.

Someone's in there.

It's the middle of the night, and someone is inside her office.

Steeling herself, Rachel opens the door.

Chapter 22

Wednesday, 12:30 a.m.

Ben is dreaming about Ellie. He is sitting on a pebbled beach watching her swim through a choppy gray sea. Not too far out, just beyond the breakers, swimming in a horizontal line to the shore, her slim arms slicing neatly into the water, exactly as he'd taught her.

Rachel is beside him, long bare legs stretched out on a towel, her thick red hair scraped up in a high ponytail, her caramel eyes soft and smiling, full lips curved to show just a hint of teeth.

He turns back to the water and sees that Ellie has been joined by someone else. He squints and feels a surge of emotion. Gemma. The two of them—his daughter and his sister—are bobbing in the waves like strange, disembodied heads, until synchronized, they begin to alter course, swimming together toward the horizon, moving away in a steady front crawl. He watches them, the ache in his chest expanding with every stroke, until the tiny bobbing heads are nothing but specks and he stands and shouts their names, feeling a rising panic, knowing they are too far away to hear, watching helplessly as the minuscule smudges disappear from view. When he turns back to Rachel, she too has vanished.

Ben's eyes snap open in the dark, instantly awake. Ellie. He should check on her.

The blue light from the clock illuminates the curly blond hair spread across the pillow beside him. Chrissie. Not Rachel. He is at home with Chrissie. Which means he won't be peeling himself from the mattress to check on Ellie. She isn't here.

The clock shows 00:31. He's only been asleep an hour or so. Which means it's going to be a long night. Rolling onto his back, Ben stares at the ceiling, waiting for his heartbeat to slow. He knows this crushing panic. The adrenaline. The nightmares. He remembers them well, his frequent night companions after Gemma's death.

Lying in the dark, he returns to the counseling session he'd attended after Gemma's death, the one Rachel had organized for him. The one where he'd sat in a quiet room on a cushion-scattered sofa and listened as a softly spoken Scottish woman had asked him about these moments of panic. How he coped. What he did.

He'd regarded her with confusion. What he did? He did nothing. He endured. He let the panic rise like a tide from the messy knot of turmoil at his core, let it engulf him. "I'm a police officer," he'd told her. "It comes with the territory."

The counselor had considered this for a moment. "Your fight-or-flight response is important for your job. It's there to protect you. But you don't want it to overwhelm you. There are things you can do, to help yourself in moments of extreme stress." She'd held his gaze. "Or in moments of extreme emotion, like fear . . . or grief."

She'd shown him how to tap into a sensory memory, one he could return to as a calming mechanism. Sitting there in the safety of her consultation room, he'd returned in his mind to a favorite afternoon at a skate park with Ellie as a young girl, where he'd watched proud as punch as she'd thrown herself down concrete ramps and runs, before they'd sat together on a bench eating ice cream, Ellie's short legs swinging as she'd turned to him and said, unprompted, "I love you, Daddy."

"How much?" he'd asked, nudging her with a playful elbow.

"More than skateboards *and* ice cream."

Such innocence. Such simplicity.

To a degree, Rachel had been right. The session had helped a little. Sometimes it was annoying being married to a therapist. But here he was, five years later, with that familiar panic rising in his chest and the sweat beading on his brow and his dreams about Gemma returning in full force, only this time shot through with his fears for Ellie. It didn't take a counselor to decipher any of it. Yet no matter how hard he tries to fix on a moment from another time, a moment when he felt happy and at peace knowing everyone was safe, he can't rid himself of this new dream, of the image of Ellie swimming with Gemma into the deep gray ocean. Terrible things happened in the world. None of the people he loves are immune. How does he live with himself, if he cannot protect them?

His thoughts drift to Rachel. He wonders if she is awake. If she is lying in bed staring up at the ceiling worrying about their daughter. If he knows anything about Rachel anymore, he's almost certain she'll be wakeful and worried too.

Ben tries a breathing exercise and after a time, feeling his pulse gradually calm, he realizes there *is* something else. Something floating just out of reach. He knows this feeling. It comes to him sometimes, when he's working a case. A tantalizing sense that there is order to be found, if only he can arrange the pieces of the puzzle into the correct order. He tries to focus. Tries to push away thoughts of Rachel and Chrissie and pull the fragments of whatever eludes him closer, but they slip away, muddling out of shape. Beside him, Chrissie murmurs. She shifts her position, but she doesn't wake.

What is he missing?

He knows the way his colleagues work, their modus operandi. The theories they'll be batting back and forth. He'd be exactly the same . . . *is* exactly the same. Keep an open mind. Follow the evidence, the breadcrumbs. But right now, the breadcrumb trail only seems to lead in one direction. Straight to Ellie. Her lies. Her bloodstained clothes. The mask from her costume. Her altercation with the dead girl up at the folly. He remembers Ellie standing in Rachel's kitchen, evading his gaze, agitated under their scrutiny. She lied to you, says a small voice in his head. What else is she lying about? What else is she hiding?

Ben's mind zeroes in. *Hiding.*

What was it Ellie had said that night? Something about the woods. Something that had caught his attention. Something that had made him think she wasn't being completely honest. He grapples with the memory, replays it over and over until her words return. *Did they check the woods?* she'd asked. *They're good hiding places.*

It had struck him as an odd thing to say at the time. Did she know something? Was she intimating that they had missed something in their search of the crime scene?

Ben slips quietly from the bed. Downstairs, perched at the kitchen island, he powers up his laptop. He might have been taken off the Sarah Lawson case, but he still has access to the central police database. Ben chews his lip, his face cast in the blue light of his screen. He logs in to the system and types *Thorncombe Folly* into the search function. The system isolates twelve or so reports that he scans through in turn, hoping something of note will leap out.

Most of the files are of criminal damage to the folly, dating back sporadically over the years, mainly vandalism and graffiti to the steel door that had once blocked entry to the tower. He filters through the rest, one relating to a clumsy arson attempt eight years ago, when some idiot had attempted to set fire to the structure; another logged by a concerned local about discarded syringes found in the vicinity. The last is a report on illegal tree-felling traced to a group of travelers who had passed through the area in 2021.

He tries another search filter, typing *Thorncombe Woods* to cast his net a little wider—too wide, perhaps, but it's worth a shot. A flurry of additional reports appears. Fly-tipping. An abandoned stolen vehicle blocking one of the woodland trails. A couple cautioned for an act of indecent behavior in the woodland parking lot. His fingers hesitate over the "death by dangerous driving" RTA report logged on the Sally in the Wood road five years ago, the date of Gemma's death. Ben sighs. It's no good. None of it seems connected to the Sarah Lawson case.

He rubs his eyes. Exhaustion is catching up with him. He tells himself to go back to bed and try to catch a few hours' kip, but there's still something nagging at him. *Check the woods*, she'd said.

They *had* checked the woods. Khan had demanded a grid search of the steep vale.

The woods are huge, she'd said. . . . *The quarry, the caves . . . they're good hiding places.*

He straightens on the stool. The caves. Why would Ellie mention the caves? Was it a place the kids frequented? It could've been a throwaway comment, but on the other hand perhaps she knew something, something they had overlooked? Had they found a way inside them?

At the team briefing, DC Crawford had assured them the cave entrances beneath the escarpment were sealed from entry. But had he actually checked? What if it wasn't about what was going on up in the woods . . . but *below* them?

Ben types *Thorncombe caves* into the search bar. He's not expecting much, but two reports flash up on the system. One about a potholer causing a kerfuffle back in 2020 by getting stuck in the caving system during lockdown. The other, a more recent incident recorded just two months ago. Ben pulls up the case of indecent exposure on the hillside above Sally in the Wood, unsure why this should've come up in his search.

He is only a few lines in when he feels the hairs on the back of his neck prickle. Two dog walkers had reported an early morning encounter with an unknown male in the woods. Rounding a corner on one of the steep walking trails above the roadside, they had come across a disheveled-looking man in a state of undress. One of the women had screamed in alarm and the man had taken off into the woods, their dog giving chase. The dog had remained in the woods, barking incessantly, refusing to return on command, and so in the end, the women had reluctantly gone to retrieve the animal. They'd found it fussing at a sealed entrance into the old quarry caving system. The women had managed to get the dog back on its lead and had returned to the trail without further incident, but they had been unnerved by their encounter and had reported it to the local station later that morning. The officer handling the case? DC Dave Crawford.

Ben sucks in a breath. Crawford had gone out to take a look but had found no trace of anyone loitering in the woods and reported the cave entrance sealed. Reading on, Ben finds the women's description of the male. "I couldn't be sure of his age, he looked rather pale, with skinny, stringy hair, but there was something all over him. Dirty black markings. Words, possibly tattoos, though I don't think so. It was ever so creepy."

Ben feels the air compress in his lungs. He minimizes the report on his screen and opens an internet search browser, typing *access Thorncombe caves*, scrolling until he finds a local website devoted to amateur potholers and cavers. He reads through the chat forum, zeroing in on a thread where a handful of cavers discuss how to gain access to the sealed caves. It's even easier than Ben had imagined. With a little determination and a few tools, it seems anyone could gain entry, if they wanted.

Ben sits back on his stool, the possibilities turning through his mind. *Good hiding places.* It could be nothing. But on the other hand? He's got nothing to lose by heading back into the woods and investigating for himself.

Chapter 23

Rachel's office door swings open to reveal a man standing over her desk, his back turned to her.

"Hello?" Fear makes her voice loud and sharp. It slices through the quiet, startling both her and the intruder. She just has time to take in his mop of thin white hair and his stooped frame, before he spins to face her, his eyes widening at the sight of her in the doorway.

"Malcolm!" she gasps. "What the hell?"

Malcolm Crowe fumbles with an object in his hands. It slips from his grip and falls to the floor, smashing with a crash of broken glass at his feet. "Dammit!" he says, taking a step back.

"What are you doing in here?"

"You reported a problem with your lamp?" He nods at the broken glass. "I came to change the bulb. You made me jump," he adds, throwing her an irritated look, as if she were the intruder, not him.

She recalls reporting the faulty lamp to housekeeping last week, but something about Malcolm's countenance makes her uneasy. The blood is rising in his cheeks, spreading across his dry, scaly face, and, as if aware of his guilty flush, he reaches up and scratches at his flaking cheeks. Rachel tries not to visibly shudder at the thought of dead skin cells drifting down onto her desk. "Why come so late? Wouldn't it be better to do this in the morning? Or leave it to the caretaker?"

He shrugs. "I don't sleep well. I have joint pain. It's worse at night, so I like to help out around the place. Besides, it's easier to get on with my odd jobs without people around. I saw you and Ellie driving back earlier and it jogged my memory." He folds his arms across his chest. "Thought it would be nice if it was sorted for you."

Rachel glances at her desk. Something is different. It takes her a moment, but then she sees it. A vase of white roses on her desk—flowers that definitely hadn't been there earlier in the day. "Oh," she says, startled. "Flowers."

Malcolm's eyes track to the vase, before he turns back to her with a strange, gummy smile. "There's a card."

The way he says it makes her stomach flip and for a horrible moment she thinks the flowers might be from Malcolm.

"You have an admirer," he adds, with an odd twitch of his eyelid that she realizes is a wink.

She crosses to the desk and snatches up the card propped against the vase.

I heard you'd been called away.

I hope everything is OK with Ellie.

Here if I can help.

Edward.

Not Malcolm, though Rachel's relief is short-lived. From the way Malcolm is still smirking at her, she knows he's read the card, which means that the gesture of Edward's flowers will no doubt be relayed straight back to Margaret. Her relief dissipates further when she realizes that if Edward is already privy to the fact she'd been called away to Ellie's interview at the station, the police interest in Ellie must be common knowledge across the school.

Malcolm's shoes crunch on the broken glass. "So how did Ellie get on today?" he asks, confirming her fear.

"Fine," she snaps.

"Strange that they carted her off in a police car." He lets the insinuation hang.

"Standard procedure." She keeps her retort breezy, but Malcolm doesn't look convinced. He hovers, waiting, as if wanting to say more. "Will you get a dustpan and brush?" she asks pointedly. "Or shall I clear this up in the morning?"

Malcolm shrugs and limps to the door, stopping to turn back, his face in shadow but for the glint of his eyes. "I'm sure you're highly qualified, and I hear these days it's all about pussyfooting around feelings and 'mental health issues,' but in my day, naughty girls got what was coming to them. Naughty girls were punished for their bad deeds."

Rachel is too startled to reply. She stares after him, watching him limp through the doorway, a sudden chill racing up her spine. What on earth did he mean, "naughty girls"? Was he talking about Ellie? She bristles. Was that who he meant? Or was he referring to poor Sarah?

Her mind spirals back to Maxwell's awful photo and the words she'd seen daubed on the girl's bloodless skin. The echo of one of them following Malcolm away down the corridor. *Punish.* She shudders. Whichever way you looked at it, it was a very odd thing to say.

She waits for his footsteps to recede, then she seizes her papers, laptop, and charging cable. As she reaches for her diary, her gaze falls on a cardboard file lying on her desk. A file that should, for all intents and purposes, be under lock and key in her cabinet. The name on the tab stares back at her: SARAH LAWSON.

Rachel frowns, her gaze darting to the open door.

What the hell was Malcolm Crowe doing rifling through Sarah's private student file? Was the light bulb his cover story, so that he could invade her records and pick through the kids' personal details? Why would he do that?

Thoroughly unnerved and unwilling to risk any further transgressions, Rachel shoves the folder back into the filing cabinet, locks the drawer, and pockets the key. Gathering up her belongings, she races for the door. There's no way she wants to be here when Malcolm gets back.

Chapter 24

Ben arrives in the woods before first light. He knows that police tape doesn't always deter people from a crime scene, and that sometimes it can do the very opposite and attract the curious or downright nosy, but it's clear as he climbs the trail from the parking lot that, so far at least, people have chosen to stay away after the gruesome weekend discovery. He can't blame them. He's not a superstitious man, but as he tramps through the fallen leaves, the cold air pulling at the lapels of his coat, he feels the eerie disquiet of the place, the lingering sensation that something bad has happened here, like the low, rumbling aftershocks of an earthquake still hanging in the air. He'd steer clear too, if he didn't have a daughter as a potential suspect and a nagging hunch to follow.

Dry twigs and the hollow husks of beech nuts crack beneath his boots as he makes his way up to the quarry basin. He navigates his guilt as he walks. He shouldn't be here. It's a clear breach of his orders from Khan; though Ben, if he were being pedantic, could argue that the Chief hadn't *specifically* told him to stay out of the woods. He was off the case, sure, but did that mean he couldn't take a scenic walk in his own leisure time? Just a quick look around, he tells himself, and then he'll be gone. If nothing else, he'll feel better knowing he's tied up a loose end.

He'd printed the amateur cavers' map back at Chrissie's and studying it now by his flashlight, he sees half a dozen entrances marked across the woods, all leading into a series of old quarry tunnels zigzagging below the escarpment. It would take days to trace them all, but he's not planning to investigate all of them. If Jasmine and Connor had seen someone lurking near the party, then it would make most sense to check the cave entrance nearest to the location of the student gathering. It would be the obvious place for a predator to hide when the boys went in search of their "watcher."

He knows it's a long shot, and perhaps his hunch about DC Crawford's attention to detail was unfair; perhaps the man had been thorough in his examination of the cave entrances. Still, anything that could help with the case—and yes, anything that might help Ellie—had to be worth a second look.

As faint light begins to spread across the woodland, creeping between the fretted branches of the trees and painting the landscape in the muted brown and orange hues of autumn, Ben reorients himself. He navigates his way to the upper lip of the quarry and studies his surroundings. Up here on the basin rim, the trees stand like silent spectators peering over the edge, thick roots clawing and spilling to hold the precarious earth in place. A dense understory of bracken, brambles, and ferns sprawls at Ben's feet. Looking down into the quarry, Ben fights the familiar, swaying threat of his vertigo.

It's hard to imagine an entry point into the earth here, but there is something: a faint line stamped into the greenery, disappearing away between the trees. He takes a few steps forward and frowns. Is it a path? He's not sure. Perhaps just a fox trail, but he plants his feet carefully and follows the tentative line a short distance, clambering over tree roots, tangled brambles, and rocks.

After three hundred or so feet, Ben reaches a rocky surface, rising as a sheer stone wall in front of him. He frowns, wondering if he's read the map wrong, beginning to wonder if he shouldn't climb down and regain his bearings, when the tree canopy shifts overhead and a thin light falls onto the stone where it catches on something silver glinting in the rock face. The sight of it makes Ben's chest thump.

Moving closer, he finds a security grill, aged with dirt and rust, fixed in place across an old tunnel entrance. He shines his flashlight through the bars and sees a dark hollow carved out beneath the rocky overhang, before it narrows and burrows away into blackness. Above him, the weight of rock and earth feels oppressive. He experiences a wave of claustrophobia at the thought of climbing into the dark void and traveling down through its underground chambers. But there is something there, something gray slumped on the cavern floor, just beyond the reach of his flashlight beam.

Ben rattles the metal grill and feels it shift in his hands. It doesn't lift, but it wants to. Ben can feel it. The fixings aren't as solid as they should be. Remembering the potholers' chat room tips, he studies the security grill more closely. One of the bolts is missing completely, so that the barrier is held in place solely by its hinges and a single fat screw in the lower right corner. This one, he finds, twists easily. He doesn't even need the tools he's brought. He unscrews it with his fingers until it slides off and lies loose in the palm of his hand. This time, when he tugs at the grate, it swings up easily on rusty hinges, revealing the dark space beyond.

The air is heavy with the fug of damp stone and soil. With

the fragrance comes an odd prickling sensation running from his scalp to his spine. He climbs through the opening and sweeps the chamber with his flashlight. The space is low and cavernous, only just room to stand before it drops dramatically, low jagged rock pressing down as the tunnel falls away into the earth. From somewhere deeper comes the sound of trickling water. He takes several steps forward, crouching lower, his eye drawn to the objects hidden in the shadows.

A pile of white ash sits beneath the overhang, nearby the blackened stumps of logs lie scattered, not quite burned through. There's a grimy sleeping bag, lumpy and twisted, lying in one corner, a half-filled plastic water carrier, and a scratched tin cup. Further away, there's the torn cardboard of a cereal box and several brown, discarded apple cores. Someone has been camping out, using the cave as a base. Kids? Possibly. A homeless person, sleeping rough? More likely.

The beam of his flashlight passes back over the detritus, his gaze catching on the red "K" of the cereal box logo. Something rattles in his memory. Cereal boxes. A shrill, indignant voice. It comes to him: Mrs. Kerridge standing in the police station, complaining about a disheveled shoplifter. *Filthy bugger . . . he just grabbed the cereal right off the shelf and ran.*

As he lifts the light to take in the rest of the space, he lets out an exclamation. "What the hell?" The flashlight almost slips from his grip. He fumbles to retrieve it before sweeping the beam back across the low ceiling.

Painted across the cavern walls are words and figures scrawled in thick black streaks. A series of childish caricatures—girls, he realizes, with triangular dresses and long hair—dancing beside a diatribe of words daubed over and over across the rock. PUNISH. DESTROY. REPENT.

With his pulse jackhammering in his ears, he moves to the sleeping bag and prods it with the toe of his sneaker. His foot connects with something small but solid beneath the fabric. Lifting it tentatively, he sees fragments of pink plastic. He frowns. Olivia Easton's anxious face returns to him. *She won't go anywhere without it. . . . An iPhone. In a rose gold case.* If it's the girl's phone, it's in pieces now.

Ben turns to leave, eager to call in his discovery, keen not to interfere any further with the evidence strewn about the cave, when he hears a noise echoing in the tunnel. There's a scuffling sound followed by the trickle of small rocks scattering across the ground, sounds that make the hairs on the back of his neck stiffen.

He swings the flashlight, the beam catching movement in the shadows. A dark form. The glow of something white and bright. Two eyes flashing in the dark, before they're gone. "Stop!" he shouts. "Police."

But whoever it is isn't stopping. They are moving fast, retreating further into the deep tunnel.

Ben's first instinct is to follow, but remembering the tangled spaghetti-scrawl of tunnels marked on the map, he doesn't fancy his chances. He knows the shafts beneath the escarpment twist and splinter deep underground. It's too dangerous to pursue his suspect alone. How could he possibly find them, let alone apprehend them? As much as he wants to play the hero, he knows what he must do.

Leaving everything where it is, he scrambles out through the grate into the muted morning and checks his phone for a signal. Nothing.

Cursing, he slips and slides his way back down the narrow trail and across the quarry basin, until one bar flashes on his phone. It's enough. With his adrenaline still pumping, he hits speed dial.

Khan's voice, when he answers, is sleepy, as if he's caught him mid-yawn. "Chase. Before you start, I know you're worried but she's—"

"Chief," Ben cuts him off, "listen. I've found something—someone—hiding out in the stone tunnels near the quarry."

"You're in the woods?" Khan is immediately alert, his voice grave.

"You can reprimand me later. But there's evidence everywhere. A camp. Sarah's phone. We need a search team now. Officers. Dogs. Trust me, Chief, you need to come. Now."

Chapter 25

Wednesday, 7:30 a.m.

They're out of peanut butter. Again. Ellie scrapes the jar, smearing the last dregs onto a piece of toast before she settles at the kitchen table with her earbuds in, losing herself in a steady crash of drums and guitars.

She's not got much of an appetite, but she needs to make a pretense of breakfast, if only to get her mum's watchful gaze off her back, so she sits for a while, allowing the music to do its work, masking all anxious thoughts trying to crowd her mind, filling any possible thinking space with noise. It's better than sitting in silence waiting for the phone to ring or the blue lights to appear outside the cottage. It's only a matter of time surely, before they drag her back to the station for round two.

Her mum stands at the kitchen sink, dressed for work in a long black dress and cream jacket. She gulps a cup of tea, then lowers the cup to the counter and starts talking, her lips moving fast. She gestures at Ellie's plate and Ellie nods. She has no idea what she's just said but her mum is still speaking and Ellie nods again, hoping it's enough.

It's not. She gestures for her to remove her earbuds.

"Did you sleep?"

Ellie nods.

"And do you think you might go into classes today?"

Ellie chews her lip. "I'm sure everyone's had a lovely time gossiping about me behind my back, but I guess I should face the music sometime. I'll look even more sus if I hide."

"You walk into school with your head held high."

Ellie doesn't answer. She plays with some stray toast crumbs on the table, moving them around with the tip of her finger.

"How's your bedroom?"

Ellie shrugs. "They went through everything."

Rachel takes up her cup again and eyes Ellie keenly over its rim. "Remember, you don't have to tell any of your friends anything you don't want to. What happened yesterday in the police station can stay private. OK?"

Ellie nods again.

The worried crease between her mum's eyebrows deepens.

"What?"

"I need to ask you something. Can you put your phone down?"

Ellie obliges with a sigh.

"Last night, on the way home, you said something about Mr. Crowe."

"What, that he's a weirdo?"

"Yes, that."

Her mum holds her cup so tightly that her knuckles are blanching white. Jeez, thinks Ellie. Her stress levels are even higher than her own. "I know." Ellie sighs. "It wasn't kind. I won't say it again." She attempts to return to her phone, but her mum isn't finished.

"No, it's not that. I was wondering if you'd ever heard anything said about him? If any of your friends or fellow students had any reason to think him . . . I don't know . . . a little . . . odd or . . . inappropriate?"

Ellie narrows her eyes, suspicious. "You only have to take one look at Mr. Crowe to know he's a little odd."

"Yes, but perhaps you've heard something around campus? Rumors, I don't know."

"Do you mean that thing about him wandering around at night spying on girls?"

"What?" Her mum visibly pales. "Spying on the female students?"

"Mum, you know what school's like. Especially this one," she adds under her breath. "Every day there's a new rumor doing the rounds. People like to make stuff up and someone like Mr. Crowe . . . he's kind of an obvious target, don't you think?"

"But who's saying these things?"

"I don't know. One little whisper and suddenly it's wildfire all over school."

"Rumors like this can affect people's livelihoods." Rachel frowns. "You didn't think to mention it to me?"

Ellie rolls her eyes. "Jesus, Mum. Boundaries! I'm not your personal mole. You can't expect me to share every stupid rumor that goes around the school. It's hard enough being here with you, without everyone thinking I'm a snitch as well."

Her mum shakes her head. "But these are serious accusations, Ellie."

"They're hardly accusations. Just gossip. I think it could've been Sarah who said it, if you must know. It's common knowledge he likes to watch the school's sports games. It's said he's particularly interested in the netball matches, if you catch my drift. But like I said, I'm not your mole."

Her mum looks horrified. "But something like this should be reported."

Ellie throws her an exasperated look. "Mrs. Crowe's hardly going to hear anything bad said against her own husband, is she?"

Fed up with the circular nature of the conversation, Ellie reaches for her earbuds and jams them back in. She glances up once or twice and sees her mother's worried frown as she washes her teacup in the sink, but then, thank goodness, she is waving goodbye, heading out the front door with her laptop bag swinging from her shoulder and that pinched frown still creasing her face.

Relieved to have reclaimed her solitude, Ellie takes a nibble of her toast. She doesn't like being a bitch to her mum. She hates seeing that wounded look on her face. It's just ever since her dad moved out, it's been so intense. Her mum hovering over her, all soft sighs and searching looks, like she's entertaining some fantasy that at any minute they're going to turn into the Gilmore Girls, all cute café breakfasts and movie nights in matching pajamas, and surely they both know that's never going to happen?

It's obvious her mum feels guilty about the way things have ended up, and she can see how hurt she is about Chrissie, because truthfully, she's hurt too. And now a baby? What the fuck? It was so gross. So unnecessary. Like her father was trying to erase them both, whitewashing all his past mistakes with a perfect new family. It felt like rejection of the worst kind.

She forces down another bite of toast, the bread like cardboard in her mouth, as her phone pings with a message. She swipes at the screen.

If you go down to the woods today . . .

She freezes, the phone suddenly white-hot in her hands. It's another message from sally@inthewood. She waits, knowing there'll be more.

Naughty, naughty girl . . .

A stab of fear hits her.

You just can't help yourself, can you?

One foot out of line . . . one misstep . . .

Sally will punish you.

She glances out the kitchen window to where the autumn foliage droops in the subdued morning light. The surrounding hills cast a heavy shadow. Someone could be out there right now, watching her, waiting for her to leave the cottage. She feels alone and exposed. Vulnerable. Prey to an unseen hunter. A mouse awaiting the swipe of a claw.

What was it her mum had asked her the night before? *If you'd like to speak to someone . . .*

Who can she talk to about *this*? Certainly not Jasmine. Ever since Saturday night, Jas has been distracted by Saul. Fawning over the boy like he was some bloody sex god. She'd seen them yesterday morning, sneaking around, all whispers and stolen kisses. Right now, Ellie doesn't fancy her chances of getting Jasmine to take anything she says seriously.

Danny had always been nice to her. He was nice to everyone. Only Danny can barely look at her now. She knows he blames her for his argument with Sarah, which is rich, given how Sarah behaved with Connor. You'd think he'd have seen for himself that night what a manipulative cow she was, without Ellie having to show him the actual evidence on Sarah's phone. More fool her for assuming he'd want to know that his crush was treating him like a simp. If he wants to deflect his guilt for leaving Sarah in the woods that night onto her, then that's on him.

So, if it's not Jasmine or Danny, who else is there? Her dad's busy playing house with Chrissie. Busy with his work. Her mum was too close to everything . . . but maybe she had a point. Maybe she could talk to her tutor, Edward Morgan? Of all her teachers, he'd always been the nicest, the most engaged, the one who'd seemed to take an interest in her right from day one, when he'd interviewed her for the sixth-form scholarship program.

"Very clever," he'd told her, thumbing through her portfolio, murmuring approval at her paintings and stenciling. "I like the way you see things. The way you subvert the expected and turn everything on its head. And these," he'd added, pointing to a series of sketches inspired by the famous graffiti sites in Bristol, "these are wonderful. Very exciting."

At that first interview, she'd sat in the art studio looking around at the incredible facilities, the immaculate workstations and tall wooden easels, the brushes and paints, the trees swaying gently beyond the floor-to-ceiling windows through which spring sunshine fell and bathed them in its warm glow. Despite herself, she'd felt a small, thrumming excitement build. "You paint too?" she'd asked.

"I do. In my spare time. It's my release." He'd nodded at a painting behind his desk. "That's one of mine."

Ellie had stared at the canvas, captivated by a landscape washed in moody grays and blues. "It's amazing."

She'd walked into her interview feeling less than lukewarm about the idea of attending Folly View, but it was Edward Morgan who'd convinced her to push aside her worries, and when the scholarship offer had landed on their doorstep in its stiff white envelope with the folly logo stamped on the reverse, Ellie knew she'd already decided to accept. Edward was a teacher who would inspire her, a teacher who would help her produce her best work. And if she was going to get into a competitive graduate program like the one at the prestigious University of the Arts London, she'd need someone like him behind her.

Since then he'd been a teacher and a mentor, pushing her to think a little more deeply, challenging her artistic practice, trying to draw her out of her shell and pull her into the school's extracurricular programs. "Come down to the set-painting day, Ellie. We need someone like you helping out. The whole cast will be there, but we could do with a 'proper' artist. Someone who understands color and perspective," he'd added. "If we leave it entirely to the actors, our Parisian streets will be *une catastrophe.*"

She'd been flattered, but had declined. She knew the Drama department types. Loudmouths and extroverts, girls like Sarah Lawson, the most confident pupils who insisted on being at the center of everything. It wasn't her vibe. She'd leave that to Edward and his crowd of adoring students. There were certainly enough of them, hanging on his every word, vying to be his favorite.

Eyeing the threatening messages on her phone, she decides to swipe the screen closed and turn it to silent. There's no one she can talk to. Not even Edward Morgan. If she ignores them, whoever is sending them will get bored. Eventually. Won't they?

She pushes her toast away. What little appetite she'd had is long gone.

Chapter 26

Wednesday, 8:30 a.m.

It feels to Ben as if backup takes forever to arrive, though in reality, it's probably no more than half an hour before the first response vehicles screech into the woodland parking lot with their blue lights flashing. There is a quick briefing, decisions about how to divide up the cave system, which entrances to man, the most effective route through the tunnels to flush out their target. Then another delay as they await the arrival of the dogs. Ben is itching to get going, concerned that every passing moment is another moment their suspect could be burying deeper into the tunnels.

His phone buzzes. It's Rachel, calling at the worst possible time. His finger hovers over the "decline" button, until he remembers his dream about Ellie. "Hey," he answers. "Everything OK?" The dog handler's white Transit van is pulling into the clearing.

"Ellie's fine. She's at home. That's not why I'm calling. I wanted to run something by you. Something that could be important to your case."

Ben watches the van navigate into a parking space, the sound of yelping and barking filling the clearing. "I've got to be quick,

Rach. I'm in the middle of something." He eyes the van impatiently, only half listening.

"It might be nothing, but I assume your team has looked into the school staff here. Specifically—"

"Rach," he turns his back on the assembled crowd and lowers his voice, "you didn't hear this from me, but we've got someone. A suspect. I'm in the woods now." He sees Khan's Volvo pulling into the parking lot right behind the dog van and lifts his hand in greeting.

"Oh, OK." She sounds surprised.

"It's good, Rachel. This should clear Ellie of any involvement."

"Yes." She still sounds distracted. "So, you guys checked the staff?"

"Yes, Maxwell spoke to all of Sarah's tutors and Khan had someone go over the teachers' files. Was there something else? Something specific?"

She hesitates. "No. I'll leave you to it. Sorry to bother you."

Hanging up, Ben goes to greet Khan. "Fill me in," says the DCI, stepping from his car, no preamble.

Ben brings his boss up to speed as they set off up the half-mile track back to the quarry. At the basin, the officers and detection dogs split into two groups. Ben veers left with the first group, back to the original access point he'd discovered, Khan tripping and stumbling behind him on the overgrown path. The others, as agreed, fan out around the far side of the escarpment where secondary points have been identified on the map. If they do flush out their suspect, they'll need to cut off any possible escape route.

Ben adjusts his headlamp and climbs through the grate, back into the cavern where the evidence he'd found earlier has already been secured and removed.

Khan is next to enter, letting out a low whistle as he takes in the cave walls. "Did Forensics get all this graffiti photographed?" he calls back to the chain of officers outside.

"Yes, Chief."

The dog leading the charge, a bouncy chocolate-and-white springer spaniel, is given the scent. She strains on her leash, eager to get going.

"Let's hope they haven't gone too far down," says Ben. "It could be hard going."

"Everyone ready?" asks Khan.

They edge through the cavern and start the precarious slide down into the tunnel, all daylight soon far behind them. The ceiling starts at a decent height, but it's not long before they are forced to crouch and stumble, the cool air and dank smell of earth wrapping around them like a musty blanket. The deeper they go, the greater Ben's unease. It's not like his vertigo, but more a general sense of claustrophobia, as if they are slowly being buried alive beneath mountains of solid earth.

Khan lets out a low whistle. "I had no idea these tunnels were here."

Ben is puffing now, crouched low, his hands trailing the damp stone walls as they move further down. "Most of the stone in Bath came from these hills. They used the caves as munitions stores in the war."

"You can see why. They're a perfect hiding place."

"Too perfect," adds Ben grimly.

They come to a split in the tunnel and the officers in front plow on, following the straining dog. Only Ben hangs back. He's not sure why, but something—instinct—makes him pause. If he were alone and seeking refuge in a cave, he would reach his limit, not wanting to go blindly further and further underground.

He stands still, then switches off his headlamp, allowing the pitch black to envelop him as the sound of the search party moves further away. He waits, trying not to let the oppressive atmosphere twist his imagination. Then he hears it.

It's a soft shuffling noise, a scrape against stone, but Ben's ears prick up. He's motionless, trying to control his breathing, wondering if he's got it wrong. Nothing more than a rat, a bat, or some other earth-dwelling creature he doesn't really want to identify, perhaps, but then he hears it again. Footsteps moving away in the direction they came from. Someone doubling back on them.

Ben waits, his heart hammering so loudly in his chest he feels certain whoever is in the tunnel must hear it too. Then, in one quick move, he flicks his headlamp on. There's a man, crouched low, making for the exit. He glances back at Ben, his panicked eyes illuminated in the headlamp beam, before making a dash for it.

Ben lets out a shout to alert the others, then follows, throwing himself back up the tunnel as fast as the narrow stone channel will allow. The man is scrabbling at the rock, but Ben closes the gap, then he's on him, shoving him down, pinning him to the dirt floor, and holding him there with the weight of his body.

The man flails and knocks Ben's headlamp, sending it skittering away, the light failing. Beneath him, the suspect is all skin and bone. He feels long greasy hair and bony joints jabbing at him. Ben squeezes, feels a sudden rage take hold, wanting to hurt the man just as he hurt Sarah, but the target cries out, and Ben releases his grip just a little as a rasping whisper curls through the dank air. "I took care of her," he hisses. "I made sure I took care."

Ben shoves the man's face into the ground. The unwashed stench rising off him makes his stomach churn. He averts his face as he slides handcuffs over the man's wrists. "You're under arrest for the murder of Sarah Lawson. You do not have to say anything.

But it may harm your defense if you do not mention when questioned something which you later rely on in court."

As Ben finishes reading the man his rights, the rest of the team emerge from the darkness behind, one of the officers moving in to escort the man from the cave, allowing Ben a moment to regroup and catch his breath. "Good job, Chase," he says, slapping his shoulder as he goes.

They trek back through the tunnel up to daylight, Ben trailing behind with one eye on the man's stumbling progress, following him out into the fresh air, grateful for the soft woodland colors and the weak sunlight. In the parking lot, Ben watches as the suspect is bundled unceremoniously into a waiting police van. He frowns as the doors are slammed shut. There's something about the man's posture, his shuffling gait, something nagging at him, like a tiny pebble caught in his shoe.

"So, what part of 'you're off the case' did you not understand, Chase?" asks DCI Khan, sidling up beside him.

"Just taking in the morning air, Chief."

Khan stands with his arms folded across his chest, trying to meet Ben's height and bulk. "I should be giving you hell, and not just because you dragged me out here again in these." He points down at his black brogues, the leather no longer immaculately polished but scuffed and smeared with mud. "You could've jeopardized the entire case with this cave stunt."

"If we'd left it to DC Crawford, we'd still be standing around scratching our arses. So much for having checked the cave entrances."

Khan tuts. "I'll be having a word."

"You got the phone?"

"What's left of it. Tech will need to work a miracle." Khan narrows his eyes. "Tell me," he asks, "what brought you out here to the cave?"

"Connor Carlisle phoned. He confirmed Jasmine Ware's story about someone watching the party from the tree line. I figured if our assailant had been scoping out the kids, but then evaded the boys' search, it made sense that a cave could be the nearest hiding place. It seemed worth another look."

Khan throws him a begrudging look. "Good police work."

Ben hesitates. "Let me interview him."

Khan frowns.

"It makes sense," Ben persists. "We're overstretched. Ferguson is still off sick. Maxwell's been flat out at the school and you sure as hell don't want Crawford doing it. Put me back on the case."

Khan sucks his teeth and Ben can see he is wavering.

"This arrest changes everything," Ben presses. "You know it. Ellie shouldn't be a suspect. Let me back on."

Khan nods. "Fine. We'll interview him together. I'll see you back at the station."

Ben punches out a message to Chrissie as he heads to his car. *Called into work. Could be a long day. Sorry babe.* Seconds later, two blue ticks light up next to the message. He waits for the typing dots to appear, but nothing comes. Chrissie's online status blinks at him, then disappears.

The adrenaline is beginning to fade as he pulls out of the parking lot. It's a massive leap forward in the case. Whoever their suspect is, Ben is hopeful they'll get him talking. They need a confession. It would certainly help to speed things up while Tech works on the phone. It's good news. The school and the local community should rest easier tonight knowing there is a man in custody. So why, Ben wonders, catching his own worried face in the mirror, does he still feel on edge? Why, when he thinks about the disheveled man they'd hauled away in cuffs, does he feel as if something has escaped him? As if something isn't right?

Chapter 27

Rachel is almost at the administration building when she senses a presence behind her. A dark car, its engine revving loudly at her back. She steps up onto the edge of the road to continue along the grass, expecting the vehicle to pass, only it doesn't. It stays at her shoulder, cruising ominously close, the deep thrum of the engine growling. Frowning, she turns to see a sleek green car, daylight glinting off the polished hood. She waves it past, but the car doesn't move.

There is something threatening in the standoff, something calculated. She squints at the windshield, but the driver's face is obscured by the cloudy sky reflected onto the glass, so she waits, all too aware of how vulnerable she is, how exposed. The car surges, forcing her to take another step back, then as quickly as it had seemed to appear, it accelerates away down the drive with a spray of gravel. What the hell? By the time she thinks to look for the license plate, it has gone.

She's still shaken as she arrives at her office to find two female students waiting for her in the corridor, their heads bent together, one blond, one dark. They look up as she approaches and she can see that one girl has been crying, her cheeks tear-streaked, her lower lip trembling. Year Sevens, small and wide-eyed, both still growing into their baggy blazers. "Are you here for me, girls?"

They nod in unison.

"Come in," she says, opening the door, flicking on the overhead light, relieved to see that the broken glass from the night before has been swept away, everything seemingly back in order. "How can I help?"

Rachel spends the next half an hour reassuring the girls that the ghost of "Sally" is not haunting their dorm room, and that it is, in fact, far more likely to be some of the more troublesome Year Nine boys playing bedtime pranks. She is also able to reassure them that the murderous screams they've heard echoing across campus at night are just the local foxes searching for a mate.

Rachel leans back in her seat. "I know it's a worrying time. I know you're feeling frightened, but you need to remember that Mrs. Crowe, all her staff, the police . . . everyone's doing their very best to make sure you're all safe."

She'd like to go further. She'd like to tell them that the police are at this very moment dealing with a very real, very human suspect, but it's not her place to share Ben's intel and all she can do is listen to them and try to allay their fears. "I'll talk to your matron. I'll ask her to keep an eye on the boys and I'm sure you'll find that the pranks settle down. In the meantime, you did the right thing coming to me. Any more scares, you come right back. OK?"

They nod in unison, conjuring weak smiles. Poor things. She'll have to raise this with Margaret. Nip it in the bud before the whole traumatized school is imagining vengeful, screaming wraiths roaming the grounds.

Ushering the girls from her office, Rachel checks the time and decides it's best to seize the moment and brave the teachers' lounge. It's already been the strangest morning. The car. The frightened girls. She knows rumors will be flying about Ellie's interrogation at the station. She should show her face. It's important to defuse the gossip quickly; to prove they have nothing to hide. Nothing to be ashamed of.

To her relief, the teachers' lounge is relatively empty when she arrives. Just a couple of colleagues occupying a sofa near the window with their laptops, their heads bent together. They look up as she enters, the half smiles freezing on their faces as she gives them a nod, before they duck back to their whispered conversation. She supposes it's better than a welcoming party peppering her with questions. Coffee, she thinks. Act natural. Drink coffee. Pretend it's any other day.

It's taken her a long time to feel part of the school. That she wouldn't fit among a more traditional, staid faculty had been one of her key worries when she'd first been interviewed by Margaret Crowe for the job. Yes, she'd worked for head teachers like Margaret before: passionate, engaged, results-oriented, educators who believed in the potential of each and every student. But there was an intensity to Margaret Crowe that had stood out at the job interview. She'd sat across from the woman in her book-lined study, drinking loose-leaf Assam poured from a china teapot and nibbling on a crumpet, baked that morning (so she'd been told) in the school kitchens.

She'd seen the zeal in Margaret's eyes, almost feverish with excitement, as she'd talked about exam results and league tables, university admissions and prestigious prizes. She'd recited a spiel that Rachel sensed Margaret had recited many times before: that she saw it as the job of every single pupil and staff member to represent, enhance, and uplift the reputation of Folly View College.

Imus supra et ultra. The woman's bosom had swelled with pride as she'd quoted the school's motto: *we go above and beyond.*

"We're a family, Rachel," she'd told her, lifting the teacup to her thin, unpainted lips. "Yes," she'd added, with a light laugh, "I realize that makes me *mother*, but as I don't have children of my own, I devote myself entirely to Folly View. This school is a complex, deeply connected system, each of us with a vital role to play, to ensure our students thrive in a stimulating and caring environment. I want my staff to feel supported and challenged, and in return, I expect the very best from them." She'd let out a little laugh. "Even my husband has been roped into the *family*. He was a teacher too—retired now—but when he's not out walking or pursuing one of his little projects, you'll see him around campus, cheering on our sports teams, or out there with a broom or a screwdriver in his hands. He likes to keep busy. That's how it is here. We all step up. We all go above and beyond to make this school the very best it can be. There's not much I wouldn't do to maintain our high standards."

Rachel had nodded. The idea of Margaret as their "mother" seemed a little out there, but she couldn't argue with the woman's passionate ethos. "A family. I like that."

"Do you have a family, Rachel?" Margaret Crowe had asked, settling her cup back in its floral china saucer.

"I have a daughter, Ellie. Her father and I are recently separated."

"Would you be looking to send Ellie to Folly View?"

Rachel had smiled. "I saw your incredible art facilities on the tour. Ellie would love it here. Art's been her passion for a long time now. But even on your generous salary," she'd added hastily, with a regretful smile, "I'm afraid the fees here would be beyond what her father and I could manage."

"We are an exclusive school, yes, but we also understand the importance of nurturing young talent, regardless of personal status and income. We have an excellent and very generous scholarship program for exceptional young people whom we feel would be an asset to the Folly View community." She'd narrowed her eyes. "You should talk to our Head of Art, Mr. Morgan, if it's an option your daughter would like to explore. We couldn't promise . . ." she'd added.

"Of course not," Rachel had jumped in. "Thank you. It's definitely food for thought."

Rachel had left her interview that day feeling impressed and inspired, and perhaps even a little afraid too. She knew she was good at her job. She knew she had a talent for connecting with students, for getting them to open up and trust her. She respected Margaret Crowe's philosophy, her desire to foster a close school community, but could she meet her exacting standards? Could she deliver a student welfare program that would satisfy such a zealous boss, such demanding parents? And most importantly, did she really want to leave the underfunded state system to work in a school that supported the rich and privileged, that offered something "above and beyond" to those who could afford it? Even with the scholarship and bursary handouts, was it fair?

Rachel had wrestled with her self-doubt and her morals for several days, but when the job offer had arrived, with the salary a third higher than any she could receive at a state school, Rachel knew she couldn't turn it down. She told herself it didn't matter. In her line of work, personal and mental health issues, learning disorders, abuse and safeguarding issues could affect kids at every school up and down the country, no matter their parents' income or social status. Yes, her new boss was a little frightening, but perhaps Margaret's intensity came with the territory. When a school charged its families such exorbitant fees, there was bound to be an immense pressure resting on the head teacher's shoulders. The woman wore it like a badge of honor.

Rachel barely had time to find a clean mug and slide a coffee pod into the machine, when she senses someone bearing down on her: Margaret Crowe, no doubt using that eerie sixth sense of hers for knowing exactly where any member of staff is at any given time. She weaves between the furniture, like a formidable ship shunting smaller boats out of her way, her focus laser-beam-sharp on Rachel at the coffee machine. Rachel feels her stomach drop. She glances around, hoping for a friendly face to act as an unwitting buffer, an attempt to deflect from whatever's coming, but the other teachers are busy or still avoiding her, their heads bent low over laptops.

"I've been looking for you," says Margaret, an accusatory note in her voice as she pulls up in front of her, hands resting on wide hips.

"Here I am," she replies, with false cheer. "How can I help?" She braces herself, wondering if this is about Ellie's police interview, or perhaps about whatever Malcolm might have shared with her of their odd, late-night encounter.

Margaret leans in, her voice lowered. "How is Ellie?"

Rachel nods. This she's expected. "All fine," she says breezily. "She's home now. Just a few routine questions," she adds, aware of her colleagues in the corner craning their heads.

"It must've been frightening for the girl to be hauled away like that? It seemed rather heavy-handed of the police," she adds, with a pointed look.

Rachel musters a smile. "Oh, you know how it is with protective fathers. I think Ben wanted to frighten her a little. He was cross that she'd lied about attending the party, so he pulled a favor with his colleagues."

Margaret eyes her with concern, as if Ben's parenting skills should be seriously questioned, and Rachel feels a stab of guilt for throwing him under the bus. Still, better Ben than Ellie.

"Terrible business. I can't believe they thought she could be in any way—"

"I know," says Rachel, cutting her off. "Everyone was just doing their job."

"Of course," says Margaret smoothly. "Well, I'm glad to hear she's OK. There is something else I'd like to discuss," she adds, sensing Rachel's desire to escape.

Here we go, thinks Rachel, the image of Malcolm's face floating before her.

"Olivia Easton has decided to return to school today."

Rachel can't hide her surprise. "Gosh, that's brave. Does she feel ready?"

Margaret nods. "I've met with her father and he seems to think that returning to a more familiar routine, as far as possible, might help the girl. It's an important exam year, of course. I've reassured them that we'll do all we can to help Olivia through."

"Absolutely," Rachel says, though she isn't entirely sure about the timing. It's only been a few days. She'd have thought the Eastons would need time to process the traumatic events as a family, to find some safety and solace in their togetherness. The summer exams were still months away.

The two colleagues with the laptops are gazing across with interest at her and Margaret Crowe, their heads ducking back down like meerkats into burrows as soon as they realize they've been spotted.

Margaret's expression grows more serious. "I don't want Olivia to feel overwhelmed by the attention from the other students, so I suggest she meets with you first. I thought you might have some kind words or counsel you could share with the girl. If nothing else, you can reassure her that we're all here for her, in whatever capacity she needs. An open door, etcetera. Two o'clock today, OK?"

"I'd be happy to talk with her." She waits, braced, wondering if Margaret will mention her late-night run-in with Malcolm, wondering if he's tried to explain it away and how she might broach the sensitive issue of Sarah's file. But Margaret Crowe, it seems, is finished with her. She turns and marches purposefully away across the teachers' lounge, her stout heels clicking across the parquet as she delivers a brisk round of nods and hellos to the remaining teachers.

Perhaps Malcolm hadn't divulged anything to Margaret about their strange confrontation last night. Perhaps he'd avoided the subject with his wife entirely. And if so, wouldn't that make it all the more suspicious? asks a tiny voice in her head.

"My mother used to warn me about frowning like that."

The deep voice at her shoulder startles her from her thoughts. Turning, she finds Edward beside the coffee machine, empty cup in hand. "Our Fearless Leader seems to have you in her crosshairs. Everything OK?"

"Olivia Easton's returning to school today."

Edward raises an eyebrow. "So soon?"

She nods.

"That's brave."

"That's exactly what I said."

He presses a button on the machine and a shot of espresso is delivered into his mug. "I heard you and Ellie had a day of it yesterday." He throws her a sympathetic look. "Everything OK?"

Rachel shrugs. "News travels fast round here."

"Sorry. It was the police car. It caused quite a stir, Ellie being whisked off like that. Tough day, I imagine. Hopefully my little gesture wasn't too much?" He waits a beat. "Sorry, maybe it wasn't appropriate." He looks sheepish, adjusts his tie, then takes a sip of coffee, throwing her a searching glance over the rim of his cup. "I just wanted to do something nice for you."

The penny finally drops. "Oh! The flowers. I haven't thanked you. I'm so sorry." She's ashamed to realize his gift has gone unacknowledged. "I appreciate you thinking of me." She's surprised to see a flush rising on his cheeks.

"My flower-arranging skills aren't up to much."

"They're lovely. Quite the surprise. I'm sorry, my head's scrambled."

"You do look tired."

She throws him a wry smile. "Thanks."

"I didn't mean . . . You look nice. You always look nice."

She's mortified to feel her own face growing red.

"But you're OK," he presses, ". . . after yesterday?"

He's being so kind, his eyes full of sympathy, but she doesn't know what to tell him. She doesn't want to talk about Ellie or what her daughter divulged to the police yesterday. She's exhausted and confused and quite frankly she'd prefer to scrub everything from her mind for a few hours. But he is waiting, expectant. "I . . . we . . . Ellie gave an interview at the station. It's fine," she adds hurriedly. "She was at the party too. She'd lied to us." She throws her hands up. "Obviously it's not great, but the main thing is that she's done the right thing now."

"Is Ellie OK?"

"She's fine. I think I just need to forget about it all for a little while, if that's all right?" She gestures to the covert glances of her colleagues across the teachers' lounge. "Keep my head down."

"Of course."

He looks a little hurt and when she thinks about the flowers sitting on her desk, the delicate white buds with their paper-thin petals just starting to unfurl, she realizes she hasn't been very gracious. "How are you?" she asks, by way of apology. "There's such strange atmosphere on campus." She glances around. "So much fear and suspicion. Are you holding up OK?"

He shrugs. "I just want to support the students. Some of the girls seem especially affected."

"I had two Year Sevens come and find me earlier. Frightened out of their wits. I hope I helped but . . . " She shrugs. "I don't know."

"On that note, I'm glad to have bumped into you," Edward says. "I had an idea. Something we could do that might help the students. I wanted to run it past you."

She nods. "Shall we fix up a time to meet?"

"I can do one better than that. Why don't you come over to my place tonight? We can talk. I'll cook for you."

Rachel eyes him, a strange, warm sensation rising in her chest. Dinner? Is he suggesting a date? The last things she needs right now are the complications of a possible romance, navigating all those unspoken rules and insecurities. But he's staring at her with a hopeful look and she's struggling to think straight. His kindness. His brown eyes. Her brain is too tired.

"Nothing heavy," he adds, filling the long silence. "Just friends, sharing a bottle of wine. I'll rustle us up a bowl of pasta and take you through my idea for the students." He eyes her with concern. "I bet you haven't been cooked for in a while?"

"Does peanut butter on toast count?"

"That seals it." He laughs. "You need a night off. Seven o'clock?"

"I'm not sure . . ." She is thinking of Ellie at home, of leaving her to her own devices, but he doesn't give her a chance to protest, leaving her with a gentle squeeze of her arm and a promise to text his address, so that Rachel is left by the coffee machine, feeling a little outmaneuvered, and perhaps, she realizes with surprise, just the tiniest bit excited.

Chapter 28

Wednesday, 1:00 p.m.

The man isn't talking. He sits slumped in a chair, tight-lipped and silent with his head bowed, lank hair falling over his face. He doesn't move much, just his blackened fingers tugging at bloody cuticles, before crawling up his arms to pick at a series of weeping scabs. Long scratches. Caused by something sharp . . . like brambles . . . or fingernails, Ben realizes with a shudder. Judging by the stench filling the room and the black grime daubed on his skin, he can only assume the man's been sleeping rough in the woods for some time.

With the man's prints and DNA samples secured, the duty solicitor had arrived to consult with their suspect. The solicitor, a thin man in a worn, gray suit, had begrudgingly given them the go-ahead to proceed. "He's noncommunicative. Won't even give a name. I'll allow you to proceed while he remains calm. The first sign of trouble, though," he'd warned, "and I'll be calling for a health care professional to assess him."

Ben had taken the lead, reading the caution before diving in with his questions. "Please state your full name and date of birth for the record."

Silence.

"Can you confirm your whereabouts on the night of Saturday, October 31?"

Silence.

"What were you doing in Thorncombe caves?"

Silence.

"Were you camping in the woods?"

Nothing.

He slides a photo of the sleeping bag taken from the cave in front of the man. "Can you confirm that these are your belongings?"

Still nothing.

"Do you recognize this girl?" Ben slides a photo of Sarah Lawson across the table, but the man refuses to even look up.

"How did you come to have this mobile phone among your possessions?"

He doesn't look at the third photo either, the one of the rose gold iPhone case shattered across the cave floor.

Ben tries a different tactic. "I understand your right to silence, but this is your opportunity to give your side of the story. If you continue like this, a court may draw their own inference as to why you are refusing to speak."

Ben waits. Nothing. Round and round he goes, a carousel of questions that raise not even the barest flicker of interest from their suspect. He might as well be talking to a brick wall.

Ben throws his hands up in exasperation, then makes a show of reaching for his cell phone to check the time. One hour and they're getting nowhere. He lays the phone on the table with a heavy sigh and reaches for his cup of water. There's a flicker of movement across the table. The suspect lifts his head, watery eyes peering between stringy hair as his gaze comes to land on Ben's phone.

It's as if he's received an electric shock. The man's body stiffens, then he is rocking back in his chair, raising his fists and beating them against his skull over and over. "Punish, punish, punish," he yells in time with his blows.

The duty solicitor slides back in alarm. "I think we should stop the interview here."

Shit. Ben knows how this is going to go. Any moment now, the suit is going to demand an assessment. They'll lose their guy into the health system and the confession they need for Sarah's murder will slip away. He throws a desperate look at Khan. He can't be the only one to recognize the significance of the man's raving. Khan gives him a small nod.

Ben leans forward, his hand still wrapped around the plastic cup. "Just tell us, is this the first girl you've killed, or are there others out there?"

"Chase," says Khan, a warning note in his voice, but Ben's question seems to have flown like an arrow straight to a bull's-eye.

The suspect's arms fall to his sides and Ben sees, for the first time, a strange marking on his upper forearm, the word "PUNISH" etched into the soft part of the skin, like a scar carved by a blunt knife.

The man lets out a low groan. The room stills in anticipation. "I didn't mean to hurt her," he says, his voice a graveled whisper. "Don't make me go back." He lifts his head and for the first time meets Ben's gaze. "I don't want to go back there."

Seeing his eyes, hooded and bloodshot, but alarmingly blue, an unexpected memory floats into Ben's consciousness and slots into place, like a key sliding into a rusty padlock. Ben does a double take.

He is painfully thin now, his hair much longer and so caked in dirt that it's hard to reconcile him with the man he'd last seen in a courtroom dressed in a misshapen brown suit, dark hair shaved close to his scalp, but Ben knows those eyes—that face. He'd know them anywhere. They were burned into his mind five years ago when he'd sat at the back of a courtroom and watched a judge sentence him for another death.

The plastic cup in Ben's hand collapses beneath his fist, sending water shooting across the table. Khan jumps back in his seat. "Chase! What the—?"

The duty solicitor, already on edge, calls out in alarm as Ben slides his chair back with a loud screech. A ferocious pulse beats in Ben's temples, his hands still clenched. He wants to lunge across the table and grab the guy, every muscle and tendon in his body straining with rage.

"Chase?" Khan warns.

It takes every fiber of Ben's being to resist the urge to pummel the man to within an inch of his life. Instead, he turns on his heel and leaves the room.

"For the purposes of the tape, it's 2:17 p.m. and DS Ben Chase is leaving the interview," Khan announces, before the door slams shut behind him.

Ben paces the corridor, tugging at the collar of his shirt, until Khan comes out to join him. "What the hell just happened?" Khan asks.

Ben feels all his suppressed rage and grief rising like a tide, threatening to overwhelm him and send him straight back into the room where he knows he will do something very stupid. He shakes his head, trying to clear the thought. "I can't go back in there."

"Why not?"

"Because I know him. It's the man who killed my sister."

Chapter 29

Olivia Easton arrives just after two. She taps quietly on the door, her nervous gaze sweeping the office, before taking one of the armchairs Rachel indicates. "I thought we could sit here," Rachel says. "These old rooms are so drafty. It's cozier by the fire."

It's not the first time Rachel has offered counseling to a grieving student. Over the duration of her career, she's met with students dealing with all manner of loss. Divorce. Illness. The death of a family member. Only today feels different. Sitting opposite Olivia, studying her stricken face and rigid posture, Rachel would be the first to admit she feels daunted, perhaps even a little out of her depth. It's one thing to try to help a child grieving a beloved family member, but it's another thing entirely to counsel a student through the aftereffects of a violent crime. The landscape they are about to navigate together feels charged and complex and, to make matters worse, Olivia looks less than happy to be sitting with her. She looks for all the world as if she would gladly burrow into the cushions and disappear.

Rachel clears her throat. "I know it wasn't your idea to meet, Olivia, but Mrs. Crowe thought this might be a good chance for us to talk about the support the school can offer you, and for you and I to have a little chat, if that would be helpful?"

Olivia's face is downcast, her blond hair pulled back into a neat ponytail at the nape of her neck, a few loose strands framing her pretty face, but there are signs of her distress, for anyone looking for them. Rachel sees them in the girl's chewed fingernails, the ink-colored shadows beneath her eyes, the restless foot tapping the floor.

"We don't have to talk about anything you don't want to," Rachel continues. "Think of this as a safe space, whenever you need it."

Olivia purses her lips. Rachel waits, but the girl remains silent, the only sound the soft drumming of her foot against the floor-boards. Rachel decides to start on safer ground. "How are you feeling about returning to school today?"

The girl shrugs. "I don't know."

"I imagine it's bringing up a lot of feelings for you?"

Olivia turns her face to the window. Outside, the day is flat and gray. A log spits in the hearth. Rachel wonders again if Mr. Easton and Margaret Crowe have got it wrong; if it's too soon for Olivia to be back. The girl is clearly still in shock. But after a long moment, she does speak.

"I guess I feel numb. But I'd rather be here than sitting at home."

"How are things at home?"

Olivia turns back to meet Rachel's gaze. "Lonely. Suffocating."

Rachel nods, but leaves space for her to explain.

"Diana's crying all the time. Dad's locked away in his study, stressed about the development and the protestors trying to stop it. Mum's doing . . . well . . . what Mum does. And Sarah's room just stands there. Exactly as she left it. I go in sometimes, just to check it's real." She bites her lip. "That she's really gone."

She can feel Olivia's loneliness as an almost tangible presence. It hangs over the girl like fine gauze. And that comment about her mother. She makes a note to circle back later. "You're hoping school will be a distraction?"

Olivia's brow creases. "Maybe. I mean, not really. It doesn't matter where I am, does it? Sarah's still . . . gone. And all these feelings I have, well . . ." Her hands return to worry the necklace at her throat. "They're a part of me, aren't they?" She closes her eyes, her jaw clenched, lips trembling. "The worst thing is that the person I felt closest to, the only one in the whole world I felt comfortable talking to, has just . . . *vanished*." Olivia's bottom lip trembles.

"You miss her."

Olivia's head jerks up, and for a split second she looks confused, but then she softens. "I keep expecting to see her. To hear her laugh. To have her burst into my room and tell me it's all a horrible joke." She swallows. "But it's not, and nothing I do will bring her back."

"I know how close you two were." Rachel waits a moment. She can see Olivia is wrestling to control her tears. "What's coming up for you as we sit here?"

The girl shakes her head.

"It's OK, Olivia. I'm not here to judge you. I'm here to listen. To help, if I can."

Olivia lets go of the pendant and burrows her hands into the sleeves of her school blazer. She lets out a long sigh. "I can't talk to you. I can't talk to anyone. It's too hard."

"You say the person you felt closest to has gone. If you could talk to Sarah, what would you say?"

Olivia glances at Rachel and shakes her head.

Too much, Rachel senses. Back off. The girl is standing at a precipice, barely holding herself together. "Losing someone we love can feel cruel and unfair. Our grief manifests in all manner of ways. Anxiety. Fear. Anger. Guilt. We can feel robbed of everything that made us feel happy, safe, and secure."

Olivia shudders at this and Rachel wonders if she's made a connection.

"That's exactly how it feels," says Olivia. "My life feels split in two now. There was the before, when I thought I understood everything, thought I saw how things were going to be. And now there's the after, where Sarah's dead and everything's been stripped away. It feels as though everything that was good in my life died with her."

"That must be hard. Disorientating."

"I feel like there's a version of me on one side of that night. And a completely different person now standing on the other. All I want is for things to be how they were." She bows her head. "How I thought they were." She shrugs. "I have no idea who I'm supposed to be . . . what I'm supposed to do."

"Why don't you tell me about Sarah?"

Olivia lets out a slow breath. "I hate being an only child. My parents are . . . busy. Distracted. It's complicated."

"Tell me. It's OK—this won't go anywhere. Your mother," Rachel asks gently, "are the two of you close?"

Olivia shrugs. "Not really. It's hard to get close to someone who isn't really there most of the time."

Rachel leans forward. "How do you mean?"

"She used to be the life and soul. She was always out—with friends, with the horses, at riding shows, throwing parties. Dad used to call her his 'secret weapon,' his 'social butterfly.' But ever since the fall, she's been different."

"The fall?"

"She was competing at the Badminton Horse Trials when she was thrown by one of our dressage horses." She glances up at Rachel. "It was bad. She was in hospital for weeks. Ever since, she's had to take pills . . . for the pain. They space her out . . . help her to sleep." Olivia sighs. "Maybe I should try them."

Rachel frowns. "I wouldn't advise it. What about your dad? Can you talk to him?"

"I used to. Dad's always been focused on his work, but he's even busier now. The housing development is all he can think about. He's been working on it for months, and just when it looked like he'd got it over the line, a bunch of local protestors throw up a whole new set of problems for him. I know he's devastated about Sarah, but he can't seem to hold the two things in his mind. He locks himself away in his study, with his plans and his phone calls." Olivia's eyes flash with anger. "These people are demanding his attention, right when we need him the most. When *I* need him," she adds quietly.

She thinks about what Olivia has just shared, and can't help wondering if this is another reason why Mr. Easton might've supported his daughter's early return to school. "It sounds very lonely at home."

"It was. It is."

"Even more so without Sarah, I imagine?"

She nods. "I argued hard for Sarah to come and live with us. She hated her international school in Dubai. She'd fallen out with a bitchy crowd after her father died and I wanted her here with us. It seemed like a no-brainer. Living with Sarah was what I'd imagined having a sister would feel like. I didn't feel so alone."

Rachel nods. She doesn't want to interrupt, not now Olivia is talking more freely.

"And it was brilliant. She was a life force, you know? Full of

ideas. Full of enthusiasm. Everything became so much more interesting after Sarah came to live with us." She manages a faint
smile. "I felt . . . I felt different when she was around."

"Different how?"

"More confident, I suppose. Having someone to share things
with. She encouraged me to be bolder. To take risks. To go after
what I wanted. It was good to have someone to bounce my problems
off. She was always there. An ear to listen when I had problems. . . .
I talked to her about everything. School. Boys. My parents." Olivia
frowns. "And now . . . now it's all been ripped away. And now . . ."
The words tumbling from her mouth come to a sudden halt. She
lifts her gaze and stares at Rachel with imploring eyes. "And now
she's . . . dead." Olivia's lower lip trembles again, her eyes swimming,
the force of her grief palpable in the small room. "I'm so angry with
her," she says, her voice barely a whisper.

Rachel can see the girl's bewilderment and pain. All normal
grief responses. Without anyone yet identified to blame for Sarah's murder, it's understandable that Olivia might find herself raging at the person she trusted to be there for her, the one who left
her. "This wasn't Sarah's fault. And it certainly wasn't your fault,
Olivia."

Olivia shakes her head.

"Trust me, anger is a part of grief."

"I took her to the party and I . . . I got so cross. I told her
we should leave. She wouldn't listen to me and I . . . I . . ." Olivia's voice cracks. She drops her gaze. "I left her there." Her voice
cracks with emotion. "It's my fault."

Rachel leans forward in her chair. "Do you remember what
you just told me about Sarah?" When Olivia doesn't answer she
continues. "You said Sarah was a life force. Was she often per-

suaded to do things she didn't want to?" She asks the question gently.

Olivia shakes her head, eyes still closed. "No."

"Did you ask her to leave with you that night? Did you remind her of the curfew?"

Olivia nods.

"Did you force Sarah to do *anything* she didn't want to do?"

Olivia is shaking her head again. "Sarah was in charge."

"Sometimes, terrible things happen—things beyond our control. It's hard to accept it when they do, but I want you to try to remember this conversation when you're working through all these big emotions. It's normal to feel responsible in some way, to question what we might have done differently, to feel angry, guilty even; but sometimes we have to accept that bad things happen to good people. It's hard, but we have to treat ourselves with the compassion and care that we know our loved ones would wish for us."

Olivia slumps back in the armchair, eyes closed. Her hands, Rachel notices, have returned to her throat, her fingers rubbing the broken heart pendant hanging there. When she opens her eyes, Rachel is disappointed to see that Olivia still doesn't look convinced. "I can't see the point of anything anymore. It's my final year," she shrugs and glances up at Rachel, "but so what? I don't care about the future now. It doesn't feel like there is one. Not for me. Not now."

Rachel doesn't like to hear Olivia talking like this. "Do you have anyone else to talk to?"

Olivia looks teary-eyed at the suggestion.

"Any other close friends?" Rachel presses. "A boyfriend, perhaps?" From Olivia's flinch, she can see she's touched a nerve. "What happened?"

"He wasn't the person I thought he was." She presses her lips together.

"Has Sarah's death scared him away? Sometimes people aren't very good at handling grief. They worry they're going to make things worse for you, so they retreat."

Olivia shakes her head. "I don't want to talk about him."

The agony of young love. Rachel feels sorry for the girl. She can't help thinking about Ellie, about her own isolation. "I'm sure there are lots of students who'd like to support you. It can sometimes look as though everyone else has their life sorted, but it's not often the case. What do you think Sarah would say to you right now? What do you think she'd want you to do?"

Olivia gives a small shudder. "I have nightmares. I see her in the woods. Alone at the folly."

Rachel kicks herself for her misstep, for conjuring a frightening image. She thinks of Ellie's night terrors, how she'd found her in bed, dazed, shaken, and sweaty. It would be the same for Olivia. They're all frightened. All fearful of the possibility of a deranged killer on the loose. "I know it's scary, Olivia, but the police are working hard. It may not be too much longer before they get a breakthrough in the case." Seeing the girl's head swing up, she kicks herself. She shouldn't have said that. "What I mean is that they're doing all they can to find the person responsible. I hope you know that. In the meantime, my door is always open to you."

Rachel watches the girl rise from the armchair, a listless energy seeming to trail her to the door. She looks so dejected, so alone. It's the thought of her returning home to a huge, empty house with two parents who barely notice her that breaks Rachel's heart. She wishes she could do more. "Olivia," she calls, beckoning her back. She goes to her desk and scribbles on a notepad, tearing off a sheet and holding it out to her. "I don't usually do this, but here. This is my mobile number. If you start to feel overwhelmed . . . like you can't see the point, please call me."

Olivia manages a weak smile, her gaze drifting from Rachel to her cluttered desk. "Pretty," she says, with a nod of her head.

Rachel turns and sees what has caught Olivia's attention: the white roses and the card still propped against the vase.

"You were married to the detective, weren't you? The one that came to our house. DS Chase?" She swallows. "He seems nice."

Rachel nods. "We're not together anymore." She says it flatly, hoping that Olivia isn't going to press for details of the investigation, but the girl's curious gaze has already returned to the flowers.

Shit, thinks Rachel, realizing Edward's note, signed with his artistic flourish, is right there for the girl to see. She kicks herself. First Malcolm. Now Olivia. The gossip will be all the way round the school by tea. "Here," she says, waving her number, desperate to distract Olivia's attention. "Call me if you need anything. We're all here for you."

Olivia tucks the note into her blazer pocket. "Not everyone," she says, her eyes welling suddenly. "Not the one person I most want to talk to." She turns as if to make for the door, then hesitates. "Is he good at his job?"

Rachel frowns, before realizing Olivia is still talking about Ben, not Edward. "Very. One thing I can say about my ex-husband is that he's a ferociously stubborn man. I know he's doing his utmost to keep you all safe."

Olivia nods, but she doesn't look reassured. "Do *you* think he'll catch whoever did this?"

Rachel nods. "He won't stop until he does."

She wishes that her reassurance could be enough, that she had made a difference, but as Olivia slips through the door, she can see the anxiety in the girl's face and knows that their time together has barely scratched the surface of her emotions. She's never felt so useless at her job in her life.

Chapter 30

Something about the cottage feels off. Ellie is at the kitchen table, trying to claw back some of the time she's lost, attempting to focus on some of the more intricate details of her artwork, but her paintbrush won't cooperate. Every stroke feels labored, every dab of paint wrong. There's a tension in her shoulders and her gaze shifts constantly to the window, where outside, dusk is already falling. The gray day mirrors her mood. Dark. Heavy. Oppressive. Beyond the unruly garden the trees loom, skeletal branches waving in the breeze, their last leaves releasing with a silent gasp before tumbling away. It's like the walls of the cottage are closing in on her, the wooded hills crowding closer, the air she breathes thick and cloying.

It had been another bad night. A night disturbed by a dream of Sarah, standing at the end of her bed, blood pouring down her face, flowing onto her hands, hands she held out to Ellie, first imploring, then reaching, pulling at the covers as she'd begun to crawl up the bed toward her.

Ellie had woken pinned by her sheets and drenched in sweat, and now all she can think about is Sarah, and that night in the woods, and what she wouldn't give to go back and do everything differently.

That stupid Ouija board. She wishes she hadn't watched their game, the way the jar had slid across Saul's improvised board. Everyone had said it was Sarah pushing it, but what if it hadn't been? What if there was an evil spirit lurking in the woods? The ghost of a murdered girl. It wasn't outside the realm of possibility, was it? The local stories had to be rooted in some sort of truth.

A noise outside the cottage draws her attention, a sharp, snapping sound, like a branch breaking. She goes to the window but there's nothing to see, just the trees swaying in the gusting wind, leaves drifting across the small, unkempt lawn. The sky threatens rain. She eyes the woods. If anything, the trees look even closer now. God, she's properly losing it.

Returning to her seat, she grabs her phone and opens a search browser.

Do Ouija boards work?
Evidence life after death?
Are ghosts real?
First signs of madness.

She scrolls the results but finding nothing of comfort, gives up and cycles through reels and posts from the activists she follows, images of protestors gluing their hands to superhighways and masked women splashing paint over a valuable artwork in Paris. She knows it's radical. Divisive even. She knows what her parents think, their worries. But isn't that the point? The world is sliding toward an irreversible ecological crisis and no one is listening. They *have* to get extreme. If they lose this fight, it's over. Start small, start local. That's what all the accounts she follows tell her. Drive change in your own community.

There's another sound outside, this time closer. She glances out, just in time to catch the wisp of something gliding past the window. Something white and indistinct, fleeting, like a feather in the wind. A chill comes over her. When her phone beeps, she knows who it will be before she's even checked. sally@inthewood.

How did you feel in the woods that night?

Blood on your hands.

Did it make you feel good?

Did it make you feel strong?

Ellie swallows, a frightening thought rising in her mind as she watches the typing dots at the top of the screen. Whoever is sending these messages knows about her fight with Sarah. Which isn't possible. The only people who know are her parents, and the police . . . and Sarah, of course.

You like to destroy things, don't you?

Unfortunately for you, so do I.

She swallows. A cold dread creeping over her. *Blood on your hands.*

Whoever else had been up at the folly that night must've been watching. Waiting. Whoever it was had seen Ellie fight with Sarah, then waited for her to leave.

Ellie rises from her seat and darts about the cottage, drawing the curtains, shrouding the ground floor in a gloomy half-light. Whoever is out there, whoever hurt Sarah, now seems to have her squarely in their sights.

Chapter 31

If it wasn't already too late, Rachel would cancel. The thought of a hot bath, a glass of wine, and a family-sized bar of chocolate on the sofa holds far more appeal than heading out into the cold, blustery night for dinner. Instead, like the accommodating people pleaser she is, she finds herself driving through Thorncombe in the pelting wind and rain, following the blue line on her GPS to an address on the far edge of town.

Ellie had been hidden away upstairs when she'd gotten home from work. The doors were locked and the curtains drawn, a few of her paintbrushes and pens scattered across the kitchen table, but Ellie was shut away in her bedroom and seemed to prefer to stay there rather than come and talk. Popping upstairs to let her know she'd be heading out again, Rachel had found her crouched on her bedroom floor, a wild array of paint and paper around her, her cell phone clutched in her hands. "Don't you knock?" Ellie had shouted, pressing the phone to her chest.

"Sorry, I was calling. You didn't hear. I'm supposed to go out, but I can cancel if you'd rather I was here tonight?"

Ellie had seemed to hesitate, and for a split second, Rachel had wondered if she were going to ask her to stay. "Go," she'd said eventually. "I'm fine."

"You sure?" She'd gone across and brushed Ellie's hair from her eyes, bending to kiss her forehead in a way she hadn't done in such a long while, treating her like a little girl, half surprised when Ellie hadn't flinched away, but leaned in, a light, warm pressure against her thigh. She supposed the past twenty-four hours had made them both feel more vulnerable. They'd certainly reminded Rachel that Ellie would always be her little girl, no matter what. "Make sure you lock the doors, OK?"

Ellie had rolled her eyes, the moment of unity gone.

A fierce wind buffets the car, sending a shower of autumn leaves spiraling onto the windshield as she navigates the deep puddles and potholes, heading along a remote lane to the mysterious sounding "Rookery" that Edward had sent her the address for. She's dressed down in jeans and an old cashmere sweater and done little more than brush her hair and apply a faint trace of lipstick, determined not to treat the evening like a date. Just two colleagues meeting for a conversation about the students and a bite to eat. Edward is being kind, and God knows she could do with a little kindness right now.

As she drives, she considers what she might've said, had Ellie bothered to ask where she was going. She would've told her the truth, though she knows it would've gone down like a lead balloon. Ellie would've considered her mother fraternizing with her favorite teacher yet another example of Rachel trampling all over their boundaries. Because, of course, it was unthinkable that Rachel might want to make her own friends at Folly View. In Ellie's eyes, everything Rachel did was purely to humiliate or embarrass Ellie. Classic solipsistic teenager.

The lane narrows into a series of hairpin bends, the hedgerows on either side pressing increasingly close, and Rachel is just beginning to wonder if she has taken a wrong turn when a tall, thin building looms out of the dark, two arched windows on the ground floor lit up like eyes. Peering out at the crooked house through the car's wildly swinging wipers, she notices it's attractive in a Gothic style, with leaded pane windows and an unusual spiked turret room jutting from the second floor. Seeing it for the first time on a wild, windswept night, it brings to Rachel's mind fantastical fairy tales and witches cackling on broomsticks.

She parks in the lane and ducks to avoid the rain as she follows a bank of ghost-white silver birches up a weed-strewn path. Closer now, she notices a faint glow behind the windows on the high, projecting turret. She wonders if Edward is up there, if he'll hear the chime of the old-fashioned doorbell as she fusses with her damp hair.

After a long moment, a blurred shape appears behind the stained-glass door pane. "Perfect timing," he says, ushering her inside with a flash of his white teeth. "What a night. Let's get you out of the rain."

The exterior of the house had hinted at a place trapped in time, dusty rooms and moth-eaten carpets. She's expecting Addams Family–style decor, but inside it's quite different. As Edward takes her coat, she glimpses a room with polished floorboards, a fire crackling in a hearth, and a low leather sofa, worn in an artful, vintage way. "Wow," she says, "your home's lovely."

"Thank you." He's wearing olive-colored trousers and a beige linen shirt, the color emphasizing the hazel flecks in his eyes. She sees his reciprocal yet subtle once-over and tugs self-consciously at her pilled sweater, suddenly wishing that she'd made a little more effort.

"Let's go into the kitchen," he suggests. "It's warmer in there with the Aga. I've already opened a bottle. Red OK?"

She nods. "Just a small one. Thanks."

Trailing him into the back of the house, she enters a sleek kitchen with an impressive range cooker and a long, mid-century walnut dining table extending toward two French doors, the glass panes casting their own pale reflections back at them. A candle flickers on the table beside a bowl of apples and an open bottle of wine. Scents of garlic and rosemary rise from the oven. The air in the room is close, intimate, as he pours two glasses. "Thanks for coming," he says. "It's nice to have the company."

"It's nice to be here," she says, and she realizes, with a jolt of surprise, that it is. After the last few days, the creeping claustrophobia of the campus, the cramped confines of the cottage, dealing with Ellie's lies and Ben's emotional land mines, Edward's house feels like a quiet, calm sanctuary. A break from the turmoil of the past few days. A chance to be Rachel, a person in her own right, not just a school counselor, a mother, or an ex-wife.

They "cheers" each other, his eyes meeting hers over the rim of his glass before she lowers her gaze and gulps at her wine, anxious that he might see how nervous she is, alarmed to find her heart racing. Stupid, she tells herself. It's just dinner. "How long have you lived here?" she asks, desperate to fill the sudden, intense silence.

"A couple of years. I inherited the house when my mother died."

"I'm sorry about your mum." She notices the streaks of green and brown on his fingers, dark against the stem of his glass. "Someone's been busy," she says, nodding at the paint.

"I was upstairs when you arrived. I lost track of time. It's not easy getting this stuff off."

She notices for the first time the framed landscapes hanging on the wall behind him, dappled trees and storm-swept valleys, moody, atmospheric scenes captured in oils. "Are these yours?" she asks, gesturing to the paintings.

He nods, looking a little sheepish. "All mine. Mum was a fan. I know they're not to everyone's taste."

"I like them," says Rachel, leaning in for a closer look. "They're brooding. Very Thomas Hardy."

"I've always been inspired by landscapes. Trees. Valleys. Moors. Big skies. I like to walk in nature. I find it helps to clear my head," he explains as he organizes plates and cutlery. Rachel moves to another artwork, this one a little different. A portrait of a familiar face. He looks a little younger, his olive skin still smooth around his brown eyes, but it's definitely Edward.

"Before you think me a complete narcissist," he says, noticing her attention, "I painted that for my mother's birthday. She requested a self-portrait. I keep meaning to take it down, but I see her disapproving face every time I think about it," he adds, with a soft smile.

"Don't take it down. It's great." She can see the brushstrokes, the subtle shading on his face, dabs of hazel in his brown eyes. Fox eyes, she thinks. "It's very expressive. I feel as though I'm looking right into you."

He steps closer, gazing at the painting over her shoulder. The hairs on her arms prickle at his proximity. "I'm not sure it was quite what my mother had in mind. She thought I looked 'troubled.'"

"Thoughtful, definitely." It takes her a moment to see it, but when she does, she's surprised that she hasn't spotted it right away—a dark figure looming behind. She wonders if it's supposed to be his shadow, but seeing Edward's painted expression, the look in his eyes, its meaning is suddenly clear as day. She's seen that exact look in another man's eyes. "You're grieving," she says, pointing to the shadow.

He nods. "You're the first person to see it. To understand. I painted this a few months after my father died. Our relationship was . . . complicated. He could be a difficult man."

Rachel can't take her eyes off Edward's haunted expression. "I don't know what I expected your art to be like," she adds, "but certainly not this. There's a darkness to it."

He nods. "We all have a propensity to darkness, don't you think?" He hesitates. "I suppose that's what I like to explore in my work. There's no light without shade."

"True. So what are you working on now?"

"I'm sure Ellie's explained the theme of their mixed-media module this term?"

Rachel is too embarrassed to tell him she knows nothing about what Ellie is working on, how anything more than a grunt or an eye roll these days is a miracle. "A little," she lies. "She can be quite secretive."

"Ellie's class are creating pieces inspired by their local environment. In turn, I've found myself inspired too. I'm using elements from the area to explore my work. I like the idea of interpreting the stories that inhabit a place, the ones that get woven into its history and passed down through the generations."

Rachel's gaze drifts back to the paintings on the wall. "Ellie said you were talented."

"Did she now?"

"Yes, you made quite an impression at her first scholarship interview."

"I'm flattered."

"You should be," she says. "She's at that stage when it's much easier to be scathing or cynical about everything than to show how much she cares."

Edward frowns. "Ellie doesn't strike me as that girl. I find her very engaged. I've seen her fired up about a number of subjects she feels passionate about. Inequality. Climate change. Art. Self-expression. I've chaired some quite heated debates in class between the students."

Rachel sighs. "I guess I'm not allowed to see that side of her anymore. Since her father and I separated, she shuts me out of most things in her life. I think it's my punishment for the marriage failing."

"Or it could just be because you're her mum, and she's a teenager, and she's hurting to realize that life isn't always a fairy tale? That try as we might, we can't always stop bad things from happening. I think all our students have had a tough week facing that truth."

Rachel nods. "A very tough week."

When she turns to face him, she finds he's standing even closer, close enough that if she wanted to, she could reach out and straighten the shirt collar sitting slightly askew at his neck, close enough to run her finger along the smooth curve of his lips. The thought sends a shiver down her spine. She clears her throat. "It can't be easy finding the time to paint?" she says, trying to lighten the atmosphere.

"I try to prioritize my own work in the evenings. My studio is my refuge."

She remembers the light shining at the very top of the house. "The turret room?"

He nods. "There's incredible light up there, even on a gray day."

"I'd love to see it. It looks like an interesting space."

His smile falters. "Sorry, it's a mess, half-finished canvases everywhere. I'd be delighted to show you when the paintings are finished." He raises one eyebrow. "I'll give you a private viewing."

She hears the suggestion in his offer, but it doesn't mask his flat "no" and Rachel is embarrassed to have overstepped. *Of course* he wouldn't want to show her his work in progress. Why would he be any different to Ellie?

A timer pings on the oven and Edward busies himself, draining pasta and retrieving a casserole dish, plating up thick strands of tagliatelle with a lamb ragu, sprinkling parsley with a flourish.

"An artist and a cook? I'm impressed. This is delicious," she says, raising her glass at him.

"Thank you."

"You wanted to run an idea past me," she says, remembering the reason for the dinner, Olivia Easton's haunted face returning to her with a lurch. "I don't feel I've helped the kids at all this week."

"Don't be too hard on yourself. I see the way the students interact with you. You have a talent for connecting with them, for drawing them out of themselves."

"I could say the same about you," she teases, "the way they cluster around you on campus. Your groupies," she adds.

He frowns, a shadow passing over his face, and realizing that he may have misinterpreted her compliment as something suggestive, she hurriedly adds, "I didn't mean . . . just that the kids seem to like you. You relate well to them."

Edward visibly relaxes. "I thought you were suggesting . . ." He gives a half smile. "I've had to deal with the odd student crush in my time, but I'm always very careful."

"I'm sure." She's mortified to have implied otherwise.

"I don't think I do anything different from you. The secret is to treat them like young adults. To listen to them. To allow them a few freedoms. I know Margaret disagrees, but I don't see the harm in school skirts being raised a few inches or allowing the kids their headphones while they work in the art studio. It's the same for you, I'm sure. It's not one size fits all. You have to adapt your approach to the student in front of you. Allow them to be their own unique selves."

"Yes, that's true." Rachel swirls her wine, thick red liquid clinging to the sides of the glass. "So, this idea to help the students?" she prompts.

"Yes. I've been thinking about you and I combining forces to run a workshop, a space where the students can share their memories of Sarah. A safe place to talk, write, paint. To express themselves and process what's happened."

Rachel nods, thinking of Ellie's locked emotions and Olivia's shell-shocked face. "It's a good idea. I worry that some of them are bottling up the trauma."

"Exactly," says Edward, leaning forward. "I knew you'd get it."

"It would be important to tread gently," she warns. "We'd need Margaret's approval and to think about the timing." She twirls a strand of pasta on her fork. "Did you hear the police have made an arrest?"

Edward's eyes go wide.

"Ben told me this morning. They've taken a man into custody."

He leans back in his chair. "Thank goodness." His face is a picture of relief. "I did wonder if you might get the inside track on the investigation." He hesitates, before asking, "How are things with Ben?"

"Fine. Separation isn't easy, on any of us, but I think it's for the best. Things hadn't been good for a while. He's moved on. His girlfriend's having a baby," she adds, a little too brightly.

"Oh. That can't be . . ." He shakes his head. "Sorry, I shouldn't have brought him up. Just curious, I guess. Being married to a police officer, I imagine that's a tough life? Married to the job, isn't that what they say?"

Rachel nods. "Something like that. I'm relieved they've caught someone," she says, steering the conversation away from her failed marriage. "It should remove the suspicion and fear that's been building all week. Feeling that everyone's a suspect."

"Sounds as if you've had some theories of your own?"

Rachel twists the stem of her wineglass between her fingers. "It seems silly now . . ."

He leans forward again, conspiratorial. "Go on."

"I don't know if I should say. I don't want to contribute to idle gossip . . ." She trails off.

"Who are we talking about?"

She eyes him. "Malcolm."

Edward lets out an amused gasp. "Malcolm Crowe? Margaret's husband?"

She nods. "I know it sounds daft."

"Wow. He's an oddball, yes . . . and that stiff way he carries himself about the place, like a disapproving Victorian grandfather . . . but Malcolm? Really? Did you have any evidence?"

"Not exactly. I found him in my office late last night. It was all rather strange." She laughs. "My mind went into overdrive." She decides she doesn't want to mention the file on her desk. "And I saw him," she says, remembering, "the morning after Sarah's death. I saw him standing at the window of the Lodge just staring up at the woods. Almost as if . . ." She shivers. "Then there's the limp," she adds, with a raised eyebrow.

"He said he fell down the stairs."

"But remember what he said before the police spoke at the school assembly on Monday morning? He made some weird comment about children being in the woods. I was wondering . . .

how did he know they were in the woods that night? We didn't know for sure it was one of our pupils at that point."

"An assumption? He lives in the Lodge, right by the gates. He must see them come and go. He's no fool."

"See. Me and my overactive imagination make a terrible Miss Marple." She grins. "Poor Malcolm. Talk about casting aspersions. You mustn't tell anyone what I thought."

Edward stands and begins to clear their plates. "Why don't we sit by the fire in the other room? It'll be more comfortable."

At Edward's insistence, Rachel leaves him to clear the table and takes her wine into the lounge. The curtains are still open and the fire in the hearth has burned down to a warm amber glow. She throws another log onto the embers, stokes the flames with a poker. Turning back to the room, she lets out a sharp gasp. Something pale and round is pressed against the window, blurry behind the rain-streaked glass, a face that vanishes into the dark as soon as she's seen it.

"What's wrong?" Edward is standing in the doorway, his glass in his hand.

"I . . . I thought I saw something." She shakes her head. "Someone at the window."

Edward looks perplexed. "What? Who?"

"I'm not sure. They were only there for a split second . . ." She trails off. "I don't know."

Edward moves to the window and peers out into the darkness. "Are you sure?"

"No." She gives a little half laugh. "Perhaps it was a cat on the windowsill. Do you have a cat?"

"A cat?" He shakes his head. "No cat. No dog." Edward peers out again. "I don't see anyone."

"Maybe it was my reflection."

Edward pulls the linen curtains closed with a flourish. "Well, whatever you saw, it's gone now." He sits on the leather sofa and beckons for her to join him.

Rachel settles onto the cushions beside him. "All that talk of Malcolm. I've spooked myself. That's all." She shakes her head. "You know, I was convinced earlier this morning that a car was trying to run me down." She tells him with a hollow half laugh.

"A car?"

She nods. "It seemed rather threatening at the time, but I realized later that it could've been Mr. Easton. Margaret mentioned that she'd met with him to discuss Olivia's return. Maybe he was in a hurry to leave and just didn't see me? Lost in his own world. He's got a lot going on right now." She frowns, doubting herself and her interpretation. Everything is so jumbled, so heightened, it's hard to know what's real, and what's being magnified or manipulated through the lens of stress and anxiety.

Edward looks troubled. "If anything like that happens again . . . any worries . . . come to me. OK?"

In the muted light of the lounge, with the shadows drawing in around them and the fire crackling in the grate, the dark intensity in Edward's eyes reminds her of his self-portrait hanging in the kitchen. The angle of his body is pitched toward her, the paint-flecked hand resting on his knee almost touching her own. Her breath catches in her throat. The moment stretches. She wonders if he's going to kiss her, wonders if this is what she wants. She imagines reaching for his hand and drawing it to her in invitation. "I'll just . . . maybe I . . ." Her voice falters. She gestures to the door. "Could I use your bathroom, please?"

He nods. "Upstairs. Last door on the right. I'll put some music on."

Her hands are still shaking as she takes the creaking staircase, gripping the polished balustrade tightly as she climbs to a wide landing, a crimson carpet runner stretching away into the shadows of the hall. A series of violent landscapes—storm-tossed seas and windswept moors—adorn the dark, paneled walls. She hesitates at the top, already forgetting which door he'd said. *Last door*, she remembers, walking the length of the corridor to open the one at the very end.

Instead of a bathroom, she sees a staircase spiraling up into darkness above. Not the bathroom, she realizes. This must be the entrance to the turret room she'd spotted from the car. Edward's art studio.

Realizing her mistake, she pulls the door shut and tries another just behind her, finding the bathroom on her second attempt. Her reflection in the age-speckled mirror over the sink surprises her. Smudged lipstick. Wine-flushed cheeks. Wide, staring eyes. She puts a hand to her heart, certain she can feel it racing beneath her rib cage. What is she doing here? Is he interested in her romantically? And if he is, does she want this? Is she ready to be with someone? Is she confusing the fear and loneliness of the last few days with a romantic spark? Perhaps it's just the culmination of everything that's making her long for closeness with another? Or a knee-jerk reaction to Ben's baby news? Could she handle a casual fling . . . a relationship, even? Would it be wise to get involved with a colleague? She eyes herself sternly in the mirror. You're an adult, she tells herself. Act like one.

Back on the landing, she hears soft music playing downstairs and the sound of Edward moving about the kitchen: clattering pans and a sink filling with water. She hesitates, her gaze drifting back to the studio door. *He's so talented.* Ellie's admiration echoes in her ears. Fuck it, she thinks, emboldened by the wine and her flush of excitement. Just a peek. It can't hurt.

The studio door swings open a second time and Rachel fumbles along the inside wall, her fingers finding a switch that brings a sudden flood of light. In front of her, the spiral staircase winds upward, the scent of dust, oil, and white spirit drifting down to greet her. After a quick glance behind her, she climbs the steps into the turret.

At first, all she sees is the trees. Dozens of them, like a towering forest stretched across a myriad of canvases angled around the room. She sees twisted branches, dark, veined bark, clawing ivy, and shafts of falling light, the sight of which takes her straight back to her early morning runs in the woods above the school. The paintings are impressionistic, propped around the circular room, enveloping the space.

An easel stands in the center of the room, its splayed oak legs visible beneath a drop cloth. Nearby, an artist's palette, daubed with thick green paint, smears of ocher and brown, rests on a cluttered table beside paint tins, a cloth roll of brushes, and a palette knife glinting silver. A strange, charged atmosphere lingers in the room, a sense of presence, as if Edward has only just thrown down his tools, pulled down the drop cloth, and left the space. An image of his hands returns to her, the green and brown paint flecks on his skin, hands she has imagined touching her own only moments ago.

Far below she hears the clash of something falling onto the kitchen tiles. Safe, for a moment. She's trespassing, invading Edward's private domain, but she can't stop herself, her curiosity and her desire to understand the man downstairs driving her toward the covered easel. Her chest tightens in anticipation as she lifts a corner of the drop cloth.

The painting appears, at first, to be another woodland study. She sees textured bark, curling green leaves transitioning to copper brown, all cast in eerie twilight. But as her eyes roam the huge canvas, she notices a startling new detail. A figure darting among the trees—a girl—her white dress streaming behind her, her golden hair caught in motion, like a ribbon blowing in the breeze.

Rachel swallows and peers more closely. The girl's face is obscured from view, but the outline of her body is clear. Backlit by the low light, the fabric of the girl's dress is sheer, revealing long, slender legs, a narrow waist, and the curved outline of one breast. Rachel feels the beginnings of a chill creeping through her.

At the edge of the sheet, she spots something glossy pinned to the easel frame. She lifts the fabric higher and the first of the photos comes into view, an image tacked beside the huge canvas. A girl. Slender and fine-boned, sitting on a stool in the very same room. The girl's body is angled toward the camera, but her face is tilted to the floor, hidden by the fall of her long, golden hair. She wears the same thin, white dress in the painting, the neckline slipping down to expose one bare, summer-freckled shoulder, the outline of her naked breast just visible beneath the light fabric.

She pulls the drop cloth higher and sees other photos tacked to the easel. A slender arm. The back of a calf. The curve of a pale neck. A hand resting on a chin, the hint of a smile playing on lips just visible at the photograph's edge. They're all odd, intimate, dismembered images of a girl's body in close-up.

Acid rises in Rachel's throat. The room feels small and hot, its curved walls pressing in on her. Her gaze slides from the photographs back to the painting. She sees the fallen leaves. The lichen-spotted bark of the trees. And, now that she is closer, she sees the final detail, the one she's missed until now: the tall folly rising like a dark spire at the very top edge of the painting. Rachel feels the truth of the photographs hit her like a fist to her stomach: Sarah was here, in this room, with Edward.

The Drama club. Wasn't that where he'd claimed their paths had crossed? He'd helped out with the sets, describing Sarah as "bright, talented." Her stomach churns. Was that how he'd lured her here? Through their connection on the school production?

All the horrifying details of Sarah's murder come rushing back. The awful photograph she'd been shown of the girl lying in the dirt in her white dress at the foot of the folly. Sarah's broken, bleeding body. There's no doubt in her mind that the painting is of Sarah. Sarah in her white dress. Sarah in the woods. Sarah running toward the tower. Sarah racing to her death.

The photographs—the ones tacked to the easel and the one Maxwell had shown her in her office—merge and blur in her mind until all she can see are white, lifeless limbs scrawled with dark words.

Edward.

Edward, beloved by all their students. Edward, Ellie's favorite tutor. Edward, the man who'd left beautiful white roses on her desk.

Her desk. The desk Sarah's file had been left open on. The penny drops. Stupid, stupid, stupid. It wasn't Malcolm who'd been rifling through Sarah's personal file. It had been Edward, perhaps checking to see if Sarah had divulged anything about these inappropriate modeling sessions between tutor and student? Checking for anything that linked him to the murdered girl? Was that what this evening was about? Asking about Ben. His friend request on Facebook, and those private messages fishing for details of the student interviews. The reason for his sudden interest in her is blindingly clear.

Dizzy with understanding, she reaches out, searching for

something to steady herself, her hand finding the table, knocking the metal palette knife, sending it clattering across the floorboards.

She wrenches the drop cloth back over the painting and stumbles down the spiral staircase, flicking off the light and shutting the door behind her, her heart hammering as she retraces her steps along the dark landing.

"You OK up there?"

She stops dead. Edward is at the bottom of the staircase, one hand on the balustrade, his face in shadow.

"I—I'm fine." She descends the stairs carefully, gripping the wooden handrail.

Edward holds the bottle of wine in his other paint-flecked hand. Seeing it, the glinting glass, the weight of it, the bloodred liquid, she feels desperately afraid. She is alone with this man in his house, miles from anywhere. No one knows where she is. Not even Ellie.

"I . . . I've just seen the time." Her mouth is sawdust-dry, the words catching like cotton-wool balls in her throat. "I should go."

She is almost at the bottom step, but he isn't moving. His body blocks her exit. "Are you sure you want to do that?" he asks, narrowing his eyes.

"I told Ellie I wouldn't be late." She grips the banister and wonders if he's noticed her trembling hands. She forces a smile. "Sorry to race away. It was . . . a lovely night."

"I can't coax you to stay for coffee? Or herbal tea, if that's your thing?"

"Thank you, but I don't want to worry Ellie. She's expecting me . . ." She trails off and it's a relief when he finally steps back, standing the wine bottle on the nearby console, allowing her past.

"Thanks for dinner." Her voice is too high in pitch. She shrugs on the coat he holds out for her, then grabs her bag. She just wants to be gone from the house, but out on the doorstep, she forces herself to turn and smile. The wind whips her hair, pulls at her coat, urging her away. "I'll see you tomorrow."

Edward is looking over her head, his eyes dark, studying the lane behind her. He nods. "Yes. Tomorrow." When he leans in, every fiber of her being screams *no* as his lips graze her cheek. Then she is darting down the path, her bag flapping on her arm as she flees through the rain, unlocks the car, her key fumbling in the ignition. As she pulls away, she allows herself a single backward glance at the crooked house, to where Edward stands on the front doorstep, his body a solid shape against the light falling through the door, one hand raised in farewell.

"Shit, shit, shit, shit," she mutters under her breath, the car jolting through deep puddles and lurching over potholes. *"Breathe."* She doesn't stop until she's at the very end of the lane where she pulls the car up onto a grass shoulder and rummages for her cell phone, praying for a connection. She glances in the mirror, at the dark lane behind, half afraid that she will see the lights of a car, or a shadowy figure running after her, or another white face looming through the rear window at her. She shudders at the thought.

"Pick up," she urges out loud. "Pick up, pick up."

Finally, there is a click.

"Hi, this is DS Ben Chase. I can't take your call right now . . ."

Fuck. She waits for the beep. "Ben," she says. "It's important." Her words come in a rush. "Call me. *Please.*"

Chapter 32

Ben shuts the front door behind him, slips off his jacket and shoes, and creeps into the kitchen where a single pendant light shines over the kitchen island. He is thinking of nothing more than down-ing a glass of water and collapsing into bed, when Chrissie's voice drifts through the open living-room door. "Where were you?"

He peers into the darkened room and just makes her out, curled at one end of the sofa, a blanket draped over her legs. She's waited up. He feels like even more of a shit than he did five min-utes ago. "Sorry. I thought you'd be in bed."

"Where were you?" she asks again. "You missed the appointment."

Ben's heart sinks. The appointment. Of course. He holds up his hands. "I'm sorry. My bad. I'll make it up to you, I promise." He clears his throat. "We had a breakthrough in the case. Something big. I had to see it through. It's good news," he adds, wondering why she isn't answering. "We arrested someone." He waits. "Chrissie?"

"I thought you were off the case?" she says, her voice monotone.

"I was. I am. At least, I don't know right now. If we can get a confession, then this whole nightmare could soon be over."

At this news, she does look up, though the pale moon of her

face remains unreadable in the dark. He reaches for the light switch. "Don't. I don't want it on." Her voice is ice-cold.

"Chrissie, please. I'm sorry about the antenatal appointment. I'll come to the next one. I promise." There's a buzzing sensation, his phone vibrating against his hip. It could be Khan, with an update. Maxwell checking in. He knows he shouldn't, he should focus on smoothing things over with Chrissie, but he can't resist a quick glance to check the caller. It's not Khan. Or Maxwell. It's Rachel. She'll have to wait. There's no way he's picking up to his ex-wife now. Not with Chrissie like this. He jams the phone deep into his pocket and reaches for the light switch again.

"I said, don't."

The shift from darkness to sudden light makes them both flinch. Chrissie turns her face away, but not before he's seen her teary eyes and the mascara streaked down her cheeks. The sight of her distress brings another sharp stab of guilt. "Chrissie, I'm sorry. My job sucks. What more do you want me to say?"

He waits, but she doesn't answer, and after a moment, he feels the smallest ember of resentment flare. She knew, when she met him, that his job required long, sometimes unsociable hours. Besides, this was an extreme case. Not their usual run-of-the-mill policing work. They had a killer to catch. One missed appointment was hardly the end of the world. The tiniest voice in the back of his head whispers, Rachel never reacted like this, but he pushes it away, aware how awful it makes him to even think the comparison. "I've had a hell of a day, love. Can we talk about this in the morning?"

"*You've* had a hell of a day?" she mutters.

He frowns and moves across the room to sit at the end of the sofa, laying one hand on her blanketed legs. "I know I've let you down. I promise I'll do better. For you and the baby."

Chrissie angles herself away and lets out a low sob.

"Chrissie, what is it?"

He is alarmed to see fresh tears streaming down her cheeks before she burrows her face into the blanket, her shoulders heaving. "What's happened?"

"You . . . weren't . . . there," she says, her words exhaled between sobs.

"I said I'm sorry. I'll come next time."

"No. You won't." She turns to him, her eyes red and accusatory. "The doctor couldn't find a heartbeat."

Ben stares at her.

"I've lost the baby." Her voice cracks. She shakes her head, lower lip wobbling. "She said the pregnancy 'wasn't progressing.' She called it a delayed miscarriage."

Ben lets out a long, slow breath. Something inside his chest plummets. A bird falling to earth. A stone dropping into a deep lake. "Oh, Chrissie." He reaches for her hand, but she slaps it away.

"Don't."

"I'm sorry."

"Are you?"

"Yes, of course I am." Ben is surprised at the depth of his feeling. The sadness rising up in him.

"I thought you might be relieved," she says in a small voice.

"Relieved?" He shakes his head. "Come here." He draws her to him, and she relents this time, allowing him to pull her into his arms so that he can kiss the top of her head and murmur what he hopes are comforting words while she cries into his chest. They might not have planned a baby, but now that they've miscarried, Ben realizes exactly what's been lost. All that life. All that joy. All that love. The pain is a sharp pang in his chest as he smooths her hair. "I'll take tomorrow off."

"What about your breakthrough?" she sniffs.

"I've done my bit. Khan's handling it from here. This is more important."

She eyes him warily. "I saw you . . . checking your phone."

"Nope, look." He pulls out his phone and makes a show of turning it off. "They can survive without me. I'm all yours. I'm going to stay home and look after you. You're the priority."

He follows her out of the room and up the stairs, helps her into pajamas, and tucks her into bed like a child. As he's brushing his teeth, he fights the urge to switch his phone on and check for an update from the station. He made a promise. Besides, the team will be pleased if he stays away, given his connection to their detainee. Maxwell can step up. She'll be glad of the challenge. This way, he's doing everyone a favor. As he slides into bed and turns out the bedside lamp, he reminds himself that he's done his bit on the case. Thanks to him, they've got their guy. He rolls toward Chrissie and traces her shoulder blade with his fingers. No more chasing shadows . . . chasing suspects. It's time to focus on what's most important. On what's right in front of him.

Chapter 33

Thursday, 6:30 a.m.

Rachel's barely slept. Whether lying awake, or caught in a fitful dream, Edward's painting has plagued her mind, disturbing images spinning in a ghoulish carousel, a horror movie she can't switch off. She's seen Sarah running in a white dress. Malcolm Crowe lumbering after her through the woods. Edward too, chasing Sarah to the folly, his footsteps echoing up the stone steps, her dress catching in his paint-stained fist, his breath on her neck, his lips meeting not Sarah's lips, but Rachel's, and with their touch, a sudden, violent shove that had pitched her backward, so that Rachel was falling, plunging from a great height . . . before startling awake.

An odd light presses at the window where her curtains don't quite meet. A ghostly white seems to smother the glass panes, casting her bedroom in a strange, muted glow. At first, she wonders if it's the remnants of her nightmare making her mind foggy, but when she pushes back the covers and goes to the window, she sees a thick fog has descended down the steep wooded slopes to shroud everything in the valley and across campus in an eerie mist. Beyond their rickety front gate, the school has vanished.

She checks for a reply from Ben, but there's only one new text message on her phone and her stomach contracts when she sees who has sent it.

I hope you got home safe and sound. E x

Rachel tastes bile at the back of her throat. At first glance it could be any other concerned message, checking up after a night out, but something in those words "safe and sound" hovers ominously, like a mild threat. She dials Ben again, not caring about the early hour, but his phone is still off and all she gets is his voicemail.

Frustrated, she drags herself into the shower and stands under scalding-hot water, dresses quickly, then heads downstairs for strong coffee and a piece of toast she doesn't feel like eating. Before she leaves, she taps on Ellie's bedroom door. "I'm going in early," she says through the crack. "Will you be OK?"

Ellie murmurs something inaudible from beneath her duvet.

"Don't fall back to sleep," she warns. "And lock up when you leave."

Out in the early morning air, it's evident that the mist isn't going anywhere. It clings to Rachel's hair and smothers her woolen coat in a fine beaded veil as she takes her usual route across campus, the path reduced to just a few feet of gravel before disappearing into white. It's eerily quiet, just the sound of her breath and her feet crunching on the path as she goes.

She can't get the image of Edward's painting out of her head. As she walks, she tries to understand his motivation, tries to square the man she thought he was with the fears now plaguing her mind. Could he have begun the painting *after* the events of the weekend? Was he creating some sort of twisted homage to Sarah? She frowns. Even if that were the case, even if he'd somehow managed to generate a prolific number of woodland studies and paintings in the few days since Sarah's body was found, that doesn't explain the photographs. Sarah had visited his studio. The evidence was there. Sarah posed in a white vintage nightdress, exactly like the one she'd been found in at the folly. Whichever way she tries to spin it, the facts are hard to ignore.

The distinct crack of a twig somewhere out in the white makes her jump. "Hello?" she calls. She stops and looks around, trying to find form in the mist, overcome by the eerie realization that someone is out there, following her. She feels certain of it, senses eyes trained on her deep in the fog. "Hello?" she calls again. "Who's there?"

There's no answer but she picks up the pace and continues along the path, reaching for her phone, thinking to try Ben again, when she hears the thud of fast footsteps coming at her, heavy breaths echoing in the blank white. Fear jolts up her spine and she ducks off the path, just as a tall teenager dressed in running gear and large headphones barrels past. "Sorry, Ms. Dean," he shouts over his shoulder, "didn't see you there."

She lifts a hand in a shaky wave, but he's already gone, one of the school's football players disappearing into the fog.

She adjusts the collar of her coat and hurries on, keen to reach the warmth and safety of her office as she leaves Ben another voicemail. "Ben, call me back. It's urgent. I know you've made an arrest but there's a man here at the school. Someone on the faculty. I think he may have been involved. Please, call me."

If Ben doesn't call back soon, she'll go to Margaret Crowe. If Edward has been fraternizing inappropriately with students, if he's hidden his involvement with Sarah, god only knows what else he's been hiding.

Chapter 34

Chrissie hasn't said much since they woke at dawn. He's brought her tea in bed and tried to coax a conversation, but she remains curled away, her eyes fixed on the wall. "You should see it out there," he says, trying a different tack. "The fog's so thick you can't see more than a meter or two beyond the drive."

She rolls over to face him and Ben can see she's not interested in his small talk. There is fresh resolve in her eyes. "I can't see a way forward," she says, her voice flat.

He reaches for her hand, but she pulls away. "We'll talk to the doctor. I'll be there for whatever comes next, I promise."

"I meant for us," she spells out. "I've been lying awake for most of the night thinking about you and me. I just can't see how we're going to make this work."

Ben reels back against the headboard. "Is this because I had to go into work yesterday?"

"No. At least, not *just* that."

This is not what he's been expecting. "If I'd known what the doctor was going to say, of course I'd have been there, but I don't have a crystal ball . . ." He trails off. It's not an excuse. He said he'd be there, and he wasn't. "I'm sorry. I let you down."

Chrissie shakes her head. "I'm exhausted, Ben. I thought if I did everything right—loved you right—it would be enough. But the truth is that this . . ." she gestures between them both, ". . . you, me, the baby—it's all happened too fast." She hesitates. "Hasn't it?"

"Chrissie—"

"You're not ready for this."

"I am. I'm—"

"You're not over Rachel," she says flatly, lifting her face so that he can see the pain in her blue eyes.

Ben waits a beat. He opens his mouth, but no words come. He can't meet her challenge and Chrissie nods, her point proven.

"Look, there's a lot going on right now with work, with Ellie. I don't know where my head's at. I'm really trying, Chrissie."

"I don't want to be something you have to *try* at. And I don't want you to feel that you *have* to be here for me. I want you to *want* to be here with me."

He nods, but the reassurances she needs are still caught at the back of his throat. "My life's complicated right now . . ." He trails off, aware that what he's saying is no comfort, aware that what she is processing and grieving is just as complex.

"I think we need some space," she says. "It would be best if you found somewhere else to stay, while we figure this out."

Ben closes his eyes, all too aware how familiar her words are, like an echo of Rachel's only months ago. Jesus Christ. Has he learned nothing? Here he is, blundering on. Making mistakes. Fucking up wherever he goes. Chrissie is right. He's not ready. "I'm sorry," he says. There's little else he can say.

She nods and rolls away from him, her gaze fixed on the ceiling. "I'm sorry too."

He goes downstairs and stands at the kitchen window listening to the sound of bathwater running overhead. The fog hasn't lifted at all. It cloaks the terraced courtyard so that all Ben can see are the planters nearest the house, drooping with brown foliage, and the faint outline of the metal table and garden chairs, still angled toward the pizza oven he'd installed less than a week ago. Was it really less than a week since Ellie had come over and they'd told her about the baby? Less than a week since Sarah Lawson had died in the woods?

You'd think by now he'd have a healthy grasp on how quickly life can change, how all it takes is one single moment to shatter a life or send it veering off course, and yet here he stands grappling with the fact still, while everything he thought was solid runs like sand through his fingers. They've lost a baby. He didn't deserve Chrissie. He didn't deserve any kind of future with her.

Seeking distraction from the emotions rising, he allows his mind to drift to the investigation. He reaches for his phone and powers it up. A steady stream of notifications lighting the screen. Rachel's name . . . then Rachel again. Followed by two more recent messages from Khan.

He tries Khan first. "What's happening, Chief?" he asks. "Has he confessed?"

"We had to pause the interview." Khan sounds weary.

Ben's heart sinks. "Why?"

"You know we have to do this by the book. We can't risk a judge ruling our evidence as inadmissible. Jamie McIvor is a disturbed individual. Seems he's been off his meds since he skipped out on his parole agreement. He's been taken to a medical facility for a full psych assessment."

"Shit," groans Ben.

"Five years inside may have kept him off the roads, but that time wasn't kind to the lad in terms of his addiction issues. You and I both know how the system can mess up an already vulnerable inmate, and the challenges prison wardens are facing up and down the country."

Ben is thinking about the man's arms, the scratches and scars, that ugly carved word scored into his skin, the type of self-inflicted tattoo meted out in prison. "But I heard him. 'I didn't *mean* to hurt her.' That's as good as a confession."

Khan releases another long sigh. "He was talking about Gemma, Ben. He was remembering your sister's death."

"What? That's not right. He had Sarah's phone. The words in the cave match the ones on Sarah's body. There's clear evidence that ties him to the girl." Ben can't keep the frustration out of his voice.

"Evidence that ties him to the scene of the crime and the body, yes." Khan hesitates. "But he's saying Sarah Lawson was already dead when he found her."

"What?" Ben leans back against the kitchen counter. "Surely you don't believe that? We've got a guy, recently released from prison for another woman's death, camping out near the scene of that crime, prowling around the woods, and just days later, another young woman's body is discovered a couple of miles away? Tell me that's not a coincidence."

"No, Ben, it's not a coincidence. We grilled him hard, at least as hard as his solicitor would allow before a medic stepped in. Maxwell made some good headway. He opened up a little. Seemed more comfortable talking to her than me. He told her that he'd returned to the woods to punish himself. He's in a bad way. Paranoid. Delusional. He's been camping out in the local caves for days. It certainly looks as though he was living rough out there, sheltering in the cave. He said he came back to be close to where Gemma died. To Sally in the Wood. He's been hearing voices. Seeing things. He thought he could find her. Say sorry."

Ben swallows, the idea of Jamie McIvor seeking Gemma catching in his throat. "That doesn't mean he's not responsible for Sarah."

"According to Jamie McIvor, he *was* in the woods on Saturday night. The party near his camp disturbed him. He wandered away, up into the woods, and was roaming around when he heard a woman's scream and went to investigate. He told Maxwell he thought it was Gemma, calling to him. Only instead, he found Sarah lying dead at the bottom of the folly."

Ben closes his eyes. "And you believe him?" He shakes his head. "He hears a scream. Goes to investigate. Finds the body. He moves her, puts her in that odd death pose, lays the mask over her face, writes odd words on her body, and destroys her phone?" Ben shakes his head. "I'm finding this hard to swallow. Why do all that?"

"If you really want to know, he said he was trying to look after her. Trying to make amends. After Gemma."

"You're shitting me?"

"The details about how he found her . . . how he moved her . . . it all fits with forensics interpretation of the scene."

"Course it bloody does. He was there when she died. He's admitted to everything bar killing her. All of this would explain his DNA at the scene, while absolving him of murder. He's no dummy, is he?"

"The medical professional I spoke to says the sight of Sarah's body in the woods may have retraumatized him."

"If he's that fragile, why was he released on parole?"

"You know as well as I do that the governors are kicking inmates out as fast as they can. Bloody cost cutting."

"Bloody reckless, is what it is."

"I don't disagree, Chase. But it became clear during the interrogation of him that McIvor was very upset about Sarah's face. How damaged she was. He says he used a mask he'd found in the woods to cover her. He pulled the twigs and leaves from her hair. Straightened her up. He must've been with her for a little while."

An echo of McIvor's rasped whisper inside the tunnel returns to Ben. *I took care of her.* "So what about the phone?"

"You saw yourself how he reacted when you produced your phone in the interview? You laid it on the table, and he went off."

Ben thinks back, remembers the moaning, the disturbing way he'd smashed his head with his fists.

"He was convicted for using a mobile phone while behind the wheel of a car. He says he took Sarah's phone and destroyed it in the cave because, in his words, 'phones destroy lives.'"

Ben lets out a long sigh.

"And get this. Maxwell took the initiative and went back over the judge's sentencing remarks in the trial six years ago. Listen." Khan clears his throat. *"Your reckless behavior destroyed the life of a promising young woman. Mr. McIvor, you must be punished. It is my belief that a period of incarceration will offer you the necessary time to rehabilitate and repent for your actions."* Khan pauses for breath. "It's there in the judge's sentencing. 'Destroy.' 'Punish.' 'Repent.' All the words he daubed on Sarah's skin and wrote in the cave. I'm told he wrote them in his cell too, even scratched them into his skin. I don't imagine for a minute a man like McIvor, with his addiction and health issues, found five years in jail an easy sentence. He's haunted by Gemma's death. Traumatized."

Ben doesn't want to hear about Jamie McIvor's trauma. The man who killed his sister doesn't deserve an ounce of his sympathy. "It wasn't an accident," is all he says, his voice flat. "It was dangerous driving. He killed my sister. And if he's this unstable off his meds, shouldn't we be asking what else he's capable of?"

"Perhaps. But we need to tread carefully. Do things by the book."

"You don't think he did it, do you?"

Khan hesitates. "Like you, I want this wrapped up as quickly as possible. Believe me, I want to know a dangerous killer is off the streets and our kids are safe. But no, after last night's interrogation, something in my gut tells me he's not our guy."

Ben stares out at the dying foliage in Chrissie's pots and fights the sudden urge to shove his fist through the window.

"Chase, you've got to admit, you're too close to all of this. Ellie. Rachel. The school. It's clouding your policing instinct."

"If you're about to tell me I'm off the case again . . ."

"No, but I want you to take a step back. Let us do things by the book. Let the emotion simmer down a little."

Ben slumps against the kitchen counter. He knows a wrongful arrest would waste precious time, spin their investigation into dangerous territory, and leave a killer roaming free. He thumps the wall beside him, frustration rolling over him. He can hear the sound of papers being shuffled on Khan's desk. "While you're there," Khan continues, "I need to ask a favor. We've had a phone call this morning. A local taxi driver by the name of John Slater called the incident hotline. He thinks he might've seen something relevant to our inquiry on the night of the murder."

"Why the delay in coming forward?" Ben doesn't like where this is heading. To him, it sounds like a time waster, looking for his five minutes.

"I wouldn't normally ask, but Maxwell's tied up here writing up the McIvor report. Can you spare half an hour to take his statement? Get it on file. Tick it off."

Ben sighs and rolls his eyes skyward. There's a part of him that resents being pushed once more to the fringes of their biggest case in years, assigned to such a menial task, certain that Khan is only asking him in order to keep him away from the action. But there's another part of him that knows Khan's right. If they're going to secure a conviction, they can't afford a single loose thread. Getting out at least keeps his mind busy and gives Chrissie the space she's asked for. "Sure, boss," he says. "Send me the address."

An hour later, Ben is standing on the doorstep of a neat, 1950s semi on the outskirts of Bath. John Slater's wife, a tanned bottle blonde in her late fifties, answers the door to him in black trousers, a leopard-print shirt, long gold earrings swinging at her earlobes. She introduces herself as Mandy and beckons him in. "Come through, love. Watch out for the cases," she adds, nudging a stack of luggage piled in the carpeted hall. "We haven't had a chance to unpack yet. John will be right down."

"You've been away?"

"A little minibreak in Tenerife to celebrate our anniversary. Still nice and warm at this time of year. It would've been the perfect trip if we hadn't been delayed getting home." She tuts. "These budget airlines . . . treat you like cattle, don't they? They'd charge you for a bloody napkin!"

He follows her down the hallway and into a cluttered living room, walls dancing with gaudy floral wallpaper, every surface holding a garish porcelain figurine. A leather La-Z-Boy chair and sofa are angled toward a large flat-screen TV streaming commercials with the volume on mute.

"John's been ever so worried since he saw the newspapers last night." She tuts again. "Something so awful happening right on the doorstep. It makes you think, doesn't it?"

Ben nods. He's trying to keep an open mind.

"Can I get you a cuppa?"

"That would be great, thank you. Milk, no sugar."

"Make yourself comfy."

He sinks into one corner of the sofa, glancing at the muted TV playing an ad for funeral plans. The screen cycles through whitening toothpaste and workplace accident claims until a huge man, tall and bearlike with a spectacular case of sunburn, appears in the doorway clutching two steaming mugs. He rests them on the coffee table and offers a firm handshake. "John Slater," he says.

Ben accepts his hand and then the mug. "How can I help, Mr. Slater?"

John perches on the La-Z-Boy, leaning forward, his elbows propped on his knees, belly straining over his waistband. "I know you're busy. To be honest, I wasn't sure about this, but Mandy said I should call you lot. She said you'd want to know."

Ben takes a sip of his tea, scalds his tongue, and places the cup back on the table. "No problem. Why don't you take me through it?"

Slater frowns and scratches at his chin. "I'm afraid it's going to sound ridiculous."

"Try me." Ben flips open his notebook.

The man clears his throat. "So, this was last Saturday night. Halloween. The night that girl was murdered, right?"

"Yes, that's right."

"I'm driving home through Sally in the Wood. Late," he adds.

"How late?"

"Gone two. Two thirty ish, from memory. I wasn't planning on working so late but two young women waved me down in Bath. No coats, shivering in their sequin dresses and devil horns, clearly the worse for wear but not *so* drunk that they posed a threat to the upholstery, if you know what I mean?"

Ben nods.

"I took pity on them. I'm too soft. Mandy tells me that all the time. But it *was* late—and cold—and Halloween does tend to bring out a funny crowd. I've never liked it, all that blood and gore and witchy nonsense. Give me Christmas or Easter any day. But I knew I'd sleep easier knowing they'd got home safe. I've got a daughter of my own, Susie, grown up now, but I remember those nights."

Ben's pencil is poised over his pad. He's still not convinced this isn't a wild-goose chase.

"So I drop the women, and I'm driving back through Sally in the Wood, trying to work out how much sleep I'll get before we leave for the airport. Not enough," he adds with a rueful smile. "Anyways, I'm going careful, because that road's seen many a driver come a cropper, right? I don't believe those superstitious stories for a minute . . . but I'm no fool either. Bloody dangerous bit of road, that."

Ben swallows. "So, you're driving through Sally in the Wood . . ." he steers, trying to get him back on track.

"Yeah, and I'm taking it easy round a corner—not fast, mind you—but it's dark and I'm tired and next thing I know, something's darting out of the trees right in front of me. Gives me the shock of my life."

"Something 'darts out'?" Ben frowns, pencil hovering. "What was it?"

"As I say, it was dark, but I saw something white belt across the road. A ruddy miracle I didn't hit it." He rubs his chin. "I told myself at the time it was an animal. A deer. You get white deer, don't you? Maybe one of those big owls."

Ben looks up from his notepad. "But now you're not sure?"

He shrugs. "I had a little whiskey when I got home, just to take the edge off. I thought it would help me sleep. But when I got into bed and closed my eyes, it came back to me and I just had this feeling, you know, that it wasn't a some*thing*. It was a some*one*."

Ben tingles as the hairs on his arms stand to attention. "A person. Male? Female?"

John Slater shrugs. "If I had to guess, female."

"What makes you say that?"

"She was fast. Running, like something was after her. And the movement suggested something white, streaming in the dark. Long fair hair. Or fabric. A dress, maybe."

"You didn't stop to check?"

The man looks regretful. "I was tired. Jumpy. Those stories about the woods, you know. As I said, I'm not a superstitious man, but Halloween had got me all jittery. Besides, it wasn't exactly a sensible place to stop. Someone coming around those corners in the dark would've driven straight into me."

"And you didn't think to report it?"

"We left for Tenerife early the next morning and to be honest, I'd pushed it out of my mind. It was only last night, when we were at the airport flying home and I saw the papers piled high with the story of the dead girl in the white dress, that the memory of it came back. Still," he says with a hopeful look, "sounds like you've caught the guy?"

Ben ignores the question and opens his phone to show Slater the photograph of Sarah that the Eastons had provided. "Do you recognize this girl?"

John Slater nods. "She's the one from the papers."

"Could it have been her you saw running across the road?"

He peers at the photo. "Like I say, it all happened so quick. I didn't get a good look." He scratches his chin again, the rasp of stubble against skin. "I guess it could've been. If it even was a girl. Like I say. I'm not entirely sure."

"Any sign of anyone else? Someone chasing her, perhaps?"

Slater shakes his head. "Nope. Just that white streak in front of the car, then gone."

Ben pulls up a map on his phone. "You must know the roads round here quite well. Do you recall where along the Sally in the Wood stretch this happened?"

Slater leans in and indicates a sharp chicane with his finger. "Right there."

Ben drops a pin on the map, then zooms out and regards the terrain. To the right, higher up into the woods stands the folly, and further on, sliding down the vale, is the quarry where the party took place. He zooms back to the pin on the map and checks the other side of the road. More woodland, and then, further on, Thornfield Manor where the Eastons live, where Sarah had been staying.

"If we assume for a moment that it was a girl you saw, tell me, which direction was she running?" He points in the two possible directions, one leading up to the folly, the other leading away toward the manor house.

"That way," says John Slater.

Ben frowns. If Sarah had been running across the road around 2:00 a.m. in the direction he is showing, then she was heading home. Why would she turn back to the folly? What would make her change her mind? It doesn't add up.

As if reading Ben's confusion, John Slater shrugs. "As I say, maybe I'm wrong. Maybe it was a deer." He raises his hands. "I'm sorry, it all happened so fast."

Ben knows the power of suggestion. It's been a few days. The newspaper stories and photos may have put the idea into this well-meaning man's head. He's obviously trying to help, but perhaps he's imagining things that just weren't there.

John Slater jerks his head at the TV screen. "It's a shame for the school, isn't it? I'm not a fan of these private institutions. Doesn't seem very fair to me that kids don't get a level playing field, but those poor students and teachers must be very upset."

Ben follows John Slater's gaze. The ad break has come to an end, replaced by a local news program with a ticker at the bottom of the screen scrolling headlines. The scene pans across the exterior of Folly View College, its clipped green shoulders, tall iron gates, and impressive signage, before it cuts to a close-up of a small gathering standing just outside. The camera zooms in on Margaret Crowe's dour face, microphones shoved close, as the ticker continues to scroll: SUSPECT ARRESTED IN FOLLY GIRL MURDER.

Margaret cuts an imposing figure in her buttoned-up black jacket. She appears to be holding court for the jostling journalists, flanked by several staff members lined up like guardsmen either side of her as she reads from a piece of paper. Ben narrows his eyes. What the hell is she doing? "Do you mind turning up the volume?"

John Slater obliges with the remote control and Margaret Crowe's clipped voice fills the room. ". . . pleased and relieved to learn the police have made an arrest in the case of Sarah Lawson's murder. We hope this development marks an end to the investigation and the start of a period of healing for our school community. I would politely request that the media respect the privacy of our teachers, pupils, and families as we mourn a much-loved and admired pupil."

Ben frowns. He's not sure who—if anyone—has given the head

teacher the go-ahead for a stunt like this, but talk about jumping the gun. "She's acting like we've got a signed confession," he mutters. It's obvious what she's doing: distancing the school from the events, projecting calm, reassuring her governors and the families who pay her salary each year that the school is healthily detached from whatever events saw Sarah meet her grisly death in the woods.

His cell phone buzzes in his pocket. He reaches for it, half expecting it to be one of his colleagues, apoplectic at the rogue PR stunt unfolding at the school. Instead, he's surprised to see Connor Carlisle's name lighting up his screen. "Excuse me," he says to John Slater, standing and moving into the hall. "Connor," he says. "To what do I owe the pleasure?"

"Are you watching the news?" There is no polite preamble. Ben can hear agitation in the young man's voice.

"I am, as it happens."

"He's right there," says Connor.

Ben wonders if he's taken something, wonders if he's going to regret giving the lad his cell phone number. "I'm a little tied up, Connor. If there's something you want to—"

"It's him," Connor says, cutting him off. "The creepy fucker who was watching us in the woods. You asked me if I'd recognize him. Well, there he is, on TV, standing right next to that old battle-ax."

Ben moves back to the open doorway to study the TV screen. The camera is still pointed at Margaret and her cohorts outside the school. "The man you saw in the woods on Saturday night is at the school press conference?"

"Yeah, mate." Connor's tone is impatient, indicating that Ben really is being rather slow on the uptake. "That's exactly what I'm telling you."

Ben scans the faces on the TV screen. Two men stand on either side of Margaret. One is familiar to him. Tall, good-looking, tufted brown hair, his arms folded across a wool blazer. Edward Morgan. Ellie's art tutor. The other wears an anorak, his thinning white hair scraped across his scalp, his lined face downturned as if studying his shoes. "Which one?"

"The one on her right. It's him. I'm telling you. He was in the woods. He was watching the party."

"You're sure?"

Connor lets out a breath. Ben can hear the long exhale of his vape as he waits. "It's him. I'm sure of it. One hundred percent."

Back in his car, he listens to the first of Rachel's urgent voicemails. "There's a man here at the school. Someone on the faculty."

He doesn't need to hear any more. He hangs up and calls the station. "You need to send a car to the school," he tells Khan. "Pronto. We've got our watcher in the woods."

Chapter 35

Ellie has been working fruitlessly on her portfolio for almost half an hour in a noisy, rudderless class of fellow Year Thirteen students, when Edward Morgan finally appears. "Sorry, gang," he says, throwing his blazer onto the back of his chair. "Mrs. Crowe asked me to attend an urgent meeting, but it's good to see you've been making progress in my absence. I know you don't need any reminders from me about your looming deadline."

Ellie casts a guilty glance at the near-blank page laid in front of her. "Progress" is not a word she can lay claim to this week.

"Is it true there was a press conference outside the school?" Jasmine calls out.

"Word travels fast, I see." Edward nods. "Yes, it's true."

"What about?"

"The police have made an arrest." There's a rising murmur from the students around the room. "I'm sure you'll be told more in due course, but Mrs. Crowe wanted to address the situation publicly. She felt it would be helpful to distance the school."

"Who's been arrested?" It's Jasmine again, but Ellie is as curious as the rest of them.

"I'm sure we'll all know more soon, but hopefully you'll all feel a little safer now that the police have taken someone into custody." Edward's gaze comes to land on Ellie and she glances away, her own experience at the police station earlier that week still all too clear in her mind. "It's been a frightening time for everyone," he adds softly.

"Does Olivia know about the arrest?" Jasmine presses.

"I believe Sarah's family have been informed. I'm sure Olivia will join us as soon as she's ready. Now, let's get back to work."

Edward moves around the studio, examining portfolios, offering advice and encouragement on their various projects. Ellie keeps her head down. She can't concentrate. She needs to finish the supporting essay that is to sit alongside her installation, but she can't focus. All she has is a heading written in bold capitals, made to look as if they drip down the page: **ART AS PROTEST.** She's tried to write more, but the words won't come. She's so incredibly tired. All she feels like doing is crawling beneath her table, curling into a ball, and sleeping for a week.

Seeing Edward circling closer, she slides off her stool and heads to the sinks. There are two boxes of brushes and paints waiting to be unpacked so she slices them open with a STANLEY knife and restocks the supply shelves, working slowly, hoping to draw out the time. When she can stall no longer, she folds the empty boxes and places the knife back on its wall hook before returning to her seat.

Seconds later, Edward materializes at her bench. He's been waiting for her, she feels sure of it. Standing at her shoulder, she knows his gaze is roaming over her workbook and she has to fight the urge to cover the empty page with her hands.

"How are you getting on, Ellie?"

"OK," she lies.

"You've been very secretive about this project. You're confident you'll hit the deadline?"

Ellie turns to find him staring not at her work, but at her. She swallows, caught out by the concern in his eyes, overcome by a sudden urge to confide in him. She wants to tell him how distracted she's been, how hard she's found it to sleep, how impossible it is to focus on anything, when all she can seem to think about is Sarah and what happened to her in the woods that night. She clears her throat, unsure how to share her thoughts in the whisper-quiet studio, reluctant to have her private worries spill out into public gossip, when the sound of the studio door squeaking open saves her.

Everyone turns to look as Olivia Easton slips into the classroom. Realizing she is the focal point, she gives a brave half smile. Jasmine, who is closest to the door, moves across and offers an awkward hug, which Olivia accepts, standing stiffly in the girl's embrace. Ellie can see Olivia's usually glowing skin is a pallid gray, her hair scraped back into a limp ponytail, dark circles beneath her eyes. Ellie thinks she looks like shit and feels a surge of sympathy.

"It must be such a relief to know they've caught the person who did it?" Jasmine carries on, clumsy in her role as the self-appointed welcome committee.

Olivia nods.

"We've got you. You know that, right?"

"Will you excuse me a moment, Ellie?" Edward leaves her side and goes to join Olivia. He tactfully disentangles her from Jasmine's clutches and sends the well-meaning girl back to her easel. Ellie watches as he speaks in low murmurs with Olivia, the girl lowering her lashes, her chin wobbling. Ellie hates herself for the small twist of jealousy that Edward's attentions should have been diverted. Olivia's been through hell. She's lost her cousin—her best friend. She wouldn't want to swap places with her. Not for anything. Who is she to begrudge her Edward's attention?

Olivia gestures to her workstation. "I'll work through break, if that's OK? I should try to catch up."

"Good for you," says Edward. "Just do what you can today. No pressure."

Tears well in Olivia's eyes and Ellie wonders if she's about to lose it completely, but then she turns and makes her way to her easel and sits for a moment as if in a daze, before reaching into her bag for a sketchbook and a case of charcoals.

Ellie is racked with guilt. Her lack of focus is even more shaming in the face of Olivia's effort. If she can haul herself into school in the midst of her grief and work on her portfolio, Ellie has no excuses.

For the next twenty minutes, Ellie attempts to write the introductory paragraph of her statement, grateful when the bell rings to signal the end of the period. As she packs her equipment, Edward returns to her workbench and pulls up a stool. "Have you got a moment? We didn't finish our chat. Tell me, honestly, how's it going?" He fixes her with a steady gaze.

There's nowhere to hide. "I know it doesn't look like I've done much, but I'll get it finished."

"I didn't mean your work. I meant *you*."

Ellie glances around the studio. Jasmine is waving to her from the door, her portfolio under one arm, gesturing something that either means she'll wait outside or see her later. The other students trickle out behind her, until only Olivia remains, mixing her paints by the sink. Ellie sighs. "I'm OK. You know . . . hard week."

"Your mum had a word with me. She's worried about you."

Ellie doesn't like to think about her mum talking with her tutors.

"I'm going to make an educated guess that you don't find it particularly easy talking to our school counselor, given that she's also your mum," he adds with a wry smile.

Ellie stares down at her feet. "I guess not."

"If you ever want to talk, Ellie, my door's always open. I told your mum I'd keep an eye out for you, and I meant it. Sometimes, it's easier to confide in someone who isn't family."

His kindness threatens to crack open that rock-hard place inside her. Emotion rises in her throat. Don't cry, she wills, brushing angrily at her eyes.

"Have you been sleeping?" he asks. "Eating?"

She shakes her head. "Not much." She casts a glance in Olivia's direction, then lowers her voice, words she's held so tightly coming in a sudden rush. "I keep thinking about the woods. The party. I think about Sarah all the time . . . if I could've done something different." Ellie takes a breath. "I wonder who hurt her. If she was frightened. If she tried to run."

Edward leans back and regards her. "It's understandable her death has affected you. Going over everything with the police must've been traumatizing."

She nods. "I know I need to focus on my work. If I want to get into art college . . ." She shakes her head. "I just can't concentrate. What happened between Sarah and me . . . I just wish . . . wish I could . . ." she shrugs, "I don't know . . . say sorry, I guess." She wipes at the tear that has spilled down her cheek.

"You can't bury feelings, Ellie. Sometimes you have to confront them head-on, even when they feel overwhelming. Bottling things up doesn't help. I bet your mum tells you that?"

Ellie nods. "Sometimes."

Edward looks thoughtful. He scratches his chin. "Do you trust me?" he asks.

Ellie nods.

He leans in and rests a hand on her shoulder, the tips of his fingers warm where they press lightly on the fabric of her shirt. "I've got an idea. Something that might help. Will you come with me?"

"Where?"

"Sometimes, we have to go back to move forward."

"I don't understand."

"Sometimes," he says, already standing, tugging at his tie and pulling it from around his neck before grabbing a set of keys and his leather jacket from a hook by his desk, "we have to visit the place that frightens us most."

Ellie looks across at Olivia. She is watching them, surreptitiously, but ducks her head behind her easel when she spots Ellie's glance.

"Come on," says Edward, slipping through the doorway, beckoning for her to follow. Ellie frowns but reaches for her own coat.

Out in the foggy forecourt in front of the studio, he surprises her by heading for the motorbike standing at an angle beneath an overhanging tree. "Where are we going?" she asks again as he removes a spare helmet from a tail pack on the rear of the bike and hands it to her.

He smiles. "You said you trusted me."

She knows there must be a hundred other things he could be doing with his time, a hundred other students he could be helping, and she certainly doesn't want to appear childish or ungrateful, so she puts the helmet on and clambers awkwardly onto the seat behind him.

"You ever been on a motorbike before?" he asks over his shoulder.

"No," she says.

"Well, you're going to have to hold on, if you don't want to fall. And lean into the bends. If you fight them, we both come off."

Clumsily, she reaches round and grabs his leather jacket.

"Tighter," he says, and she can hear the amusement in his voice. "Trust me, you'll want to hold on."

He starts the engine, then reverses the machine, walking it away from the curb before revving a couple of times. The world around them is cloaked in white, but she can just make out a figure on the top step of the art studio, one that recedes over her shoulder as they pull away. If it's Jasmine, she knows she'll never hear the end of this. A "special trip" with Edward. She'll be tormented for the rest of the year with jokes and jibes. *Teacher's pet.* Ellie feels a flash of irritation at her mum for asking Edward to look out for her, for putting her in this position. Then Edward opens up the throttle.

For a split second, Ellie thinks they are falling, the angle of the machine and their balance on it precarious and frightening. But then they are flying, the bike growling beneath them, and Ellie is lost to the adrenaline and excitement of the motion, the fog seeming to part before them as they glide across campus toward the main gates, like a stone skimming water.

She watches the blurry outline of familiar school buildings slide by, sinking down a little deeper into her seat as the ghostly forms of students emerge, then fade. At the iron gates, Edward slows, then pulls over to allow another vehicle through first, a police car moving fast, blue lights flashing.

"They weren't going to stop," she shouts, the words catching as she remembers her own ride to the station in the back of a police car earlier that week. "Wonder what they want now?"

Edward turns and shouts over his shoulder, his words half muffled beneath his helmet, "Don't think about that. Let's focus on what *you* need."

Ellie twists in her seat and watches the blue lights fade to white and the iron gates disappear into the fog. It's the strangest feeling, watching the school dissolve, as if she's vanishing entirely, being swallowed whole by the vast, white wildness around them. What *does* she need? She has no idea, but perhaps disappearing for a little while into this strange, muted world isn't the worst thing in the world.

Chapter 36

Rachel has been attempting to clear some of her mounting work-load, filing reports and answering concerned emails from parents, when Ben finally replies to her messages. *Hey. Sorry. Phone was off. There's a car on its way to the school now. Sit tight. It'll all be over soon.*

She exhales in relief. The sooner Edward is taken into custody and questioned, the safer she will feel. She still shudders to think how she sat round his house blithely eating his food and drinking his wine, feeling flattered by his attention, when all along he'd been covering up his connection to Sarah and fishing for details of the police investigation. All while that menacing painting loomed over them in his studio. It had to mean something, and whatever it was, she knew it was nothing good.

The milky fog clings to the windows of her office. It feels as if it might creep inside and smother them all, if only she opened a window to let it. Across the room, the old iron radiator clicks and groans like an old man attempting to rise from a chair, trying val-iantly to warm the drafty room. Rachel stands and turns on every lamp, eager to banish the gloomiest corners of the room, wanting light and warmth over shadows and darkness.

Returning to her desk, her gaze falls upon the vase of white roses beside her laptop. The delicate buds are open now, unfurling into generous, velvety blooms. The sight of them makes her stomach leap. She snatches up the flowers and hurls the whole dripping bunch into her wastepaper bin, relieved to be rid of them. She texts Ben back. *Ask him about the painting in his studio.*

Less than five minutes later, flashing blue lights are strobing outside the building, illuminating the fog like dry ice. She imagines uniformed officers marching across campus, barging into the art studio. Would Edward leave willingly? Would he make a fuss in front of the students? If her own sense of betrayal is anything to go by, she can only imagine the shock their pupils will feel. A man they trust and admire involved in the worst of crimes? Ellie will be shattered. They all will.

After a short time, she hears car doors slamming, an engine restarting, and the blue lights fade back to white. Rachel considers going to the teachers' lounge, where she knows the teachers will be gathering as the news begins to spread, but she's not sure she can face the drama. She needs to think about how to handle this with the students and their parents. Margaret may well ask for her advice.

She is drafting a possible response when she hears a quiet tapping on her door. "Come in," she calls, and the door swings open to reveal Olivia Easton standing on the threshold wrapped in a cream coat, a look of anguish on her face.

"You said that I could come . . . if I ever needed . . ." She trails off, looking close to tears.

"Of course. Come in."

"I didn't know what else to do."

Realizing that Olivia must've seen Edward being led away, she beckons her toward the armchairs by the fire. "You did the right thing. Come and take a seat."

Olivia shrugs off her coat and perches on the edge of an armchair. There's something about her demeanor that gives Rachel some concern. There's a fizzing energy rising off her, a distracted look in her eyes.

"Tell me. What is it?" She doesn't want to lead the girl. She wants her to say it in her own words.

Olivia crumples on the seat, her face twisting in pain. "You always want to believe the best of someone, don't you . . ."

"You're talking about Mr. Morgan?" The girl's shock is evident. Edward was in a position of authority. Olivia trusted him. Looked up to him.

Olivia nods. "I should've said something when the police first spoke to me, but I couldn't bring myself to admit it."

Rachel frowns. "Admit what, Olivia?"

Olivia drops her gaze. "I think it's all my fault."

"Oh no, Olivia. I'm sure that's not true. Why would you think that?"

Olivia lifts her head and Rachel sees tears in her eyes. "It started at the end of the summer term. Mr. Morgan . . . Edward . . . he asked me then."

Rachel frowns. "Asked you what?"

"If I'd ever done any modeling." She swallows. "He asked if I'd pose for him. For a painting."

Rachel stares at the girl, thinking she must've misheard. Edward asked *Olivia* to model for him?

"I was flattered that he thought I would be good enough. Pretty enough," she adds shyly.

"Did you do it?" Rachel asks, afraid that she already knows the answer.

Olivia nods. "He took me to his place on his motorbike. Sarah didn't think I should go, but I told her it was OK. We'd done a life-drawing class in Year Twelve, with a live model, so I knew it could be important, sometimes, to help capture the human form. Besides, it was Edward. Everyone likes Edward, don't they?"

Rachel isn't sure if she is imagining Olivia's knowing look, but she nods her agreement. "Go on."

"When I got to his place, he asked me to change into a dress he'd bought specially, from a vintage shop in Bath. It was a white, floaty thing. Pretty, but old."

Rachel's mind races back to the disembodied photo tacked to Edward's easel. The blond hair. The white fabric. The pale skin. She had assumed they were all of Sarah, but was it possible she'd been wrong? Had they been snapshots of Olivia? From certain angles, it was true the two girls were strikingly similar. *More like sisters than cousins.* Had she jumped to the wrong conclusion that night in his studio?

"What happened, Olivia?" Rachel asks gently. "What did he do?"

Olivia glances up in surprise. "Do? He didn't do anything." Understanding dawns in her eyes. "Nothing bad. Nothing like you're thinking. I changed into the dress and he took some photos. Nothing dirty," she adds, reading the suspicion in Rachel's eyes. "They were artistic. Tasteful. Afterward, we had a cup of tea and biscuits in his kitchen and he chatted to me about my university choices. He'd studied at Falmouth and I wanted to know what it was like." She shrugs. "Then I left. He let me keep the dress, as a thank-you, for being his 'muse.' He said it suited me. I thought that was the end of it."

Rachel swallows. "But it wasn't?"

Olivia shakes her head. "It was nice spending time with him one-on-one. It felt as though . . ." she shrugs again, "as though we'd made a connection. Talking to him in his kitchen . . . he wasn't like the boys at school. He seemed interested . . . interesting. He spoke to me that day like I mattered." She looks up again, shyly. "I felt a vibe between us. Electricity. I wondered if he felt it too, if that's why he'd asked me round."

A pink tinge has risen on Olivia's cheeks as she studies Rachel, clearly hoping to see agreement. Rachel doesn't know what to say, her mind is still racing to understand what she's hearing, but there's more Olivia wants to say. "I talked to Sarah, in confidence. I asked her if she thought I was mad to fancy him, to think there could be something there."

"What did Sarah say?"

"She told me I was stupid. She said Edward was an old man." Olivia sighs. "Sarah was direct like that."

Rachel manages a gentle smile.

"I tried to forget about him. I pushed the idea of him and me to the back of my mind, but it turned out I hadn't imagined the spark between us." She gives Rachel a shy smile. "A few days later, I got a Facebook friend request from Edward. That's when our messages started."

Rachel startles at the mention of the friend request, remembering her own from Edward. "Messages?" she asks. The growing dread in the pit of Rachel's stomach seems to expand.

"Yes. He suggested I set up a secret Messenger account, so we could continue our chat privately. So no one got the wrong idea. It was easy to do, with a fake name and profile picture. Look."

Olivia swipes her phone open and pulls up a screen. She scrolls back quickly over hundreds of messages, but Rachel isn't scanning the content, her gaze is caught on the small, circular profile picture at the top of the thread, the same profile picture—the one from the school website—that she has been staring at as she composed her own careful messages to Edward. The realization makes acid rise in her throat. "You're telling me that Edward Morgan has been sending you private exchanges from this account for months?"

Olivia nods.

Rachel feels sick as her eyes scan the messages, words and phrases leaping out in horrifying detail. *Wear your hair down tomorrow . . . I wish I could touch you . . . I dreamt about you last night . . . my beautiful muse . . . I want to tell the whole world how I feel. . . .* As Rachel scrolls, she notices the increasingly intimate nature of the exchanges, the sliding into an imagined future where they will be together, physically, for the first time. *It'll be worth the wait*, Edward had typed. *The most wonderful night of your life, I promise.*

She pushes the phone back at Olivia as if the plastic casing might burn her. Edward has been grooming Olivia right under their noses. No wonder the poor girl is so distraught and confused. "I'm afraid Edward has acted very inappropriately," she says. "He's used his position of authority to take advantage of you."

Olivia looks up at Rachel with huge swimming eyes. "But I thought it meant something. I thought he liked me . . . loved me even. He said we would be together. He promised if I kept it secret, we would be together when I left school."

"You kept your . . ." she hesitates to find the right word, "relationship . . . hidden from everyone?"

Olivia nods. "He said I had to. If anyone ever found out, it would be over between us. He'd lose his job. He'd lose everything."

Classic grooming, thinks Rachel. What a manipulative shit. "Did he ever . . . touch you . . . make you do anything you didn't want to?"

Olivia frowns. "No. Nothing like that. Only ever online. We couldn't risk it. We were waiting."

Rachel sighs. "Have you told anyone else about this, Olivia?"

She visibly shrinks at Rachel's suggestion. "No! He said not to."

Wow, thinks Rachel, shaking her head. He really has done a number on Olivia. On them both. "Olivia, he's made you keep this a secret because he knows it's wrong. And you do too, deep down, don't you? He's your teacher." Her mind slides back to the eerie, half-finished painting in his studio, the girl in white running through the woods. "He's fooled us all."

Olivia seems to bristle at the suggestion. "You like him too," she says sullenly, her head tilted at Rachel, "don't you?"

Rachel blushes. She doesn't want to get into any of that with Olivia. Whatever Edward has done to manipulate Rachel is nothing compared to the abuse of a student. "Olivia, I have to ask you something important." The painting is in her mind's eye. The girl in white. The folly. "Do you think Mr. Morgan was involved in what happened to Sarah last weekend?"

Olivia looks conflicted, her face a picture of anguish.

"You don't have to protect him anymore, Olivia. Think of Sarah."

"I don't . . . I don't want to. . . ." She trails off with a sigh. "I love him."

Rachel senses a "but" lingering and bites her tongue, waiting.

Olivia sniffs. "I guess he wasn't the man I thought he was."

Rachel tries to keep her voice level. "Why do you say that?"

Olivia's face crumples and Rachel can see the depth of the girl's distress.

"The time for protecting him is over, Olivia. Whoever killed Sarah *must* be brought to justice, so if you know anything, anything at all, you should speak up now."

She can see the girl's internal struggle, then, in the firm set of her jaw, the sense of a decision being reached. Olivia reaches for the phone lying in her lap and opens the thread of messages she's exchanged with Edward, angling the screen toward Rachel, pointing at the last few posts. Rachel leans in. The first message she sees was sent by Olivia on Halloween night at 17:02 p.m.

I'm scared to tell you this, but I think I blew it. Sarah knows.

Edward's reply comes at 18:12 p.m.

What happened?

She made a joke about my older man fixation. How I'm waiting for someone special. She knows.

His reply comes a minute later.

Forget it. I'll take care of Sarah.

Olivia gazes up at Rachel, her face distraught. "See?"

Rachel nods, a hollow feeling taking hold in the pit of her stomach. *I'll take care of Sarah.* She sees all too well.

The last three messages are all from Olivia, all sent the night of the party. Rachel scans them quickly.

I miss you. I wish we didn't have to be a secret. I just want to be with you. ♥ ♥ ♥

Then, much later, the last two messages.

How could you?

I'll never forgive you.

Edward hasn't replied to any of them.

Olivia is wild-eyed. "We haven't communicated at all since then. In class he acts all professional . . . sympathetic and sad, but it's all an act. I think he . . . he . . ." Her voice cracks with a sob.

Rachel's mind is spinning. Edward's motive for hurting Sarah is all too clear. He had to silence Sarah to keep his relationship with Olivia secret and his reputation and livelihood intact. Rachel feels the truth slide like a knife in her guts, twisting painfully. She feels the betrayal, the intense shame that she too was naive enough to fall for his flattery; that she too was foolish enough to think that Edward might like her, that they might share a "special connection." He has played them all like chess pieces on a board, with Edward the grand master.

"It was brave of you to tell me this, Olivia, but we have to go to the police." Seeing the fear in the girl's eyes, Rachel softens her tone. "You must understand, I have a responsibility to take this further now. What if he hurts someone else?"

Olivia's eyes flash. "That's why I came. For Ellie."

"Ellie?" Rachel frowns. "What about Ellie?"

"She left with Edward."

Rachel's stomach drops. "She can't have," she insists. "The police have taken him away for questioning. I saw the car leave."

Olivia shakes her head. "Not Edward. He and Ellie were together after art class. They left on his motorbike. I couldn't think why he would go off with her, but if he *did* hurt Sarah . . . and with Ellie's dad being a police detective on the case . . . That's why I came to see you."

Rachel feels fear clawing at her throat. All this time they've spent talking and Ellie is god knows where with Edward. "Where, Olivia? Where was he taking her?"

"I don't know. All I heard him say was that she should face her fears. He said she should return to the place that frightens her." She shrugs.

The place that frightens her? Think, screams Rachel's brain. Where does Ellie feel frightened? But then she remembers her daughter's nighttime cries, the shouts and the troubled dreams that have haunted her since Halloween evening, and she knows exactly where he's taking her, and the thought chills her to the bone.

Her mind fills with a rush of white noise. She leaps up from her chair. "I have to go."

Olivia reaches for her cream coat. "I'll come too."

"No, Olivia. It's not safe."

"I don't care." Her jaw is set, a fierce determination in her eyes. She thrusts her hands in her pockets and Rachel sees her resolve. "You shouldn't go alone. I can talk to him. He might listen to me."

"Olivia," Rachel warns, "you shouldn't be anywhere near that man right now. It's not a good idea."

But Olivia is already moving to the door, one step ahead of her, and Rachel doesn't have time to argue. Ellie is alone with Edward and she could be in grave danger. She sprints after Olivia, down the long wood-paneled corridor, and out into the cold, white light.

Chapter 37

Ben watches the interview from the surveillance room, DCI Khan leading the questions, Malcolm Crowe sitting thin-lipped and ramrod straight in the chair opposite him. Rachel hasn't responded to his last text message. He has no idea what she meant, *ask him about the painting,* but he keeps his phone nearby and on silent, just in case she does reply to shed some light.

"What took you into the woods on Saturday night, Mr. Crowe?" Khan asks, tapping his pen impatiently on a pad of paper.

Ben watches Malcolm Crowe's face. He doesn't react, just stares calmly back at Khan, his watery eyes as unreadable as deep, still water.

"Were you watching the kids? Keeping a close eye? Maybe a closer eye on one of them in particular?" Khan adds, attempting to provoke a reaction.

A flicker passes over the man's otherwise impassive face. "As I told your lot a few days ago," he says, his voice gruff, "I stayed in with Margaret on Saturday night."

Ben leans into the screen, trying to read Crowe's expression. Connor had been adamant that it was Malcolm Crowe he'd seen watching the party in the woods. Ben had put his trust in the young man's account. There hadn't seemed any reason for him to lie, but the elderly man's unwavering denial brings a moment's doubt. The old man was good. He'd give him that.

Ben had called Maxwell from outside the taxi driver's house, almost immediately after he'd spoken to Khan. "Who ran the background checks on the school staff?" he'd asked her, no polite preamble.

"Crawford."

Ben had groaned. "Do me a favor. Go back into Malcolm Crowe's records. Check for anything he might've missed."

"I'm on it," she'd said, simply, easily.

DCI Khan pushes a little harder. "We've had an eyewitness come forward to say they saw you in the woods on Saturday night. Most insistent."

Ben sees the discomfort in the man's body language as Crowe squirms on the chair. He knows Khan sees it too, knows he'll go in hard with Maxwell's ammunition.

"One of my officers has done a little digging. It seems a complaint was raised against you at your previous school, just a month or so before you took early retirement."

Ben breathes his silent gratitude once more for Maxwell's calm, can-do efficiency. That detective deserved a promotion.

"The girl was lying," says Malcolm, his voice gruff. "Goodness only knows why she'd make something like that up, but she did." Malcolm is a picture of defiance. "As good as ruined my reputation, mind."

"What was it the girl accused you of?" Khan asks lightly, flicking through his papers. "Spying on students. Being a Peeping Tom."

"I like to watch the school sports fixtures. That's not a crime, is it? The stuff she said, about me wandering through the girls' changing room, peering through windows. It was nonsense. All made up."

"And yet you decided to leave your teaching post? To take early retirement?"

Malcolm hangs his head. "Something like that shakes you. I'd given my all to that school. Twenty years as Head of Science. The girl admitted to the police that she'd made it all up with her friends, a nasty little joke, but it was too late for me. My reputation was in tatters. To hear the laughter as I walked the corridors. To see the suspicion in my colleagues' eyes. A single lie, and my career was extinguished overnight." He closes his eyes and lets out a deep sigh.

"It was agreed that I would take early retirement. The head teacher there thought it for the best. Margaret and I talked and we decided on a fresh start. She'd look for a new role, in a new county, away from all the furor. So that's what we did, here at Folly View. It seemed the right time for me to step back. To focus on my hobbies."

"Hobbies such as walking through the woods at night? Spying on the students?" Khan eyes him keenly. "Unless you have a habit of sleepwalking you haven't disclosed, I think you still have some explaining to do."

Malcolm glances round at the blank walls of the interview room, as if looking for something to rest his eyes on. His gaze lifts to the camera mounted high in the corner. With his wide staring eyes, round wire spectacles, and broad forehead, made all the more prominent by his receding hairline, he reminds Ben of the stern farmer from the famous *American Gothic* painting. All he needs is a pitchfork and he'd be a dead ringer.

In the face of his silence, Khan launches his attack from a different angle. "I believe it was Mrs. Crowe who provided you with an alibi for Saturday night?" He makes a show of flicking back through the pages of his notebook. "If you're struggling to remember, it would be easy enough for us to escort your wife to the station and question her here?"

Malcolm shifts again in his seat. "Margaret's got nothing to do with this."

"With what, Mr. Crowe? How *do* you spend your time these days?"

"I suppose some might call me a caretaker," Malcolm says flatly. "I take care of things."

"As far as I understand, you're not a caretaker in any official capacity."

He tuts. "That's as may be, but I like to help out around the place. I like to keep busy. I keep things on track, for Margaret. It's not an easy job my wife has, running an institution like Folly View. We take the school motto very seriously. *We go above and beyond*."

"Is that what you were doing in the woods on Saturday night? Going above and beyond? Taking care of things?"

"In a sense." Malcolm folds his arms across his chest.

Khan, clearly tiring of Malcolm Crowe's evasive answers, goes in. "Were you 'taking care' of Sarah Lawson on Saturday night?"

The suggestion hangs in the air. Ben sees the distaste on the older man's face and wills Khan to press harder.

"What's especially troubling to me is the conflicting alibi provided by your wife." Khan lets the point hang. "If our witness is correct, Mrs. Crowe could be found guilty of making a false statement and obstructing the course of justice."

Malcolm Crowe lets out a small *harrumph*, but his stubborn expression has switched to alarm.

"Accusations of a cover-up could be awkward to explain to the school's board of directors. Your wife's illustrious career could be at stake. And I'm sure you don't need me to tell you that if found guilty of perjury in a court of law, you *and* your wife could be looking at jail time." He pauses, allowing his words to sink in. "There's a far easier way to proceed here, Mr. Crowe, but we do need you to cooperate." Khan leans into the table. "I think it's time you stopped messing about and told me the truth."

Malcolm closes his eyes and when he opens them, he wears a new expression, one Ben recognizes as resignation. "It was Margaret who heard the kerfuffle. A little before nine. We were watching that silly dancing program she likes, and she turned the volume down and asked if I could hear a noise outside."

Khan nods encouragingly. "Go on."

"I said it was probably the foxes trying to get at the rubbish bins, but I went out to check, just in case."

"What did you find?"

Malcolm tuts. "A god-awful mess, that's what. Eggs thrown all over the front porch and windows, pumpkins smashed to bits outside the Lodge. A terrible waste and a horrid mess to clear up."

"That must've been upsetting," says Khan, careful to keep his tone neutral.

"I'm sure they thought it was a great Halloween trick, but Margaret gives her all to that school. It was disrespectful beyond belief."

"What did you do?"

"I could hear the kids moving off into the woods, so I followed them." He refolds his arms across his chest. "Thought I'd give them a piece of my mind."

"Could you identify the students who made the mess?"

Malcolm shakes his head. "No, but it was two lads. I saw that much. Not Sarah. Not the girl who died, if that's what you're getting at."

"So, you followed the boys?"

"I did. I went into the woods, but I lost sight of them. I thought they'd given me the slip, but as I neared the quarry, I saw a whole pack of them there, larking about. Up to no good. I wanted to give those boys a piece of my mind, but I wasn't going to take on the whole group. Not when things looked like they were getting a little wild."

"Wild in what way?"

He tuts. "Certainly no behavior that befitted the children of an institution such as Folly View. They were playing games. Drinking and smoking. Acting in a lewd, indecent way. There was some wanton destruction. I saw that young redheaded girl, daughter of the nice counselor lady at school. She was there, spraying her ugly graffiti. Naughty girls should be punished. As far as I was concerned, she'd got off far too lightly the last time she was caught scrawling her mess around town." He folds his arms across his chest. "Told her mother as such the other night, as it happens."

Ben thinks of Rachel's earlier message. *Ask him about the painting.* Was that what she'd meant? He frowns. It still didn't make sense to him.

"So, the kids were running wild in the woods. What did *you* do?"

Malcolm shrugs. "I stayed. I headed to the rise above the quarry and watched them from there."

"Why?"

Malcolm rubs his chin. "I suppose I didn't like what I was seeing. Some older boys had turned up. I thought things might get out of hand. Someone might get hurt."

"So, you stayed to watch? Just in case?" Khan can't hide his skepticism.

"Well, there were the bats too, of course."

"The bats?"

"Yes, the bat roosts in the caves. Horseshoe bats. They're an endangered species, you know. I've been studying them for a while. Tracing their roosts. Just a little hobby of mine. Fascinating creatures. I didn't like the thought of the children disturbing them. If I'd had to intervene, I would've."

"Intervene?"

"They're protected under UK law."

"So, did you . . . intervene?"

"No. I stayed put until one of the girls caught sight of me. I heard some of the boys say they'd investigate, and I slipped away. I didn't want them to come upon me. I knew how it might look, given the incident at my previous school."

Khan raises an eyebrow. "Like you were spying on them?"

"As I said," Malcolm folds his arms, "I was worried."

"So, you went straight home? Without incident?"

"Not exactly, no. I took a little tumble down the trail. Turned my ankle. I had to limp home. It's been causing me trouble all week."

Khan leans back in his chair, tapping his pencil on his notepad. "Why lie, Mr. Crowe? Why not tell us all this at the beginning of the week?"

Malcolm sighs. "I talked it through with Margaret. We thought it for the best that I stay out of it, given the past *unfounded* complaint. We didn't want to complicate your investigation, and Margaret was worried for the school. She was worried how it might look. She thought we should distance ourselves. Can you blame us, given our previous experience with you lot? Innocent until proven guilty. What rot!"

The door to the surveillance room opens and DC Maxwell steps inside, sheets of printed paper clutched in her hands. "Is the Chief still grilling Crowe?"

Ben nods.

"There's something—"

"Hang on," Ben says, his ears pricking up at the interview room audio. Malcolm is leaning back in his chair, looking more comfortable. ". . . really thought you'd have questioned that other teacher by now."

"Teacher?" Khan asks, eyes narrowed as he leans forward over the table. "Which other teacher?"

"The art teacher. Morgan."

"Chase," interrupts Maxwell. "I think you—"

"Sorry, Maxwell. Hold on."

". . . saw them, bold as brass, riding through Thorncombe," Malcolm continues. "The girl was on the back of his motorbike, clinging to him like a little leaf, her blond hair fluttering beneath the helmet. In retrospect, it all seems rather suspicious."

"You saw Sarah Lawson with the art teacher from Folly View," Khan asks, leaning forward. "They were riding on his motorbike together?"

"It looked just like her, yes. And now I see him sniffing around our school counselor, with his fancy flowers and cozy chats."

"Why didn't you come forward with this information earlier?" Khan is half disbelief, half flabbergasted.

"Like I said, given my previous experience with the police, I didn't particularly want to be drawn into anything. Besides, my eyesight isn't the best. I couldn't be certain it was the girl. I did a little caretaking of my own, of course. I examined Sarah's student file, to see if she was taking his art classes, or if she'd mentioned anything in confidence to the counselor about him, but it turned out that she wasn't, and she hadn't. I figured, perhaps, that I'd got it wrong. I didn't think I had enough to bring it to your—"

"Chase! Please." Maxwell's tone is insistent, cutting through Malcolm's indignant monologue.

Ben spins in his chair. "Sorry. What've you got there?"

"Tech have pulled the data from Sarah's phone."

Ben is instantly alert. "And?"

"We got lucky. McIvor destroyed the handset, but the SIM card was relatively easy to repair. You're going to want to see this."

She offers him the printouts and Ben takes them, shuffling through the pages, scanning their content. "Facebook messages?" he asks, turning back to Maxwell for clarification.

"Yes."

Ben scans the rows and rows of text and feels his eyebrows lifting. "What the hell? They're all from the art teacher. Edward Morgan."

Maxwell nods, staying silent, letting the pieces slide into place. Ben lets out a low whistle. "Malcolm Crowe was just talking about him."

Maxwell nods. "I know."

"Someone's been telling us some whoppers."

"It's a motive, right? A reason to want to hurt Sarah?"

Ben flicks through the pages and finds another stream of messages. He reads them quickly, pieces of a baffling puzzle slotting together neatly at last. John Slater's statement from the night of the murder. Everything suddenly makes sense. He lifts his head. "It's all here."

Fiona Maxwell nods at the camera. "We need to stop that interview."

"Too right," says Ben. "We've got the wrong suspect."

Chapter 38

Ellie wishes she was wearing sturdier shoes. If Edward had warned her where they were going, she would have suggested she change her sneakers. Actually, scrap that, she thinks, cursing under her breath, she would've found an excuse to avoid this batshit-crazy trip of his altogether. Tripping and skidding up the misty woodland trail, now churned to mud by the back-and-forth of the police teams earlier in the week as well as the heavy rainfall, dodging deep drifts of leaves that have come down overnight in the high winds, Ellie is bitterly regretting her decision to follow him blindly. It's obvious now where he is taking her, and the knowledge makes her queasy with dread.

There'd been no talking on the ride. It had been just the two of them, Ellie clinging to his jacket, the headlamp of his motorbike a single, narrow beam moving ineffectually over the drifting fog until they were bumping down a track and pulling into the small woodland parking lot. "Here?" Ellie had asked, feeling the first prickle of dread.

Edward had turned the key in the ignition, the deep silence of the woods replacing the thrum of the engine. He'd removed his helmet and fluffed up his hair. "I understand how you've been feeling," he'd said.

She'd nodded, but silently wondered how he could possibly know.

"Sarah's death has affected you. Deeply."

The lump that had been lodged in her throat since Saturday night seemed to swell at his mention of Sarah. She'd busied herself with removing her helmet, fumbling with the clasp.

"It's frightening, isn't it, when the blinkers come off and you understand the world is a chaotic place? No real order. It's a loss of innocence."

Ellie had frowned. Was he implying she'd been naive . . . childish? That she didn't know bad things happened in the world? Because if he was, he was wrong. That bubble had completely burst the day her aunt Gemma had died. And again, on the day her dad had moved out of the family home. She was more than aware that life could bring sadness and pain. She'd wanted to protest, but he hadn't finished.

"A place like Thorncombe can feel like a bubble, as if nothing bad could ever happen here. But no place is safe, not really. You only have to look back historically to see that."

She'd frowned, not entirely sure what he meant.

"Death isn't something many of us are skilled at talking about, or know how to cope with, especially when it comes suddenly, unexpectedly. Which is strange, don't you think, given that birth and death are the most natural processes we will experience, and the only two common certainties we all have in life?"

Ellie had tilted her head. "I guess. I hadn't really thought about it . . ." She'd trailed off. As far as she knew, there'd been nothing natural about Sarah's death, but before she could make that point, Edward was talking again, warming to his argument.

"We don't like to think about it, do we?" He'd turned to her again and she'd nodded, wanting to please him, even though she still wasn't entirely sure where his argument was leading. "We live like we're immortal. Like these lives of ours are going to go on and on forever. Teenagers are the worst," he'd added, a half smile on his lips. "You're programmed to experiment and take risks . . . live like you're invincible. That's why, when something happens out of the blue, something out of order like Sarah's death, we often don't have the language or the skills to work through it." He'd shaken his head. "It's no wonder you're struggling with the weight of it."

He'd taken the helmet from her hands, helped her down off the bike, and made for the start of the walking trail. The knot in her stomach had clenched even tighter. "What are we doing here?" she'd asked.

"Ellie, my father and I didn't have the easiest relationship," Edward had continued. "There was some bad blood between us. Some misunderstandings. He never approved of my decision to pursue an art career. When he died, I realized there were things I wished I'd had a chance to say to him. Regret . . . guilt. Those emotions can stay with you if you don't find a way to let them go. They can block you . . . emotionally," he turns to her, his eyes bright, ". . . and creatively."

Ellie had frowned. "What did you do?"

"A therapist suggested that I say all those things that I'd never had a chance to say to him. To find a place that reminded me of him, and to tell him everything that was on my mind. So, I did."

Traipsing behind him, Ellie had found herself curious. "Did it help?"

"I didn't expect it to, but yes, it did. And I think it might help you too."

"Me?"

"You said earlier that you wished you could say 'sorry' to Sarah, that you can't stop thinking about her. About what happened between you both in the woods on the night of her death? So, how about we go up there," he'd jerked his head in the direction of the trail, "and you say all the things you want to say to Sarah. In the spot where you were last together?"

Ellie had felt her eyes go wide. "That sounds kind of . . . weird."

"Perhaps. But what if it helped you let go of some of these overwhelming emotions? What if it meant you could focus again? You've got a full-on year ahead of you, if you want to get to UAL. There's a lot at stake. It's worth a shot, don't you think?"

"I don't know," said Ellie, secretly horrified by the idea. "I don't think I want to talk to Sarah. Not in front of you."

"You don't have to speak the words out loud. Talk to her in your head, privately, if that feels easier. I'll just be there for moral support."

Ellie had pulled a face, still skeptical. How could she tell him she didn't want to do it, when he'd shared all that stuff about his own father? When he'd gone to the trouble of bringing her out here? How could she tell him that the last thing she wanted to do was go up into the woods again—to the place where this whole nightmare had begun?

But Edward was already moving toward the path, tugging his jacket collar up against the cold. She'd sighed. If it had been her mum or dad, she would've simply told them where to go and refused to budge, but this was Edward—her teacher. She'd hesitated a second, eyeing the bike and the route back, a jittery feeling creeping up her legs. Everything in her body had seemed to scream *don't go*, but Edward was beckoning to her and she could see the hint of impatience creeping over his face. With a sinking feeling, she'd started to follow him up into the fog. It hadn't seemed as if she had a choice.

Stumbling along behind him now through the mist-cloaked woods, cursing her stupidity for blindly climbing onto the back of his bike, rather than finding some excuse to take her back to the safety of the common room, she focuses on the back of his leather jacket, and on her breath ballooning before her face. *Stupid, stupid, stupid*, she chants internally to the beat of her footsteps.

"You know these woods are supposed to be haunted?" he calls back to her.

Ellie doesn't really want to think about that. The place is creepy enough on a normal day, but after everything that's happened, and with the fog slinking between the trees, it seems to have taken on an even more sinister feel.

"You've heard the story about the girl murdered in the folly?"

"It's just an old wives' tale," says Ellie, with more bravado than she feels. She glances around, trying to read shapes in the fog. Just tree trunks, looming out at her, branches grabbing and clawing, and Edward forging on up the trail. "You know, I'm really OK with not doing this," she says. "I'm sure I'll feel more like myself in a few days."

But he isn't listening. He's talking again, his voice trailing down the slope toward her. "I've been planning a series of paintings based on the local stories from this area," he calls over his shoulder. "Did I tell you that?"

"No," she puffs, trying to keep up, putting on a sudden sprint to reach him where he's waiting for her beside a gnarly oak.

"Yes, I was inspired by you lot. You've been working on art projects drawn from the local landscape and I thought I'd do the same in a new collection. I've always been interested in the echoes a place holds. I'd been thinking about the story of the girl at the folly, and now here we are. Such a strange coincidence. I was working on a painting of the folly." He turns to regard her. "But I probably won't ever show it now."

"Why not?" She's grateful for the moment to catch her breath.

"It wouldn't be right."

Ellie glances around. She has the strangest feeling, as if someone might be watching them. It feels as if Sarah could slide out of the mist in her white dress and stand before them. The thought makes her shiver.

When they finally emerge from the trees into the folly clearing, the tower looms high in front of them, its apex disappearing into the white. Piles of copper leaves have fallen since she was last here, blown into high drifts against its stone walls. Ellie sees the tatters of police tape dangling from branches in forlorn scraps and hangs back, feeling sick to her stomach to be at the place of Sarah's death. At the place where they fought.

It's ominously quiet, the mist only seeming to muffle the silence of the place, making it feel as though they've stepped into a vacuum, somewhere out of place, out of time. Not a single birdcall. Her gaze trails up the stone walls, dark against the swirling fog, that gaping void at the top from which Sarah had plunged. A reel of imagined images flickers through her mind. She shudders. Poor Sarah.

"It's fear that's blocking your creativity," says Edward, seeing her reaction.

Ellie shrugs. "Perhaps. I mean . . . I don't know . . ."

"Do you know how you eradicate fear?"

She shakes her head.

"You face it head-on. You can't squash it. So, feel it, and then act anyway. Do that and you're free. Invincible."

Ellie frowns. She's still not sure what he's talking about, or what they're doing here. Seeing her confusion, he moves a little closer.

"What's the thing you're most frightened of, Ellie?"

She glances up at the folly towering over them.

Edward follows her gaze. "That's it. That's where we'll go." He is already marching toward the yawning black entrance, stepping through the open doorway before stopping to look back at her. "Come on, what are you waiting for?"

"I . . . I don't want to go up there."

He turns to look up at the internal shaft of the tower, then glances back at her. One foot is still poised on the bottom step, his teeth shining white, though his eyes remain unreadable, cast in the shadow of the folly. "It's not so frightening when you're in here. Come on."

There's more than a hint of impatience about him now. She can tell Edward is growing frustrated that she isn't embracing his idea and Ellie is frightened not just of the tower, but of letting him down, of disappointing him. He only wants to help. She glances back at the trail and the trees, sees the mist slinking around their trunks, then makes for the tower, stepping through the doorway and following Edward into the shadows.

Chapter 39

Rachel drives as fast as the fog will allow, her adrenaline firing as she careens along the twisting lane. If her hunch about where Edward is taking Ellie is right, the woodland parking lot offers the best access point to the trail. It's the quickest route.

She punches Ben's number over and over, willing him to pick up, but the signal drops out and it takes several attempts before she hears ringing and then, blessedly, Ben's voice answering. "Rachel. What's—"

"He's got Ellie, Ben. He's taken her into the woods."

"Wha—" Crackling static breaks his words. "—mean got Ellie?"

"You said you were taking him into custody, but he's still out there and he's got our daughter." Her voice is rising in pitch, fear constricting her throat. The tires hit a patch of mud and the car's rear swings out, forcing Rachel to wrestle with the wheel. She swears and feels Olivia's startled glance in her direction.

"Rachel. Slow . . . not making sense . . . to Khan now." She's only getting every few words, the patchy reception playing havoc with the line.

"I'm with Olivia. She saw them leave, Ben. Edward's been lying to everyone. And now he's got Ellie. I'm frightened about what he might do."

There's a long silence as the line drops out again. Rachel curses before Ben's voice fills the car in a rush. "—are you? Don't go any-where w—"

"I have to get Ellie away from him."

"Rachel . . . it's dangerous . . . new information. You need to protect . . . Olivia . . . Ellie."

"That's what I'm telling you, Ben!" She thumps the steering wheel.

"Just stay—"

His last words are lost as the line cuts out. Rachel glances across at Olivia. The girl is white-faced, one leg jerking up and down, her hand thrust deep in her coat pocket, moving agitat-edly, as if she turns a pebble over and over in her fingers. Guilt washes over her. She shouldn't have brought her. It's too danger-ous and she's been through so much already. "I can drop you here. I'll go on alone."

Olivia shakes her head. "Here? In the middle of nowhere?"

Rachel glances out at the foggy lane. She has a point. "What do you think he wants with Ellie?" She swallows. It's a question she hasn't wanted to ask, but now she's voiced it, all manner of frightening possibilities seem to rise up.

Olivia shrugs. "I don't know. I thought I knew him. I thought he loved me. But I see now that I had no idea who he was."

Rachel thinks about Ben's broken words. *You need to protect . . .* "When we get to the woods, you're to stay in the car. Understood?"

Olivia doesn't answer and Rachel presses her foot to the accelerator.

Chapter 40

Ellie takes the crumbling steps one at a time, her hand trailing the damp stone wall, her footsteps echoing through the hollow chamber as she climbs the tower behind Edward, the two of them rising toward the platform high above their heads. She refuses to look down, painfully aware of the sheer drop to her right and the unforgiving stone floor far below.

At the very top, with her feet finally braced on the solid wooden platform, she lets out a shaky breath and moves to grip the nearest wall. Above her head, the pitched rafters are slung with gray cobwebs fluttering like dirty rags in the breeze.

"Come and look," says Edward, beckoning for her to join him near the arched opening. "It's quite amazing."

His body is solid against the white sky. She shakes her head, too frightened to take the final steps to close the gap.

"Come on. I've got you. Face the fear, remember?"

Tentatively, she creeps forward, arms outstretched until she is standing next to him. Beyond the opening, she can see the black spears of treetops rising out of the mist below, the rest of the valley erased in a deep blanket of fog. "Oh," she says, the word a soft breath leaving her body. The sight is surreal and strange and, she agrees with Edward, quite amazing. She turns to look at him and offers a tentative smile. "I've never seen anything like this."

"See?" he says. "Not so frightening after all."

Ellie nods, but as eerily beautiful as it is, it's hard not to think about Sarah, about what she might have experienced up here on the night of her death. What would it be like to plunge from the top? To feel yourself falling through the air, and the ground rushing up to meet you? She shudders at the thought and seeing her reaction, Edward places a firm hand on her shoulder. "Is this the place? Do you want to try talking to Sarah here?"

She nods, still not sure this is exactly what she wants, but needing at the very least to prove to him that she is trying. To get this over and done with. Looking out at the white horizon, she attempts to conjure the words and feelings she's had churning in her mind since Saturday night. Words of regret and apology. Sorry, sorry, sorry, she thinks, remembering the stupid fight, the fury she'd felt at Sarah's taunts, her too-hasty response. Sorry that I let my temper get the better of me. I wish I had stayed. I wish things had turned out differently. I wish I could have protected you.

A blackbird lifts off a tree branch and flies out like a dart across the white. Tracing its path, she watches it land, then lets out a sharp breath as just below, stepping from the mist, she sees the figure of a girl in white. Ellie stares down at her long fair hair and her heart-shaped face, tilted up toward the apex of the folly. "Sarah?" she gasps.

Ellie stumbles a little, reaching for the stone wall. She is imagining it. She has to be, because Ellie doesn't want to believe in ghosts and the only way Sarah could be here with them now is if these woods have conjured her, pulled her vengeful wraith from the trees.

"What's wrong?" asks Edward, sensing her shock, taking a step forward to follow her gaze.

Ellie opens her mouth to speak but no words will come. She is imagining it, she thinks. She has to be. But when she turns back to Edward for reassurance, she can see the alarm in his eyes.

"What the hell . . ." he says, gazing down at the girl. "What is *she* doing here?"

Chapter 41

For all her intention to make Olivia stay in the car, the moment that they pull into the woodland parking lot, screeching to a halt next to Edward's motorbike, Olivia bolts, taking off up the misty woodland trail, leaving Rachel still wrestling with her seat belt. "Wait, Olivia!" she calls, setting out after her, but her voice, muffled by the fog, is met only by the eerie silence of the woods. She tries to keep pace with the girl, every so often catching a glimpse of her cream coat flashing ahead among the trees, but then she's gone again, lost in the mist.

The path is slippery with mud and leaves, treacherous with rocks and sprawling tree roots. Near the top, Rachel staggers and trips, falls to her knees, then rises and presses on, ignoring her scrapes and grazes. Something about the deep silence stops her from calling out again. Nearer the crest of the escarpment now, she is afraid of alerting Edward to their approach, afraid of what he might do if he knows they are close.

Stumbling into the folly clearing, she sees Olivia standing beneath the tower, gazing up at its high stone walls. Rachel's own gaze tracks upward. She lets out a sharp gasp. Like a bird on a branch ready to take flight, Ellie is right there, poised at the edge of the opening, facing the sheer drop below. At her back looms Edward, tall and threatening. Any words of warning catch in her throat. All he'd have to do is stretch out a hand and shove. The thought chills her to her marrow.

Ellie has one hand on the edge of the opening and is staring down at Olivia, a startled look on her face. As Rachel steps out from the line of trees, she sees her daughter's head shift, her gaze coming to land on her. "Mum?" The word echoes down to her. "What's going on?"

Rachel lifts her hands, as if she would push her daughter away from the high drop. "Ellie, move back from the edge."

"But what are you doing here?"

Rachel scans for Olivia, but the girl has disappeared, perhaps around the other side of the folly, or back into the line of trees flanking the clearing. She doesn't have time to think about her, because a movement is pulling her attention back to the top of the folly. Edward has taken a determined step forward—closer to Ellie. "Stay away from her, Edward."

Edward doesn't listen. He takes another step to join Ellie at the ledge, peering down at her. "Rachel?"

"I'm warning you, Edward, if anything happens to Ellie . . ."

He lifts his hands. In her mind's eye she sees her daughter jerk forward, her arms reaching for something to grab on to, finding nothing before plunging over the edge, falling, falling, a replay of the nightmare she'd woken from earlier that morning.

"No," Rachel screams, screwing her eyes shut, but there is no awful *thump* of impact, and when she opens her eyes again, Ellie is still there, staring down at her from the top of the folly.

"What are you doing here?" asks Edward, sounding genuinely alarmed.

"Let her go, Edward."

"Who? Ellie?"

"I've seen the messages, Edward. The photos. The painting. It's over. Let Ellie come down and we'll talk. Just the two of us. But first, let her come down, safely."

Edward shakes his head. "What messages? What are you talking about?"

"I know all about the grooming. The coercive control. The secret relationship."

Edward peers down at her. "Rachel, are you OK? I have no idea what you're on about."

"Mum?" Ellie looks frightened. She grips the arched stone opening. "What's going on?"

"Edward, I saw them. The painting. The photos in your studio. The messages on Olivia's phone."

A flicker of shock crosses his face. "You saw the painting?"

She nods. "It'll be better if you come down. Ellie first. Then you."

Ellie is twisting to look at Edward.

"I can explain," Edward protests. "The painting was a mistake. I never should've asked Olivia to model for me that afternoon. It was silly. I didn't think it through. There was no way I could've known that the painting would somehow end up mirroring what happened to Sarah. It's an eerie coincidence. Not a sign of guilt." He lifts his hands. "You know me. You know I'd never hurt anyone."

He sounds smooth, convincing even, and Rachel sees how he has fooled them all for so long.

"But it wasn't just one afternoon, was it? You've been conducting a private relationship with Olivia for months now."

"No," insists Edward. "That's not true."

"There's no point lying. I've seen the messages. All those words. All those promises." He looks baffled, but she isn't buying it.

"Rachel, truly, I don't know what you're talking about. There's nothing going on between us. Olivia is just a student to me. Nothing more."

A high sound rises from inside the folly, cutting Edward off, a wail that echoes through the hollow stone tower, before flying out of its dark apertures, screeching across the clearing. It's a shriek of torment and indignation. A cry of pain. Rachel sees Edward spin around as a third figure rushes up onto the platform, joining Edward and Ellie at the top. Olivia.

She staggers into view, something silver flashing in her hand, rushing forward, heading straight for Edward and Ellie at the ledge.

"Olivia! No!" screams Rachel, her heart in her mouth, but it's too late.

They tussle on the brink, a tangle of flailing limbs, and Rachel watches in horror as one falls back. A shout of surprise. Arms pinwheeling in the air, reaching helplessly for the sky as they plummet like a stone to the earth below.

Chapter 42

Ben is almost at the clearing when he hears the scream. It echoes down through the trees and sends a bird flapping from a nearby branch. It's enough to spur him on, to make him push harder up the steep trail, his muscles straining and his lungs burning. He hasn't stopped since he took Rachel's desperate call about Edward, racing to the woods, finding Rachel's car and the motorbike abandoned in the parking lot, before following muddy prints up the folly track. What an unholy mess. He only hopes he isn't too late.

Emerging into the clearing, it's strangely quiet, the folly standing as a silent monument in the white mist, a soft sobbing noise drifting on the damp air. He spots Rachel a short distance away, crouched over something lying in a deep drift of autumn leaves. Ben blinks and the object takes shape—not a thing, but a person. A body.

Rachel is checking for signs of breathing, clearing airways, gently but firmly tilting a chin. He races forward, his heart in his mouth, relief flooding through him when he sees that it's not Ellie lying sprawled in the leaves, but the teacher, Edward Morgan, one leg twisted horribly beneath him, his face ashen, blank eyes staring at the sky, blood trickling from his mouth.

"Where are the girls?"

Rachel jerks her head at the folly. "Up there. Safe. Thank god you're here. He has a pulse, but it's weak. I don't think he's going to make it."

Ben lifts his head as the soft crying spirals in the air. "Backup's on its way. I'm going up to the girls. Will you be OK?"

Rachel nods. "Yes. He can't hurt us now."

Ben shakes his head and holds a finger to his lips. He doesn't have time to explain. "Stay here," he murmurs. "I'm going to Ellie."

A low groan lifts from Edward, drawing Rachel's attention. She lowers her mouth to his ear. "Edward, it's Rachel. Help's coming."

Ben knows there's nothing more he can do for the man that Rachel isn't already doing. He needs an ambulance. Urgent emergency care. Leaving Rachel's side, he makes his way to the folly entrance, stepping into its dank cavity, feeling his legs give a little as he looks up at the spiraling steps leading to the upper reaches of the tower. His heartbeat is already galloping at the thought. Get a grip, he tells himself. You can do this. It's just a few steps, that's all. Do it for Ellie.

"Dad?" Ellie's voice echoes down to him. A frightened tremor in that one word that pierces his heart and forces his foot onto the first step. "I'm coming, sweetheart. Stay where you are."

Step by shaky step, he climbs the tower, almost to the top when a second voice calls out to him. "Don't come any higher."

Ben grips the stone wall and glances up at the rafters above his head, immediately regretting it as they spin kaleidoscopically, his legs threatening to collapse beneath him. The sensation that he could topple at any moment down the open shaft is overwhelming. Vertigo has him in its grip.

He takes a couple of deep, ragged breaths before he answers. "Olivia, I just want to come up and talk. That's all."

He takes her silence as acquiescence and forces himself up the last steps, until he is through the gap in the wooden platform.

Olivia stands by the arched opening, one arm wrapped around Ellie, a STANLEY knife in her hands, its silver blade pressed against Ellie's throat. Tears streak down Olivia's cheeks and he can see the desperation in her eyes. A girl on the edge. Ellie, in comparison, is still and wide-eyed. Good girl, he thinks. Don't move. Stay calm. He tries to reassure her with his gaze.

Ben assesses the gap between them and knows there's no way he can cross the space fast enough. Even if his faltering legs allowed it, if he rushed at Olivia, he risks both girls going over the edge, or Olivia hurting Ellie with the blade. Instead, he holds out his hands in a placatory gesture. "It's over, Olivia. We know what happened on Halloween night. It would be best all round if you came down now, safely." He edges forward.

"Don't. That's close enough," calls Olivia. She presses the knife firmly against Ellie's skin and he hears his daughter's whimper.

Ben doesn't want to risk it. He drops his hands. "I'm not moving."

Olivia blinks slowly. "Is he dead?" Her question is soft, tremulous.

He doesn't want to lie. "Edward's in a bad way, but help's coming."

"I didn't mean to hurt him. I love him," she adds, the tears glistening on her cheeks. "I love him so much."

"I know, Olivia. I know everything. Just put the knife down."

"But if I let Ellie go, it's over, isn't it? I just want everything to go back to how it was—how I *thought* it was."

"Olivia, no one else needs to get hurt."

The girl's hands are shaking. "I just wanted Sarah to tell me why she'd done it. Why she'd pretended. Why she made a fool out of me." Olivia's voice trembles with emotion. "Six months she kept it up. Six whole months. Nothing but a sick game. Like a cat toying with a mouse."

"We know she faked all the messages to you from Edward. We've got her phone now, Olivia. Catfishing, that's what they call it, isn't it? Using a fake identity to deceive someone."

Olivia nods slowly.

Talking is good, thinks Ben. Talking means she's not think-ing about Ellie, or the blade in her hand. Ben needs to keep her talking. "It was very cruel," he says. "How did you find out? What gave her away?" He edges forward, his gaze never leaving Olivia and the blade shining against Ellie's throat.

"It was at the party. Connor gave Sarah a dare and she went in on him. Kissed Connor right there and then. I couldn't believe she'd do that to Danny. It was so mean. So childish. I was sick of the party. I just wanted to be at home, so I sent Edward a text from my secret account to tell him I was missing him."

Ben takes another step forward.

"The next thing I know, Ellie's making a huge deal about some-thing showing up on Sarah's phone. A notification. She was wav-ing it around, trying to get Danny's attention. It was only when Danny read it out to the group, demanding that Sarah tell him why someone was missing her and sending heart emojis, that I realized it was *my* message, arriving in Sarah's inbox. He'd read it out word for word."

Ben locks eyes with Ellie. He tries to reassure her that he is there, that he won't let anything happen to her.

"I didn't believe it at first," continues Olivia. "I thought I'd made a mistake, but I took the phone off Danny and I saw it there. My message, from my secret account. MU5E123. I just knew. All that time. All those lies. It was Sarah pretending to be Edward on-line. Bouncing messages back and forth, pretending to be him . . .

pretending to be in love with me. Telling me I was special . . . his muse. Making me confess my deepest feelings . . . making me believe we were in a relationship when all along it was just Sarah, trolling me . . . laughing at me."

"That must have been very painful."

Olivia nods, her lower lip trembling. "That night I lost the two people I trusted most in the world. One because she'd been lying to me. The other because he'd never really existed, at least not as I knew him." She takes a shuddering breath. "It all suddenly made sense, why Edward had been so good at covering up in class, his offhand demeanor whenever we saw each other in person. I thought he was a great actor, but to him, I really was just another student. Our love affair was a complete fiction. I was never special. Never really his muse." She lets out a small sob, her hand shaking, the edge of the knife shimmering in the white light. "He never loved me. He never really existed."

Ben nods. "Sarah played a very cruel trick on you."

Olivia lets out a sob. "I didn't want to hurt her."

"Put the knife down and we'll talk it all through, calmly."

"But you don't understand." Olivia shakes her head, her eyes darting wildly. "I left them all at the party, but when I got home, I couldn't sleep. I needed to know why she'd done it. I waited up. Midnight came and went. Then it was 1:00 a.m. Still no Sarah. I sent her messages. I sent them from my secret account to her 'Edward' account, and then from my phone to her phone. I wanted her to know that I knew. I could see she'd read them, but she didn't reply. Too chickenshit to face me."

Olivia's face twists with rage. Ben knows he needs to keep her calm if he's going to help Ellie, but she's ranting now, spilling her secrets like a bloodletting.

"She wasn't going to face me, so I slipped out of the house. I could see on the location app that she was still at the folly and I found her here alone, hanging out on the top platform, drinking from a bottle of wine, her nose all busted up, blood smeared down the front of the white dress I'd loaned her. *My* dress."

Ben notices Ellie wince in recognition.

"She'd promised to look after it, but it was ruined. She'd trashed the only thing Edward had ever given me—his thank-you gift for that afternoon in his studio and the only remnant of anything real and meaningful between us." Olivia's eyes flash. "Sarah blamed you," she says, spitting the words at Ellie. "She said you'd fought, that you'd broken her nose. She said you had blood on your hands. That she'd make you pay."

Ben sees Ellie's eyes widen, a jolt of recognition. "It was you," she says softly. "You sent me those messages."

Olivia's eyes glitter with emotion. "Sarah was laughing at you, Ellie. She told me you were raging at her, ranting on and on about how you were going to stop Dad's development. She was laughing about it, but she didn't see it from my point of view. She didn't see how everything you and your lot do to block Dad's project only keeps him away from us, keeps him away from me and Mum. You wouldn't understand anything about that though, would you, Ellie? Because your mum and dad actually notice you."

Ben sees Ellie's eyes welling with tears. *Easy*, he tries to warn her. *Stay calm.*

"It wasn't fair," says Olivia. "You had everything, and you were causing trouble for my family, trying to stop the development. Then Sarah died and Dad still couldn't be there for me. He didn't have time, did he? He was too busy worrying about illegal protests and conservation covenants and the whole development slipping through his fingers. I needed you to back off, Ellie. To give up your crusade, so the project could go ahead and I could get my dad back."

Ben doesn't like this shift in Olivia's focus. He needs to keep her trained on him. Not Ellie. Not the knife in her hand. "Olivia, look at me. Tell me, why did Sarah do it? Why did she pretend to be Edward? Did she explain?"

Olivia's expression twists. "She had the audacity to say she did it to help me, to boost my confidence. She said she wanted me to feel 'worthy of love.' But I didn't buy it. I think it was a power trip. She did it to Danny too, pulled his strings, kept him dangling. I think she enjoyed toying with us all, making us her pawns, watching us dance to her tune. It was all just a sick game to her. But she'd humiliated me. She took away the one good thing I thought was mine."

"What happened?"

"We fought up here, at the top of the folly." Olivia glances around, wild-eyed. "I was sick of her excuses. I couldn't stop myself. I pushed and scratched her and we were so close to the edge when I shoved her and she . . . she staggered." Olivia shakes her head. "One minute she was here, holding on to the opening, and the next she was gone."

"She fell?"

Olivia shrugs. She doesn't meet his eye. "I don't know. I mean, she didn't even scream. Just dropped, silently, no sound but her body hitting the ground." She shudders.

"When I got to the bottom, I found her lying face down in the dirt. I knew she was dead. I screamed. I was so frightened. I didn't know what to do, but I heard something in the woods, rustling noises, coming closer, and I panicked, thinking someone might've seen me. I ran away."

McIvor, thinks Ben, remembering the man's insistence that he'd heard a woman's scream, piecing together the details, the man's strange, reverential care over the body he'd found there, Sarah linked in his disturbed mind to Gemma's death all those years ago.

"I ran all the way home. I was so frightened, in such a blind panic, that I darted out in front of a car as I crossed Sally in the Wood. It almost hit me. It was only when I got into bed that I realized Sarah's phone was still at the folly. It had every message on it. Every last piece of evidence about what she'd done. I thought when you turned up at the house that first afternoon that you'd have pieced it all together, that you'd come to arrest me. It was only when I heard about the words on her skin and the mask you'd found on her face that I got really scared. I'd never do anything sick like that. You have to believe me."

"I do believe you, Olivia. We know you didn't do those things. We know everything now. I just need you to put the knife down and everything will be OK."

A look of relief crosses her face, a softening in her eyes, a slight relaxation of her arm against Ellie's body. Yes, he thinks, and for a split second he believes it will be all right, that she will let go of Ellie, until Rachel's panicked voice rises up from below. "Ben," she calls, her voice desperate. "He's stopped breathing."

A sob leaves Olivia's lips. "Don't let him die," she implores. "I love him." She glances down into the clearing below, and Ben sees the pain and anger rising again on her face. "Not that he loves me. He wants *her*," she spits. "I've been watching them. Together at his house. A cozy dinner for two. Bet you didn't know that, did you?" she adds, shaking Ellie, casting an angry glance at Ben. "He wants her, not me, and there's nothing I can do about it."

Ellie throws Ben an imploring look. He can see the silver edge of the blade pressing against her skin, the beads of blood where the pressure is intensifying. He screws his hands into fists. "Help will be here soon, Olivia. Edward will be OK," he lies. "No one else needs to get hurt."

He can see it in her face, the hesitation as she teeters between two choices, the shift as she decides.

"No!" he shouts, but it's too late.

In one fluid motion she shoves Ellie away and turns to face the drop.

Ben lunges for her.

Olivia seems to balance for a split second, precarious at the edge, before she steps out into the air.

He dives forward and catches her arm, feels her pulling him over, his body slipping on the rough wooden boards, gravity threatening to drag him over the ledge with her. He groans, his arm nearly wrenched from its socket as he takes the full weight of Olivia and holds her over the void.

Olivia screams, a cry of fear and anguish, but he doesn't let go and then Ellie is there, beside him, dropping to her stomach, reaching down for Olivia's other hand. "Don't let go, Dad," she says, and they don't, slowly hauling the girl up until all three of them are lying on the platform, gasping and panting, tears streaming from eyes. Ben holds a sobbing Olivia tightly in his arms, part restraint, part comfort, as Ellie clings to her dad, the three of them locked together safely, until the sound of voices and the static crackle of police radios echoes through the mist, breaking the silence of the folly.

Chapter 43

December 12, 12:00 p.m.

Gold and silver decorations have been strung across the atrium and a tall Christmas tree twinkles its gaudy lights as they make their way through the hospital entrance to the orthopedic ward. This is the second time she's visited with her mum and Ellie knows the way now, knows what to expect through the heavy double doors where Edward lies strung up in traction.

He'd been lucky to survive the fall, the pink-cheeked nurse who was clearly already a little bit in love with him had told them on their first visit, counting off his long list of injuries like impressive battle scars. Internal bleeding. Severe concussion. A cracked skull. Shattered pelvis. Broken wrist, collarbone, and femur. "He'll be like the bionic man when we're finished with him," she'd joked, leading them to his bedside.

"I don't know how he survived it," Rachel had murmured. The only explanation seemed to be the dense autumn leaves blown like a snowdrift against the high walls of the folly, which had gone some small way to breaking the severity of his fall, and Rachel's Herculean CPR efforts to keep him alive before help had arrived. Without those two things, everyone agreed he would have most certainly died. Instead, Edward was staring at a long road to recovery, months of healing and physio, but with life all the same beckoning on the other side.

"Put it this way," he'd told them with a brave smile, "I don't think I'll be riding my motorbike anytime soon."

His face visibly brightens at the sight of them at his cubicle and Ellie adjusts the folder in her arms so that she can give him a small, shy wave. He looks different, and not just for the convoluted contraptions and machines all around him. His hair has grown out into wayward feathers and he sports a dark, unruly beard.

"It's good of you to visit again," he says, looking genuinely pleased. "I can't tell you how tired I am of staring at these ceiling tiles."

"We've brought you some things," says Rachel, offering him headphones and an iPad. "So that you can watch movies and listen to podcasts while you're stuck in here."

"That's really thoughtful. Thank you." He beams at Rachel, before turning his attention to Ellie. "What's that you've got there?"

"Mum thought you might like to see my art portfolio."

"Your mum's right. I'd love to. I heard you smashed the assessment. Highest possible marks, and you got the whole town talking too from the sound of it. Very clever."

Ellie nods. "It was only up for twelve hours. I had to take it down after that. But I got loads of photos and a bit of press coverage too. It's all in here. I'll show you."

She lays the folder across the bed and talks him through the various stages of her creation, the replica advertising hoarding she'd created, mimicking the CGI display of Easton Developments' plans for the wildflower meadow. At first glance, it looks like the original, but on closer inspection it's clear she's stripped away the glossy sales pitch. All the details of the happy scene have been subverted. The trees are leafless and dying. The grass is brown. The baby in the carriage is wailing. The cars in the cul-de-sacs send out plumes of emissions. The houses have cracks, missing roof slates, and broken windows. There's dog shit on the pavements and most striking of all, a tiny cemetery of crosses, marking the graves of all the wild animals destroyed in the build, a river of blood flowing down from the woods and weaving among them.

"It was so big I had to work on it in sections. Some of it in spray paint, some of it in oils. I kept my kit at a site in the woods so I didn't have to drag everything back and forth from campus all the time. When it was finished, I went out after dark and assembled the design over the original with a time lapse to record myself. What's fun is that I caught all the cars on the video the next morning, slowing down to look at the art piece, people getting out to take a closer look or snap photos."

"I heard the housing development is under council review?"

Ellie can't hide her delighted smile.

"Yes," says her mum, full of pride. "Ellie's certainly galvanized community feeling. A news station came out to talk to her. But it's not all thanks to Ellie. There's Malcolm Crowe too. His studies of the horseshoe bats roosting in the quarry caves have got a national conservation group fired up. They've found evidence to suggest the wildflower meadow is an important bat corridor. Any major development on the land will disturb their path and could put them at risk. They're an endangered species so it's looking pretty open-and-shut. Between Ellie and Malcolm, not even Christopher Easton will be buying his way out of this one."

Edward throws her mum a wry look. "I heard he'd been buying inside intel from a dodgy copper."

Rachel nods. "Yes, Ben was pleased to see DC Crawford dismissed. I'm told, on the down-low, that he'd been a total liability throughout the Sarah Lawson case."

Edward turns back to Ellie. "Your project's a triumph, whichever way you look at it. I hope you're putting it all into your college admission forms. This is the sort of stuff they'd love to hear about, details that will set you apart from the other applicants."

Ellie flushes pink. "Our substitute teacher isn't nearly as good as you, but she's helping me with all the uni forms."

"I'm pleased, Ellie. You've got a bright future ahead of you."

Talking about her future is exciting, but it brings another less pleasant thought to mind. "What's going to happen to Olivia? Does anyone know?"

"That's up to the courts," says Rachel. "I believe a date's been set for a hearing. In the meantime, Ben says she's being held in youth detention." Rachel turns to Edward. "He told me you're reluctant to press charges against Olivia for the assault at the tower?"

Edward tries to shrug but winces instead. "She's already facing criminal proceedings for Sarah's death. After the emotional distress of what Sarah put her through, followed by the traumatic events of that week, the state of her relationship with her parents, well, I think she's been through enough already. The most important thing is that she gets the help she needs. I don't know how the system will treat her, but I hope there is some room for compassion."

Her mum nods. "You can withdraw your statement, but you must know the Crown Prosecution may continue, regardless? It's unlikely they'll let it go," she warns.

"Whatever happens, I felt it was important that Olivia knew *I* didn't blame her. I hope it's a small comfort, whatever lies ahead for the girl."

Her mum shakes her head. "I still feel so awful that I assumed . . . that I thought you capable of . . ." She trails off.

Edward shakes his head. "Don't, Rachel. You've already apologized. The evidence she showed you, everything she said. What were you supposed to think?"

Ellie considers Edward's generosity toward Olivia. She wonders if that's why she hasn't told anyone about Olivia's creepy messages, the taunting words sent from sally@inthewoods in the days after Sarah's death. She thinks she understands why Olivia sent them now. She's talked a lot with her mum in the aftermath, trying to make sense of Olivia's state of mind and put the events at the folly into some kind of order in her head. "I think Olivia was desperately lonely," her mum had explained. "After Sarah's betrayal, after losing trust in her best friend and a man she thought truly loved her, after the awful fight at the folly and Sarah's death, she desperately needed love and care. Sadly, I suspect Olivia's mother hasn't been able to care for her in a long time, not since her riding accident, and her father was so caught up with his work, so determined to fight anyone who put up resistance. She needed her family more than ever after Sarah's death, and there was no one there for her."

Ellie had understood then that Olivia's anonymous messages had been her attempt to keep Ellie from stirring up trouble. A way to scare her from her disruption of the project and the plans she had shared with Sarah up at the folly, which Sarah had in turn shared with Olivia. Olivia had been trying to smooth the path for her father's development so that she might, in turn, draw him back into her life.

Shining a light on Olivia's screwed-up home life and desperate behavior had made Ellie feel sorry for Olivia, rather than frightened of her. She guesses, from what Edward's just said, that he feels the same way. Was this what he'd meant by "facing your fears"? That opening them up and understanding them a little better somehow removed them of their power?

"You might be interested to know," says her mum, "that I did a little digging into Sarah's life, before she moved to the UK. I spoke to the head teacher at her previous school in Dubai. He told me that this wasn't the first time Sarah had pulled a catfishing stunt, that she'd tricked her former best friend in a similar way, creating and managing a fake profile on social media—a fictional boyfriend—to interact with her. When it all came out, she was shunned by her peer group. It was one of the reasons for her move here. The Dubai school agreed to keep it quiet. They didn't want the scandal getting out. The Head told me they went easy on Sarah, given her father's death and the fact she'd decided to withdraw from the school. The incident was never written up in her file."

"I still don't really understand why she would do such a thing," murmurs Ellie. "Why catfish your best friend? Your own cousin? It's *so* weird."

"It is, but it does happen. I imagine manipulating the people closest to her brought Sarah a feeling of power or control," explains her mum. "She'd lost her father not long before. Her life might've felt out of control and frightening. Her behavior may have been a reaction to his death. Grief can do funny things to people," she says. "It can isolate us, make us angry, resentful. It can make us feel detached from the people we love." Ellie appraises her mum and has the distinct feeling that she's not just talking about Sarah anymore.

"I was sorry not to make it to Sarah's memorial service," admits Edward. "I would've liked to have been there."

"The school did a lovely tribute," her mum admits.

"Did you go, Ellie?"

She nods. She'd felt uncomfortable about attending, frightened that the service would churn everything up again, but her mum had told her it was important to go; that it was a chance to honor the best parts of Sarah's life. It would give everyone the opportunity to process her death and say goodbye. In a way, her mum had been right. Hearing the tributes from Sarah's teachers and fellow students, listening to the choir perform some of Sarah's favorite songs, had stirred her emotions. It had helped Ellie to remember Sarah as the living, breathing girl who had lived alongside them all, not just the girl in the woods, the girl from her nightmares. Some of the more complex feelings Ellie had been wrestling with had seemed to soften in the aftermath of the memorial.

"What's the plan for Christmas, Ellie?" asks Edward, changing the subject, steering them toward lighter topics.

"Not much. Christmas morning at home with Mum. Then the afternoon with Dad in his new flat. There's an end of term sixth-form ball at school. Just a little celebration . . . *on campus*," she adds, with a wry look. "Mrs. Crowe thought the year group deserved something fun, after everything." She tugs at her sleeves. "It'll probably be lame, but I think I'll go. Jas and Danny say I have to. No excuses. So . . ." She shrugs.

"Good for you."

"It's a shame you can't come."

Edward pulls a face. "My best Nineties dance moves in the school hall?" He waves at the bed and the surrounding equipment. "See, there is a silver lining after all."

Ellie smiles, but she can see he's putting on a brave face. It must be awful being trapped on the ward for goodness knows how long. "You will be OK, won't you?"

Edward nods. "A few more weeks in here and a whole lot of

physio to come, but they've promised me I'll be an all-new and improved version of myself when I'm done."

"I'm sorry this happened to you."

Edward shares a sad smile. "I'm sorry it happened to you too."

When it's time to leave, her mum gathers their coats and makes promises to return again. Ellie waves goodbye, then makes a tactful retreat, allowing them a private moment.

"You didn't have to do that," says her mum as they walk back into the atrium. "There's nothing going on between us."

"Nothing?" asks Ellie. "I wouldn't mind, if you did want to date someone."

"Good to know," her mum smiles, pulling her in for a hug, "but right now, I think I'm steering clear of anything heavy. For a little while, anyway. I've got some things I still need to figure out."

They exit through the automatic doors, leaving the overheated hospital and stepping out into the cold, bright day. Her father sits on a bench beneath a tall plane tree, right where they left him, waiting to escort them home. He takes the portfolio from her hands and tucks it under one arm, folding her free hand into his. "All OK?" he asks. His gaze is fixed on her mum, a hopeful look on his face.

"All OK," says her mum.

Ellie notices how she holds his eye as the three of them turn toward the car. Interesting, thinks Ellie, a small smile playing on her lips. Very interesting.

Acknowledgments

"Sally in the Wood" is a curved stretch of road on the Somerset–Wiltshire border that cuts through dense woodland near Bath. Various explanations exist for the location's strange name and much has been speculated and written about the history and mythology of the area. While this novel is loosely inspired by the place and stories of Sally in the Wood and the nearby stone folly, I've taken liberties to create other fictional surroundings. These places are drawn purely from my imagination. I hope readers who are familiar with the area will forgive my creative license.

The idea for this novel took root a few days after my daughter completed a Girl Guides night hike to the stone folly above the very spooky Sally in the Wood. So my first thank-you goes to Gracie, for telling me about her walk, and for sharing how creepy it was. It's thanks to her, and a few rambling walks with the dog, that this novel exists.

My thanks as always go to Sarah Lutyens, the very best agent I could wish for, whose support goes way beyond what I dreamed of years ago as a new writer. Muddy twilight walks and homemade kombucha mornings on the farm are now my favorites. I also owe my gratitude to the entire Lutyens & Rubinstein team, who have to deal with my awful admin skills and tax questions. (Sorry, Lily.) Big thanks to the wonderful David Forrer at Inkwell, for steering me so well in North America. Chatting with David over champagne and olives is the best!

I love being part of the Simon & Schuster team. Thank you to my publishers, Clare Hey, Kaitlin Olson, Cassandra di Bello, Anthea Bariamis, Adrienne Kerr, and everyone across all the departments at Simon & Schuster around the world who've been involved in turning this messy manuscript into a book. I'm so grateful.

Thanks a million to the booksellers, librarians, reviewers, and bloggers who keep the literary world thriving. A special shout-out to Graham at Paper Plus, Whakatāne, in NZ, for making me laugh with his Instagram reels. I'm looking forward to that sausage roll, one day.

Thanks to Adrian Thompson-Boyce for answering some of my research questions. Any mistakes in this book are mine alone.

Big love to my sister Jess, always my first reader, cheerleader, and general sounding board.

Love and gratitude to my amazing family and friends, especially Matt, Jude, Gracie, Noah, Zac, and Sadie. You guys are the best.

Last, but by no means least, thank you to you, the reader, for picking up this book. I love being a storyteller, and it's because of you that I get to be one. I hope you enjoyed the read. If you'd like to let me know what you thought about this book or any of my previous novels, you can find me online.

 @hannahrichell

 @hannahrichellauthor

hannahrichell.com

About the Author

Before becoming a writer, Hannah Richell worked in the book publishing and film industries in both London and Sydney. She is a dual citizen of Great Britain and Australia, and currently lives in the South West of England with her family. Richell is the author of international bestsellers *The House of Tides* (2012), *The Shadow Year* (2014), *The Peacock Summer* (2019), *The River Home* (2020), and *The Search Party* (2023). Her work has been translated into twenty-one languages.